A Mortal Terror

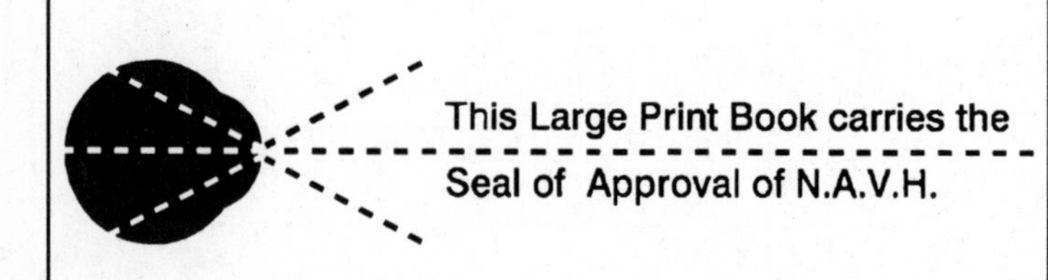
This Large Print Book carries the
Seal of Approval of N.A.V.H.

A BILLY BOYLE WORLD WAR II MYSTERY, BOOK 6

A MORTAL TERROR

JAMES R. BENN

KENNEBEC LARGE PRINT
A part of Gale, Cengage Learning

Detroit • New York • San Francisco • New Haven, Conn • Waterville, Maine • London

Kennebec Large Print® Superior Collection.
The text of this Large Print edition is unabridged.
Other aspects of the book may vary from the original edition.
Set in 16 pt. Plantin.

LIBRARY OF CONGRESS CATALOGING-IN-PUBLICATION DATA

Benn, James R.
A mortal terror : a Billy Boyle World War II mystery / by James R. Benn.
p. cm. — (Kennebec Large Print superior collection)
ISBN-13: 978-1-4104-4385-4 (softcover)
ISBN-10: 1-4104-4385-X (softcover)
1. Boyle, Billy (Fictitious character)—Fiction. 2. World War, 1939–1945—Italy—Fiction. 3. Soldiers—Crimes against—Fiction. 4. Americans—Italy—Fiction. 5. Serial murder investigation—Fiction. 6. Large type books. I. Title.
PS3602.E6644M67 2012
813'.6—dc23 2011038501

Published in 2012 by arrangement with Writer's House LLC.

Printed in the United States of America
1 2 3 4 5 15 14 13 12 11

FD348

This book is for —

Camille
Claudia
Emma
Luke
Nathaniel
Noah
Oliver

The future.

swift there came
a mortal terror;
voices that I knew.

The Epic of Hades, Book II, Actaeon

■ ■ ■ ■

Part One: Switzerland

Chiasso, Switzerland
Swiss-Italian border
January 1944

■ ■ ■ ■

Chapter One

Kim Philby owed me one. I'd helped him out back in London, and he told me to ask if I ever needed a favor. Well, now that I needed one, I didn't hesitate. I wanted to be there when — not if, when — Diana Seaton returned from her mission.

Philby was the only person who could make that happen, so I was glad he was in my debt. As head of the British Secret Intelligence Service's Mediterranean operations, he controlled all the spies, saboteurs, and agents operating in neutral nations and behind enemy lines from Portugal to Turkey. That included Diana Seaton of the Special Operations Executive, who had been sent into Rome, disguised as a nun, to establish contact with a pro-Allied circle within the Vatican.

How do I, a lowly lieutenant, know all this? Because Diana Seaton is the love of my life, and I worry about her day and night. A lot of people worry about each other in this war, but unlike them, I can do something about it. I work for General Dwight David Eisenhower, which gives me access to secrets out of the reach of most colonels and many generals. The fact that in private I call him Uncle Ike doesn't hurt either. It allows me to get involved with men like Kim Philby. When Philby called two days ago to tell me he was good for the favor I'd asked, Uncle Ike gave me a five-day leave and told me to stay out of trouble. I'm going to Switzerland, I told him, how much trouble could there be in a neutral country?

As I stamped my feet on the station platform, trying to keep warm, I thought I might have been off the mark. It was cold, and the sun was casting its last feeble yellow rays sideways from the west. I watched the German and Italian border guards, about fifty yards away, their frosted breath trailing like plumes as they walked. Chiasso is a border town, and the railroad runs right through it. The platform stretches from the station on the Swiss side south to the Italian border, marked by a customs house and crossing gate. Philby and I had been waiting an hour, nervously watching the train halted behind the gate, still on Italian soil. Diana was on board, or so I'd hoped, until a half dozen men in leather trench coats entered the train, and a platoon of German soldiers with submachine guns surrounded it. The black locomotive released a sigh of steam from its boiler, as if straining at the leash for the final stretch.

"Gestapo," Philby had said. "Not to worry. She has good travel papers, signed by the German general commanding rail transport in Northern Italy."

"The Gestapo can sniff out phony papers, no matter how good."

"Oh, they're the real thing, old boy," Philby said, clenching his pipe between his teeth. "This general is quite the churchgoer, especially since he arranged for the transport of several thousand Italian Jews."

"To where?" I knew the Nazis were rounding up Jews everywhere, and shooting a lot of them. But I didn't know where they kept transporting them to, or why. It didn't make sense when they needed railroads for troops and supplies, but then nothing in this war made much sense.

"To those camps in the east we keep hearing about. This old general began to feel guilty, more so after we landed in Italy. He let it be known he'd be glad to do a small favor for the Vatican now and then."

"Isn't it dangerous to give him Diana's

name? Or whatever name she's using?"

"Yes, it would be," Philby said absently, as he knocked the ash from his pipe and jammed it into his coat pocket. "That's why she's coming out with a group of twenty nuns. Didn't want to tell you the details before now, you understand."

"Sure, security. Lot of that going around."

"The cover story is that they're being sent to a convent outside of Zurich, to relieve crowding in the Holy See. Solid on all counts. Look there," he said, pointing to the train. A rush of black leather exited, accompanied by shouted orders. The troops surrounding the train trotted to their vehicles. The Italian border guards stood back, melting into the shadows, mere spectators on their own soil. Two burly Gestapo men stepped down from a train car, holding a civilian by his elbows, guiding him to the waiting sedan. The civilian looked around, his head swiveling wildly as he sought some way out. He dug in his heels, but the two goons carried him easily. Then he dropped, as if he'd fainted. One of the Germans pulled back his leg to give him a kick, and all of a sudden the prisoner was up, pushing his tormentor and twisting free. He ran along the train, his arms pumping, and leapt from the platform, hitting the ground hard, rolling and coming up at a run, limping as one leg threatened to give out. Pistol shots cracked and gray dust kicked up at his feet. Then an MP40 submachine gun sounded, the harsh burst slamming into his back. He took another two steps, perhaps not realizing that death had burrowed into muscle and bone. His momentum propelled him forward, almost in a cartwheel, until his body fell limply across the track. The sigh of steam flowed from the locomotive again, a mournful sound that seemed to apologize for the sudden death of a passenger so close to his final destination.

The Germans pushed the Italian border guards forward, ordering them to retrieve the body. As they grabbed the fellow by his feet and pulled, they left a streak of crimson that pointed, like an arrow, to the Swiss side.

"Lucky fellow," Philby said. "That was at least quick."

"One of yours?"

"No. Some poor bastard on the run. Deserter, maybe. Probably betrayed by some other chap looking to save his own skin. Here we go," he said as the gate was raised and the train finally lurched forward, its giant steel wheels rolling over the bloodstains as it left Nazi territory.

The train arrived at the platform, and

lights switched on above us as the sun gave up and set below the looming mountains. To the south, a blanket of darkness settled over occupied Italy, where the blackout was complete, not a glimmer allowed to guide Allied bombers. The Swiss side seemed gaudy in comparison, bright lights shining on gray pavement and orange tile roofs. Maybe I'd gotten used to the blackout in London, but the glare of streetlights and lamps was blinding. I shaded my eyes and strained to see into the compartments as they rolled by, the train moving slowly until its caboose was safely on neutral ground.

The compartment doors opened, and the passengers spilled out with a mix of nervous chatter and ashen faces. Some looked like businessmen, others refugees. Wartime travel to a neutral country provided for odd traveling companions. Then I saw them, two cars down: a procession of black habits, led by an older nun. They wore cloaks against the cold and white wimples encased their faces, their black veils prohibiting sideways glances, their eyes focused on the ground at their feet.

"Hold," Philby said in a low voice, placing his hand on my arm. "Don't say anything. We don't know who may be watching the station."

I saw her. Not her face, but her walk. Nothing could hide that confident swing of her shoulders, the aristocratic posture, the determined steps. It was Diana, her head bowed a fraction less than the others. The nun in the lead said something in Italian, and they turned to enter the open doors of the station. Diana glanced up, looking in all directions. Her eyes met mine and flashed wide for a split second, then disappeared as she assumed the obedient, demure posture of a nun following her abbess.

Philby and I fell in a few steps behind them as I watched for signs of anyone trailing us. I pulled my hat brim low over my eyes, blending in with the crowd, while trying to spot anyone who didn't. I was in civilian clothes, and if it hadn't been for the threat of German agents in similar attire, not to mention the blood on the tracks, I might have talked myself into enjoying this Swiss interlude. Instead, I saw everything with suspicious eyes, not trusting that anyone was who he said he was. I wasn't, Diana certainly wasn't, so how could we assume we were surrounded by harmless Swiss neutrals?

We trailed the procession of nuns out onto the street. They walked up the Corso San Gottardo, each clutching a small black suitcase, dodging the pedestrians strolling along the thoroughfare. Wind whipped at their cloaks and veils, the black fabric snapping like flags in a parade. Passing restaurants and shops with unaccustomed light spilling out into the street, the nuns made a beeline for the Chiesa di Santa Maria, a bronze-roofed church in a small, park-like setting. Trees surrounded two buildings to the rear, and I guessed this was where they'd be staying. As they entered the church, Philby guided me down a narrow side street, where a gray sedan sat idling. We got in the backseat and the driver took off without a word, circling around to the rear of the church. The car stopped and Philby got out, holding the car door open. A church door opened, the light from inside briefly framing the silhouette of a nun, who dashed to the car and slid into the backseat. Philby slammed the door and got in the front, a split second before the driver accelerated and sped along the gravel drive and out onto the road.

"Billy," Diana said, glancing toward Philby, her eyes showing a curious mix of surprise, joy, and fear. "Why are you here? Is something wrong?"

"Nothing wrong, my dear," said Philby. "I simply owed Lieutenant Boyle a favor and brought him along to see the sights."

"Then you *have* been busy since I last saw you," Diana said to me, her face relaxing. We'd last seen each other in Naples, a month ago, before an assignment from Uncle Ike cut our time together short.

"Yes. I asked if I could tag along when your mission was finished. I never thought you'd be brought out so soon."

"It was . . . sudden," she said. Her voice wavered, and I thought tears welled up in her eyes, but she regained her composure in an instant, running the rosary beads she wore through her fingers. "What's the connection?" Diana asked in a low voice, nodding toward Philby.

"It's a long story."

"They all are," Diana said, as she took my hand in hers and gazed out the window. She rubbed the moisture away and stared at the traffic, the streetlights, the glow from windows — all the signs of normalcy that had become so abnormal in these years of war. She blinked rapidly as the tears returned, and one dropped onto the back of my hand.

"Are you okay?" I asked.

"Long and sad," she said. "Every story is so long and so sad." She gripped my hand until her knuckles turned white. We drove on through the peaceful streets in silence broken only by the sound of muffled sobs.

Chapter Two

The Hotel Turconi was located just north of Chiasso. It sat atop a hill at the start of a wave of foothills and high ridges cresting the Alps themselves. It was a small place, perfect for knowing who your fellow guests were, and for watching the winding road that led up from the border town. When we'd first checked in, the owner nodded to Philby like a long-time customer, the kind who liked to be left alone. He didn't blink at our passports, both Irish, and reserved a table in an alcove for our meals, set apart from the other diners. Our papers and our names were phony, but the money Philby handed over wasn't. I hoped he wasn't stingy with the king's pound notes, since I didn't like the idea of German agents paying us a visit while we slept.

The owner himself served us. Wild mushroom soup and roasted duck breast with apples, washed down with a couple of bottles of Merlot Bianco — from his cousin's vineyard, he was proud to tell us. It beat dining in London, with all the rationing restrictions, even though Diana was still dressed as a nun.

"Why don't you change?" I asked as our host cleared the dishes and Philby fired up his pipe. "Do you need clothes?"

"Kim," Diana said. "Didn't you tell him?"

"Tell me what?" I wanted to know.

"The mission isn't over," she said, lowering her voice. "I needed to report something in person, so I asked to come out. I'll go back as soon as I can."

"I will be the one to make that decision, my dear," Philby said in his best professorial tone. "That's why I didn't tell Boyle. I'm not sure myself if you should go back. First, I need to hear what was so important, and how you came to learn of it. The Germans are great ones for playing games, and it could be false intelligence designed to draw out an agent, forcing you to take the sort of intemperate action you did."

"This is not the sort of intelligence they would plant," Diana said. "And I am not intemperate." She drank her wine and set the glass down hard, punctuating her statement.

"Very well," Philby said, shrugging his acceptance. "We can discuss the matter later, in private."

"No," Diana said. "This is not something to be hidden away and kept secret. Billy does work for General Eisenhower, after all." She made it sound like Philby was an idiot, not her spymaster boss.

"And I am in the business of managing secrets," Philby said. "Not broadcasting them before their usefulness can be determined."

"I saw a report from the bishop of Berlin, Konrad von Preysing," Diana said, ignoring Philby, who refilled his wine glass and eyed her with faint amusement, as if she were a precocious child on the verge of misbehavior. "It was sent directly to the pope, and one of his secretaries typed a copy . . ."

"If you insist on proceeding, move on to the facts," Philby said. "There is no need to detail your sources for Lieutenant Boyle." It was a way for him to assert his authority while allowing her to continue.

Diana waited for a heartbeat, then nodded. "Kurt Gerstein is an *Obersturmführer* in the SS. A lieutenant. He joined the Nazis in 1933, but quickly became disillusioned and spoke out against their anti-religious policies. For his involvement with various Christian youth groups, he was thrown out of the party, severely beaten, and briefly imprisoned for anti-Nazi activities."

"So how did he end up in the SS?" Philby asked, an eyebrow raised in disbelief.

"In early 1941, his sister-in-law died in a mental institution."

"Nazi euthanasia?" Philby asked.

"Yes. At that point, Gerstein became committed to acting against the regime. He apparently decided the best way to do that was from within. A few months after her death, he joined the SS. Either they didn't check his records, or his technical skills made them willing to overlook them. He had an engineering degree, and had completed his first year of medical school. So they brought him into the Technical Disinfection Department of the SS."

"What, do they clean garbage cans?" I asked, wondering where all this was leading.

"No. They are in charge of disinfecting the clothes of all the Jews they kill. Jews, Gypsies, Communists, opponents of the regime, anyone who is sent to the extermination camps."

I'd read about the concentration camps, where enemies of the Nazis were sent, and I knew the SS and the Gestapo had no qualms about shooting whomever they wanted. But this felt different. A whole structure dedicated to extermination? It was bigger than wanton slaughter, beyond evil, beyond believing. Everything I'd read or seen in newsreels about the Nazis made me angry. This made me sick.

"We know the Nazis have treated the Jews terribly," Philby said. "As they have many others. We know many die in the camps in the east, but extermination? Surely they use them for labor, and many die, but you can't mean wholesale slaughter?" Philby's normally suave demeanor faltered for a moment as he took in what Diana was describing.

"The Technical Disinfection Department also provides a gas called Zyklon B. It is used in gas chambers, in large quantities," Diana said, her lips compressed, as if the words were too terrible to let loose into the world. "Kurt Gerstein is in charge of the delivery of Zyklon B. He delivered large quantities to a number of camps in Poland, including a huge complex of camps at a place called Auschwitz."

"Unbelievable," Philby said, and I couldn't tell if he simply did not credit Diana, or was stunned at the enormity of what she was telling us.

"In 1942, he visited several concentration

camps, including Belzec, in Poland. While he was there, he witnessed the gassing of three thousand Jews. This was what he had joined the SS for. To gather evidence of outright extermination. He described what he had seen to the Swedish diplomat Baron von Otter, and the papal nuncio in Berlin, Father Cesare Orsenigo, as well as to the bishop. All promised to send word to London, and each did. When nothing but silence came of that, Bishop von Preysing wrote directly to the pope."

"Diana," Philby said, leaning forward to whisper to her. "Are you sure this chap isn't mad? Surely I would have heard of such a report coming from Berlin. Perhaps he had an attack of conscience and fabricated the worst he could imagine."

"You don't understand," Diana said. "What do you think is happening in these camps? Gerstein witnessed it all, the trains coming in, the few able-bodied separated to be worked to death, all the rest ushered into the gas chambers. They have them marked as showers, to disinfect for typhus. Jewish trustees tell them to fold their clothes and leave them on benches, to remember where they left them. Then they enter the chamber and the doors are locked behind them. The Zyklon B is dropped through vents in the ceiling. In twenty minutes they open the doors and pull out the dead. They pry the gold from their teeth and incinerate the bodies."

"The very Zyklon B that Herr Gerstein so thoughtfully provided?"

"Yes. So that he could witness what was being done. So he could tell the world. But so far, the world hasn't listened." She slammed the table with the flat of her hand and her glass fell, staining the tablecloth with wine before it rolled off the table and shattered.

Philby sat in silence, haunted perhaps by visions of mass killing, or worried that he hadn't been privy to reports smuggled out of Nazi Germany. Finally he stirred enough to chastise Diana about overreacting to Vatican gossip and to tell me to keep quiet about what I'd heard, and then left the table.

"What do you think, Billy?" Diana said, now that we were alone. I knew Diana was counting on me to believe her, to back her up. I squirmed in my seat, trying to find the words she wanted to hear, but I didn't know what to say. It was all so insane, it was hard to come up with a logical thought. Then I remembered Sammy.

"I had a friend in high school, Sammy Vartanian. He was Armenian, and his father used to curse the Turks for killing over a million Armenians in 1915. I'd never heard of it, and I figured maybe Sammy's old man was off his rocker. So I looked it up in the encyclopedia. Sure enough, there is was. The Armenian Genocide. I figure if something like that happened a few decades ago, and I never heard of it, then you could be right. Besides, I believe in you."

"I'd heard talk among Jews we have hidden in Vatican City, but I thought it might be nothing more than rumors. Not the deportations and shootings, all that is well known. It's the sheer scale of it all. Like a giant assembly line of death."

"But you believe this report from Gerstein?"

"Yes. It all checks out. Bishop von Preysing vouches for him, and he's completely reliable. He's been anti-Nazi and quite outspoken about it, unlike most other German bishops. And thank you."

"For what?"

"For believing in me." Diana reached her hand toward mine, and her skin held an electrical charge. I pulled away, looking around to see if anyone had seen this Irish civilian hold hands with a nun. Diana blushed, the red flush stark against the white surrounding her face.

"Let's go," she said, and I followed her up the stairs, aware of the movement in her hips beneath the black cloth. My heart was beating fast, and I wondered if I should feel guilty about desiring her so soon after discussing the fate of millions. Then I wondered if I was going to hell for lusting after a nun, even a phony one. That made my heart beat even faster, but I didn't have time to decide which to worry about, since we were in front of Diana's door. Guilt and hell were pretty much the same thing in my upbringing, and I knew I could never explain this situation to a priest and ask for absolution.

"Listen," I said, as she turned the key in the lock. "I'll understand if you want to be alone, you know, after your long trip and all."

Diana eyed me, then the hallway. It was empty. The only sounds were those drifting up from the restaurant two floors below. She pressed her body against mine, her face warm, her eyes half closed, her lips moist as we kissed. Our arms encircled each other, and I tasted the sweetness of her mouth and the saltiness of the tears that streaked her cheek. I reached for the unlocked door, pushed it open, and we entered like two dancers in tune with the music of longing. I kicked it shut as Diana pulled the white coif from her head, letting her long hair loose. She carefully removed the cross she wore around her neck and the rosary beads from her woolen belt, placing them on a small table by the gable window. Then she removed her scapular — the black apron draped over her shoulders — and covered them with it.

"I've missed you," she said, kicking off her shoes and wiping a tear away.

"Is that why you're crying?" I asked, taking her in my arms, feeling warm flesh beneath the nun's habit and trying not to think about all the real nuns I'd known. This was not the time for visions of Sister Mary Margaret.

"I don't know. It's everything. The war, the innocent deaths, all the lives ripped apart. It's too much to bear. I don't want to think about it anymore, at least not now."

We struggled out of our clothes, not wanting to separate for a second, eager to release our bodies from the confines of belts and buttons. I laughed when Diana pulled off her tunic, half expecting all the saints in Switzerland to barge through the door.

"What's the matter, haven't you ever seen a nun undress before?"

I laughed some more and Diana giggled

as the pile of clothes by the side of the bed grew, layers of her undergarments mixing with my civvies, until we were under the duvet, basking in the warmth of our flesh on a cold winter night, safe from the murderous conflict that threatened from all points of the compass. The world had shrunk down to the two of us in this room. The war had burned away all the petty arguments, all the ill will that we'd let come between us. There were no questions about tomorrow or the next day, no expectations of the future, no wondering what would become of us. Fear, blood, and death had washed us clean, leaving only what survived, or what had burrowed deep into our hearts, as far from the danger as it could go and still be remembered. We caressed each other, coaxing those memories out, letting them breathe the air of joy and freedom before we put them away again.

We laughed, but I can't say we were happy. We made love, but it was desperate and burning hot, as if we were keeping evil at bay by the very act. We cried, but our woes were so small that I was ashamed of the tears. We held each other, and knew it would not last.

We slept, but could not rest.

Chapter Three

The next morning, he was waiting for us. A young guy, his face smooth and pink. He sat at our alcove table, pulling at his shirtsleeves to best display his gold cuff links. I squeezed Diana's hand and stopped before he saw us. I watched as he sipped his coffee, resting his hands just so, allowing the gold to sparkle. A leather briefcase was on the chair next to him. His hair was brown and wavy, his expression bored, his fingers manicured. He'd been out in the sun, most likely on a ski slope. He had the healthy, athletic look of a college boy, and the well-tailored look that came from a rich daddy. His eyes weren't on the other guests or the entrance. He didn't even notice us a dozen steps away. He sipped his coffee and looked at his copy of the *Neue Zürcher Zeitung,* the major Swiss daily newspaper. Probably checking his stocks.

"Let's go back," I whispered, pulling Diana by the arm. She wore a silk blouse and tweed skirt from the clothes that had been provided for her and the sensation was appealing.

"Why? Because that boy is at our table?" She stood closer to me as we edged against the wall. Feeling the smooth silk against her skin, I hated the thought of leaving her so soon.

"He's from the embassy. It can only be trouble."

"How can you be sure?"

"He's American. He's not an agent, unless he's in disguise as a Harvard twit. He's too young to have any clout, which makes him a messenger boy. And messages from embassies are like telegrams — always bad news."

"All right," Diana said in a low voice, her face close to mine, close enough to feel the heat of her breath on my cheek. She backed away and I followed as she took the stairs. Two at a time.

Sunlight streamed in, warming us as we huddled under the white duvet.

"Do you think he's still down there?" Diana asked.

"Yeah. He's probably knocked on my door a couple of times by now. If he's got half a brain he'll start asking questions and figure out I'm in your room."

"Perhaps Kim will shoot him. Or have him shot, more likely." She laughed, and it sounded like wind chimes on a warm spring day. But it was winter, a war winter, and this hidden moment with a bit of sunshine was all we had. It was enough, I decided, and laughed along with her, until we lay exhausted and the sun rose higher in the morning sky, leaving the room in a gloomy chill.

Dressed again, we went down to the restaurant. It was nearly empty, with no trace of the messenger boy. The waiter brought coffee to our table and said the young man had gone off to look for me. He smiled and Diana blushed.

"I hope they don't have microphones in the rooms," Diana said as the waiter left.

"Could they?" I asked, and then saw she was trying to hide a laugh. "Make a nice souvenir," I added, trying to cover up.

"Mr. McCarthy?" It was the embassy kid, looking at a photograph and checking it against my face. It took me a moment to remember that was the name on my Irish passport.

"In the flesh," I said, and Diana gave an abrupt laugh, her hand covering her mouth as she looked away. "Please join us."

"I'm sorry, but I need to speak to you in private."

"Unnecessary, as I'm sure Mr. Gallagher has told you." That was Philby's cover name.

"Very well," he said, taking a seat and waving off the approaching waiter, probably having had his fill of coffee. "Julian Dwyer, Assistant Commercial Officer, American Embassy."

"Sorry we missed you earlier," I said.

"How do you know I was here earlier?"

"Because I saw you and figured you were bad news. So we skipped out."

"My time is quite valuable, Lieutenant Boyle," he said, whispering my name and rank in a hiss.

"No it isn't. There's not much commerce these days between Switzerland and the U.S. And the fact that you couldn't find me and you stand out like a virgin in a whorehouse means you're not a spy operating under diplomatic cover. I bet you just graduated from Harvard or one of those snobby schools and daddy got you a posting so you wouldn't have to associate with the lower classes and dress in khaki."

"Yale," Julian said, sounding offended more by the Harvard remark than anything else.

"I'm not a college football fan, so it makes no difference to me. It boils down to the fact that you're the only guy they could do without up in Bern and not insult whoever sent the message to be passed on to me. You dress well, I'll give you that."

"Billy," Diana said, placing her hand on my arm. I was getting steamed, and poor Julian was the perfect target. It wasn't his fault, but he was right in front of me, and I never liked his type much anyway.

"It was my grandfather, not my father," Julian said. "Six-term congressman. And I have a punctured eardrum, not to mention flat feet, so khaki was never in the cards. But I would look good in it."

"Okay, Julian, sorry. But I'm not wrong, am I? About bad news?"

"I guess you would call it bad news," he said, eyeing both of us. "Your orders, Lieutenant Boyle, are to proceed immediately to Naples, Italy. I've booked you on a flight from Zurich to Lisbon tonight. From there you'll travel to Gibraltar and then via military transport to Naples."

"Tonight?"

"Yes. The orders came from London. From a Colonel Samuel Harding."

"Thanks, Sam," Diana said, with an edge of bitterness.

"I still have three days of leave," I said, knowing it was futile.

"Sorry. I have the orders right here, along with a file," Julian said, popping open his briefcase.

"I believe you," I said. "It's got to be important if Colonel Harding sent it. My leave was approved by General Eisenhower, so if he's overruling that, he's got good reason. Have you read the file?"

"The file is for you," Julian said.

"Right. It's not sealed, so stop making believe you haven't looked at it. This has got to be the most interesting thing that's happened since you got here."

"Not quite as interesting as some of the Swiss girls I've met skiing at Gstaad, but you've got me dead to rights. You're sure?" He nodded to Diana.

"Spill, Julian. She's got higher clearance than either of us."

"There have been two murders in Naples," Julian said. I could see the eagerness in his eyes. He was excited, and I was sure this bit of cloak-and-dagger was the high point of his life.

"Only two? Must've been a slow night."

"Both U.S. Army officers. First guy was found in the 3rd Division bivouac area at Caserta, outside Naples. Lieutenant Norman Landry. Found behind a supply tent, his neck snapped. The other officer was Captain Max Galante, M.D., of Fifth Army medical staff. He was found the same night, outside headquarters at Caserta, strangled."

The waiter came to our table with a tray of warm rolls, butter and jams. Conversation ceased as he laid everything out. As soon as he was gone, I buttered a roll, not knowing when or where my next meal might be.

"Forgive me for asking, Julian," Diana said, flashing him a warm smile, "but terrible as these murders are, they don't seem to warrant your presence here. Why the orders from London? Fifth Army must have plenty of military police to sort this out."

"Like the lieutenant said, I'm only the messenger. But there is something here that may explain it. Pictures of the bodies." He pulled two black and white photos from the file, face down. "They're a bit gruesome."

"Gruesome is par for the course," Diana said. "Let's see them."

They weren't pretty. Lieutenant Landry was on his back, head lolled to one side. His field jacket was open, and his .45 automatic was still in his holster. His hair was curly, and a splash of freckles decorated his cheeks. He looked young — too young to be leading men into combat. A canvas tent was visible in the background. A piece of paper appeared stuck in his shirt pocket. As if in answer to my unspoken question, Julian laid the other photo on top. It was a close up.

"The ten of hearts," I said.

"A brand new card," Julian said. "No other playing cards were found on him."

"You read this pretty carefully," I said.

"There wasn't much else to do, waiting for you."

"Okay, okay. What about the other guy?"

"Meet Captain Max Galante," Julian said. Captain Galante was older, late thirties maybe. Stocky, dark haired. His throat was heavily bruised, his eyes bulging, the terror of death still on his face. Landry probably died instantly. This guy didn't. What looked like a playing card stuck out from his shirt pocket as well.

"Don't tell me," I said.

"The jack of hearts?" Diana asked.

"Yes," Julian said, laying down the close up as if he were dealing a poker hand.

"When did this happen?" I asked.

"The bodies were found yesterday morning. As soon as Fifth Army put two and two together, they sounded the alarm. German agents, Mafia, Italian Fascists, they're seeing them all behind every rock."

"There must be a lot of nervous majors, not to mention colonels and generals," I said.

"From the cables in the file, I think it's a general who sounded the alarm. But he probably got a major to do the work. Count in the British, and there are probably a thousand majors within five miles of Caserta Palace. And they're all worried it will be them next."

"No one else killed?"

"Not since we got that report last night in the diplomatic pouch from London."

I leafed through the paperwork. Orders to proceed without delay to Naples and report to Major John Kearns at Fifth Army HQ. Maybe he didn't like the odds. Maybe he knew Harding and called in a favor. There were more photos of Galante. I guessed that once the MPs realized there was a link between the two murders, they paid more attention to the crime scene. Close-ups of the neck, front and back.

"Interesting," I said.

"What?" Julian and Diana said at the same time, leaning in to study the photo.

"The killer used a lot of force, and the good doctor fought back. These bruises and abrasions go up and down the neck, as if

Galante struggled to get away. You can see the thumbprints where the killer squeezed. There's also a bruise here at the base of the neck, from the excessive pressure."

"So the killer was angry? Probably not uncommon," Julian said.

"Look at Landry," I said, placing that photo next to Galante's. "No signs of a struggle. His pistol still in his holster. This killing was quick, professional. No sign of anger."

"Two murderers?" Diana said.

"Maybe. Or two entirely different reasons. Can't really tell much, but it's something to look into. The cards could mean something, or be nothing at all."

One of the photographs was a long shot, taken several steps back from the body. Galante lay against smooth gray boulders bordering a pool of water. It looked familiar, the waterfall and the sculpture of a pack of dogs bringing down some guy with antlers on his head. Not the kind of thing you forget.

"I've been here," I said. "These are the gardens in back of Caserta Palace. The palace is at the top of a hill, and the gardens, fountains, and waterfalls go on forever, down the hill at the rear."

"The Fountain of Diana must be beautiful," Julian said, looking at the photo.

"Huh?"

"Oh, I see," Diana said. "Diana and Actaeon, right?"

"Exactly," Julian said.

"Is that somewhere in the file?" I asked.

"No, it's nothing about the murder. Just a bit of Greek mythology, the kind of thing you pick up at Yale. Or one of the fine English schools, I'm sure," he added, smiling at Diana.

"Okay Yalie, explain it to the one of us who didn't pay attention in public school."

"Diana was the virgin goddess of the wild places. One day she and her maidens were bathing in a forest stream. Naked. Actaeon was out hunting with his pals. They'd bagged their share of stag, and he was heading back with his pack of hunting dogs when he saw Diana. He was stunned by her beauty, but she could not allow a mere mortal to tell the world what he had seen. So she turned him into a stag, and his own dogs hunted him down and tore him apart."

I studied the picture. Galante, dead in front of the sculpture that told a story of death from thousands of years ago. What had he seen in his last moments? Not the beauty of a goddess.

"When do we have to leave?"

"We should go now."

"Give us half an hour."

Diana and I walked along the road, arms wrapped around each other. I didn't have to apologize. It could have been Kim Philby sending her off suddenly as easily as Julian Dwyer coming for me. We'd both donned our coats without speaking to spend our last few minutes outside, under blue skies. It was quiet away from the hotel, a farm on each side of the road, cowbells sounding from a hillside pasture.

"I thought you might want to tell Julian about Kurt Gerstein and the camps," I said.

"I'd rather be with you. He's not a bad sort, really, but it would be beyond his grasp."

"What do you think Kim will do?"

"About Gerstein's information? I don't know. He seemed at a loss, which is unusual. I want him to send me back, but I think he's upset about me coming out for this. He'd rather have hard information about troop movements, that sort of thing."

"Be careful," I said. "Of him and the Germans."

"Good advice. It's not bad, you know, inside the Vatican. We're safe there."

"Okay," I said, knowing that anything else

would only get Diana angry and me worried.

"You be careful, too. This seems like an odd business, with the playing cards. What do you suppose the killer is up to?"

"Sowing confusion? Or maybe it all makes sense to him. Or them. I'll be careful, I promise."

"Okay," she said, echoing my own words, and probably my thoughts, as we leaned into each other. "I'll only ask one thing."

"What's that?"

She stopped and turned to face me. "That whatever happens, to either of us, you keep a place in your heart for me. Always. Don't ever forget I love you."

I couldn't speak. I held her close. I stared into the blue sky, drinking in the distant and near beauty, filling that space in my heart that was already feeling the claim of the war on it, the draw of the dead waiting for me, their stories, their desires, their final moments. I felt Diana's cheek, her skin cold in the mountain air, like the sheen of ice on a pond in December.

Chapter Four

I shed my civilian clothes in Gibraltar, and transformed from an Irish businessman into a piece of military cargo. I was tossed in the back of a B-24 Liberator making an early morning run to Naples, carrying mail, a couple of war correspondents, a congressman, and me. A supply sergeant had met me at the airfield with a duffle bag full of government-issue duds and a .45 automatic. The congressman had come on board with a fifth of bourbon, and shared it with the reporters in hopes they'd mention his name. I didn't work for anyone who bought ink by the gallon, and he wasn't from Massachusetts, so the bottle didn't come my way often. I settled in on some mail sacks. B-24s weren't built for passengers, and there was damn little room in the narrow fuselage.

As they boozed it up, I read through the file Julian had given me. The initial report about Lieutenant Norman Landry was brief, the kind of cop shorthand I was used to. Perfunctory, describing the physical condition of the body, but little else. The kind of report a patrolman might write up after finding a drunk knifed in a doorway off Scollay Square at three in the morning. Dutiful scribbling doomed to the unsolved file, unless the victim turned out to be a Cambridge boy or a Beacon Hill gent.

Landry's death was attributed to the usual "person or persons unknown" with no speculation as to why someone had snapped his neck. A doctor from the 32nd Station Hospital had listed cervical fracture as the cause of death. I could tell as much from the angle at which Landry's head canted on the ground. He had been killed in a bivouac area near San Felice, a small village about five miles from headquarters. His regiment was resting and refitting there after being pulled out of the fighting along the Volturno Line, where he was one of thousands of GIs. A report from the MP noted that Landry had been popular with his men, a platoon he'd led at Salerno and on the road to Cassino before they were pulled off the line for rest outside of Naples. The fact that he'd survived, and that his men liked him, told me two things: he was a good soldier, and he led from the front. Lots of platoon leaders get killed quickly. Others who survive do it by staying behind their men. If Landry's men, especially the veterans, liked him, then he wasn't one of those.

The last person to see him alive, other than his killer, was Lieutenant Kenneth Dare, the chaplain attached to Landry's battalion. I wondered if it had been a social call or if something more serious was bothering Landry.

The photographs showed the ten of hearts clearly. In the close-up, it was easy to see the card was brand new, clean and crisp. It must have come out of a new deck and gone straight into Landry's pocket. Maybe the ten of hearts was his good-luck charm, who knew?

The report on Captain Max Galante was more detailed, not surprisingly. Even before the MPs got the playing-card connection, this murder had been a priority. Captain Galante was a medical doctor assigned to the Fifth Army headquarters staff at Caserta. He got noticed, if not for his rank, for his proximity to the high and mighty. General Mark Clark, commander of Fifth Army, and his boss, British General Harold Alexander, of Fifteenth Army Group, both called Caserta Palace home, along with a passel of rear-area brass.

The MP's report included the duty roster from the 32nd Station Hospital, where Galante worked. He'd gone off duty at 1800 hours, and planned to meet two other doctors for dinner two hours later, at eight o'clock civilian time. The other doctors rented an apartment in town and paid their rent in rations, which their landlady cooked for them. Galante never showed.

The hospital and the apartment were on the south side of the palace. A hand-drawn map was paper-clipped to two photographs; the first showed the hospital and the tree-lined boulevard with the palace at the end. The second photo, according to the map, was taken from the opposite side of the palace. Gardens and walkways sloped gently downward, over a mile of it all, leading to the end where the statues of Actaeon and Diana stood against the backdrop of a waterfall. That gave me the basic layout, but no answers about why Galante ended up at the far end of the gardens.

I went through the photographs again studying the position of the body. While it appeared that Landry had been left where he fell, Galante's body looked like it had been laid out, tucked alongside the rocks that bordered the pond fed by the waterfall. Had he even been killed there? From what I could tell from the photos, there were no scuff marks in the grass, no telltale gouges of earth where a heel dug in during a struggle. But I had no way of knowing for sure; whoever took the shots hadn't bothered to show the surrounding area, away from the body and the pond. Within the pond were the two sculptures, one of Diana and her maidens, all aflutter at Actaeon seeing her naked, and opposite was poor Actaeon with the head of a stag, being killed by his own hounds. Death and beauty sharing the same tranquil spot. Was Galante killed by one of his own? Had this spot been chosen for some reason other than its seclusion?

The jack of hearts stuck out of Galante's pocket, just as the ten was positioned in Landry's. Side-by-side shots of the two cards, front and back, showed that they were from the same pack — or at least the same kind of pack — and apparently unused. Probably no fingerprints. Maybe Galante and Landry had been in a card game together and kept souvenirs. Maybe they'd won big, and a killer, or killers, had decided to grab their cash.

All I knew for sure was that I had two stiffs waiting for me at Caserta, not to mention all the self-important brass throwing their weight around, demanding protection. The two cards were a flimsy connection, and the different ways the bodies had been left to be found didn't seem like the work of the same killer. I gave up thinking about it, and wished I had a drink.

The plane lurched as we hit some turbulence, and the file containing the photographs fell to the deck. A close-up of Galante's head and neck sailed farthest, ending up on the congressman's toes.

"What the hell is this?"

"A guy who didn't share his booze," I said, grabbing it from him before the reporters got too interested. The aircraft shifted sideways in heavy winds as the pilot descended.

"It's all gone," he said, slurring it into one barely understandable word. The newspapermen moved away from him as he swayed in his seat, his face gone pale. I grabbed the files and moved as far away as I could just as the bomber hit another pocket of turbulence and the congressman vomited his share of the bottle into a bucket.

A few hours ago, I'd been looking forward to a day with Diana, strolling down a peaceful country road, and hoping for at least one more night together. Now, here I was, the stink of bile and whiskey in the air, hoping this crate would land in one piece so I could search for a card-carrying killer. The air had grown colder, and I shivered as one of the reporters made his way over to me, balancing on the narrow gangplank.

"Phil Einsmann," he said as he sat. "International News Service."

"Lieutenant Billy Boyle." We shook hands. "You're not going to be sick, are you, Phil?"

"No worries. I've flown worse than this. Combat mission over Germany a few months back, and I wish I'd had a bottle for that one."

"I didn't know correspondents went on bombing raids," I said.

"They don't, anymore. A few months ago, the Eighth Air Force decided to train a handful of reporters and send them on a few missions, to get the story out for the folks back home. We've been in ground combat, so they figured why not? Be good press for the flyboys. So they train about a dozen of us. How to adjust to high altitudes, parachuting, even weapons."

"You actually volunteered?" I asked, thinking that air travel was bad enough without flak and tracer rounds shredding the aircraft.

"Yeah, crazy, huh? Some joker starting calling us the Writing 69th, and it stuck.

They chose a few of us for the first mission. Me, Walter Cronkite from United Press, this kid Andy Rooney from *Stars and Stripes,* Bob Post from the *New York Times.*"

"I think I remember hearing about Post," I said.

"Yeah," Einsmann said. "The one thing they didn't think through was the bad press if one of us got it. Post was killed over Germany. His B-17 blew up midair. Our first mission was our last. I'll tell you, if Bob hadn't been killed, I don't know if I could've gone back up there. I've never been so scared."

"Get a good story?"

"Best thing I ever wrote. Making it back in one piece focuses the mind wonderfully."

"You and your pal headed to Naples?"

"I'm going back, believe or not. I was supposed to go to London. I left last night, and when I got to Gibraltar there was a cable from the home office. Return to Naples. Caserta, actually. I was billeted near Fifth Army headquarters. Something must be brewing."

"News to me," I said, and we both laughed at the unintended joke.

"Does that photograph have anything to do with why you're headed to Naples, Lieutenant Boyle?"

"Call me Billy, everyone does. And I'm going to Caserta, too. Maybe I can give you a lift. You and your pal."

"He's the competition, Reuters, and he's on his own. You're pretty good at not answering a question."

"Used to be a cop, so it's second nature to ignore reporters."

"Hmm. An ex-cop, first lieutenant, traveling way above his pay grade, with pictures of what looks like a strangled officer. You know they bumped a colonel to make room for the congressman?"

"How come they didn't throw you off instead?"

"Billy, I've found that the promise of a mention in a news story works wonders with all sorts of people."

"Including the noncom in charge of the flight manifest," I guessed.

"Sergeant Randolph Campbell, of Casper, Wyoming, soon to be mentioned in a little piece about Americans stationed at Gibraltar."

"Based on your extensive research there."

"Yep. Two hours on the ground. Talked to Randolph and a bunch of other guys. Dateline Gibraltar: the unsung heroes who keep men and material moving in the Mediterranean Theater. Sounds good, doesn't it?"

"Yeah, and I'm sure Randolph's mom will think so, too."

"See, you can answer a question! So fill me in on the dead guy."

"I can't, Phil, sorry."

"Listen, Billy. You're headed to Caserta, so that's obviously where the killing took place. I've been there more than a month, I know the place inside out. Odds are I'll get the dope on this guy before I change my socks. And I really need a clean pair."

"Okay," I said, deciding he had a point. It had been a while since I'd been to Caserta, and Galante's death was probably the main topic of discussion at the palace anyway. It might be interesting to hear what Einsmann had to say about it. Plus, there was no reason to mention Landry. "The name is Captain Max Galante, M.D. He was strangled two days ago — no, three days ago — his body was found two mornings ago."

"Where was he killed?"

"Not sure, but his body was found next to that pool with the statue of Diana and the guy who got eaten by his dogs. You know it?"

"Actaeon. That's a ritzy neighborhood," Einsmann said.

"How so?"

"Engineers just finished building bungalows for generals, pretty close to that fountain. Tennis court and dance hall too. Seems like the palace is too run-down and drafty for the big brass, so they ordered up a little complex for themselves. The CO of the engineer unit wrote up an official complaint, saying his men came over here to win a war, not build vacation homes for generals."

"You gotta love an idealist. How close to the fountain?"

"A stone's throw if you have a good arm, but there's trees and shrubs bordering the place."

"You didn't hear anything about this? You were still there when the body was discovered." It was odd that a newsman wouldn't be all over a juicy story like this, even if the censors would probably keep it under wraps.

"I went down to Naples for a couple of days there before flying out. Painted the town red with a couple of guys from the BBC. You said Galante was a doctor?"

"Yeah, he worked out of the hospital near the palace."

"Must be the 32nd Station Hospital. I've interviewed lots of boys there. Nurses, too," he said with a raise of the eyebrows.

"I bet. Ever run into Captain Galante?"

"Name doesn't ring a bell, but I paid more

attention to the female staff. CID, that's the new Criminal Investigation Division, right? Are you CID?"

"No."

"Who do you work for, then?"

"Listen, this has to be all off the record, okay?"

"Sure, Billy. If there is any news in this, I might follow up with you, but that's got nothing to do with this conversation. Strictly background."

"Okay. I work for General Eisenhower. Actually, I work for Colonel Sam Harding, who works for the general. He sent me down here to investigate."

"Well, well. My boss turns me around and sends me back to Italy, and your boss sends you down here to check on a dead doctor. There's more to this story, Billy. I mean, it's terrible that Captain Galante was killed, but people are killed every day in this war."

"Where is your boss?"

"London."

"I can't see how he found out, or even if he did, why he'd send you back. This is small potatoes, Phil."

"Maybe," he said, eyeing me. "Are you Ike's personal cop?"

"Sort of," I said. "It's a long story." I told him the whole thing, about how the Boyles viewed this war as another alliance with the British, who were seen as the real enemy in my strongly Irish Republican household. About Uncle Frank, the oldest of the Boyle brothers, who was killed in the Great War, and how Dad and Uncle Dan didn't want to lose another Boyle in the second round. A few political strings were pulled, and after Officer Candidate School I was sent down to Washington D.C., where I was supposed to sit out the war in safety, on the staff of an obscure general laboring in the War Plans Department.

It had been a great idea. Mom was related to the general's wife, and we'd met him a few times at family events. So it was Uncle Ike whom I went to work for, and he jumped at the chance to have an experienced investigator on his team when he was chosen to head U.S. Army forces in Europe, back in 1942. It had been quite a surprise to us all.

I left out the part about my not being all that experienced. I'd been promoted to detective, sure, but with the Boyles, the Boston Police Department was sort of a family business. Especially when Uncle Dan sat on the promotions board and Dad was a lead homicide detective.

Of course I made detective; I'd just needed a little more time to actually learn the ins and outs of detecting. A little more on-the-job training with Dad would have gone a long way. But Emperor Hirohito had other ideas, and I ended up on Uncle Ike's staff, trying not to make a fool of myself. Because if I did, I knew I'd end up as one of those lieutenants leading an infantry platoon with a life expectancy of weeks, if not days.

Some things are better left unsaid.

■ ■ ■ ■

Part Two: Caserta, Italy

■ ■ ■ ■

Chapter Five

We'd landed at Marcinese airport, between Naples and Caserta, where a jeep and driver were waiting. I'd let Einsmann tag along, leaving the drunken congressman and the Reuters reporter on the tarmac looking lonely and confused. We dropped Einsmann off at a cluster of tents pitched on the south lawn of the palace, and he and I agreed to meet up later at the officer's bar.

The driver parked near the side entrance, had me sign for the jeep, and took off. A light mist began to fall and the palace loomed against the gray sky, large and formidable. I could see the gardens descending on the north side, but the rain obscured the distant fountains. I turned up the collar on my mackinaw and ran inside.

When I'd last been here, the town had just been captured. The palace was a mess, everything of value looted or destroyed. Now it hummed with activity, spruced up as purposeful men and women in the uniforms of half a dozen nations and services scurried along, a few like me pausing to gape at the high gilt ceilings. I worked my way to a desk at the base of the main staircase, where a corporal sat at a desk, directing traffic. I asked him where I could find Major John Kearns, and he pointed to a chart behind him, which contained a layout of the building.

"G-2, third floor, quadrant two," he said, and then went back to his paperwork. The diagram showed all five floors and four sections of the building, each with its own courtyard. I figured out where I was and spotted the rooms allocated to Fifth Army Intelligence. I took the staircase, got lost a couple of times, tripped over communications wire strung across a hallway, watched a rat scamper out of an empty room, and finally found a door with G-2 painted above it. I knocked and entered. The room was cavernous, with a row of deep-set windows at the far side. Maps were mounted on the walls, desks pushed together in the middle, telephone line strung like a clothesline above my head.

There were three noncoms in the office. One staff sergeant and a master sergeant ignored me, leaving it to a corporal to handle stray officers. The corporal looked at me, one eye squinting against the cigarette smoke that drifted from the butt stuck in his mouth. He went back to the photograph he was studying through a magnifying glass, looked up again a few seconds later, and finally spoke when it was apparent I wasn't going away. "Help you, lieutenant?"

"I'm looking for Major John Kearns."

"What's your business, sir?" The corporal leaned back in his chair as he spoke, while the two sergeants stood and moved to opposite sides of the room, one of them resting his hand on the butt of his automatic.

"That's between me and the major, who asked me to come here. Ease up, fellas, I'm not carrying a fifty-card deck."

"You'll have to excuse us, Lieutenant Boyle," said a voice from a narrow hallway at the far end of the room. "The boys are a little overprotective these days. Come on in." I caught a glimpse of a tall, lean figure as he disappeared into the shadows. The noncoms relaxed, but watched me in a way that made me nervous to show them my back.

The hallway was dark, paneled in wood that gave off a musty smell of rot and centuries of dust. It opened into a large room with a fireplace big enough to stand in and windows ten feet high. Marble pillars flanked the windows, and the arched ceiling was painted with scenes of Roman soldiers and pudgy women in white flowing gowns.

"Quite a place, isn't it?" Kearns said, gesturing for me to sit. He had high cheekbones and close-cropped hair with a hint of gray creeping in. He wore a .45 in a shoulder holster and looked like he was on friendly terms with it. He took his place opposite me at a long table strewn with maps and glossy black-and-white photographs, a confusion of shorelines, mountaintops, and gun emplacements. I didn't think the question really needed an answer, so I nodded and waited for him to explain things.

"How's Sam?" he asked.

"Fine, Major. You know him well?"

"Sam Harding and I were in the same class at West Point," he said, holding up a hand to show me the West Point ring. "We were roommates." He went silent, as if that explained everything. Maybe it did.

"How did you come to ask for me to be sent here, sir?"

"Sam and I got together a few times in Naples, when he was still in Italy. He told me about you. Said you weren't half bad at snooping around."

"That's not something I've heard from him very often," I said. Never was more like it.

"No, you wouldn't. But like I said, we go way back. Even though he had a few drinks in him, I knew he meant it. Tell me he was right."

"Snooping is easy. Finding a murderer is another thing, especially when there are thousands of guys within a few miles, all heavily armed and trained to kill."

"I need you to find this guy, Boyle. Find him and stop him."

"What about the military police? CID? I'd think the new Criminal Investigation Division would be all over this one. Solving it would make the guy in charge a hero."

"Make, or break. There's no guarantee CID can close the case. I want someone on the job who's got nothing to lose. Find the guy or not, you go back to London when it's over. Work with CID, but you get this killer before he deals another card."

"How is G-2 involved? Is this an intelligence matter?"

"Everything is, until I understand what's behind it. Right now, I don't know if this is a German agent, a stay-behind Italian Fascist, or someone who wants a promotion the easy way. And I don't like not knowing.

CID is not under my jurisdiction, but you are. Understood?"

"Sure, Major, I understand that. What I don't get is what's so damned important that you needed to pull me in. Do you have any reason to believe you're next?"

"We have more majors here than we know what to do with, Boyle. As a matter of fact, I worry more about some trigger-happy major plugging the next poor slob who taps him on the shoulder to ask for a light. But that's my worry. I've got two things I want you to worry about." Kearns leaned forward, folding his arms on the table, his head inclined so that he stared at me with his eyeballs nearly rolled up. I waited ten, fifteen seconds, and then knew it was up to me to ask.

"What two things, sir?"

"One, finding the killer. Two, what I'll do to you if you ever again suggest that I called you here for my personal protection." He nodded toward the hallway. "Corporal Davis has your billeting information and will tell you where CID is. Ask for Sergeant Jim Cole. Now get out."

I did, thinking that he and Harding must have gotten along well at West Point.

The corporal gave me billeting papers and directions to CID. Quadrant one, second floor. As I climbed the stairs, I wondered about Kearns and his attitude. Not that I didn't care about anybody — major, private, or civilian — being murdered. But there were murders everywhere, not to mention deaths in combat, and the mass killings going on in occupied Europe. All over the continent, people were being shot, strangled, gassed, knifed, bludgeoned, and poisoned. Some because of who they were, others because of the uniform they wore, and often because someone they loved — or once had loved — lost his or her temper in a rage of jealousy and possessiveness. Death was everywhere, commonplace. So why was I here? Kearns didn't impress me as the kind of guy who needed a bodyguard flown in, and I knew Harding wouldn't have cooperated if that were what he'd wanted. Maybe he wasn't too worried about dead majors or even dead colonels. Maybe it was the ace of hearts that kept him up at night.

As I navigated the maze of hallways and descended a marble staircase, I counted officers. By the time I found CID, I'd given up counting majors after a dozen. There'd been six lieutenant colonels and four full bird colonels, three brigadier generals, and one major general. All within five minutes. Brigadiers were the lowest-ranked generals, and there were probably plenty within Fifth Army HQ, as well as those with the divisions and brigades. A major general, with two stars, was just below the exalted level of three-star lieutenant general. The only one of those I knew around here was General Mark Clark, Fifth Army commander. And maybe his boss, 15th Army Group commander General Harold Alexander, but I wasn't certain of his exact British rank.

As I entered the Criminal Investigation Division office, I considered the possibility of an operation aimed at assassinating Clark or Alexander. It would have answered the question of why Kearns and G-2 were involved, but it didn't make much sense otherwise. If it were a German plot, why would they announce their intention by starting with junior officers? It didn't add up, and I decided to wait until I learned what Sergeant Cole had dug up before I tried out any theories.

CID had a string of rooms, connected by a passageway running along the outer wall. Each was decorated in a different color, the paint peeling and curling off the walls. The first room housed military police, and one of the snowdrops — so named for their white helmets — sent me two rooms to the right. I shivered as I walked past the tall windows, feeling the damp cold seeping through. Rain splattered against the glass, which rattled as the wind gathered up and blasted the casements.

The next room was long and narrow, with two rows of desks facing each other. On the walls, mirrors in fancy frames were set into panels, reflecting what light there was into each other, except for the gaps where the glass was missing or shattered. With his back to a busted mirror, a sergeant stood over a desk covered in playing cards. He wore his field jacket buttoned up, probably against the breeze that seemed to run through the high-ceilinged room. He scratched absently at his chin, appearing to be lost in thought.

"Sergeant Cole?"

"Jesus!" His eyes widened in surprise as he took a step back, then recovered. "Sorry, Lieutenant, I guess I didn't notice you walk up."

"You are Sergeant Cole, CID?"

"Yes sir, I am. You must be Lieutenant Boyle? Major Kearns said to expect you." Cole sounded worried, as if I were here to fire him. His eyes darted about the room.

"That's me. What have you got here, Sergeant?" I pointed to the cards on the desk, but kept my eyes on Cole. He was jumpy, and I had to wonder if he was hiding something, or hiding from someone.

"Do you know the details of the case, Lieutenant? How the bodies were found, with playing cards?"

"Ten and jack of hearts," I said. "I read the files."

"These are the originals," he said, opening a drawer and taking out a small manila envelope. "No fingerprints, and they seem brand new."

I slid the cards out onto my palm and studied them, lifting each by the edge. They were crisp and clean all right. No soft edges from repeated shuffles, no bend in them at all. The backs were red, the usual swirling vines pattern that you never paid much attention to. I put them back and handed the envelope to Cole.

"Trying to match them?"

"Yes sir. As you can see, it's a common deck. I was able to buy the same kind, with blue or red backs, at the post exchange in Naples, and get them for free at the Red Cross center or at the hospital."

"The same hospital where Captain Galante was stationed?"

"Yes, the 32nd Station Hospital. Why do you ask?"

"How long have you been in CID, Sergeant?" I asked as I took a seat. He lit a cigarette and sat, taking his time with the answer, fiddling with his lighter.

"I'm fairly new. About a month."

"Were you an MP before?"

"No."

"Cop before the war?"

"No."

"Fair to say then that you've got a lot to learn. Let's start with this: Asking why I want to know something is a waste of time. An investigator needs to know everything about a case, everything that has the slightest connection. You never know when something is going to fit in later on. So explore every angle. Don't ask why, because I don't know why. By the time we know that, the investigation will almost be over. Make sense?"

"Yes sir, it does."

"You have any problem working with me on this, Sergeant Cole?"

"No sir."

"How about your commanding officer?"

"Captain Bartlett, sir. He's in Naples, working on a black market case. He said to cooperate with you." Cole looked at the doorway, as if he expected Bartlett to return and check on him.

"Okay, good." It sounded like Bartlett was not eager to dive into this one. He was giving me a rookie and leaving it in my hands. If I failed, it was all on me. If not, as soon as I was gone he'd claim the credit. Cole seemed oblivious. "What else do you have?"

"Not much, sir. Landry was well liked by his men. No trouble from that quarter. He took good care of them, if you know what I mean."

"Unlike some other officers?"

"I don't mean any offense, sir."

"Don't worry, Cole, I'm not all that big on officers above lieutenant myself," I said with a smile that was meant to put him at ease.

"Some officers, you know, they look out for themselves first."

"So I've heard. What about sergeants?"

"Harder to get away with it," Cole said. "Everyone sees what a sergeant does. His men, his superior officers. If he screws up, it makes his lieutenant look bad, then his captain, and before too long he's in big trouble."

"Landry's sergeants are a good bunch?"

"Sure. Steady guys, you know?"

"Any of them make Landry look bad? Did he make life miserable for any of them?"

"Lieutenant Landry wasn't like that. He got his guys out of scrapes when they had too much to drink, and in the field he was always up front with them."

"Sounds like a stand-up guy," I said.

"So why would someone want to kill him?"

"Good question, Cole. Any of his men have a theory?"

"No, nothing."

"What about Galante?"

"What about him? He was a doctor, he helped people. Killing him makes no sense."

"Unlike Landry?"

"No, I didn't mean it that way." Cole shook a fresh cigarette out of a pack and lit it from the stub of the other one. His hand shook, the faintest of tremors sending ash onto the playing cards on the desk. I sat back and waited as he crushed the first butt out in an ashtray. A wisp of smoke curled up from it, but Cole didn't notice. He inhaled deeply, and blew smoke toward the ceiling, his politeness a good cover for not looking me in the eye. I didn't speak.

"What I meant was, why would anyone kill a doctor? There are plenty of captains around here. Why pick one who actually helps people?" His voice had a tinge of panic to it, as if the thought of anyone who'd murder a doctor was too much for him to bear.

"Sergeant Cole, what did you do before

you were assigned to CID?"

"I was with the Third Division. Squad leader, after Sicily."

"Been with them long?"

"Since Fedala," he said, and brought the cigarette to his lips with his left hand. The right sat on his lap, out of sight. Fedala was the invasion of North Africa, fourteen months ago. That had been a long haul, being shot at by the Vichy French, Italians, and Germans along the way.

"Let me guess," I said. "You got your stripes because you were the only one of the original squad still standing."

"You learn something by staying alive, can't deny that," Cole said, as if he were confessing a mortal sin. "All the other guys — killed, wounded, captured. I lost track of dead lieutenants, and saw four sergeants killed before they promoted me. Replacements kept coming, most getting it pretty quick. Not much I could do about it either. They'd panic, forget everything I told them, run around when they should stay put, stay put when they should advance. They weren't ready."

"Were you? At Fedala, fourteen months back?"

"Hard to remember. That was a lifetime ago." He lit another butt, unable to hide his shakes. He gripped his left arm with his right hand, over the stripes, as if he'd been wounded.

"After Sicily they made you squad leader. Then Salerno."

"Then Salerno. Then the Volturno River crossing. That's where I got hit. Shrapnel in my leg."

"Not a million-dollar wound," I said. Not bad enough for a stateside ticket on a Red Cross ship headed westward.

"Nope." Cole smoked with a determination that was impressive. He didn't talk with smoke flowing out of his mouth like some guys. He savored each inhale and exhale, as if the burning tobacco held the kiss of an angel.

"Anything else I should know?"

"Nope. What are you going to do next?" Cole was a cross between nervous and relieved. Relieved that I was here to tell him what to do, and nervous that he might have to do it. Buying up playing cards seemed to be his limit.

"Find where I'm billeted, dump my stuff, and get some sleep. I've been in the air more hours than I care to count." I wanted to meet Einsmann and see what he'd found out, and there was no reason to take Cole away from his cards and smokes. I handed him my billeting papers and asked him how I could find the place I'd been assigned.

"On the Via Piave?" he said when he looked at the address. "Jesus, that's Captain Galante's apartment!"

Chapter Six

Kearns had apologized, saying that the corporal was supposed to have told me. Space was at a premium, and his idea had been that I might as well be given that bunk, where I could talk to the two doctors who shared the apartment. It did have a certain logic, but I wondered what Galante's pals would think of it. Their feelings weren't high on Kearns's list, so I headed out of the palace to meet my new friends and interrogate them.

I swung the jeep out of the parking area and onto the Via Roma, watching for the turn Cole told me would take me to the Via Piave, a side street of relatively intact structures, two- and three-story stone buildings, most closed off by large iron gates or strong wooden double doors leading into a courtyard. Halfway down the street, two homes were destroyed, heaps of blackened rubble still spilled out onto the roadway.

The rain was falling harder now, and the smell of charred timbers and ruined lives filled my nostrils. Through the gap where the houses had been I saw a row of B-17s lined up, their giant tail fins shadowed against the darkening sky. Except for when weather like this grounded them, it was going to be a noisy neighborhood.

I found the building, its masonry decorated by a spray of bullet holes. Most centered around one window on the upper story where hinges held the remnants of wooden shingles. A sniper, maybe, drawing fire from every GI advancing up the street, as they edged from door to door, blasting at any sign of movement, not wanting to die from the last shot of a rearguard Nazi. Or a curtain fluttering the breeze, catching the eye of a dogface who empties his Garand into the window as the rest of his squad joins in, excitement and desperation mingling with sweat and noise until all that remains is the smell of concrete dusk and nervous, jumpy laughter.

I parked the jeep in the courtyard and turned off the engine. Rain splattered on the canvas top, reminding me of distant machine-gun fire. I took a deep breath, telling myself this was way behind the lines, and there would be no snipers lurking in third-story windows. Wet as everything was, I swore I could smell concrete dust in my nostrils. Shaking off the memory, I grabbed my duffle and took the stairs up to the main door. I was about to knock when it opened and a short, stout, gray-haired Italian woman unleashed a torrent of language at me, beckoning me in with one hand and pointing to my feet with the other. I didn't need to understand Italian to get it. I wiped my wet boots on the mat and hung my dripping mackinaw on a peg. She must have decided I passed inspection, and led me down a hallway into a kitchen, allowing me on the tile floor as she pointed to another room beyond. I wanted to linger and savor the smells coming from the pots on the stove, but the old woman had her back to me, busy with whatever was cooking.

"You must be Boyle," said a figure in an armchair, seated before an old coal stove. I was glad of the warmth, and stood close, rubbing my hands. He watched me, folding the newspaper he'd been reading, as if he thought I might be of greater interest. He was a British captain, the Royal Army Medical Corps insignia obvious on his lapels.

"You were expecting me?"

"Yes. We got a note that you'd be taking Max Galante's room. Terrible thing, him getting it like that. Bradshaw's the name," he said, extending his hand. "Harold Bradshaw."

"Doctor Bradshaw?"

"Oh, please. Leave the doctor and military business out of our little home, will you? There's enough of that outside these walls. Hope that doesn't spoil things for you, Boyle. Sit down, why don't you?"

"If I wasn't taking a dead man's bed, I think I'd feel at home here," I said, settling into another chair drawn near the fire. "I hope you don't mind."

"Not at all. Can't say I knew Galante all that well, and this is war, isn't it? Still, one hopes for a quick bullet on the field of battle, if one has to buy it. Not a brutish attack by one of your own."

Bradshaw packed a pipe and fussed with it the way pipe smokers do. He was in his forties, with a bit of a paunch and receding hairline. His uniform was worn and wrinkled, and I guessed this was about as much spit and polish as the army was going to get out of him. I stretched my legs and let the stove warm my boots.

"You're both doctors at the same hospital, and you lived together, but you didn't know him well? How come?"

"What's your concern with this, Boyle?"

"They didn't tell you I was investigating the murders?"

"No," Bradshaw said as he blew out a plume of smoke. He admired the coals for a moment before continuing. "Only your name and that you were to be billeted here. So you're with the American CID?"

"Working with them. I'm curious about your remark, if you don't mind me asking." I figured the best way to interrogate Bradshaw was to keep it casual, pal to pal after a tough day at work.

"Not at all. Galante kept to himself. There were four of us here, all medical men. Two American, two English. We work long hours, not much time for socializing. And at my age, not the same inclination as the younger lads."

"There are two other doctors living here?"

"One, at the moment. Stafford got transferred, then Galante got himself killed. That leaves Wilson. Captain Jonas Wilson. Yank, like you."

"Was he any friendlier with Galante than you were?"

"Well, I wasn't unfriendly. The way you put it makes it sound like I disliked the fellow. No, he was pleasant enough company. He and I often chatted at meals. We all tried to arrange our schedules to be here for dinner. Signora Salvalaggio can work wonders with any kind of ration. Even bully beef."

"The lady in the kitchen?"

"Yes. She lives downstairs. Keeps house for us, cooks and cleans. We all pool our rations and share with her, pay her a bit as well."

"Is Captain Wilson here?"

"Not yet. Should be soon, though. You're welcome to stay and eat with us, but if it's going to be a regular thing you'll have to throw in your share."

"Thanks. Not tonight. I have to meet someone. Is there anything else you can tell me about Captain Galante? Did he have any enemies you know of?"

"He never mentioned anyone. He was transferred to the hospital only a month ago, hardly time to generate a blood feud."

"Where was he before the transfer?" That was something that hadn't been covered in the file I'd been given.

"An infantry division, part of the medical battalion," Bradshaw said. "Can't recall which one."

"You really don't know much about the man, do you?"

"Hardly a thing, Boyle. We didn't work together at the hospital. I specialize in skin conditions, or at least I did in civilian life.

Here I deal with trench foot, frostbite, burns, that sort of thing. Galante was a surgeon, but he was also interested in shell shock. Nervous exhaustion. He'd talk a blue streak about it if you let him." There was something disapproving in Bradshaw's voice.

"You're not as interested?"

"I served as a private in the trenches back in '18. Saw enough shell shock to last a lifetime. Didn't want to talk about it." Bradshaw held the pipe stem in his mouth with grim determination and looked away from me, out the window, into the darkness.

"Did Galante talk about anything else? Interests?" I knew the topic of shell shock was closed, but I didn't want Bradshaw to clam up totally.

"He knew Italian history, and spoke some of the language. Chatted with Signora Salvalaggio now and then. About what, I have no idea. I recall that he was intrigued by the Royal Palace. Quite a place in its time, I'm sure, but a drafty flea-ridden ruin now."

"Fleas?" I resisted the urge to scratch.

"Fleas and rats. Never go near the place if I can help it. Ah, here's Wilson."

Bradshaw introduced me to the other doctor, telling him I was with CID. Close enough.

"Are we suspects?" Wilson asked as he took a seat and lit a cigarette. He was younger than Bradshaw, but not by much. Dark hair, thinning. Dark eyes, glancing at Bradshaw, who only grunted.

"Where were you the night he was killed?"

Wilson's eyes widened. Apparently his question had been a joke.

"Here, I think. We had a lot of casualties in from the Liri Valley that day. We all worked late. Bradshaw and I were both back here by eight o'clock or so. Galante never showed, but that was normal for any of us. We often sleep at the hospital if needed. After dinner, I sacked out. We're not really suspects, are we?"

"Listen," I said. "Most investigations are about ruling people out. I'm sure no one thinks of you as suspects, or they wouldn't have me staying here. Were you close with Galante? Friends?"

"Friendly," Wilson said, relaxing into his chair. "Not pals. He hadn't been here long, and like I said, the hours can be long."

"So the 32nd Station Hospital does more than care for calluses on the backsides of HQ types?"

"Fair amount of that," Bradshaw offered. "When you get this many generals in one place, you tend to see a lot of normal ailments, the type of things you'd see in peacetime. Colds, influenza, gout, bad back, the list goes on."

"A lot of them would like their own personal physician too," Wilson said. "But we get a lot of battle casualties brought in from the line. Wounds and illnesses. We've had over a thousand cases of trench foot, not to mention frostbite."

"Worse among you Americans," Bradshaw said. "Your army needs better waterproof boots. The way it rains around here, your chaps end up living in constant mud in the mountains."

"Could Galante have been at the palace to treat a general?" I wanted to get the conversation back to the main topic. Shortage of winter gear was a whole separate crime.

"Maybe," Wilson said. "Hasn't CID checked that already?" "I'll check tomorrow. I only got in today, so I need to get up to speed."

"From where?" Wilson asked.

"I was on vacation in Switzerland," I said.

"Just what we need, a joker. Come on, I'll show you to your room."

The room was spare. One bureau with a washstand. One narrow bed. One small table and chair. One light hanging from the ceiling. One window. I tossed my duffle on the floor and sat on the bed. The springs creaked. The room smelled faintly of dust and stale air. I went to the window and opened it, despite the weather. I leaned out and lifted my face to the cold rain, hoping it would help me rally against the tiredness that was creeping through my bones. It was fully dark now, the B-17s on the airstrip lost in the gloom. I heard a jeep start up and saw headlights casting their thin glare on the rain-slicked road. Time for me to go too. Drinks at the palace. What a war.

Chapter Seven

I grabbed a meal at the officer's mess at the palace. Not the senior officer's mess, which I had first mistakenly blundered into. I knew something was wrong when I saw the white tablecloths set with gold-trimmed porcelain and crystal glassware. GIs wearing white jackets carried trays of broiled steaks and other delicacies to tables graced by elderly colonels and generals who looked more like businessmen at a hotel than soldiers not far from the front. I'd backed up to the doorway, not wanting to draw attention to my silver lieutenant's bars. I watched the diners, staff officers most likely, and wondered what they wrote home about. The atmosphere was muted, soft and swanky, the hefty clink of real silverware on porcelain somehow reassuring.

GI waiters crossed in front of me, taking orders, clearing dishes, pouring wine looted from only the best cellars. I saw one guy trip, a little stumble, losing his balance enough to send his load of plates crashing down. It was loud, the tile floor sending echoes of shattering sounds across the room. Heads rose from beefsteaks, irritated at the interruption. Turning to leave, I noticed another GI huddled in a corner, hidden from the diners by a sideboard that held glasses and dishware. He gripped the sideboard with one hand, pulling himself up, the other hand held over his heart. His face was white, his mouth open as he gulped in shallow breaths of air.

"You okay, buddy?" I asked as I took his elbow.

"Yeah . . . yes, sir, I'm fine. The noise, it surprised me, that's all. I'm fine." He stood, embarrassment flushing his face red. At least it gave him some color. He tossed me a weak smile and left, glancing around guiltily in case anyone else had noticed.

There were no fine tablecloths in the officer's mess. The food was warm and filling, even if I had to serve myself, and I didn't linger. But there was plenty of lingering in the room that served as the officer's club. A bar was set up beneath a towering gold-relief sculpture of an angel holding a scroll, with two doorways twenty feet high on either side. The floor was inlaid marble, with plush carpets set out in the seating areas to keep the noise down, but that did little to drown out the chatter that rose from every corner of the room. It was a lively bunch, officers of all ranks, nationalities, and services, with a liberal sprinkling of WACs, ATS, and other females, some wearing decidedly civilian outfits. Those ladies were surrounded by senior officers, guys who wouldn't be questioned about their choice of female companion.

I saw Einsmann and he nodded to an empty table at the far end of the room. I got a whiskey at the bar and joined him.

"How are things, Billy?"

"Better for some than others," I said, raising my glass in a toast and glancing at the brigadier general with a woman who looked like a movie star on his arm.

"You got that right," he said. "This war is a real racket for some guys."

"I saw the senior officer's mess upstairs. Talk about easy street."

"I ate there a couple of times. Nice thing about being a reporter is that when the brass wants to butter you up, you eat well. You know the chef they got up there worked at the Ritz in New York?"

"He should've brought over his own waiters. Those GIs dressed up in white jackets are lucky they aren't paid in tips."

"Better than white coats," Einsmann said with a sharp laugh.

"Why do you say that?"

"They're all convalescents from the hospital. Bomb-happy, you know what I mean? They got the jitters all the time. Somebody figured it was a good job for them while they waited to go back up the line."

"Interesting choice of occupation," I said.

"How so?"

"Waiting hand and foot on senior brass, watching them devour steaks, knowing they're the guys ordering you into the mountains, to live on K rations in a muddy hole. Must be great for morale."

"I never thought about that. Could be a story in it, Billy."

"Everybody's got a story," I said, not certain where Einsmann might be going with this. Some of those convalescent boys had had it tough, and I didn't want an overeager newshound making it tougher. "Did you find out anything about what I told you?"

"Not much, Billy. Word is Galante was kicked upstairs, sent to the 32nd Station Hospital because he didn't get along with a senior officer on the 3rd Division staff."

"Galante was with the 3rd? That's the

same outfit Landry was from."

"Yeah, but he was with the Medical Battalion. Unless Landry had been wounded, chances are he wouldn't run into him. There are probably over twelve thousand guys in the 3rd Division right now, especially with all the replacements coming in."

"Okay, so what was the problem?"

"Shell shock, or nervous exhaustion, whatever they're calling it these days. Galante had his own ideas about treating it, and he clashed with a colonel named Schleck. Seems Schleck doesn't buy the whole concept, and blames any GI's failure of nerve on poor leadership."

"Combat fatigue," I said, recalling what I'd heard back in London. "They're calling it combat fatigue now."

"Yeah, well, there's plenty of it going around, whatever the moniker. The boys in the 3rd Division have been at it since North Africa. I wrote a piece about them a month ago. They hit the beaches at French Morocco, then ten months later in Sicily. Then more landings at Salerno, fighting along the Volturno River and up to Cassino. They finally got pulled out of the line a couple of weeks ago."

"Is that why they're here, to rest and refit?"

"Who knows? Maybe the brass is fattening them up for the kill. Me, I don't know how the infantry does it. It's one thing to fight the Germans in this terrain. It's another thing to live up in those mountains, with the rain, cold and knee-deep mud. But to do both at the same time? No wonder some guys go off their rocker."

There wasn't much to say about that. I tried to imagine what it was like, winter in the high Apennines; Germans dug in behind every ridgeline, trying to kill you while you worked at not freezing to death. Yeah, no wonder. I sipped my whiskey and tried not to think about the guys who were up there right now, dying. There were times to think, and times to drink. If you knew which to do when, you might stay sane. I took another sip, then slammed back the rest of the booze, waiting for the warmth in my belly to spread while visions of cold and wet GIs faded from my mind.

They didn't. As Einsmann and I gabbed, about the war, the women in the room, the brass, all the usual bull, I knew they were out there. I'd been there too, not as high as in those mountains, but out in a foxhole with cold water pooled at the bottom, hot lead flying above, and the cries of the wounded all around. I could see it now, even as I watched Einsmann return with a couple of fresh glasses, and for a moment it felt like there was no time at all, but simply here and there, the bar and the mountains, and I could as easily be in one as the other. I must be tired, I thought, too much travel. We talked, and drank, and the noise of the conversations in the room rose into an incessant buzz as it grew more crowded. I could barely make out what Einsmann was saying and had to lean closer when I heard him mention ASTP.

"What did you say about ASTP?" My kid brother Danny was in the Army Specialized Training Program back home. He'd enlisted as soon as he was eighteen, and the army put him into ASTP after basic training. It was a program for kids with brains, sending them to college for advanced courses while keeping them in uniform. The idea was that they'd graduate as officers, keeping the army supplied with second lieutenants as the war went on. It was tailor-made for Danny; he was a bright kid in some ways, but he was too young to have any common sense about staying alive. A college campus was the safest place for him.

"Working on a story about it," Einsmann said. "The army is pulling most of those kids out of college."

"Why?"

"They're short on infantry replacements. The brass figures it doesn't make much sense to keep those boys in college when they need bodies now. They pulled over a hundred thousand of them out, about two-thirds of the program."

"When did this happen?" I'd had a letter from Danny a month ago and he hadn't mentioned a thing about it.

"Few weeks ago. There's a transport landing in Naples tomorrow with the first batch for Italy. Most are going to the 3rd. I'm going down there to interview some of them. Then I'll follow up in a few days when they've been assigned to their platoons. Ought to be interesting."

"My kid brother is in ASTP, but I guess I would have heard if he'd been called up. I can imagine these veterans giving college boys a cozy welcome, especially since they've been sitting out the past few months on campus." I hoped Danny wasn't among this bunch. They'd have a hard time before they ever got to the front.

"I figure that's what will make it interesting," Einsmann said. "Word is some non-coms think the ASTPers will have a monopoly on promotions when they hand out new stripes. Especially the Southern boys."

"Everything will probably smooth out once they get up on the line," I said. *Yeah, it'll be peachy up there, one big happy family united by butchery and misery.*

I saw Major Kearns making his way through the crowd, with two *Carabinieri* officers in tow. They both wore dark-blue dress uniforms, with the flaming grenade emblem of the Italian national police on their service caps.

"Lieutenant Boyle," Kearns said, after a nod of greeting to Einsmann. "This is *Capitano* Renzo Trevisi, and *Tenente* Luca Amatori. Capitano Trevisi is in charge of the local Carabinieri garrison."

"Billy Boyle," I said, standing to shake hands.

"Pleased to meet you," Trevisi said in heavily accented but precise English. He looked to be about forty, with a thick, dark mustache, a slight paunch, and a friendly smile. "If I can be of any assistance, I am at your service. Major Kearns has told us of your investigations. I do not think there is any civilian involvement in this unfortunate matter, but please ask should you require anything."

"Thank you, Capitano, I will."

Trevisi spoke in Italian to his lieutenant, who had been silent during the exchange in

English. I heard Galante and Landry's names mentioned as he gestured to me. "Tenente Amatori will provide whatever you need if I am not available. *Buona sera.*"

"Interesting," Einsmann said as they moved off.

"What?"

"I've never seen Italian officers here before, army or Carabinieri. I wonder what's up?"

"Well, the Italians are on our side now. They have a combat group fighting near Cassino, and most of the Carabinieri are loyal to the new government. Stands to reason they'd show up at HQ sooner or later. Plus there have been two murders."

"Yeah," Einsmann said. "But the killings are an army matter. No way they'd let the locals in on that unless they needed them for something."

"Well, not my problem," I said as I watched Kearns and the two Italians huddled in conversation. Maybe it was somebody else's problem, maybe not. I decided I had enough to worry about without adding Italian cops, and got back to the subject of Galante.

"This Colonel Schleck, who got Galante transferred out. Where do I find him?"

"Personnel section, 3rd Division HQ, over

at San Felice."

"I'm headed there tomorrow. I'll see what he knows."

"What can he tell you? I doubt he killed Galante because they disagreed about combat fatigue."

"No, but if he had it in for Galante, he had to know him, right? You can't have a beef with a guy and not get to know him, even if it's only his weaknesses."

"And Galante's weakness might tell you about who killed him?"

"It's all I have right now," I said.

I finished my drink and made my way out of the room, passing a group of colonels and women in low-cut dresses. The colonels were flushed and loud, their lips smacking with drink and lust. The women laughed, a harsh, high laugh that echoed off the marble floor and stayed with me as I stood in the rain, looking toward the invisible mountains to the north, where men shivered, suffered, and bled.

Chapter Eight

San Felice was a fair-sized village, or at least had been before the fighting passed through. Now it was a fair-sized pile of rubble, with the few intact buildings housing the 3rd Division staff. In front of a burned-out church, a water pipe stuck up from the ground, a spray of water gushing into the air. Women and children with buckets were lined up, eager to haul the fresh water home. At the base of the pipe, a gleaming white stone arm lay on the ground, its fingers gracefully pointing to the sky. Debris and masonry cascaded from the buildings into the street, making it hard to tell where the outline of homes and shops had been, but it was obvious this had been the piazza, the center of the village. Now it was crammed with shattered stone, a line of black-clad women, and American military vehicles.

I found G-1, Personnel, on the ground

floor of a two-story school that was missing its roof. Colonel Raymond Schleck was seated at a desk near a boarded-up window, a tin bucket catching drips of rainwater from the ceiling. Files were stacked in wooden boxes all around him, and two clerks at the other end of the room pecked at typewriters, making piles of forms in triplicate, some nearly a foot high. They had the grimly bored look of men who knew there was probably an easier way to do this job, but also understood it had to be done the army way.

"Colonel Schleck?"

"See one of my clerks, Lieutenant, I'm busy." Schleck cranked a field telephone, barked a few quick questions into it, listened, and slammed it into its leather case without comment. He crossed off names on a list and consulted a personnel file. Without looking up, he spoke again. "You still here?"

"Yes sir. I need to speak with you about Captain Max Galante. I'm afraid one of your clerks won't do."

"And who the hell are you to tell me what won't do?" Now I had his full attention. I showed him my orders. He gave them back, frowned, then waved in the general direction of a chair.

"You've heard Captain Galante was murdered?"

"Yeah. Tough break. I lost a good platoon leader too. Landry. What can I do for you, Boyle?"

"Tell me about Galante. You two had a disagreement, right?"

"You think I killed him because of that?" He gave a small chuckle and shook a Chesterfield from a crumpled pack. He lit up and tossed the match into the bucket.

"You had him transferred out of the division, so I doubt there'd be a reason to kill him. But what did you think of him?"

"I thought he worked hard, and was sincere in his beliefs."

"Listen, Colonel," I said. "It's nice not to speak ill of the dead, but that doesn't help me find who killed Galante and Landry."

"Okay," Schleck said. "He was a snotty prig who thought he was smarter than everyone else. I mean it when I say he worked hard, but he had a bad attitude."

"About combat fatigue?"

"Listen, Boyle," Schleck said, sitting up straight and pointing his nicotine-stained finger at me. "You start telling these boys that all they have to do to get out of the line is to go on sick call with the shakes, pretty soon you'll have empty foxholes all across these damn mountains. You can be damn sure the Krauts don't believe in combat fatigue."

"You think it isn't real?"

"I don't say there isn't something to it. But Galante and I differed on the cause. In my book, there's only one way to explain why one unit, on the line as long as another, has a completely different rate of combat fatigue cases."

"What's that?"

"Leadership, Boyle. At every level, from generals to second lieutenants. That's what makes the difference. Poor leadership leads to excessive cases of nervous exhaustion, or whatever the shrinks call it. In a unit with good leadership, the cases are fewer. When the men trust their officers, they have confidence, and that keeps them going."

"But it still happens, in every unit."

"Some men are cowards. It's unpleasant, but it's true."

"Was this the reason you had Galante transferred out?"

"It was on my recommendation, yes. We needed to send a message, that there was no easy way out of combat duty. Galante was always trying to ease the burden on the men, with all good intentions, I'm sure. But the fact is, it's a heavy burden they face. It's not fair to them to make believe it's anything but."

"Okay, I get what the beef was about. You described him as snotty. Why? Because of his attitude?" I understood the difference of opinion. But the use of "snotty" spoke to something deeper, a disdain that made me suspicious.

"Holier than thou, by a mile."

"You also said he was a prig. What does that have to do with anything?"

"Nothing. That's just me spouting off. He liked art, Italian history, that sort of thing. He preferred to spend his off-duty hours chatting with the locals and visiting museums. He wasn't much of a poker player or drinker."

"He wasn't the only guy to visit a museum over here. Did he think he was better than you?"

"I didn't say that. He just didn't pass the time like most guys. We do have a few other oddballs who keep to themselves, but they do their job and don't get anyone hurt."

"You make him sound dangerous," I said.

"He was. He got an entire squad killed."

"How?"

"Ask Sergeant Jim Cole. He's one of your CID buddies, isn't he? Now get the hell out. If you need anything else, see my assistant,

Major Arnold, next office. He will cooperate as required, but I don't want to see you step foot in my office again."

That was that.

Major Matthew Arnold wasn't in, and his clerk said he was busy organizing the new replacements. I showed him my orders and told him to inform the major I might have questions for him. The clerk said everyone had questions for Major Arnold, like how many replacements would they get, and were any experienced men coming in. I got the impression I was everyone's lowest priority.

I thought about Cole not saying anything about knowing Galante. That made me suspicious. If Galante did get a squad wiped out, then there would be plenty of guys looking to even the score. Maybe Landry was involved? But why hadn't Schleck told me more, and why hadn't anyone else mentioned it? I hoped the guys in Landry's platoon could explain things. I drove out of the village, toward the 7th Regiment bivouac area, following the signs as they led me along roads that were little more than dirt tracks soaked from recent rains. Heavy trucks plowed the mire in both directions, splattering my jeep with thick, yellowish

Italian mud.

I drove until the road turned into a field, churned into a thick ooze of ankle-deep mud by countless wheels and thousands of GI boots. Beyond was a sea of tents, rows of olive drab stretching in every direction. I gunned the jeep before I got stuck, and parked on a patch of high ground in a line with other vehicles. As I got out, my boots sank in the muck, and it began to rain. I turned up the collar of my mackinaw and ran, as best I could, to the rows of tents marked 2nd Battalion, Easy Company.

Within the tent city, planking had been set up between rows, and the going was easier. There were mess tents, medical tents, supply tents, assembly tents, and command tents. The smell of wood smoke hung in the air, as small tent stoves tried to beat back the wet chill. Around the perimeter deuce-and-a-half trucks backed up to the large supply tents and disgorged crates of food, ammunition, and all the other necessities of life and death. Communication lines were being strung throughout the encampment, wire parties carrying spools of the stuff, unreeling it through their leather-glove-clad hands.

"Third Platoon?" I asked a corporal

weighed down with bandoliers of M1 ammo.

"Follow me," he said. After a couple of turns, he nodded to a small two-man tent. Then he left, distributing the bandoliers to neighboring squad tents. I pulled aside the tent flap, wondering if a new lieutenant had been assigned yet to take over Landry's slot. Two-man tents were usually reserved for officers.

"Close the damn flap!" I did, and wiped the rainwater from my eyes. "Lieutenant," a voice added as an afterthought.

Seated on one cot was a staff sergeant, cleaning his Thompson submachine gun and giving me the eye. Across from him a second lieutenant fed pieces of wood into a small stove. Between the two cots and footlockers, cases of supplies, the stove, and the two guys, there wasn't much room.

"Looking for someone, Lieutenant?" the staff sergeant asked.

"Is this 3rd Platoon? Landry's outfit?"

"Landry's dead," he said. "This here is Lieutenant Evans. He has the platoon now."

"Andy Evans," the other fellow said. He had an eager smile, a fresh face, and shiny lieutenant's bars on the collar of his wool shirt. We shook hands, and I introduced myself to both of them.

"Gates," was all the sergeant said. He was no more than a couple years older than Evans, but all the freshness was long gone from his face. He worked intently on reassembling his Thompson, the scent of gun oil rising from his labors.

"Platoon Sergeant?" I asked, pointing at his stripes, three chevrons and a rocker.

"Yeah," Gates said. His eyes narrowed as he glanced at Evans, and back to me with the faintest glimmer of interest. "You assigned to us?"

"No," I said. "I'm here to investigate the murder of Lieutenant Landry."

"I hear he was a good man," Evans said. He'd understood what Gates was getting at and was trying to assert his authority. Problem was, he wouldn't have much pull with a veteran like Gates until he survived a few days in combat without getting anyone killed for no good reason.

"Good or bad, he's dead," Gates said, wiping down the assembled Thompson. "Not much we can do about it."

"Let me guess," I said, taking a seat on Evans's cot, glancing at the red hair sticking out from under his wool cap. "They call you Rusty."

"Yeah. Since I was in short pants. What do you want, Lieutenant?"

"To find out who murdered Landry. You want justice for him, don't you?"

"Andy," Gates said, ignoring my question. "Be a good time to check on the men, see that they got a full load of ammo."

"Good idea," Evans said, as if he'd been about to do just that. He put on his helmet and field jacket and left, looking happy to leave this talk of his predecessor behind.

"Justice," Gates said. "You look like you been around enough to know there's no justice up front."

"The murders didn't happen at the front."

"No, but sooner or later your number's up. At least Landry went out clean and dry. Odds were he wouldn't last much longer anyway. Good platoon leaders seldom do. Lucky guys and cowards have a better chance. Sorry, but I can't get all worked up over it. I've seen too many come and go to care how they get it."

"That's a helluva attitude," I said.

"It's the way it is. If I can help you, I will. But I have my hands full right now with this platoon and a green second louie. They're getting ready for something, and it's going to happen soon. They pulled us off the line a few weeks ago, gave us clean uniforms, hot showers, good food, and plenty of passes. Not to mention replacements. There's something brewing, and it ain't good news, let me tell you."

"Why do you say that?"

"You ever get good news in the army?"

"You have a point. What do you think of Evans?"

"Nervous. Eager to show he's got what it takes. He got transferred in from a supply outfit in Acerra. At least he ain't right off the boat. He'll screw up, then either figure things out or get himself or us killed. The usual."

"Landry figured things out?"

"Yeah. He came to us from battalion staff. He knew some of the guys, didn't have to prove anything. Made sure we had hot chow when he could, never volunteered, kept his head in a fight. Can't ask for much more."

"Except not to get killed in bivouac. Any idea who had it in for him?"

"Not a clue. No one, really. He must have seen something, or ran into someone who had a secret. Someone who knew how to break a neck."

"Who found the body?"

"Don't know. Some private from the transportation company, I heard. It was stashed behind a supply tent."

"Stashed? Why do you say that?"

"I went over there as soon as I heard.

Landry was next to the tent, and a set of guy wires ran above his legs. He couldn't have fallen there. So someone stashed his body, out of sight."

"Makes sense. Can you show me?" The photo I'd seen of Landry hadn't shown the lower part of his body, so I'd missed the fact that he'd been placed there. And Cole hadn't mentioned it. Was he a rookie at this, or did he have something to hide?

"Come on," Gates said with a sigh. He donned a poncho, his helmet, and slung his Thompson, barrel down, over his shoulder. We headed out into the rain. The supply tents were at the edge of the area, a double row, back to back. There was just enough space between the guy wires from each tent to walk without tripping over them. The ground was soaked, but it hadn't been ground up into mud yet.

"It was dry when he was found," I said.

"Yeah, we had a clear spell for a while. It's been raining off and on since. You looking for anything special?"

"No, just trying to get a feel for things. I saw one photograph, but it only showed his upper body. You're right, he wasn't killed here. So someone had to carry him from someplace else."

"What difference does that make?"

"Don't know yet. Maybe he didn't want the body found until he got to Galante."

"I heard his body was sort of hidden too. Tucked away by those fancy fountains."

"Rusty, for a guy who doesn't care about this investigation, you seem to know a lot about it."

"Not much else to do around here but clean weapons and listen to scuttlebutt. You seen enough?"

"Yeah," I said, looking down the long row of tents, a back alley of olive-drab canvas. Landry had been killed somewhere close and hidden here. It had to be close. It took some nerve to snap a man's neck and then carry him when you could be seen at any moment. Even in the dark, you could trip over a tent stake, create a racket, and be done for. I didn't have a good feeling about this.

"Let's get out of the rain," Gates said.

Chapter Nine

We sat in the mess tent, clutching mugs of hot coffee as rainwater dripped from our clothes. Gates wiped his Thompson down and leaned it against the bench.

"Not everybody here goes around armed," I said.

"Not everybody here has been around since Tunisia, Sicily, and Salerno. I notice you keep your .45 close at hand."

"You never can tell," I said. "Especially in my line of work."

"That's what I tell the men. If you're always loaded for bear, the bear won't win. It's got to become a habit, if you want to stay alive."

"Evans hasn't picked it up yet," I said. He was a couple of tables away, playing cards with three other lieutenants. Not a weapon among them.

"No. He says it's safe here." He shook his head at the futility of explaining things to officers, and sipped his coffee. "He hasn't fired a weapon since he's been in Italy, so you can't blame him. Too much."

"Do you know Sergeant Jim Cole?"

Gates's eyes flickered for a second. "Jimmy Cole? Sure. He's over at CID now, right?"

"Yeah, he's working this case with me. How about Captain Galante? Did you know him when he was with 3rd Division?"

"Knew of him," Gates said. He looked away at nothing in particular.

"What did you think of him?"

"I think he's dead, and I have the living to worry about. Now I have a question for you."

"Okay."

"Do you think I killed them?"

"That's not how it works. If I could —"

"Do you think I killed them?"

I looked at his hard eyes. I looked at his strong arms, and at his weapon close by. He held ready violence like a whip at his side.

"I don't think so. But I've been wrong before."

"Fair enough," Gates said. "You want to talk to the other sergeants?"

"Sure," I said. "But tell me about Cole and Galante first."

"No need for that. Come on." Gates rose, and I followed him out of the mess tent. I knew I wasn't going to get anything more out of him about Cole, but I didn't know why. Rusty Gates was hiding something, but I didn't think it was murder. He was a deadly killer, yes. But everything he did was about surviving. He wanted to live, and he wanted his men to live. Landry had been a good platoon leader, and there was no percentage in seeing him dead. But as I told Gates, I'd been wrong. Dead wrong.

The rain was heavier now, and we dashed along the plank boardwalks to a tent in the Easy Company area. Gates held the flap as we entered, and the warmth from a glowing tent stove was welcome. Crates of supplies were stacked to the rear, and next to the stove a table was set up, with three noncoms lounging around it. Two lanterns hung from the ceiling, shedding light on a stack of cash, empty bottles, cigar butts, and other debris from what looked like a long night of poker.

"Game busted up, boys?" Gates asked.

"Yeah. Flint finally cleaned the padre out. He was the big winner all night, and when he caved, the other guys left. Couple of corporals from Baker Company, they shoulda quit hours ago. Who's this?" A stubby hand gripping a smoldering cigar waved in my direction.

"Lieutenant Boyle. He's looking for whoever killed Landry and Galante. He wants to talk to you guys."

"Call me Billy, fellas. Everyone does. Who made the killing?" All three of them looked at me, mouths agape. "I mean, who was the big winner?" I pointed to the pile of scrip.

"That'd be me, Billy. Amos Flint."

"Flint has Second Squad," Gates said. "Louie with the stogie there has First Squad, Stump the Third."

I shook hands with Flint. He had a ready grin, but who wouldn't, after raking in all that dough? He had startlingly blue eyes, and was neatly attired in a chocolate-brown wool shirt, usually reserved for officers. He had the satisfied calmness of a winner who'd known he'd win all along.

"Louie Walla, from Walla Walla," the cigar-chomping sergeant said as he extended his callused hand. "Last name is Walla, and I'm from Walla Walla, Washington. How 'bout that?"

"Amazing, Louie," was all I could say. Louie was short, with black curly hair, a raspy voice, and an easy grin wrapped around his cigar.

"Don't mind Louie, he gives everyone that speech," the next sergeant said. "Marty Stumpf. They call me Stump, on account of the Kraut-sounding name." Stump was sandy-haired, with high cheekbones and eyes that didn't seem to miss a thing.

"Yeah, if we called him Stumpf up on the line, one of his cousins might answer," Flint said, and they all laughed at what sounded like a familiar joke. Stump rolled his eyes.

"You guys answer Billy's questions. I'm going to pull Evans away from his bridge party. Weapons inspection in one hour. Have your men ready."

"Aw, Rusty, we been up all night," Louie said.

"Yeah, and look where that got you. One hour," Gates said as he left.

"He's right," Flint said to the others. "We gotta stay on our toes, and show the rookies what's what." The other sergeants groaned but did not argue.

"Anybody have an idea about who might want Landry dead?" I asked, watching their eyes for the downward glance, the rapid flicker, anything that would signal hesitation, the censoring of thought into words.

"Nobody south of the Bernhardt Line," Flint said, referring to the name the Germans gave to their current main line of defense, stretching across the Italian mountains south of Monte Cassino.

"You got that right," Stump said. "Landry

was one of the best."

"That's what everybody says," I said. "Funny that he got murdered. What do you think, Louie?"

"I think I'd like to get my hands on whoever done it. Now we got ourselves a ninety-day wonder for a platoon leader, like to get us all killed if he ain't smart enough to let Rusty run things."

"I think Billy is asking what we think about who might have killed him, Louie," Flint said. "Not about his replacement."

"Yeah, sure. Well, no one had a beef with him that I know of. He was real good to us, on the line and off. Kept the MPs off our backs, that sort of thing."

"He a big gambler?"

"No," Stump replied, and the others shook their heads in agreement. "No more than the average Joe. Helps to pass the time. But he didn't owe anyone, I'm pretty sure."

"You think that's why the ten of hearts was left on him?" Flint said. "Like a warning not to welsh?"

"No, you don't kill a guy who owes money, unless it's to make an example."

"Hell, if the Lieutenant needed dough, any of us woulda been glad to cough up what we had," Louie said. "We all looked out for each other. I woulda given the shirt off my back for the guy. Saved my life just a coupla weeks ago. Pulled me outta the way of a Kraut 88. Took the arm off a guy not twenty yards behind us. And Flint, he saved Landry's life more than once, right?"

"Yep," Stump said. "He plugged that Kraut officer we thought was dead. He was about to put a slug into Landry's head. Flint shot him from fifty yards out, square in the back of the head."

"Nice shooting," I said.

Flint shrugged. "Lucky. I was just hoping these guys would hit the dirt. The guy only had a Walther."

"Worked, didn't it?" Stump said. "I dove into a shell hole filled with mud. I would have shot that sonuvabitch just for getting me wet. Landry gave that Walther to Flint, and he sold it to some headquarters weenie for a load of booze when we got sent here." He grinned.

"Yeah, there's no percentage in carrying a Kraut pistol," Louie said. "You get captured, especially by the SS, and they take exception."

"Don't like it much myself," Flint said. "Finding a Kraut carrying around anything from our boys." There were murmurs of agreement, and I knew I was in the presence of hard men, men who knew how to survive, to put away mercy until another day. Kinder men than them were buried in graveyards for hundreds of miles behind us.

"You guys have any trouble with the military police?"

"Naw, nothing that you'd call trouble," Stump said. "We ain't had time to get into any real trouble. A few twelve-hour passes that got us as far as Acerra, a town about an hour south. It ain't much, but it's still in one piece, so it's the best place to go if you can't get to Naples."

"Landry go down there much?"

"A few times, sure," Flint said. "We saw him having dinner with some other officers at a café, that sort of thing. He and I had to go down there the night before he died, as a matter of fact. One of the men in my squad started a fight, broke up a joint pretty bad. We had to square it with the locals."

"What kind of joint?"

"The kind with booze and broads," Louie said, grinning as he clamped the cigar in his mouth. "We didn't want the MPs to declare it off-limits, so we took up a collection, fixed things with the owner."

"Landry knew it would be better all around to keep things quiet," Flint said. "Give the boys a place to blow off steam, and keep a good soldier out of the stockade.

All it took was a wad of occupation scrip."

"No hard feelings with the locals?"

"No," said Flint. "And even if there were, no civilian could make it in here, never mind get the drop on Landry." He was right. I'd had a flicker of hope that this could be traced back to a barroom brawl, but it didn't add up. This killer was in uniform, invisible to everyone around him. A strong, experienced killer.

"You all know Landry a while?"

"Yeah," Stump said. "He was with battalion staff when I got transferred in, back in Tunisia. Landry brought Louie with him when he got the platoon just before Sicily. Flint's been around the longest, since Morocco, right?"

"Yep," Flint said. "Not many of us left from back then."

"Any other sergeants in the outfit?" I asked. "Assistant squad leaders?"

"We *was* the assistant squad leaders," Louie said. "We got promoted due to sudden vacancies opening up. Ain't enough noncoms to go around, so no more assistant squad leaders. Just a bunch of green replacements."

"We're supposed to have twelve-man squads," Flint said. "We each have two or three experienced men, but none ready for corporal's stripes yet. Plus about a half-dozen replacements."

"Are you getting any of the ASTP replacements coming in?" I asked.

"Them college boys? Be more trouble than they worth," Louie said, crushing out his cigar.

"Aw, you never know," Stump said. "Keep an open mind, will ya?"

"My kid brother is in ASTP," I said, unexpectedly bristling at Louie's insinuation. "I think he'll do alright if it comes to that."

"No offense, Lieutenant," Louie said. "You know how it is with replacements."

"Yeah, I know. Tell me, did any of you know Captain Galante?"

"He patched me up once," Flint said. "Got a piece of shrapnel in the calf, and he took good care of it. Let me lay around the hospital for a couple of days, with all those pretty nurses. He was a decent guy."

"That's what I heard too," Stump said. Louie agreed.

"Any idea who'd want him dead?"

"No," Stump said, looking at the others, who shook their heads. "He wasn't like a lot of the other officers. Didn't drink a lot, kept to himself. Didn't you tell me, Flint, he had a thing for Italian art?"

"Yeah, right," Flint said, snapping his fingers. "He told me all about the fancy artwork they have in the churches here. I don't remember the names of the artists, but he knew them all. He knew all about Italian royalty too. Me, I didn't even know they had a king over here until he fired Mussolini. King Victor Emmanuel, it was. Galante told me all about them, how the royal family used to have fancy dance balls right here in Caserta, in the palace."

"A real bookworm," Louie said.

"Louie, you got no class," Stump said. "Billy, you got any other questions? We gotta go get our boys ready for inspection. Everybody gets a pass into town once we're done."

"Just one. What about Jim Cole?" There was silence, and three sets of eyes looked everywhere but at me. "What's the big secret?"

"Nothing," Stump said. "Cole's a good guy."

"Yeah, leave him out of this," Flint said. "Let's go."

Louie shrugged, and they all stood.

"Don't you feel bad taking all that dough from the padre?" Stump said.

"I'm going to give it back, most of it anyway. For some worthy cause," Flint announced with a grin. "I just wanted to hang onto it for a while, make believe it was mine."

"Who's the padre?"

"Father Dare," Flint said. "Regimental chaplain."

"Last guy to see Landry alive," Stump said.

"Not counting the guy what killed him," corrected Louie Walla from Walla Walla.

The rain had let up, so as the three sergeants went to organize their squads, I walked back to where Landry's body had been found. Smoke mingled with the fog and dressed everything in a dull, damp gray. I stood in the narrow pathway in the rear of the supply tents, an alleyway bordered by stakes and ropes from the tents on either side. I planted my feet where the killer must have stood to drop Landry's body, and saw how he must've had to drag him by the collar to get him under the guy wires and up against the tent.

Where did you come from? I thought as I looked around. How far did you carry him? Why did you bring him here? I went back to the boardwalk and looked in every direction. More tents, more open space. Was Landry killed in a tent? No, then he could have been left there. I walked in front of the supply tent, and noticed the tire tracks in the mud. Trucks had been bringing in supplies constantly, backing up to the supply tents for easy unloading.

Here, Landry was killed here. In between trucks parked for the night. No, not for the night, just for a while. That's why the killer had to move the body, if he didn't want it found right away.

But why did he need the body not to be found? Why hide both bodies in places that only delayed their discovery? To show someone else? To frighten someone — a major, maybe? Or was it simpler than that? Maybe he had to go get a deck of cards. If that was it, then the cards were an afterthought.

So what if they were? That and a nickel would get me a phone call.

I shivered, mostly from the chill creeping up my boots, but also from the presence of murder. Here, on this meaningless patch of dirt, a man's life ended. The air was different here, choked with mist, as if the specter of violence oozed from the ground. I looked around, feeling I was being watched, trying to pick out a pair of eyes focused on me and this patch of dirt. Nothing but GIs hurrying back and forth, killing time while waiting to be killed.

Maybe Landry would have been dead anyway in a week, maybe two, when they went back to the line. But that made those two stolen weeks all the more precious. Some bastard had taken that from him, and I was going to make sure he paid for his sins.

Before he added to them, I prayed.

Chapter Ten

"I was wondering when you'd pay me a visit," Father Dare said as he invited me into his tent. He had his gear laid out on his cot, and was stuffing his field pack with thick wool socks. A communion kit lay open, the brass chalice gleaming from a fresh polish. Rosary beads lay curled on the wool blanket. "Have a seat, Lieutenant Boyle."

"How'd you know I was here, Father?"

"Word travels fast, especially about the dead," he said, as he sat opposite me in a folding camp chair, surrounded by stacks of hymnals. He sighed, leaned forward, and looked straight into my eyes. "How can I help you, son?"

Father Dare was maybe thirty or so, hardly old enough to call me son, but with the silver cross on his collar and the paraphernalia of the church all around him, I let it slide. He was a tall guy, with dark hair and thick eyebrows that almost met when he furrowed his brow. His eyes were bloodshot, likely from the night of poker and cigar smoke.

"No one else has been much help," I said, unsure of exactly what I hoped to learn here. "It's pretty much the same story everywhere. Lieutenant Landry was a good man, an officer the men could count on. Well liked. Captain Galante didn't get along with Colonel Schleck and got himself kicked upstairs to the hospital at Caserta. He kept to himself, didn't seem to bother anyone other than Schleck. What can you add to that?"

"That about sums it up. Landry was solid. Galante was a good doctor, I saw him in action many times. Are you Catholic, by any chance?"

"Yes, I am."

"I thought you had the look of the altar boy about you. Am I right?"

"Yes, sir. Back in Boston. How can you tell?"

"Oh," he shrugged. "I'm not really sure. Something in the eyes. A great disappointment at the ways of men and God. It comes from youthful adoration dashed on the rocks of death and despair. I see it in you, son. It's clear the war has marked you. Have you been to confession recently?"

"Thanks, I'll pass for now." Not that I thought a chaplain could be a suspect, but until I figured out who was who, I preferred to keep my deepest and darkest to myself. "The war has marked everyone, don't you think?"

"Yes. Some more than others. The sensitive ones, the ones who had ideals, they have it the worst."

"Who does best?" I asked.

"The boys who had nothing, who were used to tough times. Not that sudden death and dismemberment are easy to take, but anyone who's been hardened by life has a thicker skin, if you know what I mean. But sooner or later, it gets to everyone. It's just a matter of time."

"Is that what Captain Galante thought?"

"That every man has his breaking point? Yes, he did. That's what didn't sit well with Colonel Schleck. He didn't like the idea that all the men under his command would break in time. I think it made him feel too responsible. It was easier for him to insist that some men are cowards, and the rest have to be led by example."

"Just as long as I'm not the one to lead them."

"No one likes being responsible for other

men's lives. I'd bet you have been, and the experience didn't sit well with you."

"Really, Padre, I'm okay. I don't need to tell it to the chaplain."

"Well, I'm here if you need me. For a while, anyway."

"Pulling out soon?"

"The signs are all there. Plenty of supplies, extra socks, and ammo. Good food, replacements coming in. Not hard to figure. It pays to be ready."

"From what the noncoms tell me, things have been pretty rough for your outfit."

"Yes," Dare said, looking right through me for a fleeting moment, as memories danced just out of his field of vision. "Rough. There seemed to be no end to the minefields, machine guns, and mortars." He kept looking into that middle distance, the place where the mind's eye sees everything it wants to forget. Finally he rubbed his eyes and sighed. He stayed quiet, and I wondered if he were praying.

"Sorry," he said, standing. "We lost a lot of men before we came off the line after Monte Cesima. Took the starch out of my collar." He forced a weak smile. "The men get torn up horribly. I never imagined there were so many ways to be wounded and still live. I work with the litter bearers mostly."

"It's hard to imagine there's someone living in the midst of this carnage and committing murder," I said, trying to bring Father Dare back to the present.

"Evil exists in the world, we know that to be true," he said. "It saddens me, but comes as no surprise. This person must have a tortured soul. Perhaps the exposure to so much violence has released demons that might have stayed buried in peacetime."

"That's generous of you."

"No, not generous — realistic. Being a man of God means that you also have to accept the devil for what he is. Why wouldn't the prince of darkness haunt a battlefield, probing for weaknesses, uncovering what lies beneath our civilized exteriors?"

"I was a cop in civilian life. I found the reasons for murder were more mundane. Love and money usually topped the list."

"Don't you think it takes the devil to turn what once was love into murderous intent?"

"Maybe," I said, not wanting to get into a theological argument. My money was on the devil within us, not the guy with horns and a pitchfork. "Did Landry or Galante have any problems with love or money?"

"There's little time for love of the kind you mean. Lust can be satisfied for chocolate or cigarettes, I understand. I have no idea what Landry may have done while in town, but I know Captain Galante was not the type to pursue lust. He was a not a lighthearted man. He took his responsibilities seriously. Any free time he had he spent studying Italian culture. He loved the language, the history, everything about it."

"So I've heard. The only guy he seemed to antagonize was Colonel Schleck."

"The colonel does his job the best way he knows how. So did Galante; he just didn't care whose feathers he ruffled. Can't say why. No one really knew him well. There was another chaplain, a rabbi, who he got along with, but he was wounded in Sicily and shipped home."

"Galante was Jewish?"

"Yes, he was. Does that matter?"

"I don't know. Maybe some guy said something, you know, 'dirty Yids,' that sort of thing. And Galante took offense." I tried to sound like I neither approved nor disapproved of the term, so I could go along with the good Father whichever way he went.

"Some people aren't too used to Catholics either, but they don't murder them. Landry was Protestant, I believe. I never heard anything about remarks directed against Galante's religion."

"I'm trying to find a way to look at this, Father. So far, there's no reason I can find for anyone to do more than pin a Good Conduct Medal on these guys."

"Yes, I understand. It's a bit like my line of work, isn't it? People seem to be fine on the surface, but it's their eternal soul that I worry about. It takes some digging to find out the truth about a soul."

"Sounds like you didn't dig anything up on Landry or Galante."

"No, and I'm not keeping anything from you. Neither took confession with me, or shared confidences. Perhaps they were what they seemed."

"What about Sergeant Jim Cole?" I was getting a little tired of people singing the praises of the living and the dead. I needed to hear their secrets, not their eulogies. "Did he do his job?"

"He did," Father Dare said, not meeting my eyes. He stood and began taking things out of his field pack and repacking them.

"Past tense?"

"I'm sure he's doing a good job at CID as well."

"When was he transferred out of the division?"

"After Monte Cesima, about a month ago."

"Why?"

"Jim Cole is a good man. He was one of the most selfless leaders you'd ever hope to find up on the line. He never asked a man to do what he wouldn't do, or hadn't done a hundred times. Night patrols, taking the point, it didn't matter, he was always there."

"Was he in Landry's platoon?" I couldn't believe Cole would leave that out if he was, but I was beginning to wonder what he had left out.

"No, he was with 1st Platoon."

"But same company? Did he know Landry and his men?"

"Damnation, Boyle! Of course they knew each other. There weren't but a few dozen who'd been with the outfit that long. Everybody knows everybody, except for the replacements, until they're dead or veterans."

"What happened to Cole, Padre?"

"Leave him out of this."

"I've been told that before."

"Then I don't need to say it again." He threw a few decks of cards into his pack. He had a cardboard box full of them.

"Where do you get the playing cards?"

"Quartermaster. Chaplains are morale officers, among other things. I'm issued sports equipment, cards, that sort of thing.

I don't think there will be much time for baseball when they ship us out."

"Do you usually play poker with the enlisted men?" Chaplain or no, it was frowned upon for officers and men to gamble together.

"All the time, Lieutenant Boyle, all the time. They're a lot more fun than most of the officers, who never let me forget I'm a priest. And I love poker. I cleaned up at the seminary." He grinned, and I couldn't help taking a liking to him.

"But not tonight."

"No, Flint won big. I can read most people. It comes with the profession, and it's useful in poker. But Flint is different. Bluffing or holding four aces, it's all the same on his face. Unreadable. The best damn poker player in the platoon."

"They asked him if he was going to give the money back. Why?"

"It's sort of a tradition. If I win, I use the money to help out any boys who need it. Problems at home, that sort of thing. Sometimes for the local children, if we're in a village. When I lose big, the winner will usually pass some scrip back to me."

"Like tipping the dealer."

"Sort of. Word got around it was good luck, so my private goodwill fund is never entirely depleted."

"Pretty creative, Padre. Did you play cards with Landry?"

"A couple of times. He didn't like to gamble with the men under his command. Said he didn't want any of them owing him money."

"Because someone might question who he chose to take point?"

"I think so," Father Dare said. "It's strange, though. He'd gamble with a captain or major who might send him to his death, but he wouldn't play with an enlisted man whom he might have to give the same order to. Doesn't really add up, does it?"

"It makes sense to the army," I said, giving up on understanding the logic of military rules. The padre gave a short snort of laughter and continued with his packing.

"How was Landry the last time you saw him? Was there anything unusual?"

"Not that I recall. Of course, everything here is unusual when you know you're being fattened up for the kill. Everyone is a bit jumpy."

"Anyone in Landry's platoon a big loser? I mean in hock to another guy?"

"Louie. I'm sure he's introduced himself to you."

"Louie Walla from Walla Walla."

"That's Louie. He owes a few guys money from cards and craps. He won't have much left next payday, but he's good for it. Anyway, that couldn't be a motive. He didn't gamble with Landry."

"No, I guess not. What about Stump and Flint?"

"Stump's been up and down at cards, and he stays away from the craps games. Flint usually wins, like I said. He's got a good poker face. Otherwise, he's the life of the party, a real charmer most of the time."

"Most of the time?"

"He's also got a temper, but you don't see it too often. I heard he got into a fight with three Italians in town and laid them all out."

"What was it about?"

"No idea. A woman, a bottle, who knows? The boys don't go to museums when they get a pass. They wander around, eat and drink, look for women. It doesn't always put them in the best neighborhoods." He stopped stuffing wool socks into his pack and sighed, shaking his head. "Listen, for all their faults, they're a good bunch. They just like to blow off steam once in a while."

"You ever been to that joint in Acerra? The one where one of Flint's men had a fight?"

"That's where Flint took on the three

locals, from what I hear. Bar Raffaele on Via Volturno. And no, I haven't been there. A chaplain would definitely put a damper on things for all concerned. Now let me finish getting my gear together so I can catch some shut-eye. Unless you need spiritual counseling."

"Thanks for your time, Father." As I rose to leave, he pulled a .45 automatic from his duffel and loaded a magazine into it. "I thought chaplains were men of peace."

"We are. Trouble is, we're at war. The Geneva Convention allows medics and litter bearers to be armed, in order to provide protection for the wounded. Sometimes it's necessary to guard the flock. You know what it's like in battle, I expect. Men are on edge, their fingers on the trigger, waiting for the next threat, the next person trying to kill them. They don't always see the red cross on a helmet or that a man is down and wounded. All they see is the uniform, and the threat it implies."

"You think you're going to stop a berserk German with a Schmeisser submachine gun with that?"

"I may be a man of God, but I don't plan on being a martyr. I'll do what I have to do to protect those under my care."

Chapter Eleven

The afternoon was dark and gloomy as I sat in a line of military traffic, inching along in my jeep. We had to pull over for a truck convoy heading into the 3rd Division bivouac area. Men, artillery, and supplies flowed along the mud-caked road, nearly bumper to bumper. Something was happening, but in true army fashion, I'd be the last one to know if all my suspects shipped out to parts unknown.

I needed several things. I needed to know if the division was shipping out soon. I needed to see where Galante's body had been left. And I needed help. I needed Kaz. Kaz would be an extra set of eyes and ears, not to mention someone smart enough to figure out what was going on. I needed Lieutenant Baron Piotr Augustus Kazimierz.

Kaz had been my best friend since I got shipped over here in 1942. He'd been on

General Eisenhower's staff as a translator, mostly as a courtesy to the Polish government-in-exile. Kaz was the last survivor of his family, alive only because he'd been studying in England when the Germans invaded Poland. His entire family had been killed, wiped out by the Nazis as they eliminated the educated elite of the country. Kaz wanted to serve, but a heart condition had kept him out of uniform. He finally talked his way in, as a translator for Uncle Ike. He was a skinny, bookish kid, and the idea was he could work in an office and do his bit.

Kaz's father had seen what was coming, and deposited the bulk of the family fortune in Swiss banks. As a result, Kaz was filthy rich. Rich enough to permanently keep a suite of rooms at the Dorchester hotel in London, the same suite where he and his family had celebrated their last Christmas together. I bunked with Kaz when I was in London and felt the ghosts of his past life drift by us in the ornate high-ceilinged rooms. One of those ghosts was Daphne, the love of Kaz's life. Sister of Diana Seaton. Maybe that's why I worried about Diana so much. I didn't want to become scarred like Kaz.

Kaz wore a physical scar as well. An explosion — the same explosion that had killed Daphne — had ripped his face from the corner of one eye down to the cheekbone. The injury and the loss had changed him. For a long time, he hadn't cared whether he lived or died, and I felt it was my job to keep life interesting enough for him to hang around. Lately, he'd turned a corner. He'd begun working out, building himself up, but for what I didn't know. All I did know is that he had more brains than ten other guys put together and wasn't afraid to use the Webley break-top revolver he wore. I could use both kinds of firepower. I decided to radio Colonel Harding and ask for Kaz to be sent down from London.

The column finally passed and the traffic moved along, toward Caserta. I ran through the leads I had to follow. Pay a visit to Bar Raffaele in Acerra and see what the scuffle was all about, and why Landry and Flint went down there to pay damages. Find out whom Louie owed his next paycheck to. Go back and find Major Arnold, Schleck's second-in-command, and see if he'd be more talkative. Ask Sergeant Jim Cole why he didn't tell me about knowing Landry and Galante. An infantry division is a big place, about fourteen thousand guys at full strength. He should have mentioned it, even if it was only a coincidence. He didn't, and I wanted to know why. I also needed to find out how Galante had gotten a squad killed, and why Cole was supposed to know about that. Maybe it was just a rumor that Schleck glommed onto, but if true, it would be a motive for revenge. Then ask the same question around the 32nd Station Hospital, and see what Galante's colleagues had to say.

It was a lot of legwork, and none of it might end up being important. But it gave me the illusion of being on the right track, and I might get lucky and stumble onto something I'd recognize as a clue. After an hour of stop-and-go traffic, I parked in front of the Caserta HQ and went to see Major Kearns. My plan was to send the radio message to Harding, then look at where Galante's body was found before it got too dark. Then Cole, then chow, and onto the officer's club to practice my interrogation skills at the bar. It was a good plan, except that it didn't hold much promise in terms of solving the murders.

"Billy!" A familiar voice echoed in the hallway leading to Kearns's office.

"Kaz," I said, turning to find him behind me. "What are you doing here? I was on my way to radio Harding to ask for you."

"He sent me immediately, but we had

aircraft trouble and I was stuck at Malta for a day. It's good to see you, Billy." We shook hands warmly, both of us glad to be working together again. As usual, Kaz looked perfect in his tailored British battle dress uniform, complete with the red shoulder patch with "Poland" inscribed in bold letters. His blue eyes shone eagerly behind his steel-rimmed spectacles, and as usual the Webley revolver was at his hip.

"Do you know what's going on here?" I asked.

"Yes. Colonel Harding briefed me in London, and I saw Major Kearns twenty minutes ago. He told me to find Sergeant James Cole in CID, and that he'd tell me where you were. But he wasn't in."

"I'm glad you're here, Kaz."

"As am I," he said. We stood in silence for a heartbeat, the bonds of mourning, suffering, and hardship still strong — so strong that there were no words for it, none that I understood, anyway.

"Let's take a walk," I said, putting my arm around Kaz's shoulder. "I haven't seen where Captain Galante's body was found yet. Then we'll look for Cole." We walked through the gardens, beautiful even with tents and vehicles marring the landscape. A waterway led from the palace down the gentle slope to the Fountain of Diana and Actaeon. As we drew closer, the formal gardens became wilder, and smooth marble gave way to rough stone, creating the effect of entering a wilderness.

"Apparently the major was lured here," said Kaz. "One wonders why he was placed in this particular location."

"Out of the way?"

"Surely. But why was that important?"

"I don't know. Not a lot about this makes sense."

"Ah," Kaz said as the final pool of water came into sight. "Diana and Actaeon. You know the story?"

"It was explained to me," I said. "Guy got turned into a stag for daring to look at a naked goddess, then got ripped apart by his own hunting dogs." A small waterfall descended over moss-covered rocks, between two sculptures. Diana on one side, covering her nudity, and Actaeon on the other, being brought down by hounds. It was an oddly private place, sunken from view, surrounded on three sides by trees and shrubs. Not a bad place to stash a body. "I saw this place once before, but I'd forgotten how hidden it was."

"The report said Galante's body was laid out at the wall of the pool," Kaz said.

"Over here. There are still some chalk marks," I said.

"Interesting," Kaz said. "He's facing Actaeon."

"So?"

"Perhaps nothing," he said, squatting down to get a corpse-eye view of the fountain. "It just strikes me as odd. This is a public place, although hidden from view until you come upon it. I don't think the killer's objective was to hide the body, at least not for very long."

"Right," I said. "He could've put it in among the trees and shrubs. That would have bought him more time."

"I wonder if this placement was a statement."

"What kind of statement?"

"That Captain Galante had seen something, as Actaeon had. Something that must be kept hidden from human eyes. Once he'd seen it, his fate was sealed."

"Listen, Kaz, this is a nice quiet place, a good place for a killing. The murderer brings Galante down here under some pretense, strangles him after a short struggle, then rolls his body next to that wall. Short and sweet. No mythological psychiatric mumbo jumbo."

"Perhaps, Billy. I admit to a weakness for

the old myths. The killer might also." I looked at the statues, and thought about my father telling me there was no such thing as a coincidence.

"You might be right about Galante being killed because he saw something. We have to find out what." This was why I needed Kaz, to help me see what was staring me right in the face.

"What do you make of the playing cards?" Kaz asked as we trudged back to the palace. The sky was darkening with low, gray clouds rolling in.

"It could be part of some crazy game. Or it could be to throw us off the scent. Maybe these two guys were the only targets, and by using the ten and the jack, he's got us worrying about the next victim instead of focusing on Landry and Galante."

"It could have been just one of them, with the second man killed to confuse us."

"I'm confused enough as it is. The only thing I've found out is that Cole held something back from me. He's only been with CID a short time. Before that he served in the 3rd Division and knew everyone in Landry's platoon. They all refuse to talk about it, as if they're protecting him. Colonel Schleck, who runs Personnel for the division, says Galante got a squad killed, and that Cole knows all about it."

"Do you think it's true?"

"Schleck seems convinced. What's more important is why Cole held that story back, especially any relationship he had with Galante."

"If Galante was somehow responsible for an entire squad being killed, that could be a strong motive," Kaz said.

"Yeah, and I wonder if any of those guys were Cole's buddies."

"Let us find the sergeant," Kaz said, "and discuss this with him."

"Maybe after we get some chow. I'll fill you in on my Swiss vacation."

"Switzerland? How . . ."

"What's going on over there?" I said, interrupting Kaz and pointing toward the palace. To one side, among the jeeps, trucks, and ambulances lined in neat rows, a growing mass of people was gathering, many of them pointing to the roof of the palace. We hurried closer, curious as to what the hubbub was all about. GIs, officers of all ranks, nurses, and civilians began to jostle us, eager to get closer to a break in the endless routine of headquarters work. No one seemed to know what was happening, but no one wanted to miss it.

Vehicles were started and headlights lit

the wall of the palace. Lights went on in windows as they were thrown open and heads peered out, looking up, then down at the crowd, then up again. The sun had begun to set, and the roof, a full five stories up, blended into the dark gray sky. The headlights only made it worse with their bright angled glare. Someone found a searchlight mounted on a truck and switched it on. A harsh white light played across the building, and I could see people in the windows covering their eyes, turning away. The beam darted back and forth until it caught a pair of boots dangling from the edge of the roof. Then the full form of a GI, his hand shielding his eyes. Even at that height, with the mask of an outstretched palm covering his face, I knew we'd found Sergeant Jim Cole.

I raced up the stairwell, looking for a way to the roof. Kaz was right on my tail, keeping up as we hit the fourth floor. Not too long ago, he would have stopped, gasping for breath halfway up. I didn't know if his heart could take it, but I figured Kaz was more interested in living what life he had than worrying about dying.

One more floor, and we found Kearns at the base of a narrow set of stairs, with a couple of MPs keeping the curious at bay.

"It's Cole," he said.

"Yeah, I saw him. What happened?"

"You tell me. He came to see me this afternoon, looking for you. Next thing I hear, he's on the roof. What did he say to you?"

"Nothing, I just got back from 3rd Division."

"Well, get up there and talk to him, dammit! Bring him in, Boyle."

"Yes sir. I'll need some rope."

"You're going to tie him up out there?"

"No. It's for Kaz. Tie it around his chest and anchor it to the stairs. Then send him out. I may need something to grab onto and it'd be nice if it stayed put." Kearns sent an MP and I took the metal stairs, holding onto the thin rail as the walls narrowed and ended at a small wooden door. I opened it and had to duck to squeeze through.

It was windy. Windy and dazzlingly bright, as the searchlight caught me square in the eyes. I stumbled back, grabbing for the door, but it had shut in the wind. I grabbed air, slipped, and felt myself sliding down a section of roof, panicking in my near blindness. My leg jammed up against a low wall, but my head kept going until it hit granite. It hurt, but not as much as the idea of falling. The searchlight moved on.

"I've been thinking about shooting out that light," Cole said, his voice even and low, eyes on the crowd below. We were on a flat section of the roof, a narrow catwalk at the corner of the building. Above us the roofline sloped into the night. Below us, a long fall to hard ground. A knee-high wall was all that separated me from air. It did less for Cole. He sat on it, his boot heels dangling into space. A .45 automatic rested in his hand, and he gestured with it lazily toward the searchlight.

"I'll do it for you," I said, hoping for a chance to establish a common bond. I untangled my legs and stood. Or more accurately, leaned against the roof, as far from the edge as possible.

"Don't come any closer," Cole said.

"Yeah. Or else you'll jump. Pretty obvious. What's with the gun? Can't make up your mind which way to check out?"

"What? Why'd they send you out here anyway, Lieutenant, to crack jokes?" He still didn't look at me.

"No, I'm serious. I was a cop back home, saw my fair share of suicides. Usually they picked one method and stuck to it. Did you have a plan when you came up here?" One thing my dad taught me is that it's a rookie move to tell any jumper that this too shall pass, you'll feel better in the morning, that sort of stuff. It's likely he's already heard it, and it didn't stop him from climbing to the top of the highest thing he could find. Sometimes a person would jump just so he wouldn't have to listen to another idiot lecture him. No, best thing was to go right at him, ask him what he planned to do. It let him know you took him seriously, that you knew he was in pain. Then, maybe, he might talk.

"The gun is for anyone who tries to stop me," Cole said, finally giving me a quick glance.

"Listen, if you think I'm going to grab you and let you wrestle me off that ledge as you make your swan dive, you got another think coming. This is as close as I get. Tell me what happened today."

"Today? What do you mean?"

"You didn't come up here yesterday. Or the day before. Not that I know of, anyway. So what got you on this ledge today?"

"You wouldn't understand. You couldn't, or you'd be up here yourself. I keep seeing them. Especially the little girl. I see her in my dreams, and she's alive. She's holding her doll, like kids do, you know? Then I wake up, and I know she's dead. I can't go on any longer, I can't." Cole spoke in a deliberate, slow voice. The voice of a man who was sure of himself. This wasn't a cry for help; this was a guy in the last moments of his life. I needed to get him thinking in a different direction.

"Why were you looking for me today? Was it about the case?"

"It's nothing. Meaningless."

"Come on, Cole, help me out. If you jump, I'll be all alone on this investigation. Tell me what you know." What I knew was that this wasn't the time to ask about dead squad mates from the 3rd Division.

"I don't know anything. Except that nothing matters, no matter what you do. You try to do good, but it turns evil. You try to save lives, but you end up taking them."

"This is war, Cole."

"Innocent lives. I can't forget them. He won't let me. I can't carry this any longer." He thumped his chest, once, then again, harder. "It'll never go away, never."

"Who won't let you?"

"He was my friend," Cole said, his voice breaking. "I see it in his face, see everything all over again." He began to sob now, rocking back and forth on the ledge. I reached out to steady him, but his gun hand was up in a flash. "Don't touch me!" His face was contorted in agony as tears streamed down his cheeks.

"Okay, okay. Just tell me, Cole. Who are you talking about?"

"Everybody wants something, don't they? You do, the army, the Krauts, you all want something. Answers. Blood. Promises. But I've got nothing left to give. I'm going crazy, I can't take it anymore. I don't want to see that face for the rest of my life. I see that doll too, a rag doll in a red dress. Even when I'm awake, I see it. I don't want to live like that. I can't."

I heard a noise behind me, and hoped it was Kaz.

"Shoot the light," I said. "Shoot the damn searchlight!" It was all I could think of.

"There's people down there. Are you nuts?"

"You're a combat infantryman, Sergeant Cole. You telling me you can't hit a big, blazing searchlight dead center at this range?"

"What do you care?"

"You're the one about to kill yourself, so what do *you* care?" It was like daring a kid to break a window back home. *What are you, chicken?* I heard the door move on its hinges.

"Okay," Cole said, taking the dare. "But first, in case someone shoots back, I have something to give you." He reached into his pocket, and tossed a double strand of pearls into my hand. Pearls? Smooth white pearls. I was dumbstruck.

"What's this?"

"You're the detective," he said. He stood, balancing his weight, and raised his arm, aiming the .45 at the searchlight. A murmur rose up from the crowd, and I hoped it covered the sound of Kaz coming through the door.

It didn't. I leapt, but Cole saw my move and sidestepped away from me. I came down hard on the edge of the granite wall, Kaz hanging onto my legs, the breath knocked out of me. I looked up at Cole, surprised at how agile he was, and tried to think of what to say.

"Don't jump." It was all that I could come up with, and it came out in a wheeze as I gulped air.

"I'm not going to," he said, and took another careful step away from me, sliding his feet along the narrow ledge. He raised the automatic and placed the muzzle under his chin. He didn't move as the searchlight played over him and the crowd below gasped. He stood, rock solid, until the slightest movement of his finger shattered the night with a sharp noise, blood, and bone.

Chapter Twelve

"Who was that up there?" Phil Einsmann asked. He'd been coming upstairs as Kaz and I headed down, and he turned to descend with us. He handed me a handkerchief, and I must have looked at him dumbly because he made a rubbing motion. I ran the handkerchief across my face and it came away red-streaked. I've never gotten used to the tremendous power of the human heart, and I don't mean its capacity to love. I mean as a pump. The last mechanical function at the moment of death by violence, the release of crimson as if the body is leaving its final mark upon this Earth. And on anyone who happens to be close by.

"It's not a story, Phil. Not one his folks back home need to read, anyway."

"I'm not asking as a reporter, Billy. I have a lot of friends here. Who was it?"

"Jim Cole. Sergeant with CID. Did you know him?"

"No, not really. I heard he was new with CID, saw him around, but those guys are a tight-lipped bunch. What set him off?"

"Hard to say." I meant it.

I handed Einsmann his handkerchief, but he told me to keep it. Couldn't blame him. I introduced him to Kaz, and then left him to go to CID. I didn't feel like talking right now, and Kaz could tell. He took the handkerchief and wiped the side of my neck. The top of my jacket was covered in tiny dots of drying blood, and I hoped it wasn't too noticeable. We walked among people filtering back to what they had been doing before the crazy sergeant shot himself on the roof. Shaking their heads, telling each other it was unbelievable, the poor guy must have been off his rocker. All the things people say to put as much distance between their own lives and the suddenness of death.

That was one of the terrifying things about being on the line. There was so little distance. Death was all around you, and not just during combat. It could be a mine where you didn't expect it, a sniper shot, or a random shelling. It's why you lived in a hole in the ground, getting as much distance as possible between yourself and the rest of the world.

I found myself standing in front of the

door to CID. Staring at it. Kaz was standing by, patiently. I rubbed my eyes, shook my head, and wished I had a hole to crawl into.

"We don't have to do this now," Kaz said.

"Yeah, we do. I don't want anyone going through Cole's stuff. Might be a clue there." I put on my cop face and opened the door.

An MP sat at his desk, a cigarette smoldering between his fingers. "Jeez, Lieutenant," he said, shaking his head. "Can you believe it?"

"Did you see it?" I asked.

"Yeah, we were trying to keep people back. That shot. The blood. I couldn't believe it was Jim."

"Was he acting strange at all?"

"No more jumpy than usual. He spooked easy. But I never figured he would kill himself. Jesus."

"Did you see him leave here?"

"Yeah, I did. He went into his office, then came out a few seconds later. He must have gone straight to the roof. Jesus."

We left the MP and went into the office Cole shared with the other CID investigators. It was empty. Cole's desk was clean as a whistle except for the white phosphorus grenade set square in the middle of it.

"What is that?" Kaz asked, stopping short

of the desk.

"It's a new kind of grenade. M15 white phosphorus." I walked around the desk and studied it. The safety lever and pin were both securely in place. It was about the shape and size of a beer can, painted gray with a yellow stripe around it. "When it bursts, the phosphorus makes white smoke, good for cover. It also burns incredibly hot, thousands of degrees, I've heard. It's used for taking out pillboxes or fortifications, if you can get close enough."

"Why would a CID agent have one?" Kaz asked.

"No reason at all," I said, opening the two drawers on the side of the desk. The playing cards Cole had shown me were there, along with forms, pencils, an empty holster, and an Armed Services Edition paperback — *Deadlier Than the Male,* by James Gunn. I flipped through it and two photos fluttered to the floor.

One photo was of Cole standing in front of the Caserta Palace with two people. One of them looked like Captain Max Galante. That was a surprise, but not as much as the other.

"This is Signora Salvalaggio, Galante's former cook and landlady," I said. "What was Cole doing with them? For that matter, what was Galante doing with her?"

"We can ask her tonight," Kaz said. "I am billeted with you."

"Good, because she doesn't speak English," I said, as we studied the other photo, which was much more worn at the edges. It showed three GIs, arms around each other, weapons slung over their shoulders and wine bottles in their hands. It looked like a hot and dusty summer's day. Sicily, maybe.

"That's Cole, on the left," I said. "And Sergeants Louie Walla and Marty Stumpf. Third Platoon. Let's find these guys. It's time for secrets to be told."

We asked the MPs on duty about the WP grenade. No one had noticed it, or seen anybody bring it in. I carefully put it in my jacket pocket and we headed for the jeep. On the main floor I spotted Father Dare, and he made a beeline for me.

"Is it true? Cole killed himself?" He looked stunned, his eyes wide with hope that I'd tell him it was all a mistake.

"Yes, Father, I'm sorry to say it is. I'm heading out to find the other sergeants now. Anything you want to tell me about Cole before I do?"

"I wasn't there, Lieutenant. Better let them tell you," he said. "You don't have to look far, they're all over at the NCO club.

Passes were cancelled, so they drove over here to have a few beers. They told me about Cole."

"They saw it happen?"

"Yes, Rusty told me. They were walking to the NCO club when they saw all the commotion. Was that you up there with Cole?" He glanced at the stains on my jacket, then locked eyes with me. "What did he tell you?"

"Not nearly enough. Where's the NCO club?"

"Across the way from the main entrance there's a row of Quonset huts. It's marked, you can't miss it."

"What were you doing here, Father?"

"I came for a good meal at the officer's club. I have a feeling we're pulling out very soon. More replacements came in today; we're almost back to full strength. I think I've lost my appetite, though. Good night, Lieutenant."

"Good night, Father. I'm sorry."

Father Dare walked away, looking distraught.

"Isn't the clergy supposed to comfort others?" Kaz asked.

"Yeah," I said. "What do you make of a poker-playing padre who carries a .45?"

"You can be religious and still wish to defend yourself. And to gamble."

"No law against that. Listen, while I talk with these guys, will you ask around and find out if there's an armory in this joint, or nearby? Some place where they have M15 WP grenades?"

"Do you think it had anything to do with Cole's suicide?"

"I don't know. It could be evidence from some other case, for all I know. See what you can find, and we'll meet at the officer's mess and compare notes."

It's not unheard of for an officer to grab a drink or a meal at a NCO club, but as a courtesy he's expected to ask permission of a senior noncommissioned officer present. I spotted Rusty Gates and figured a platoon sergeant was senior enough.

"Mind if I join you fellows for a while?" Gates was sitting with Louie Walla from Walla Walla, Flint, and Stump. It was a subdued crowd. "Be glad to buy a round."

"You just bought yourself a chair, Lieutenant," Flint said, making room at the table. Gates gave me a nod, then signaled to the bar for five beers.

"Call me Billy, fellas. I was a cop back home, and I still turn around and look for my father when someone calls me lieutenant."

"You're in the family business, then?" Flint said.

"Until the war, yeah."

"Looks like you're still keeping your hand in," Stump said. "Asking all those questions."

"And I've got more. That's why most cops don't have a lot of friends outside the job. Always asking questions, it tends to get on people's nerves."

The beers came, and I waited to see who would say it, if anyone would. I held onto my bottle, half-raised in a toast.

"To Jim Cole," Gates said. They all repeated his name, then we clinked bottles and drank.

"Was that you up there with Cole?" Louie asked, gesturing with his beer bottle to the rust-colored stains on my jacket.

"Yeah. Major Kearns thought I should try talking him down. You guys saw it all, right?"

"We did," Gates said. "Now I suppose you want to know the whole story?"

"Yep. And why you all held back."

"It was for Jim," Louie said. "We was doin' him a favor, goddamn it."

"It's okay, Louie, it's okay," Gates said. "Flint, tell Billy what happened."

Flint took a long draw on his beer, set it down hard, and pursed his lips. He shook his head before beginning, as if he wondered if this was a good idea. "I was assistant squad leader. Cole was my sergeant. He came over from First Platoon after we lost a couple of guys. He knew what he was doing; he'd been with the company longer than anyone."

"Since North Africa," I said.

"Yeah. That had started to bother him. You know, with so many guys killed and wounded, and not a scratch on him. He kept saying his number was up, it had to be."

"Everybody worries about that," Gates said. "That wasn't the problem."

"Right, right. The problem was Campozillone," Flint said. He gulped the rest of his beer. "It's a little village near the base of Monte Cesima. The division was advancing on Mignano, and we had to clear Campozillone of Germans. It was a small place, but it overlooked the main road. It was on a hill, with a big stone church at the top, like a lot of these villages."

"Good place for an observation post," I said.

"Yeah. Landry and the rest of the company stayed on the main road while Third Platoon hustled up this dirt track. The village had taken an artillery barrage the night before, and we hoped the Jerries got the message and cleared out. When we got there, it was all narrow streets, like switchbacks, heading up to the church. The buildings were real close together, made from white stone, like granite. Solid."

"Them switchbacks were perfect for an ambush," Louie said.

"Yeah. It was real quiet at first. Some buildings were piles of rubble. Others were fine. It was hard to tell if they were homes or shops or what. They were all shuttered up. So we keep going, checking out alleyways and side streets, advancing up toward the church. No sign of Germans or civilians."

"It was hot," Stump said. "I remember sweating. Hot for November, even in Italy."

"Hot," Flint agreed. "We were almost to the church, and it seemed like the Germans might have pulled out after all. There was a set of steps leading up to the road, so we took them, our squad. The others went around the bend in the road, and we went up the steps, figuring to save time."

"It wasn't a bad move," Louie said. Everyone nodded their agreement.

"Then the Krauts opened up. Machine gun in a cellar window, at the head of the steps. They had the road and the steps covered. We lost two guys right away. One, MacMillan, had been with us a while. The other was a replacement, I never got his name."

"We was pinned down," Louie said. "Stump and me. Rusty was with us. We had one guy wounded, out in the middle of the street, but we were all holed up in doorways, nowhere to go."

"We started lobbing grenades," Flint said. "But they'd miss the window and bounce away. Some of these buildings had real narrow basement windows, and that's where the Krauts set up. Like a pillbox. The building between us and the Krauts was nothing but rubble, which blocked all the entrances on our side. We couldn't get at them."

"Bishop was out in the street, hit pretty bad in the legs," Gates said. "They left him alone, hoping one of us would try to get to him."

"We was screwed," Louie said.

"What happened?" I asked.

"The MG42 stopped," Flint said. "A few rifle shots, then they were gone. The medics got to Bishop, and we kept going. But now we knew they were probably setting up somewhere between us and the church. Everyone was mad. We wanted to get those bastards. Mac and Bishop, plus that kid —

it got us all pissed off. You know how it is, when one minute you're so scared you just want to get into the deepest hole you can find, and then something happens, your blood's up, and you're doing something that might get you killed. It was like that. We moved up, hugging the walls, watching for those basement windows, waiting for shutters to swing open and the MG to open up again."

"We were all jumpy," Stump said. "Lots of firing at shadows."

"Our squad was in the lead," Flint said. "Cole took point. We were about fifty yards from the church, only one more switchback to go. I was looking at the bell tower, watching for snipers. I heard Cole say something and saw him point to a building at the top of the road. The roof had been caved in, but the rest of it was intact. It had stone steps leading up to the front door, and two small windows with bars on them on either side of the steps."

"I heard him yell for covering fire," Gates said.

"Yeah, then everyone started shooting. He ran toward the building, and I followed, shooting and yelling. We were all a little crazed, you know? Cole was screaming about the basement, that he saw movement, and to fire at the windows. I did, and as we got close, he pulled out a WP grenade, one of those new M15 gizmos, you know? And I figure, good idea, even if he misses, some of that Willie Peter will spray into the basement and fix those Krauts good. So he throws, and Jesus, it was a beautiful shot. The windows were a bit high off the ground, which made it a little easier, but it sailed in there perfectly. You saw it, Louie, wasn't that a shot?"

"Right between the bars," Louie said. "Cole had a helluva arm."

"Flint," Gates said in a low, quiet voice. "Tell Billy what happened."

"Well, we took cover. You know that stuff flies everywhere and burns like the devil. But when it went in, we moved up, covering the door, figuring Krauts might come spilling out."

"But there weren't no Krauts," Louie said, helping Flint along. I felt the weight of the grenade in my pocket, as well as the weight of what I knew was coming. I thought about the fact that someone had left this grenade on Cole's desk hours — or minutes — before he'd decided to kill himself.

"No. Smoke was pouring out, and inside was a white-hot glow. We heard screams. We got to the window, and there was this guy, this Italian. He was on fire, his back was blazing. He had a little girl, he must have shielded her from the blast, and he was trying to push her out between the bars, but he couldn't. Cole grabbed at the girl, but he came up empty. Except for a rag doll she'd been holding."

"It was a whole family," Gates said. "Father, mother, couple of kids. They'd evidently taken shelter during the bombardment. When the roof caved in, it blocked the stairs to the basement. They were trapped."

"Cole just stood there," Stump said. "Holding that rag doll. And I mean he stood there, looking into that burning basement. We couldn't move him."

"We found those Krauts," Louie said. "They was hightailing it outta the church, four of 'em, makin' for an olive grove. We'd split up, a squad on either side of the church. Soon as they saw us, it was *kamerad, kamerad.* But we wasn't in the mood."

"What happened with Cole?" I thought about pulling out the grenade and plunking it down on the table, but I didn't know what that would tell me. If one of these guys put it on Cole's desk, he might expect it. The rest would think I'd lost it.

"Landry came up with some medics and

they checked him out, but he wasn't wounded. Flint brought him to the aid station, just to give him a rest," Gates said. "Since he wasn't hurt, they didn't know what to do, so Father Dare took over and took care of him for a couple of days. The padre brought him back, and he seemed okay. Quiet, not out of his head or anything. So we think everything is back to normal, that he got over the shock. We're closer to Mignano now, and the next morning we shove off to occupy another hill. I left Cole's squad in reserve, but we come up against a farmhouse with a bunch of Krauts holed up in it. I needed Cole to move his squad down an irrigation ditch to get closer, so I send him out. It's good cover, and they get close, but they stay in the ditch. I crawl down there to see what's the problem, and everyone's looking at Cole, waiting for the order. But he won't move, won't speak. So I gave the squad to Flint, and we took the farmhouse. No casualties."

"Did he say why he froze?"

"He said he just couldn't do it anymore," Flint said. "He was okay as soon as he got away from the shooting. But he said there was no way he could ever go up on the line again."

"He wasn't shaking in his boots or anything. He just said he couldn't do it no more," Louie said.

"It wasn't like some guys who try to talk their way out of it," Gates said. "He was ready to take whatever the army dished out, but he sure as hell was not going up on the line ever again."

"Fourteen months, since Fedala," Stump said. "That's how long it took. Fourteen months and one morning in Campozillone."

"We got Father Dare to talk to Captain Galante," Flint said. "He'd just been assigned to the hospital here, and we knew he was an okay guy. If Colonel Schleck ever found out about Cole freezing, he would have transferred him to another company and court-martialed him if he didn't fight. We didn't want that to happen."

"Schleck claimed Galante got a squad killed," I said. Now that everyone was in the mood to tell the truth, I wanted to get as much out of them as I could.

"Bullshit," Gates said. "That wasn't Cole anyway. It was another old-timer from Dog Company, couldn't get out of his foxhole. Said he'd be dead if he did. Guy had the Bronze Star and two Purple Hearts, so he wasn't goldbricking. Galante pulled him off the line and that very day his squad got caught in the open. The Bonesaw cut them to pieces."

"So Galante got Cole transferred to CID?"

"Yeah," Gates said. "That's how it went. Cole was fine knowing he still had a job to do, but that he was off the front line. But we figured no one needed to know the whole story. No reason to embarrass him."

"You all were okay with that? No one felt left in the lurch by Cole?"

"There but for the grace of God," Gates said, to nods all around.

Chapter Thirteen

"There are no arms or weapons storage in the palace," Kaz said as we settled in at the officer's club. Neither of us had felt like eating, so we went directly to drinking. "There is a rule against carrying grenades within headquarters, but it is not well enforced."

"Who'd want to go up against some guy fresh from the line?" I enjoyed the vision of a mud-encrusted, filthy GI, grenades hanging from his web belt, M1 slung over his shoulder, as he sauntered through the palace, scaring the pants off clerks and typists, not to mention the residents of the fancy mess hall upstairs. He would seem to be from another world, a wraith who lived underground and only came out to kill or die.

"The rule was made after a major posed for a photograph, kitted out like a combat soldier," Kaz said, grinning. "Apparently he had political aspirations, and wanted a picture to impress his future constituents. Somehow he managed to pull the pin, then dropped the grenade and ran. The photographer threw it into a latrine, which thankfully was empty. The ensuing odor and destruction brought about the regulation against grenades as fashion accessories."

"So the WP grenade probably came from a combat outfit."

"Or it could have been stolen from a supply depot," Kaz said.

"Basically we'll never know. Hundreds of people were in and out of this place tonight. All of Cole's sergeant pals, his padre, CID staff, even those Italians," I said. I cocked my head in the direction of two Carabinieri officers in their dark-blue uniforms.

"Billy, the Italians are fighting on our side now. The First Motorized Combat Group performed admirably around Monte Cassino. They took heavy causalities."

"Yeah, I heard about that. It's just that Italians have done more shooting at me than I like. Takes some time to get over that."

I finished my whiskey and got refills for both of us. I filled Kaz in on Cole's story as I'd just heard it. When I was done, Kaz got the next round. We drank in silence; any words we might say would only seem trivial.

"What do we do now?" Kaz finally asked.

"What do you know about pearls?"

"What has that to do with anything?"

"Excellent question," I said, leaning in closer. "There wasn't time to tell you before, but Cole gave me something before he shot himself. Pearls." I withdrew the necklace from my pocket, keeping it balled up in my fist. I passed it to Kaz under the table. "No one knows about this, so keep it out of sight."

"Did Cole say anything?"

"You're the detective."

"Billy, this is —"

"Lieutenant Boyle, is it not?" I hadn't noticed the two Carabinieri approach our table, but I was glad to see Kaz had, as his empty hand emerged from his jacket pocket.

"Yes," I said. "Capitano Trevisi, this is Lieutenant Baron Piotr Augustus Kazimierz." I remembered the captain from when we met the other night, but I drew a blank on the lieutenant by his side.

"Renzo Trevisi, at your service. Baron, this is Tenente Luca Amatori."

"Please join us," Kaz said, with a slight bow and a graciousness I would not have pulled off.

"Thank you," Trevisi said. "We do not encounter many titled personages here, other than military, that is." He spoke

English well but with a thick accent, and slowly, so it took a second to realize he had made a little joke.

"Ah, yes. My title is a minor one from the Polish petty nobility. I was about to tell Lieutenant Boyle about the Italian House of Savoy, and the grand balls held in this very palace."

"King Umberto and the great Queen Margherita of Savoy did reside here," Trevisi said. "I am from this very town, and remember as a child watching their carriages parade through the streets. It was magnificent. Such a pity Umberto was assassinated."

"At least it prevented Margherita from staying on the throne. She was a notorious Fascist supporter," Luca Amatori said. His English was rapid and perfect. He was younger than Trevisi, and he had the impatient look of a guy who was tired of agreeing with his superior officer.

"Now Luca," Trevisi said, in a weary parental tone. "Many of the wealthy and the aristocrats wanted stability after the last war, and they weren't alone."

"You're not a fan of royalty, Tenente Amatori?" Kaz asked.

"On the contrary, Baron. I have the greatest respect for King Victor Emmanuel. He ordered the Carabinieri to arrest Mussolini, after all."

"Yes, the Carabinieri were not great supporters of Fascism. The king felt safe to call upon us when it was time to get rid of *Il Duce.* Mussolini," Trevisi clarified, for our benefit. "Old habits, you know. We had to call him that for so long, it is difficult to change."

"Certainly," I said, as I noticed Amatori glance away, his knuckles white where he gripped the chair. I decided it was time for a change of topic. Murder was safer than politics. "Does your jurisdiction extend to Acerra, by any chance?"

"Yes," Trevisi said. "Does this involve your investigation?"

"Perhaps. We need to find an establishment that caters to soldiers. Liquor and women, nothing fancy from the sound of it."

"Are you looking for a recommendation?" Trevisi asked, one eyebrow raised in conjecture.

"No, Capitano," Kaz said. "I believe Billy is looking for a specific establishment, in connection with the investigation."

"We have a name," I said. "Bar Raffaele."

"Capisco," he said. "Tenente Amatori would be glad to accompany you. Tomor-

row? Perhaps he could meet you here in the morning."

Luca Amatori was happy to guide us through the fleshpots of Acerra, mostly to get away from his boss, as far as I could tell. We made our arrangements, more drinks arrived, and we toasted to victory. I could picture Trevisi making the same toast with schnapps not too long ago.

"We interrupted your discussion of the palace in the last century, I think," Trevisi said. "Little is left of its former grandeur. You should have seen it before the turn of the century. *Era bello.*"

"Yes, I was about to tell Billy about Queen Margherita. A very elegant woman, a patron of the arts, she revitalized the Italian court, made it fashionable. She held balls and parties that became famous all across Europe."

"People loved her," Trevisi said, nodding his approval. "They called her the Queen of Pearls."

"I'd guess all queens like pearls," I said, trying to sound casual.

"Oh, but Margherita loved them. She wore huge strands and had many different necklaces. She was renowned for her pearls," Trevisi said.

"Wasn't there a theft at one point?" Kaz asked.

"Yes, back in the 1890s. She and the king held an anniversary ball here at Caserta. As I recall the story, a small box containing a three-strand necklace was stolen from her dressing room. It was never recovered, and apparently has never turned up. The Carabinieri chief resigned in disgrace. Very unfortunate."

"You have an excellent memory, Baron," said Amatori. "I haven't heard that story since I was a child."

"I was a student before the war. One tends to accumulate bits of information."

"Indeed," Amatori said. "And you, Lieutenant Boyle? Were you a student in America?"

"Not for long," I said. "I was a police detective."

"Ah, a fellow officer of the law! Of course we will assist you in every way possible," Trevisi said. We had another round to toast our cooperation, then finally parted ways.

"The Queen of Pearls?" I said as we got into the jeep and Kaz tossed his bag into the back. It had started to rain, a steady, incessant spitting that sounded like drum rolls on the canvas top.

"As I was about to tell you when your Italian comrades showed up. Billy, if Sergeant

Cole had these, there may be more. Perhaps he found them in the palace and was being blackmailed. Or threatened by an accomplice?"

"I don't think that's why he jumped. What happened in Campozillone caused him to jump."

"But why this particular night? That was months ago, and as you said, he'd found a place in CID where he could still be useful." Kaz turned up his coat collar against the blowing rain. "You know that I have thought about it," he said in a softer voice.

"Yeah, I do." I placed my hand on Kaz's shoulder for a moment. There was nothing left to say.

"There were times I missed Daphne so much. I missed everything. My family, my way of life, my country. When things got difficult, as they did in London recently, it was a temptation."

"An end to all your problems."

"Yes, that is the answer for some. But for me, it seemed like defeat. They would finally win, those who took everything from me. So we must think, who won with Sergeant Cole? Who defeated him, months after that dreadful incident?"

"He said he couldn't forget the innocent

lives he took. *He won't let me* is how he put it."

"Who was he talking about?"

"He didn't say. Only that it was a friend, and that he could see it all in his face, see everything that happened."

"Someone from his unit, who reminded him of that day. Someone he'd felt close to, and now his face only reminded Cole of what he had done."

"Maybe," I said, turning a corner and sending up a sheet of water that drenched the hood. "Or he had a friend who was a jewel thief on the side. Right after he said that, he handed me those pearls. It was the damnedest thing."

"Could the pearls have anything to do with the murders?"

"I don't know. Maybe Cole found the queen's pearls. All I know is I've had too much to drink and it's been a long day. We're almost home."

"In good weather it must be difficult to sleep," Kaz said, looking out over the B-17s lined up on the airfield across the road. He was right. When the skies cleared, they'd be revving engines and flying overhead all day.

"Good weather? What's that?" Right now GIs in the mountains were huddling in trenches, caves, dugouts, wherever they could find cover from shrapnel and storm. Roads were turning into mud pits that could suck a heavy truck down to its axles and stall a Sherman tank. Sunny Italy. I'm sure it existed in some other time and place, but not in this winter of 1944.

Signora Salvalaggio greeted us at the door, watching as we hung up our dripping coats and stamped the wet from our boots. I assembled some of the few Italian words I knew and attempted an introduction. *"Salvalaggio di Signora, questo è il Tenente Baron Piotr Augustus Kazimierz."*

"Il barone? Da che la famiglia la sono?"

"Siamo discesi dalla casa principe di Ryazan," Kaz broke in. *"È un piacere incontrarla, Signora."* He made a little bow as he took the old lady's hand and kissed it. She accepted it without surprise, and graciously escorted us through her kitchen and into the living room. Before I had time to ask Kaz what the exchange was all about, Captains Wilson and Bradshaw were on their feet and I made another round of introductions. The heat from the coal stove was a relief after the cold rain.

"Welcome, Lieutenant," Bradshaw said. "We had a message from Major Kearns this morning that another investigator would be taking the spare room. Haven't found the murderer, Boyle?"

"Not yet," I said, pulling my chair closer to the stove. "We'll probably be at the hospital tomorrow afternoon, asking the staff about Doctor Galante. Anybody there he was close to?"

"I saw Galante talk more to our landlady than anyone at the hospital, outside of medical business anyway," Wilson said. "They were always chatting in Italian. Galante said he liked the practice."

"An odd duck, that one," Bradshaw said. "Not to speak ill of the dead, but he did keep to himself, more interested in artwork and Italian history than anything else. I believe he said he was Jewish, so I wonder what the fascination was."

"His family was Italian," Wilson said. "He once told me he hoped to get to Rome when it was liberated, to see his mother's birthplace. Her family emigrated at the turn of the century. According to him, she was descended from one of the oldest Jewish families, been around since Roman times."

"Any idea what he and the signora talked about?"

They didn't. I wondered why I cared, as the warmth from the coal fire seeped into my body.

Chapter Fourteen

The next morning I found Kaz in the kitchen, seated at a worn wooden table, drinking espresso as Signora Salvalaggio hovered over him, filling his tiny cup and laying out a plate of cheese and bread. He'd told me last night that she knew of the clans of Poland, and had asked him which princely family he was descended from. I didn't even know that there were princely families in Poland, so this old landlady had a leg up on me.

"Buon giorno," she said, placing a cup of steaming, thick coffee in front of me. It tasted strong and sweet.

"Molto buono," I said.

"Billy, are you becoming a student of languages? I didn't know you'd learned Italian," Kaz said.

"Picked up a few sentences, that's all. Hard not to."

Kaz spoke to the signora, pointing at me,

and they both laughed.

"You two became pals pretty quick," I said, smiling to let her know I could take whatever Kaz had dished out.

"Signora Salvalaggio used to work at the palace, as a seamstress. She understands the distinctions of European royalty, even the minor nobility. She is very well educated for a woman of her time. She knew Queen Margherita personally."

At the mention of the queen's name, I thought the signora stood a little straighter, as if the memory of her royal service brought back the posture of her youth. For a moment, I saw her as that younger woman, not a gray-haired lady in the typical black garb of the elderly. Taller, dressed in finery at the court, with smooth skin and glossy black hair. Her dark eyes met mine, as if to say, yes, I was once beautiful, can you believe it? She smiled, and returned to tidying up the kitchen. I wondered if she'd been around when the pearls were stolen, and if she might be able to help us identify what we had. Maybe she'd recognize the queen's pearls, or might know if these were cheap imitations.

"I wonder if she was there when the pearls were stolen," I said.

There was a crash, and Signora Salvalaggio stood with her hand to her mouth, a glass shattered at her feet. "Have you found them?" Her voice trembled, as if she were on the verge of tears, the precise English a shock to us both.

"Signora, please sit down and tell us what you know," Kaz said, as he pulled out a chair. *"Per favore."*

"Do you have them, the pearls?" Her voice was now insistent. Kaz glanced at me and I nodded. He took the pearl necklace from his jacket pocket and placed it on the table. She gasped, and reached for them, but stopped herself. "The last time I saw that necklace, I dressed the queen myself and put it around her neck. It is the same clasp, the same length. It is the queen's."

"Signora Salvalaggio, I had the impression you did not speak English," I said. "You are quite fluent." I didn't know which surprised me more, her perfect English, or her claim about the pearls.

"I did not let the Germans know I spoke their language either," she said. "There is nothing to be gained by idle conversation."

"Yet you spoke with Doctor Galante often."

"Yes. He was cultured, and from one of the ancient Roman families, even if he was a Jew. The *Italkim,* they call themselves. He understood the nature of things."

"He appreciated Italian culture, the language and history."

"Yes. Not many men in the army do. Any army. They use the palace as if it were a barracks." She spit out that last word.

"Tell us about the pearls, Signora," Kaz urged her with a gentle hand laid on her arm.

"I was a seamstress, but it was not a commoner's position," she said, waving her hand as if dismissing a servant. "I came from an old family, honorable but impoverished. My husband had died one year after we married, from the cholera, and I almost succumbed myself. The queen heard of my plight and brought me to Caserta, to be in charge of her gowns — sewing, repairing, and altering. Oh, you should have seen them! Silk, velvet, satin, gold embroidery, nothing was too precious to go into her gowns. 'Inspire the popular imagination,' that's what she used to say about her gowns and jewelry. She saw it as her duty."

"What happened to the pearls?" I asked.

"It was on Their Majesties silver wedding anniversary, in 1893. She wore a long parure of rubies with this short three-strand pearl necklace. It was a grand party, the emperor and empress of Germany, the queen of Portugal, the grand duke and duchess of Russia, so many of Europe's finest were there." Her eyes were focused on a distant memory of the old century, long-dead aristocrats dancing in the now rat-infested palace. Meanwhile, I was trying to figure out what a parure was.

"When did they go missing?" Kaz asked, in a whisper.

"That night. I was supposed to put all the jewelry away, it was a sign of the trust the queen had in me. But I rushed through it, since I had fallen in love with a young man, a lieutenant, like you two gallant gentlemen." She smiled, and looked away, a faint blush showing on her wrinkled cheeks. "He was waiting for me downstairs, and in my hurry I left the necklace in its black lacquered box on a table in the dressing room. It should have gone in a locked armoire, where I'd put it many times before. But the heart is always in haste, at least for the young," she sighed.

"What happened?"

"In the morning, the lacquered box was gone. When I last saw it, all the guests had departed, and very few people left the palace after that. Because of all the royalty gathered, there were guards on all the doors throughout the night."

"Except for you and your lieutenant."

"Yes. The Carabinieri suspected us, of course. We were questioned for days. We had walked through the gardens under the moonlight. It was beautiful, and I had no way of knowing it was the last truly happy night of my life."

"You lost your position?" Kaz asked.

"Yes. For my negligence. And my lieutenant was transferred to Sicily, in disgrace. I never saw him again."

"No one else was questioned?"

"The others were all too exalted to be questioned. But the theft made the guests nervous, and they all left the next day. I was somehow always certain it was waiting to be found. Where was it?"

"I don't know. It was given to me."

"Ask the person!" It was an order, and in the set of her face I could see her lineage. Impoverished and disgraced, she still had the aristocratic bearing, the readiness to issue orders that commoners must obey.

"He's dead. He shot himself moments after he handed me the necklace."

Signora Salvalaggio crossed herself. "That such beauty could ruin so many lives," she said, shaking her head.

"Did you stay in Caserta to search for the pearls?" Kaz asked.

"Back then, I had no such thought. I had nothing, no family left, no place to go. I walked into town and looked for work. A good seamstress can always find employment, and I did. Not sewing fine gowns, but it kept me alive. I often wondered where the pearls were, and if the Carabinieri had their eye on me. If they did, I disappointed them. I never ran off with my fortune."

"But now you have been vindicated," Kaz said, gathering up the necklace. "We can tell the authorities."

"Ha! Do what you wish. It does not matter. Who is left alive to remember a theft in 1893? The old king and queen are both dead. The Carabinieri headquarters was destroyed in the fighting; any records they had went up in flames. I am simply an old seamstress with her stories of grand balls, lost love, and other ancient memories. Please, take it away."

"Did you tell Doctor Galante all this?" Kaz asked as he carefully swept the necklace into his pocket.

"Not at first. But the *dottore* was so interested, he flattered me with his attention. Foolish for an old woman, I know. I found myself telling him the story, describing the rooms, where the nobles and servants slept, where the jewels were kept. He would come back and tell me about what he'd seen and how the rooms looked. It was all so sad to hear, but at the same time, it brought back memories of the good times, before the pearls cursed me."

"He never found anything?"

"No. I believe he would have told me if he had. We had become friends, of a sort. A lonely man, more of a scholar than his colleagues, and an old woman with a sad but interesting story. Will you find who killed him?" Her lip trembled, and I knew that she had valued Galante's friendship. A cultured man, who respected her and her stories of royalty and palace balls.

"That's why we're here," I said, sounding confident but avoiding a direct answer.

"It wasn't over the pearls, was it? Please, no."

"There seems to be no connection," Kaz said. I wasn't so sure.

"Did you know another American, Lieutenant Norman Landry?"

"No," she said. "I know very few soldiers, only those they send for my rooms and cooking. But I do know the priest, *Prete* Dare."

"How?"

"He came to visit *Dottore* Galante. Twice. Once he dined with him. Your American priests are very different from ours, I think."

"Father Dare is one of a kind. Did he know about the pearls?"

"I don't know. I never heard the dottore speak to him about it."

"What did they talk about?"

"Nothing I recall. Other soldiers, the war. The dottore spoke often of *sgusciare la scossa,* you know?"

"Shell shock," Kaz said. "Combat fatigue."

"Yes," she said. "I did not know these terms, but Dottore Galante explained them to me. It was his life's work, he said, to learn about this. He was very annoyed with some officer who kept him from it, and had him sent to work at the hospital."

"Did he and Father Dare speak about this?"

"Yes. When he came for dinner, it seemed the padre was asking his opinion about soldiers they both knew. But I did not pay attention to names. American names are so strange to me, especially the names soldiers use."

"What do you mean?"

"What is the word? *Soprannome?*"

"Nicknames," Kaz supplied.

"Yes, yes. It makes it so difficult to understand, especially with the Americans. One of the men they talked about, he had a

French name, at least to my ears. And there was something about a ridiculous town he was from. They always laughed when they said it."

"Louie Walla from Walla Walla?"

"Yes!" She slapped her hand on the table. "The dottore was worried about him. Why, I cannot say. I was too busy preparing *la Genovese.*"

"Were the other doctors at the dinner?"

"No, they were both working. I think Dottore Galante wished to dine alone with Il Prete."

"*La Genovese?* Is that the Neapolitan beef and onion ragout?" Kaz's concentration on the case had apparently been broken.

"Yes, Barone. I will make it for you, if you can find some good meat. Not horse meat, although it will do in a pinch," Signora Salvalaggio said, with a conspiratorial smile.

"Why do they call it *la Genovese,* if it comes from Naples?" I asked.

"A mystery," she said, with a shrug.

A real mystery. Priests and doctors, suicide and murder, hidden pearls and Willie Peter grenades. Nothing made sense, nothing connected. I drank the last of the espresso, now gone cold, the harsh taste gritty and sour on my tongue. Kaz and the signora chatted on about cooking while all I could think of was who was going to be dealt the next card.

Then I recalled seeing women in Sicily, squatting at the side of the road, their knives slicing into the bodies of horses killed in the German retreat. The animals were still in harness, flies buzzing around their eyes, as the Sicilian women butchered them and carried slabs of flesh home, blood staining their shoulders. I watched Signora Salvalaggio, and wondered what she might be capable of. To what lengths would she go to recover her honor? Or the pearls?

Chapter Fifteen

"What should we do with the pearls?" Kaz asked as we drove to the palace to pick up Luca Amatori, our Carabinieri guide for our trip to Bar Raffaele in Acerra.

"I'm not sure," I said. "I wish I knew if they were a dead end or a connection to the murders. There might be some percentage in letting it slip that we have them."

"Meaning a fair chance that someone will try to kill us for them. I'd prefer a different plan, Billy."

"Well, that wouldn't have worked anyway. If word got out, CID would want us to turn in the pearls. They'd sit in a locked file somewhere until a colonel with a key decided to bring home a souvenir. No sense in letting that happen."

"What would you do if this were Boston?"

I wanted to say, *Whatever the patrol sergeant said to do.* My experience as a detective was limited to the few weeks between my uncle calling in a few favors on the promotions board, and the attack on Pearl Harbor. Before that, I'd been a beat cop, working different parts of the city, and helping Dad out when he needed a few extra bluecoats at a crime scene. Dad was a homicide detective, and it was his plan to bring me up in the family business. It was a good plan, but the war had gotten in the way. Instead, I said, "It's not the same. I doubt we'd ever find a dead queen's pearls in Boston."

"What about one of the old Boston families? The Brahmins, as you call them. You find jewelry from a theft that happened fifty years ago. The original owner is dead. The family is stupendously wealthy. No one is pursuing the case. What do you do?"

I took a corner harder than I needed to, sending Kaz rocking in his seat. Only fair, since he was putting me in a corner too.

"You forgot the old family retainer, living a life of shame."

"What if there were one?"

"I know some cops who'd split it with her. Not many. A few would turn it in, a few would keep it for themselves."

"What about the rest?"

"My dad always said you couldn't trust a guy who was either too honest or too crooked."

"I don't understand," Kaz said.

"I didn't either, at first," I said. It was hard to explain. "Okay, for example. There was a fire, a few years before the war, in Mattapan Square. Big two-family house, four-alarm blaze in the middle of the night. Everyone got out, and the firemen kept it from spreading to the neighbors, but the building was ruined, had to be torn down before it caved in on itself. So the next day, I'm there with a few other cops to keep the onlookers at a safe distance while the wrecking crew takes it down. There's a fire truck too, in case anything's smoldering under the debris."

"Are there any Boston Brahmins in this story?" Kaz asked.

I responded with a hard stop at an intersection, but he'd braced himself for it. "Wait. There was an attic, used by the two families for storage. But it used to be an apartment, back before the turn of the century. No one remembered who'd lived there, or where they went. When they pulled the front of the house down, a wooden crossbeam came loose and hit the ground, rolled right into one of the workers. Broke his leg. So we push the crowd back to make room for him, and as we're standing around while the firemen rig a stretcher, a cop named Augie Perkins notices a coffee can sticking out from the horsehair lathing on a section of interior wall. It was from the attic. Stuffed full of fives, tens, and twenties, all rolled up tight."

"Why leave money inside a wall?"

"You'd be surprised what you find hidden in old houses. Lots of people don't trust banks or their relatives, so they keep money hidden. Trouble is, they don't tell anyone, and end up taking their secret to the grave."

"Who owned the house?"

"I'll get to that. The lid was off, and Augie sees that there's a ton of dough in that can, and he thinks no one else sees it. So he eases over, kneels down to tie his shoe, pulls it free, and stuffs it under his jacket."

"But you saw him, right?"

"No, a pal of mine did. Joe Leary, one of the firemen. He waits until the worker is loaded onto the ambulance, and the crowd breaks up. Then he clocks Augie good, opens his coat, and shows the rest of us what he'd taken."

"And you arrested him?"

"No. Joe told us the building was owned by a rich guy named Frederick Perkins. Almost a Brahmin. Good enough for one of them to marry his daughter, and his money, anyway. We weren't in a hurry to give him a tin can of cash he never knew about. So there's ten of us, not counting the guy with the broken leg. Joe suggested we split it thirteen ways."

"Why thirteen?"

"A share for each of the families that were burned out, one for the guy with the broken leg, and the ten of us. Even Augie, but we had to cut him in, just to keep him quiet."

"It sounds like an admirable plan."

"Except for Teddy Booker. Augie was the greedy one, and Teddy was the too-honest one. He threatened to turn us all in if we didn't give the money to the owner of the property. Joe threatened to bash him one, too, but Teddy didn't give in. He took the money, and reported both Augie and Joe for pilfering."

"What happened?"

"No one would speak to Teddy after that. They called him By-the-Book Booker. He quit the force and moved to Chicago. Augie and Joe lost their jobs. Frederick Perkins got a can of cash, had a heart attack two weeks later and died."

"And the moral of the story?" Kaz asked.

"Like my dad always said, don't trust anyone too honest or too crooked. They'll both get you in hot water."

"I still don't know what we're going to do

with the pearls. But at least now I know not to give them to Augie or Teddy," Kaz said.

"Which do you think Luca Amatori is?" I said, as we pulled onto the gravel driveway leading to the palace to pick up our escort and former enemy.

"I think we'll find out more without his boss around," Kaz said. "Capitano Trevisi didn't seem to think much his Tenente's opinions."

"Buon giorno," the Carabinieri lieutenant said as he walked to the jeep. He was right on time. Kaz got in back and the lieutenant thanked him.

"After enduring Billy's driving, you might not thank me, Tenente."

"Please, call me Luca. We are all lieutenants, yes? It would be tiresome to hear of it constantly."

"Certainly, Luca. Call me Kaz, which is Billy's version of Kazimierz."

"Been stuck at *tenente* long?" I asked as we shook hands.

"Stuck? Yes, and at war also," Luca said, pulling his blue service cap down tight on his head. "It has been a long time since we have known peace. Here, take this turn for Acerra," he said as we came to the main road. We drove south, past horse-drawn carts loaded with firewood, blackened ruins, the odd intact farmhouse, and fallow winter fields, sodden from recent rains. The weather was clearing, low gray clouds tumbling across the sky, making way for the sun and the bombers that would follow.

"Have you been stationed at Caserta long?" Kaz asked, leaning in from the backseat.

"No. I was transferred here with others from my battalion, two months ago. We had been in Yugoslavia, but returned to Italy with the armistice. I think we are about to be sent somewhere else. We have received new arms and supplies, and there are many rumors."

"Not the first time I heard that. Any idea where?"

"No. No one tells us anything. We wait, we patrol, and we do what we can against the black market, but it is hopeless."

"Do you have much trouble with GIs?"

"Yes, but we can do little about it. Only the military police and your CID may arrest your soldiers. We work closely with them, but it is understandable that they take care of their own in a foreign country."

His words made sense, but I could tell from his tone that it bothered him. It would bother any good cop, so I liked that about him. "Any scuttlebutt about where you're going?"

"Pardon me?"

"American jargon," Kaz said. "Rumors, loose talk."

"Ah. We will be flown into Rome after American paratroopers take the airport. Or, that we will land on the beaches west of Rome with our own San Marco Marine Regiment. We are going to protect the pope, we are escorting the king into Rome, take your choice. They all involve fantasies of heroics and reclaiming our national honor. I suspect the reality will be somewhat less glamorous."

"Rome is not that far away, maybe a hundred and twenty miles. It's not impossible."

"Except for the Germans dug in along the Bernhardt Line, and on Monte Cassino, it would be a pleasant drive," Luca said. "Although machine guns do spoil any outing."

"A seaborne landing does make sense," Kaz said, more usefully. "To go around them."

"I'll be sure to tell General Eisenhower next time I see him," I said. Getting to Rome sounded fine to me. Maybe I could go along and find Diana.

"If only generals would listen to lieutenants," Luca said.

"This general will. Billy is his nephew. We are attached to General Eisenhower's headquarters," Kaz said, with a touch of pride in his voice.

"Really?" Luca looked like he had a hard time believing we worked for Uncle Ike.

"Yeah, really. Now tell us what you know about Bar Raffaele."

"How can I say no to the nephew of General Eisenhower himself? The bar is run by a pimp named Stefano Inzerillo. He took over a bombed-out building, cleaned it up, put in a rough bar, a few tables, and serves terrible wine at high prices, which soldiers are willing to pay."

"The women?"

"Inzerillo is smart. He does not employ them directly, and they do not use his premises for their services. He has kept out of trouble, and probably pays someone not to declare the place off-limits."

"But he did have trouble recently, according to the men in Lieutenant Landry's platoon. He made them pay for damages."

"I had not heard. Inzerillo has at least two men at the bar at all times to prevent fights."

"Bouncers?"

"If you mean men who will break an arm

or a kneecap, then yes."

"Thugs," Kaz said.

"Yes, thugs," Luca said, nodding his head. "If anyone caused damages, they must have been damaged themselves. Inzerillo is not one to be caught unawares."

We drove on, passing a crumbling castle perched on a hilltop, surrounded by olive trees. Destroyed in another war, centuries ago, Luca informed us. It was nice to know we weren't responsible for every ruined building in sight.

"Billy," Kaz said from the backseat, "there's a jeep following us. It's been there since we left the palace, hanging back."

"I see it," I said, checking the rearview mirror. With the canvas top up, it was hard to tell who or how many were in it. "You sure it's following us?"

"Either that or they left for Acerra right after us."

"There is an AMGOT office in Acerra," Luca said. The American Military Government for Occupied Territories ran government functions in areas that had been liberated. "I've made the trip on several occasions with American officers in a jeep. Nothing unusual about it."

"Keep an eye on it anyway, Kaz." At that moment, two jeeps came around a curve and passed us in the opposite direction. A common enough sight, as Luca said. I drove on, past olive groves, the trees with their silvery leaves in straight rows, marred by the occasional shell hole and shattered, blackened trunks.

We followed Luca's directions into Acerra, winding through narrow streets, past a walled castle, complete with moat and drawbridge, where American and British flags flew next to the Italian banner. That had to be AMGOT. We entered a neighborhood of even narrower streets. Clothing hung from lines strung between buildings, adding odd traces of color to the dingy and shadowed roadway. Shops and homes were shuttered, and only a few civilians were on the street, eyeing us with indifference, suspicion, fear, or avarice, depending on their intentions. I was pretty sure that covered all the bases in this part of town.

We pulled over in front of a building with a gaily painted sign announcing this was Bar Raffaele. The sign was the nicest thing on the street. Empty wine bottles, cigarette butts, and other debris littered the sidewalk. The sour smell of spilled wine mingled with the tang of urine and rotting garbage.

"Welcome to Acerra," Luca said.

"Reminds me of certain parts of Boston,"

I said. "Scollay Square, right outside the Crawford House, for instance. Makes me a little homesick, almost."

"It makes me ill," Kaz said. He pounded on the locked door. "I hope it smells better inside." There was no answer.

"Aprire, aprire!" Luca thundered, hammering on the door with the butt of his pistol. *"Carabinieri!"*

I heard the creak of doors and shutters opening all around us, as people risked a look at the commotion. I turned around and they all shut, no one wanting to take a chance on being seen and dragged into an unknown situation.

"Carabinieri? *Italiano?*" came a voice from behind the door. It sounded fearful and weak, not what I was expecting.

"Si, aprire ora," Luca said, and the door cracked open far enough for a bloodshot eyeball to peer out at us. It flickered at each of us, growing wide as it lit on me. Luca said something calming in Italian, and the guy finally undid the chain lock and opened the door.

He was holding a sawed-off shotgun. But that wasn't what surprised me. It was his face. Ugly purplish-red bruises covered it. His other eye was swollen shut, and he winced as he stepped back, the shotgun pointed to the floor.

"Posare il fucile," Luca said, in a tone that I would have recognized in any language, coming from a cop. *Put the gun down.* He did. *"Che è successo a lei?"*

"Who is the *Americano?*"

"A friend. Now tell us, what happened to you?"

Inzerillo steadied himself with one hand on a chair, then eased himself down into it. Broken ribs. I could tell by the way he moved, and by the sharp intake of breath between clenched teeth. Two fingers were taped together on one hand, probably broken. His knuckles were about the only part of him that wasn't bruised, meaning that he hadn't even gotten a good punch in.

"You were beaten by someone who knew what they were doing," I said, walking around the table to look at Inzerillo from all angles. "Somebody who took his time, who wanted to inflict as much pain as possible, and still leave you conscious. He broke your fingers, cracked your ribs, worked on your face, but didn't hit you in the head. Or your mouth, so he wouldn't have pieces of your teeth in his fist. A connoisseur of pain, a man who enjoyed his work."

"I fell down the stairs," Inzerillo said in his thick accent. If he could have moved his face more, he would have sneered.

"A man who might come back," I said.

"When did you fall down these stairs?" Luca asked him as he holstered his pistol and then removed the shells from the shotgun.

"Last week, I don't remember. *Venerdì?*"

"Did anyone see you fall down the stairs last Friday?" Luca asked. Inzerillo shook his head. "Where were your men, your bodyguards?"

"Ask them, if you can find the bastards!"

"What was the argument about?" I asked.

"I told you, I fell down the stairs. Am I under arrest?" He sounded hopeful.

"No, Signor Inzerillo," Luca said with a sigh. "We have nothing to arrest you for. Clumsiness is not a crime. Gentlemen, do you have any other questions?"

"Talk to us off the record, Inzerillo," I said, pulling up a chair and sitting across from him. The stand-up interrogation was not going to work, so why not try the one-guy-to-another technique? "We know a GI did this to you. Just tell us what you know about him and we'll keep it quiet."

"I do not know you," Inzerillo said. "So I don't trust you."

"He is the nephew of General Eisenhower," Luca said. Inzerillo rolled his eyes.

The eye I could see, I should say.

"Were these the damages Lieutenant Landry came back to pay for?" I said, gesturing at his face and hands.

"The lieutenant never paid me for anything."

"You knew Landry?"

"Sure. He has a favorite girl. Always trying to get her to quit, but she makes too much money. I think she breaks his heart."

"What about a doctor, Max Galante? Or an army priest, Father Dare?" The chaplain had said he never came here, but a pistol-packing priest deserved a bit of distrust.

"We have a doctor who takes care of the girls, but his name is not Galante. And priests do not come here, thank God. What is Landry going to pay me for?" The wheels had started to turn in his beaten, larcenous head.

"One of Sergeant Flint's men broke up the place?"

"No. Only I have been broken."

"Falling down the stairs." He nodded, as if I'd finally figured it out. "You know Landry's sergeants? Gates, Flint, Stump, Walla?"

"Louie Walla from Walla Walla," Inzerillo said. "Louie likes to have fun. Sure I know them, I know many GIs. It is my job to help them relax, to enjoy *vino* and *amore.*"

"What you sell here is not fit to be called either," Luca said. "Come, he is not worth our time."

"You sure you won't let us help you?" I asked, giving it one last try. He laughed, coughed, and winced again.

"Thank you for your cooperation, Signor Inzerillo," Kaz said. "It will be duly noted in our report."

"What do you mean, *Inglese?*"

"I am Polish, Signor, but I do wear the British uniform proudly. What I mean is that we will report to the Army Criminal Investigation Division, and to the Third Division headquarters, that you have fully cooperated and an arrest of the soldier who attacked you is imminent."

"Huh?" Inzerillo said, trying to follow Kaz. *"Imminente?"*

"Yes, imminente. You should probably give the Signor his shotgun shells back, Tenente. He may need them."

"No, you wouldn't. It is a death sentence, and I am an innocent man!"

"I doubt that," Kaz said. "Innocent men have nothing to hide."

"La santa madre di dio," Inzerillo said softly. "Talk to Landry. He will tell you."

"You don't know?" Luca said.

"Know what?"

"He is dead. *Assassinato.*"

It was a rookie move to tell Inzerillo that Landry was dead. He hadn't picked up on the past tense when we'd mentioned his name; his English wasn't that good. Luca was more of a military man than a detective, so he didn't get that if Landry knew whatever Inzerillo was trying to keep covered up, and Landry had been killed, Inzerillo would see the same thing might happen to him. Kaz's ploy had been a good one, but after hearing Landry had been murdered, Inzerillo clammed up tight. There was nothing to be learned from him.

We left Inzerillo's neighborhood behind, gladly, and took Luca's suggestion to stop for lunch off the main piazza. The Trattoria La Lanternina was a different world. Clean sidewalks, delicious smells from the kitchen, tablecloths, and several Carabinieri at their midday meal. Any joint where bluecoats ate was okay by me. Luca stopped to chat with two officers and we grabbed a table.

"Friends of yours?" I asked when he joined us.

"Yes, we served together in the Fourteenth Carabinieri Battalion. I haven't seen them for months. Tell me, was this trip worthwhile?"

"It was," I said, before Kaz could say anything about Luca blowing our chances with Inzerillo. No point in showing him up. "We know that Landry knew something about what happened to Inzerillo, and was killed a day later. There might be a connection."

"But no connection to Doctor Galante," Kaz said. "He showed no recognition of that name."

"Still, it's interesting. And why did he deny that Flint and Landry went to see him? All the sergeants agreed that they had."

"Maybe Landry went to see that girl he liked. Maybe that's where the money went," Kaz said. "Perhaps Inzerillo was afraid to admit there had been a fight, in case he would be closed down."

"Could Landry and Flint have beaten him like that?" I wondered aloud. "Maybe he harmed the girl, and they took it out on him."

"Or your Lieutenant Landry was insanely jealous of this prostitute, and killed her," Luca said. "And then her family attacked Inzerillo and killed the lieutenant."

"You don't really believe that, do you?"

"No, but with no evidence, it makes as much sense as your conjectures."

"I'll talk to Flint and see what he says. I'll

bet the girl fits in somewhere. Any chance of finding her?"

"A prostitute, yes. A specific prostitute, never. If anything did happen with Landry, she will have disappeared. If not, she would not allow herself to be found by the authorities for obvious reasons."

"Well, I don't know of anything else we have to go on. Luca, if you hear of anything else from Inzerillo, please let us know. Kaz and I will check out the hospital and see what the staff has to say about Galante."

Luca ordered as the waiter delivered a decanter of wine. "Since we spoke last night of Queen Margherita, I thought you should taste the dish named after her. Pizza Margherita. It is said that she scandalized the court by eating pizza bread from street vendors when she visited Naples. It used to be sold plain, rolled and eaten by hand. The story goes that she noticed the poor eating it and ordered a guard to bring her one. She loved it, and the people of Naples appreciated her for noticing their native food. A chef created a pizza dish in her honor, using tomato sauce, mozzarella cheese, and basil leaves, to represent the colors of the Italian flag: red, white, and green."

"Quite a lady," I said. "Pearls and pizza." Kaz nearly choked on his wine.

The pizzas were good, thinner than I was used to from the North End, but tastier. The place was crowded, and I was glad to see normal life returning to this little part of Italy.

"What was it like in Yugoslavia?" Kaz asked Luca as we relaxed after the food.

"Garrison duty, mostly boring. A few times we went out with the army to hunt for partisans. We never found them, which was frustrating, since they could always find us when they wanted to. We lost men on guard duty, throats slit. Terrible."

"Did you have a hard time with the Germans, when the king declared the armistice?"

"No. There were no *Tedeschi* in our area. The Carabinieri stayed loyal to the king. Other units did as their commanders told them. Some even joined the partisans to fight the Germans. It was a difficult time."

That was that. I got the impression Luca didn't want to talk about it, and I wondered if he had friends or family who had gone over to Mussolini's puppet state in the north.

"Boring, frustrating, difficult," I said. "You add terrifying and you pretty much sum it up for all of us, Luca."

No one disagreed.

Chapter Sixteen

The 32nd Station Hospital was buzzing. It was a complex of buildings that might have been Italian Army barracks from a couple of wars ago. Outside of the headquarters building, a line of ambulance trucks, their sides painted with huge red crosses, pulled into the central square. Doctors, nurses, and orderlies spilled out of half a dozen buildings, unloading stretchers and directing the wounded to different wards. The patients were all bandaged and wearing army-issue pajamas; these weren't fresh casualties, but transfers from evacuation and field hospitals closer to the line.

At the same time, GIs were loading a pair of trucks parked next to the dispensary, as a nurse with a clipboard checked the inventory while talking with a doctor. He wore a wrinkled white lab coat, a major's gold leaf, and a neatly trimmed mustache. He looked like the guy we'd come to see.

"Excuse me, Major Warren?"

"I'm a little busy, Lieutenant. See the adjutant if you're looking for a buddy, or Ward 13 if you've got the clap." He spoke without looking at me, and went back to reviewing the inventory with the nurse. She wore the army-regulation white dress and blue cape, which looked snazzy, but wasn't very useful closer to the front lines, where nurses wore whatever army fatigues they could scrounge.

"It's about Captain Galante, sir."

"Listen, Lieutenant," he said, turning to face me. "I've talked to CID and gave them a statement. I don't have time to go over that again, so check with them. Some sergeant was here, I forget his name."

"Sergeant Cole?"

"Yeah. Talk to him, I'm busy."

"He's dead, sir. He killed himself."

"Jesus! Was that the guy who shot himself on the palace roof?"

"Yes sir. I just need a few minutes of your time."

"Perhaps I can assist with the supplies, while the doctor speaks with my friend?" Kaz said to the nurse. She was pretty, but I knew Kaz was going to interrogate her while I talked to the doctor. Major Warren agreed, and led me to his office. The sign above the door read Chief of Medical Services.

"Sorry if I barked at you, Lieutenant, but I've been up to my eyeballs in work today, starting before dawn." He fell into the chair behind his desk and I sat across from him, waiting as he lit up a Lucky. His desk was stacked with patient charts, an overflowing inbox, and an empty outbox. "Accident on the road from Naples. A truckload of replacements — ASTP kids — goes over an embankment. Broken bones, lacerations, the usual for a road accident. Poor bastards hadn't been off the boat for a full day yet, and they're all banged up already."

"I hear there's a lot of replacements coming in," I said, trying not to think of my brother Danny and worrying if he was headed for trouble.

"Indeed. Some of us have been told to get ready to move out. There's a big push going on somewhere, that's for sure. Now, what can I do for you?"

"I need to ask some questions about Doctor Galante that Sergeant Cole may not have asked. Did he frequent prostitutes?"

"Galante? That's a good one, Lieutenant. He probably never even thought about it. I never heard him speak about much of anything except medicine and Italian culture."

"You're sure? This won't be part of any official report, in case you're worried about his family finding out."

"I'm sure. Have you talked to the doctors he roomed with? Wilson and Bradshaw?"

"Yes, they didn't really know him well. Ships passing in the night. Galante was transferred from Third Division. You know anything about that?"

"Just what I heard. He got into a dispute with a colonel and got booted upstairs. He wasn't happy about it, I can tell you that."

"You all must work hard, but this place does look pretty comfortable."

"It is. Long hours every day of the week, but clean sheets and decent food every night. A far cry from battalion aid stations near the front lines. The Luftwaffe bombed us once, but that's as close as we've come to real danger here."

"What was it that Galante didn't like?"

"He wanted to work on combat fatigue cases. Exclusively. He was almost a bore on the subject." He looked at me shrewdly. "You probably know that's what the beef with the colonel was about. Sending him here was a real punishment. We don't treat psychiatric disorders. We have dentists, physical therapists, surgeons, even a dietician, but no psychiatrists."

"So what happens to combat fatigue cases?" I sensed that there had been no love lost between Warren and Galante, especially on this topic.

"We don't often get casualties direct from the front. Like the boys who just came in, they've already been patched up and sent here for further treatment. They have to be actually wounded to be sent here." He crushed his cigarette out.

"What's your opinion on combat fatigue?"

"Not sure. I'm a surgeon. If I can't cut it out or sew it up, I'm at a loss. I know some cases are sent back to headquarters to do menial work. Seems sort of pathetic."

"I agree. I've seen the waiters in the senior officer's mess."

"But Galante's theory seems weird too. A hot meal, change of clothes, a good night's sleep, and then *wham,* back to the front."

"Isn't that what you do? Patch them up so they can go back as soon as they're able?"

"That's what Galante said. I guess the difference is some of the brass don't mind GIs in a hospital bed if they have holes in them, but they don't like the idea of able-bodied men getting a rest from combat."

"Able-bodied, yes. But what about their minds? Their spirits?" I thought about Jim Cole. No surgeon could ever cut out the memory of that basement, remove the guilt, and patch it all up.

"Like I said, I cut, I stitch. And I do a damn good job of it, as well as running this place. I've seen the inside of men's bodies, I've operated on the brain more times than I like to recall. But I never saw evidence of a spirit in there. Sorry. I wish I had." I wasn't so sure he was. Anyone who looked for the soul between bits of bone and blood didn't know what they were looking for.

"Did Galante have professional differences with another doctor over this? Anything more than a medical disagreement?"

"Far as I know, his serious disagreements were all with the brass at Third Division. We may debate medicine here, Lieutenant, but we're usually too exhausted to do much about an opposing opinion. But there is someone you should talk to. Doctor Stuart Cassidy. He's in Radiology, but he's the closest thing we have to a shrink. He interned with a psych department in Chicago, I think. He and Galante were friendly, as far as that went with the late doctor." Major Warren made a call, and told me to hustle out to the trucks that were being loaded. Cassidy was one of the doctors being transferred to parts unknown.

I found Cassidy sitting on the tailgate of a

truck, leaning against his duffel bag. He looked young for a doctor, with wavy blond hair and an easy smile. Behind him the truck was loaded with medical supplies, stretchers, blankets, cots, and rations.

"Taking a trip, Doctor Cassidy?"

"I am, Lieutenant. Naples harbor is all I heard. You know anything about what's happening?"

"Not a clue," I said, introducing myself and giving Cassidy the short version of the investigation. Like everyone else within twenty miles, he knew about the murders and the suicide. "Anything you can tell me about Max Galante would be helpful."

"Max was brilliant," he said, without hesitation. "Too brilliant, maybe, for his own good."

"What do you mean?"

"I happen to agree with his ideas about combat fatigue. Other units are using the same approach, and it's working well. But Max was so sure of himself that he didn't suffer fools gladly. Sometimes he forgot he was in the army and didn't hold his tongue. It's a problem with us doctors. We think we're gods, but the army has other gods who outrank us."

"Like Colonel Schleck, Third Division."

"Right. Him and his assistant, Major

Arnold. Max made a big stink about how they were incompetent Neanderthals for not taking combat fatigue seriously, as a disease. If he'd been more diplomatic, he'd probably be alive today."

"You're not saying there's a connection?" Did Cassidy know more than he was letting on?

"Not — I just mean he would have been with his unit, and wouldn't have run into whoever killed him. Is there a connection?"

"Not that I can see. If every guy who ran afoul of incompetent Neanderthals got killed, there wouldn't be anyone left to fight this war." Cassidy gave a knowing laugh. "Anything going on in Galante's personal life that might have gotten him in trouble?"

"Can't see it," Cassidy said. "He spent time reading medical journals, when he could get them. Visited museums when they weren't bombed out. He liked his landlady, said she was helping him improve his Italian. He couldn't wait to get to Rome, poor guy. His family hailed from there, went way back to Roman times, according to him. Other than that, I can't think of a thing."

"Did he ever mention Sergeant Cole?"

"Sure. He got him transferred to CID after that incident in Campozillone. He was worried about him."

"Any guys from his old outfit come to see him here?"

"Yeah, Landry, the other guy who got killed. He and Galante got on well. I know Max went to their bivouac at least once. Cole dropped by a couple of times after he started at the palace." That was the first link I had between the two victims, not to mention Cole.

"Do you think Cole was unbalanced? Did Galante think he should have been hospitalized?" I wanted to know more about Galante and Cole, and anyone else he knew in Landry's platoon. Like the killer, maybe.

"No. Not in the way you mean. We call it Old Sergeant's Syndrome. Unofficially, of course."

"What's that, some sort of combat fatigue?"

"It's more than that. According to current thinking, combat fatigue can be dealt with by rest and a short period of relative safety. But for those men who have fought and endured for long periods of time, there finally comes a point at which they become fatalistic. They're usually sergeants, because simply by surviving for months in battle, they've been promoted. In most cases, they are the only man left of their original squad, if not platoon."

"So hot chow and a cot won't do it for them?"

"Nope. You can send them back on the line, but they'll just tell you they know their number is up. They become ineffective as leaders, see themselves as dead men. They've reached the breaking point, and if placed in danger, they simply can't function. And remember, these are men who, by virtue of their survival, have won citations and been praised for their bravery. Like Sergeant Cole. The incident in that village just hurried along what was about to happen. The wonder is not that he succumbed to it, but that he endured so long."

"What's the treatment?" I asked, starting to think about Cole, and what strings Galante had pulled to watch over him, or what regulations he'd broken. Who else knew about that?

"Well, that's the good news. All that's needed is to remove these men from immediate danger, and to give them something useful to do. They still want to serve, so any position off the line makes them feel useful. Once the threat of death in combat is removed, they become healthy again, especially if they have a job to do. CID was perfect for Cole."

"But you said Galante was worried about

him." Or maybe he was worried about what Cole knew. Was there a reason Cole ended up in CID, working in the palace, where he'd have a chance to search for pearls?

"Yeah. What happened in that village produced a burden of guilt that was unusually strong. It must have weighed on him more than we thought."

"Well, it could have been something else entirely," I said, wondering again about the pearls and what part they played in this. The truck engine turned over, and Cassidy jumped down, hoisted the tailgate, and we shook hands.

"Good luck, Lieutenant. I hope you catch the guy. Gotta run."

"Keep your helmet on and your head down, Captain." I liked Cassidy, and hoped he wasn't headed into dangerous territory. Sometimes keeping your head down just wasn't enough.

I watched the trucks leave, with Cassidy and another doctor as passengers and enough gear and supplies for more casualties than I wanted to think about. Replacements, doctors, Naples harbor, leaves cancelled. It was obvious that a force was shipping out, but for where? They could be headed to England for all I knew. Or maybe southern France. Or Rome, who knew? Was that why Diana had to get back so quickly? No, don't let it be Rome, I prayed silently. I don't want her in the midst of a battle. And don't let Danny be one of the nameless replacements either. I decided I should find a church and send up some prayers before it was too late.

"Billy," Kaz said, strolling out of a nearby ward. "What is wrong? You look lost."

"Just thinking. About Diana, and my kid brother Danny." I told Kaz about the ASTP program being curtailed, and how some had been among the replacements flowing in. I told him about the accident, and that I wanted to be sure Danny wasn't among the injured.

"Come, I will ask Edie to check," he said.

"Edie?" I said as I followed him.

"First Lieutenant Edie Embler, of Long Island, New York. She is an operating-room nurse, and is heartbroken over the departure of Doctor Cassidy. But I will console her, if we ever solve this case."

"Will you now?" I was glad to hear it, but I didn't want to act like it was a big deal, so I needled him a bit. He ignored me.

"Edie," he said when he found her. "Could you put my friend's mind at ease, and check the names of the young men from the truck accident? He is worried his brother could be among them. Humor him, please."

"Sure, Piotr. What's the name?" Edie had a faint trace of freckles across her nose, and curly black hair pulled back and stuffed under her white cap.

"Danny Boyle," I said, as she grabbed a mimeographed sheet from a pile on her desk.

"Boyle," she said, tracing her finger down the list. "No, not a Boyle among them. Feel better?"

"Yes," I said, but I didn't. I couldn't shake the feeling of dread that hung over me. Was it Diana I was worried about? Danny? I felt connected to both, and certain that one of them was in danger.

"Edie," Kaz said, "tell Billy what you said about Captain Galante."

"He had an argument," she said. That got my attention. "The day before he was killed."

"With who?"

"I don't know his name. He was an infantry lieutenant, I could tell."

"How could you tell?"

"You just can. The way they carry themselves. It sounds funny, but I just know. He wasn't pretending at anything. And he wore the Third Division patch, the blue and white stripes. Probably a platoon leader."

"What were they arguing about?"
"I don't know, but the lieutenant wanted help with someone, or something, I don't know. I wasn't really paying attention. Captain Galante finally agreed to help him, and then he left in a big hurry."
"Help him how?"
"He just said, 'Okay, okay, I'll do it.' That was it."
"Thanks, Edie. And thanks for checking the list."
"No problem. You two boys come back if you need anything."
I said we would, but I knew she meant Kaz. I think she was already consoled.
"That was interesting," I said to Kaz as we drove up the main road to the palace. "Had to be Landry. Who or what were they arguing about?"
"And did it have anything to do with who killed them?"
"Right. There has to be a connection there, to a person or persons unknown, or to someone we know. Inzerillo, Cole, who else?"
"Didn't Signora Salvalaggio say that Galante and Father Dare discussed Louie Walla?"
"From Walla Walla," I said automatically. "We should talk to Louie and the other

sergeants. They held out before, protecting their pal Cole. Maybe they're protecting somebody else now."

"Landry? Perhaps he asked for help for his prostitute girlfriend. Perhaps she needed medical care."

"Hmm. That would explain the argument. Galante was a straight arrow. He probably drew the line at brothels."

"Or was drawn into one," Kaz said. "Do you think we should try to find her?"

"It would eliminate a whole lot of questions if we did, either way."

"Without Luca, perhaps we could persuade Inzerillo to tell us where she is," Kaz said. His voice was harsh, and I knew he meant business. Kaz had been a gentle soul when I first met him, but now there were times when his intent was as grim as the scar on his face.

I remembered my first meeting with the sergeants of the Third Platoon, and the discussion about carrying captured souvenirs. Neither side liked finding evidence of how their comrades' bodies had been looted. In the same breath that they condemned the Germans for mistreating captured GIs with German sidearms, they'd all but admitted doing the same.

Mistreating prisoners, or shooting them? I

didn't know, but I knew that in most units there was always one guy you didn't detail to escort prisoners to the rear, if you wanted them to survive the journey. Hard men, I had thought at the time. Damned hard men, I thought as I turned the wheel and drove in the direction of Acerra, determined to get to the bottom of something in this cursed investigation.

Chapter Seventeen

We smelled the smoke from the center of town, and I had a bad feeling. Another bad feeling, on top of all the others. Black smoke churned above the rooftops ahead, and if I didn't know where I was going, I could have used it as a beacon. Vehicles clogged the road near Bar Raffaele, and we left the jeep to walk the last hundred yards. A long flatbed truck marked *Vigili del Fuoco* stood in front of Bar Raffaele, two hoses attached to a large cylindrical tank pumping water onto the building.

The bar wasn't the only thing burning. A U.S. Army truck in front of the main entrance was engulfed in flames, its burning tires producing most of the black cloud we'd seen from a distance. More smoke billowed out from the two windows, both partially blocked by the truck, which had been pulled up against the door, blocking the exit. Firemen tried to get near the windows but were driven back, gasping and coughing. We followed two of them down an alleyway, to the rear of the building that housed the bar. Empty bottles and rotting garbage were piled against the wall beneath a pair of windows, iron bars set into the masonry, probably to discourage thieves. One wooden door was set low, down a short flight of steps. A torrent of flame gushed up from the door, and I could make out a jerrycan at the base of the steps.

"Truck up against the front door, and a can of gas ignited at the back door," Kaz said.

"He must have seen us," I said, realizing I could scratch Jim Cole off my list of suspects.

"Who?"

"The killer. He saw us here and decided not to take a chance on Inzerillo staying quiet. But he knows Inzerillo's guard is up, that he's barricaded himself in there. So he uses it against him."

"Cunning," Kaz said as we stepped out of the back alley and went around the front. There, the flames had died down amid the swirls of acrid black smoke, and the fire truck pulled out to circle around the block. Kaz spotted a Carabiniere talking to onlookers and approached him as I tried to get a look inside. The wreck of the truck was too hot to get close to, and all I could make out was a gray haze inside the building. No telltale smell of burned flesh, but no sound of movement, no cries for help. The heat or the smoke must have gotten him. In his weakened condition, he couldn't have moved fast enough to escape.

"He says witnesses saw the truck pull up alongside the entrance, but paid little attention," Kaz told me. "Two of them saw an American soldier take something from the truck and walk around back. It was common knowledge that Inzerillo dealt in the black market, so it was not seen as unusual."

"Could they indentify the GI?"

"No. He wore a helmet and had his collar turned up. They can't say if he was an officer or enlisted man. Both claim not to have seen the fire start, front or back. The Italian officer says they are scared to talk, that if a tough bastard like Inzerillo could be killed, no one is safe."

"I think that was part of the message."

"It worked. These people look genuinely frightened. Should we check the truck?"

"No, it's probably stolen. He used the spare gas can for out back, then probably lit a rag stuffed into the fuel line. Hoofed it back to his vehicle, and was gone before the local fire brigade got here."

"There's only one piece of good news in all this," Kaz said. "He hasn't played the queen of hearts yet. Perhaps the cards were a feint, to distract us."

"Or maybe he had loose ends to tie up before he moved onto bigger and better things. Let's get back," I said. I didn't think much of Inzerillo, but I didn't like him added to the list of victims either. He was a loose end, and now no one would have to worry about him unraveling. I should have seen this coming. I should have seen Cole's death coming, for that matter. I don't know what I could have done about either, but that didn't stop me from feeling responsible.

As we turned to leave, the Carabiniere whom Kaz had spoken to called him over and I watched as they talked, the conversation growing heated at the end.

"What was that about?" I asked as we walked back to the jeep.

"He asked if we had a vehicle to tow the truck away. He thought we were from the AMGOT headquarters in town. When I said we were not, he began to ask what our interest was with Inzerillo. I told him it was part of an investigation that Lieutenant Luca Amatori was involved in. He didn't like that answer."

"He probably didn't like being kept in the dark, especially since the investigation involved an Italian civilian. Can't blame him."

"No, it wasn't that. It was the mention of Luca's name. He called him a Fascist, and a friend to the Nazis."

"Strange," I said as I started up the jeep. "The Carabinieri aren't known for Fascist tendencies. And Luca didn't come across as a Nazi sympathizer."

"Would you, after the king deposed Mussolini and the government went over to the Allies?"

It was a good question, and I gave it some thought as we drove back to Caserta, even though I couldn't see how it had a damn thing to do with our card-dealing killer and the murder of Inzerillo. But I did wonder what Luca had done to deserve the contempt of a fellow officer, to generate so intense a disdain that it would be brought up to a stranger, an outsider. Maybe it was nothing, some guy with a beef, spreading rumors about Luca. I didn't want to know. I had problems of my own.

We drove to the 3rd Division bivouac area. I wanted to see who had been where this afternoon. But the going was slow, the roads crammed with long convoys of trucks, all headed east, toward Naples and its big harbor. Huge GMC deuce-and-a-half trucks, some pulling artillery, most crammed with GIs huddled together on the open bench seats. Ambulances, flatbeds with Sherman tanks, and jeeps overflowing with soldiers and gear, some so top-heavy I was surprised they made it around the next bend. It was a constant flow of men, so many that it seemed we must have emptied out entire towns and schools to get all these soldiers, all these anonymous clean-faced boys, their hands clenched around the barrels of their M1s, heads bowed low against the wind, as if they were murmuring their nighttime prayers.

There was little traffic in the opposite direction, but we were held up at every intersection. As we came to the outskirts of Caserta, a flight of P-40 fighters flew over, heading for a landing at the Marcinese airfield. One plane trailed the others, smoke rhythmically sputtering behind it.

"Do you think he'll make it?" Kaz said, following the P-40's progress.

"He's close, he should," I said, and glanced upward. The puffs of smoke stopped and the aircraft hung in the air for a moment, then began a lazy twirl straight down, as if a giant hand had swatted it out of the sky. There was no evidence of a pilot trying to regain control, nothing but dead weight descending to a stony field where it blossomed into a fireball, a final violent eruption of flame and smoke marking the spot.

We drove on.

An hour later we pulled into San Felice, home of the 3rd Division headquarters. I wanted to quiz Colonel Schleck and Major Arnold about their disagreement with Max Galante over combat fatigue. From what Doctor Cassidy told me, it had been more personal than professional. Maybe they'd also tell me how much longer the division was going to be around. I had a feeling it wouldn't be for long.

The bombed-out school that served as headquarters had its own fleet of trucks parked outside, tailgates down and GIs loading them up with boxes and crates of whatever it was you needed to run a division HQ. Typewriters, carbon paper, and Scotch were high on the list.

We parked the jeep and worked our way inside amidst the heavy lifting.

"You back again? Boyle, wasn't it?" Colonel Schleck growled, heading out in full battle gear. Grenades hung from his web belt, Thompson submachine gun at the ready, helmet on. You might have thought the Germans were right outside the door.

"Still is, sir. I wanted to talk to you and Major Arnold if I could."

"You can't. We're pulling out, and Arnold is AWOL. If you see the bastard, shoot him. My clerk is still in the office upstairs. Talk to him if you need anything. You find that killer yet?"

"No sir. The whole division pulling out?"

"Headquarters is staging to Naples, that's all I can say." And that was all he did say. He got in a waiting jeep, signaled with his hand like a cowboy at a cattle drive, and a small convoy of trucks followed him.

"Interesting fellow," Kaz said as we headed to the G1 office. "I'm not surprised he doesn't believe in combat fatigue. He looks like he's enjoying the war."

"Some guys do. They get rank and privileges they never had in civilian life, and if they're just behind the front lines, in a headquarters outfit, they wear combat gear and get their picture taken to show the folks back home. I'll bet a lot of them will get into politics after the war."

"I fear for your nation," Kaz said, as we entered the office. Boxed files were stacked everywhere, and a corporal with his sleeves rolled up was pulling sheets from a type-writer, separating the carbon paper from the duplicates, as he looked up.

"Sorry, Lieutenant. No more replacements, we're all sold out."

"I don't want replacements —"

"Well, if you don't like the ones you got, sorry, can't do anything about that either. Those ASTP kids are wet behind the ears, but we gotta take what we can get."

"No, no, listen. I need to talk to Major Arnold. Colonel Schleck said he was AWOL?"

"Lieutenant, you got a complaint about the guys in your platoon, lodge it with me. It's better than bothering the officers. What's the beef?"

"No beef, Corporal. It's a murder investigation."

"This war's murder. You mean the guy with the cards? Thought that kinda died down, so to speak." He laughed at his own joke.

"Corporal," Kaz said, in a low and even voice. "Tell us where Major Arnold is or the killer may start working the deck in the other direction. An eight of hearts would do quite nicely for you."

"I've heard guys say they'd kill for my job, but no one ever threatened me outright," he said, and again laughed at his little joke. We didn't. "Okay, okay. This morning we got the last truckload of replacements in, right off the boat, twenty ASTP kids to farm out. The colonel was eager to leave, so he told Major Arnold to handle it. He tells me to pull the list of platoons still short on guys. Problem is, there's been trouble in some squads. The ASTP guys hang together, the noncoms resent them since they come out of college and the officer program, you know how it is. It ain't easy keeping everyone happy."

"Does this story lead to Major Arnold anytime soon?"

"Yeah. So the major wants to place these kids one per squad, figuring they'll fit in better if they have to buddy up with a non-ASTP guy. See?"

"Sure," I said, not really caring about the psychology of replacement handling.

"So he takes my lists, and has the driver take him to the bivouac area, and doles out the kids, one per squad, where they're needed most. Takes him an hour or so, then he comes back here. Tells me he's going to his tent to square away his gear, and I ain't seen him since."

"Why did Schleck say he was AWOL? He told me I could shoot him if I found him."

"The colonel sent for him, sent runners everywhere. To his quarters, back to the bivouac area, but nobody could find him. Colonel Schleck is a man of little patience."

"Did he have much patience for Max Galante?"

"At first, he tolerated him 'cause he was a good doctor and he worked right up front. But when he started pestering the colonel about nervous exhaustion or whatever, that did it. Colonel Schleck does not believe in it, therefore it doesn't exist, so Galante got his walking papers."

"What was Major Arnold's opinion of Galante?"

"His opinion was that his immediate superior is correct in all things. Makes it easier to get through the day around here. Which reminds me, I got to get everything packed and shipped to Naples. Anything else I can do for you?"

"Where is Major Arnold?" I asked, one hand on his shoulder in a fatherly gesture, the other hand on the butt of my .45 automatic.

"Honest, I don't know, Lieutenant. He should have been back long ago."

"Is there something about the major you're not telling us?" Kaz asked. "Some place he might go? A woman, perhaps?"

"No, he wouldn't disappear for a dame. The only thing I can think of is that he's a real souvenir hound. He's always trading with the dogfaces. Nazi knives, pistols, flags, all that junk. He's a teetotaler, so he has his officer's liquor ration to swap with. The boys love that."

"So he's off hunting souvenirs?"

"No need to, the guys come to him. But he might be packing them up and shipping them home. Check the field post office. It's a busy place, he might have gotten held up."

"You didn't mention this possibility to Colonel Schleck?"

"The major and I get along. I'm no snitch."

"Okay, just tell me this. Who might get a pass today to go into Acerra? Or have business there?"

"All passes were cancelled last night, and I don't know of any official reason for anyone under the rank of general to go to Acerra. That's AMGOT territory. We got guys going to Caserta all the time, but that's usually for headquarters errands. No one minds a quick stop once business is taken care of, since it's so close, but for Acerra you'd need a pass, and there ain't none."

The corporal gave us a description of Major Arnold and we headed to the field post office, looking for a short, wiry officer with curly brown hair and parcels tucked under each arm. He wasn't there, and no one remembered him coming in. We decided to check his tent, and if we didn't find him there we'd move on. Where to, exactly, I wasn't sure.

Officers' tents were pitched in a field behind headquarters. It was high ground, free of mud, a good deal for guys who didn't rate a real roof over their heads. There were four rows, each marked with the occupant's names and a wood-slat walkway.

I opened the flap and called the major's name, but no one was home. He kept the place neat, his cot made, books and papers stacked on a small folding table. His gear was all there. Footlocker, carbine, field pack. The insert tray from the footlocker was on the cot, shirts precisely folded. In one corner sat two wooden boxes, a hammer and nails and a roll of twine perched on top of them.

"Souvenirs?" Kaz asked, testing one of the lids. It came up, and revealed Nazi daggers, belt buckles, a black SS officer's cap, iron crosses, and other medals.

"Check the other," I said, studying the rest of the area. There had to be some clue as to where Arnold was. It looked like he had stepped out in the midst of packing and never returned.

"It says fragile," Kaz said. Arnold had marked the contents as china. Kaz opened it, and there were four plates, wrapped in newspaper. Beneath them was a Nazi flag, the black swastika on a field of blood red. "What's this?" He unfolded the flag and a Walther P38 pistol fell out.

"Major Arnold could get himself in trouble. It's against regulations to mail weapons home."

"There are two magazines as well," Kaz said. "But at least the pistol isn't loaded."

"He was probably banking on the post office being too busy to ask questions, with everyone pulling out. I don't even know how much attention they pay anyway. I heard a story about a sergeant shipping a jeep home, one part at a time."

"Impressive," Kaz said. "Should we look further for the major, or is this a dead end?"

A dead end. A missing major. I looked again at the footlocker, and pushed it with my boot. It was heavy, and I had that real bad feeling again. I'd been sidetracked by the fire, and hadn't thought about the next victim since then. There was a padlock in the latch.

"Why is this locked, if he hadn't finished

packing?" The tray, its compartments filled with shirts, sat on the cot.

"Perhaps he has his valuables inside?" Kaz sounded hopeful, but it was that false hope, the hope you feel when you go for an inside straight. Brief, insubstantial, useless. I took the dagger from Arnold's souvenir box and began working the latch. The footlocker was plywood, not built to withstand a steel blade. I dug around the top latch, loosening the screws until I could pull the latch free. I hoped that all I'd end up with was a chewing out from a superior officer for destroying his footlocker, but that was inside-straight thinking. I lifted the top, and the only card I saw was the queen of hearts, stuck between the dead fingers of Major Matthew Arnold.

He was short, which was a good thing. He was on his side, knees to his chest, hands up to his face, as if at prayer. The card stuck out from between two fingers, the red heart at odds with the pale face of the dead major.

"Strangled," I said. "Strangled and stuffed in a box. Why?" His neck was bruised and the blood vessels in his eyes had burst.

"It had to be a major," Kaz said. "The odds were it would be one from the Third Division, since the first two victims had been."

"No, I mean why stuffed in a box? The killer didn't hide either of the first two bodies. Galante was tucked against a wall, but he was in plain sight. Why hide the third victim? It's not the same pattern."

"To delay his being discovered?"

"Has to be. In order to give the killer time to get away. Which means he was seen by someone, and he needed to put time between that and the discovery of the body."

"We should go back to division headquarters," Kaz said. "Report and contact CID."

"Not yet," I said, shutting the footlocker. "Let's go."

"It's more important that we find out where the GIs in Landry's platoon have been today," I said as I gunned the jeep down the muddy road to the bivouac area. "It all started with him and it has to go back to him. Galante, Cole, Inzerillo, they all connect to Landry and his men. If we reported the body now, we'd be tied up for hours with CID and filling out reports. We'll go back as soon as we talk to Sergeant Gates and get an accounting of where his men have been."

"I suppose Major Arnold is in no hurry," Kaz said. Traffic was light, and I was glad we hadn't stumbled straight into the entire Third Division pulling out. I turned into the churned-up, muddy field and drove to the same small rise I had before, claiming what dry ground I could. Before us was the bivouac, rows of olive-drab tents of all sizes, with vehicles loading and unloading supplies around the perimeter, just as before. But there was something different.

"Those are British trucks," I said. The men unloading them were British. Not a Yank in sight. As we drew closer, I noticed a pile of white-painted signs at the end of each row of tents. Signs for units of the 3rd Division, no longer needed.

"Has the Third Division pulled out?" I asked a British sergeant leading a work detail of Italian civilians. Brooms, shovels, garbage cans, wheelbarrows. I guess more than ten thousand GIs can leave a fair-sized mess.

"Whoever the Yanks were, they've gone," he said. "Got to clean up for our lot to move in tomorrow. Can I help you, Lieutenant?"

"No," I said. "I doubt it."

I walked along the perimeter until I saw the signpost, lying on the muddy ground. 2nd Battalion, Easy Company. Soon I found the tent where the poker game had been in session. Third Platoon territory. Everything was cleared out, nothing but folded cots and the debris of a departing unit. Empty wine bottles, mostly. Crumpled paper, odds and ends that men had accumulated when in camp but tossed out as unnecessary when they were on the move, back to the sharp end.

Garbage cans had been placed along the wooden walkway, but not enough to handle the last-minute discards. The one in front of the poker tent was overflowing with bottles, broken crates, and other indefinable rubbish. On top was a single tan leather glove, holes worn through the fingertips, the kind the wire crews had been wearing when I first came here.

"This is what he wore," I said to Kaz. "Leather gloves. A new pair would give enough protection."

"You mean whoever beat Inzerillo?"

"Yeah. I wanted to check the knuckles to see who'd been using their fists. But leather work gloves would do the trick." I tossed the glove back on the pile, and wondered if that new pair, complete with bloodstains, might be at the bottom of the can. It would prove the connection I was certain of, so I tipped the can over, glad that the British sergeant and his work crew weren't in sight.

I moved stuff around with my boot, but didn't see another glove, bloodstained or not. Out of the corner of my eye, I did catch something red poking out of the mess. It looked familiar, as if I ought to know what it was.

"What is it, Billy?" As soon as Kaz spoke, I knew exactly what it was. A rag doll in a red dress.

CHAPTER EIGHTEEN

I watched as CID agents searched Arnold's tent, knowing they'd come up empty. I had. The rag doll was in my jacket pocket, and I was keeping quiet about it for now. Without Gates and the others to confirm it was the same doll from the girl in the basement, it didn't mean much as evidence. Even then, it was only my word that Cole had said he'd seen the doll, in his dreams and while awake. I had thought he meant he saw it in his mind's eye, but now I knew different. Someone had kept that rag doll from Campozillone, someone who wanted to spook Cole, to terrify him, to push him over the edge. Or was it to control him, keep him dependent?

He was my friend, Cole had said. *I see it in his face, see everything all over again.*

A friend, a buddy from 3rd Platoon, who kept the memory fresh, the wound open. Manipulating Cole, keeping him under control. For the pearls? Were they wound up in the killings, or was it something less sinister? Looting went on all the time; maybe this was just a higher class of loot. Who wouldn't scoop up a pearl necklace found hidden behind a wall or in a drawer with a false bottom? It was like the house on Mattapan Square. Original owner long gone, no questions would be asked. But had Cole stumbled on it, or had someone told him where to look? What difference would it make? Maybe a life-and-death difference. I tried to make sense of what I knew for certain.

Cole and Inzerillo, dead. No evidence they knew each other. One a suicide, the other beaten up and then burned. His death could have been a Mafia hit for all I knew.

Landry, Galante, Arnold, dead. Ten, jack, queen. All killed up close, the same calling card left on their corpses. They all knew each other to some extent. Arnold must have processed Cole's transfer at Galante's request; I doubted Colonel Schleck would have approved it.

The rag doll bothered me. Or was I reading too much into it? Maybe Cole just couldn't take it anymore. Maybe seeing his pal, whoever it was, was too much of a reminder. Maybe the pain was too much to bear. Maybe Inzerillo antagonized a mafioso, or didn't pay a debt. First a warning, then the torch. Maybe Cole found the pearls on his own, by accident, and had no idea of the story behind them. Maybe. But the rag doll was real, in a place where it shouldn't have been.

If all those maybes held water, then I had less to go on than I thought. Three dead officers, with the king and ace waiting to be dealt. A colonel and a general. Did the killer have them picked out already? Or was it simply a target of opportunity? If the killer was in the 3rd Division, it made sense that he'd have more contact with 3rd Division officers than anyone else.

If, maybe. I didn't have much to go on. The only good news was that colonels were not as easy to come by as more junior officers.

Arnold's body was carried out on a stretcher. Luckily rigor mortis wasn't fully established yet, probably due to the warmth in the closed footlocker.

"We have to find out where Third Division is headed," I said to Kaz as the stretcher passed us. They loaded it into an ambulance, which drove off at a sedate pace, no sirens, no rush for the late Major Arnold.

"No one knows, or admits to knowing,"

Kaz said. "I found several officers packing their gear, and they all claim ignorance."

"It shouldn't be hard to find an entire division. The front line is about thirty miles north. If we follow the main road, we should catch their tail soon."

"But Colonel Schleck said they were staging to Naples. That's due south."

"That might mean the coast road north from Naples, or the harbor. They could be shipping out to England for all we know."

"We should report to Major Kearns," Kaz said. "He may be able to tell us."

"Not that we have much to report. I'm sure he's heard about Arnold by now. I'm sure every colonel and general at the palace has."

We made a stop in San Felice, figuring it might be worth it to search Arnold's office desk and files, unless his corporal had packed everything up and shipped out too. We were in luck. There was still a skeleton staff at 3rd Division headquarters, the corporal included. Most of his crates and boxes were gone, but he was still on duty, clacking away on his typewriter.

"You've heard about Major Arnold?" I said.

"Yeah, word travels fast. You really find him in a trunk?"

"We did. In his tent. Did he mention meeting anyone there?"

"Nope. But if it was souvenir trading, he wouldn't have. He made it clear he preferred things on the QT."

"We found two boxes of souvenirs, ready to be shipped home. Including a Walther P38."

"Jeez. You ain't supposed to send Kraut pistols to the States, are you? Where is it now?"

"It's evidence, sorry."

"What a waste. The major, I mean."

"Yeah. It's important that we find out where the division is going. Do you know, or can you find out?"

"You think the Red Heart Killer is one of us? That's what they're calling him, I heard."

"Yeah, catchy. I asked you a question."

"Sure. I mean, no, I can't. They got this thing locked down tight. If we were going back up on the line, we'd all be there by now. But they're staging everyone on a staggered schedule. Naples is all I know. Maybe we're going to be garrison troops, that'd be nice."

"I don't think that's in the cards," I said, disappointed that no one laughed. "Tell me, do you remember paperwork on Sergeant Jim Cole, transferring him to CID?"

"Sure I do. Doc Galante came in, waited until the colonel was gone, and spoke to Major Arnold. He knew Schleck would never go for it."

"But Major Arnold did?"

"Yeah, no problem. Routine stuff."

"We're going to search the major's desk, okay?"

"Be my guest," he said, pointing to the far corner. "I ain't packed it up yet."

I sat at Arnold's desk as Kaz wandered about the room, looking through paperwork stacked up on a table, ignoring the corporal's stares. There were half a dozen personnel files on top of the desk, all new second lieutenants who had just transferred in from stateside. They weren't suspects, and they were safe, at least from the card-dealing murderer. The Germans would probably get half of them within days, most of the rest within weeks. I put the files aside.

Mimeographed orders from the division chief of staff were stacked by date, the latest directing Arnold to await transport to Naples until the rest of the headquarters unit arrived there. All the others had to do with the mundane daily routine of any HQ. Boring, repetitive, useless.

I went through two drawers and found nothing of interest. Forms in file folders, lined up alphabetically. In a bottom drawer, under a copy of *Stars and Stripes,* was something more interesting: a Luftwaffe forage cap, filled with wristwatches, rings, and a few German pay books. *Soldbuch,* they called it. It contained a photograph of the soldier, his unit, rank, that sort of thing. I dumped the lot onto the desk.

"The major collected those books," the corporal said.

"And he had a nice sideline in watches too. Taken from the dead, stripped from POWs. Interesting guy." I flipped through one Soldbuch, looking at the photo of a young kid who could have been wearing any uniform. I didn't like looking at war souvenirs. It made me think of some fat Kraut pulling my wristwatch off.

"I'm not seeing anything here but evidence of a tidy mind and an acquisitive nature," I said.

"Billy," Kaz said. "You should look at this." He held a clipboard, one of six hung from nails on the wall.

"Those are replacement lists," the corporal said, "the latest batch. I ain't had time to file them away yet."

"What?" I asked Kaz. His finger pointed to a list of names, and traveled down three from the top. A column of serial numbers and names.

BOYLE, DANIEL P., PVT.

"What is your brother's middle name?" Kaz asked.

"Patrick," I said. I felt sick as I said it, and leaned on the table for support. "Daniel Patrick Boyle."

"Hey, you found a relative?" the corporal asked. "Lucky guy."

"Is this the ASTP group you were telling us about?" I pointed to the clipboard.

"Yeah. Those are the replacements Major Arnold brought out. Before he got it."

I'd been hoping for that inside straight to come along, and how did I finally manage to beat the odds? By having my kid brother show up and join a division about to end up in combat, if my guess was right. Replacements were flowing in to Caserta, filling the ranks after other replacements had been killed, wounded, or captured. I traced the line with his name on it to the right, past numbers that meant something to the army and nothing to me, until I came to his unit. Private Daniel P. Boyle had been assigned to the 3rd Division, 7th Regiment, 2nd Battalion, Easy Company, 3rd Platoon.

Right in the goddamn middle of not only the shooting war, but my investigation.

■ ■ ■ ■

Kaz drove us back to Caserta. I was in a daze, unable to get my mind off Danny. The plan was to report to Major Kearns and find the 3rd Division. I was certain of two things: my kid brother was headed for trouble, and the Red Heart Killer was going to strike again.

Kearns was busy, so I waited outside his office while Kaz went to check on something he said was bothering him. A lot of things bothered me, so I didn't ask what it was. I watched messengers, aides, high-ranking officers, British airmen, and a couple of civilians scurry in and out of the Intelligence section, everyone in a hurry. I bet none of them gave a hoot about my kid brother and all the other green kid brothers heading up to the line. I was upset, and the more I watched them, the more I wanted to deck one of them, just to see how they liked it. But I held back, because of the two MPs on duty outside Kearns's door, and because while I knew it would be satisfying, it wouldn't help me find Danny.

"Boyle," Kearns said, appearing in the open doorway. "Get your gear and be back here in one hour. We're shipping out."

"We, sir? Where?"

"You'll drive with me to Naples. We're joining VI Corps staff."

"Third Division is part of VI Corps, isn't it?"

"Yes," Kearns said. "That's why you're coming with me. I've been transferred, and you need to find this killer. Something big is about to happen, Boyle, and we can't have one of our own gunning for the brass. One hour, you and Lieutenant Kazimierz."

"You've heard about Major Arnold then?"

"Me and every GI, Italian, and Brit within ten miles. The damn Krauts probably know by now."

"Where are we going?"

"That's top secret. You'll know when you get there. Now hustle, goddammit."

He was steamed, so I hustled out of sight. I waited for Kaz, who showed up twenty minutes later. I told him what Kearns had said and we beat feet to the jeep and made for Signora Salvalaggio's. We grabbed our gear and said our good-byes. The signora promised to cook la Genovese for Kaz when he returned, and gave him a curtsy that wouldn't have been out of place at the palace, a lifetime ago. She didn't ask about the pearls, and I was glad, because I had no idea what we were going to do with them.

"What were you doing, back at the headquarters?" I asked Kaz as we drove to meet up with Kearns.

"Asking around, about the Fourteenth Carabinieri, the unit our friend Lieutenant Luca Amatori served with. I was curious, after the reaction of the officer in Acerra."

"What did you find out?"

"The unit served primarily on the island of Rab, off the coast of Yugoslavia. As concentration camp guards."

Part Three: Anzio Beachhead

CHAPTER NINETEEN

For the hundredth time in this war, I sat in a jeep at a crossroads, watching a convoy of trucks crossing an intersection ahead of us. Worrying. Everyone was worried, about getting killed or wounded, about fear and what your buddies thought of you, about trench foot and the clap, about chickenshit officers and insane orders, about *Schu*-mines and what your girl back home would do when she heard you were alive but minus your private parts.

Everyone worried, everyone sat, everyone waited. But now I had a new worry. My kid brother. When Dad would get mad at Danny and me, he'd say that if he could put the two of us in a sack and shake it up good, he might end up with one son who was smart enough to stay out of trouble, and strong enough to get out of it when it came looking. Trouble was, Danny was a skinny kid, smart enough in class but just plain dumb anywhere between home and school. I was always stronger than most, but I used up all my smarts before I got to the schoolhouse door. We'd come home with our fair share of black eyes and pants torn at the knee, usually as a result of trouble Danny got into and I got him out of. Or in deeper, he claimed. I wondered if he had any idea how deep this trouble was.

I got tired of worrying and watched the scenery instead. On the left, a drainage ditch was filled with sluggish water, and beyond that a ruined farmhouse sat crumbling into the earth as weeds and vines worked their way through the masonry. On my side, an open field sloped gently away, down to a long green patch where water flowed, a real stream, not a ditch, maybe with frogs in the warm weather. Maybe fish. What did they fish for in Italian streams? I didn't know, but the memory of springtime at the grassy edge of a stream came back to me, and I wanted to run through that field, feel the sun on my neck, scoop up fresh cool water and splash my face.

A line of pine trees ran up to the road, forming a neat border to the side of the field. In the field itself withered brown plants and faded grasses hung on, and occasional rock outcroppings provided a shape and contour that gave the land its own definition. This was a place that people knew well, perhaps by name, a natural field where sheep could graze, kids could play, and lovers could go for a walk. I spotted a flat limestone rock that would be great for a picnic, and a tall one that would be perfect for shade in the summer.

I wanted it to be summer. I wanted to be in the field, exploring it with the intensity of a child, the barely remembered sense of discovery and awe that a new place, a new object, a new sensation could bring. I closed my eyes and saw Danny and me running through a field much like this one, racing for the stream, splashing in the water and laughing without quite knowing why, or caring. It seemed, in that moment, that the field encompassed everything good, life at its best. Nature, youth, innocence. This field, and all the ones in my memory, held life.

I opened my eyes. Above, a bird glided high across the sky, circling the field. A hawk. No, it was a falcon, a peregrine falcon. As he turned, the sun lit his blue-gray wings, a dead giveaway. A hunter on any continent. A flutter caught my eye, far beneath the soaring falcon, and I knew if I saw it, he saw it even more clearly. He tucked in his wings and dropped in a fast, steep dive, heading straight for a blackbird lazily making for the trees, about ten feet off the ground. The falcon hit the blackbird, hard, claws outstretched and wings wide, braking before the momentum brought them both to ground. A flash of dark feathers, and it was all over. The falcon carried his limp prey to the flat rock, set it down, and began to rip the bird apart. The falcon paused and gazed in my direction. Maybe he was worried we were a threat. Maybe he was telling me to get a grip, or reminding me that the field was death as well as life.

As the column moved through the intersection, I did not look back.

The road was ours the rest of the way, two hours straight to the Naples docks. The column snaked through the narrow streets leading to the waterfront. On each corner, Italians sold bottles of wine, fruit, and anything else GIs would fork over cash or cigarettes for.

"Major," I said, leaning forward as the driver weaved the jeep between crates of supplies and lines of American and British soldiers. "Can you tell us now where we're headed?"

"Not until we board ship. It's all top

secret, not to be revealed until we are sequestered from the civilian population. We can't take a chance on Fascist spies getting word to the Germans."

"Okay," I said. Next to me, Kaz shrugged. We could wait. The traffic stalled, and we bought some oranges from a skinny young girl doling them out from a burlap sack. Following her was a short, pudgy guy with a thick black mustache, selling postcards. He held a stack in his grimy hands, fanning them out for all to see.

"Naples harbor, Anzio. Good-a luck, boys. Nice-a women in Anzio. Post-a cards, Anzio, Nettuno here." He kept up his singsong pitch. Army security, you gotta love it.

"Anzio. That's about a hundred miles north of the German lines, Major," I said.

"Yeah, well, I guess the cat's out of the bag already. We ship out in the morning, hit the beach the following day. Anzio and Nettuno are two seafront villages about a mile apart. The idea is to get behind the Germans and cut off their supplies from Rome. Something along those lines."

"Something?" Kaz said.

"We'll talk when we're on board," Kearns said. He seemed to be in a bad mood. Maybe it was finding out our target was common knowledge, or the vagueness of the battle plan, or the fear that a colonel and a general would get their necks snapped. None of these things made me happy either.

As we entered the harbor, MPs waved trucks to their unloading areas, and after a quick check of Major Kearns's orders, we were directed to the main wharf where Liberty ships and landing craft of all types were lined up, taking on men and the machinery of war.

"Here's our ship," Major Kearns said. "The USS *Biscayne,* command vessel for the invasion. You'll be traveling with the brass. General Lucas is on board."

"And a number of colonels and other generals, no doubt," Kaz said.

"Yep, so keep your eyes peeled and don't get in the way."

We followed him up the gangplank and a swabbie showed us where to stash our gear. Kaz and I had a cabin about the size of a janitor's closet with two double bunks. Plenty of room, as long as the four guys didn't all get out of their bunks at once.

Up on deck, we gazed out over the five-inch guns on the bow and watched the parade of troops boarding vessels all along the waterfront. LSTs had beached themselves beyond the wharf, their bow doors dropped onto flat rocks where GIs used to sunbathe and fishermen had dried their nets. Now, Sherman tanks backed in, their engines growling as they slowly made their way onboard. Shouts and curses drifted up from the ships as the traffic jammed up on the docks.

"What do you know about Anzio?" I asked Kaz.

"In ancient times it was called Antium. Both Nero and Caligula were born there. Actually, that is where Nero was when Rome burned and he famously played his lyre. He had a summer palace in Antium, and Rome is only forty miles away; the sky must have glowed with the flames. I hope we shall get to see the palace ruins."

"I bet there will be plenty of ruins. Just not all two thousand years old. What about Caligula? Wasn't he the crazy one?"

"A bloodthirsty killer, a megalomaniac, yes. But Nero was no prize either. He had his own mother killed for plotting against him."

"Both sons of Anzio," I said.

"Ironic that we are pursuing a killer, perhaps a madman, to that very place."

"Is he a madman? It seems he has a plan, of sorts. The playing cards, plus the murder of Inzerillo, pushing Cole to suicide. These aren't sudden or random. They're deliberate, linked in some way we can't yet understand."

"Billy, we don't know for certain that Inzerillo's killer is the same man."

"It's a good bet. His joint was frequented by the Third Platoon, Landry was mixed up with some girl there, and we have conflicting stories about damage done. Somebody's hiding something, and I think that has something to do with Inzerillo being silenced. What I don't see anywhere is a motive. For any of this."

"Caligula was a madman, but he managed to run an empire. Being insane doesn't mean one is out of control. It is another way of seeing the world."

"So our guy has his own set of rules?"

"Yes, rules that make sense to him. Perhaps he views us as out of step with reality."

"Being in the army, it would be hard to keep to your own rules, your personal sense of reality."

"It is difficult, maintaining individuality in such a large organization that demands obedience and discipline."

"Yeah, it's hard enough for guys like us," I said. I felt I had the thread of an idea, but didn't know how to put it into words. "But our Caligula, he'd have a real hard time of it, wouldn't he?"

"Are you getting at his motive?"

"Maybe. I've been trying to think of the usual motives. Greed, passion, revenge. But what if it's beyond that? Something we can't imagine, but that he desperately needs to cover up?"

"That would mean the victims all knew something. Something that got them killed."

"A lieutenant, a captain, a major, a pimp, and a sergeant. What did they have in common, and what did they know?"

"Perhaps we should be asking which colonel and which general have something in common with them," Kaz said.

"We're not going to get a senior officer to admit knowing a pimp. And Captain Galante wasn't really part of Landry's Third Platoon crowd."

"But Landry and Galante were connected. They knew each other from before Galante was transferred to the hospital at Caserta. Sergeant Cole was transferred to Caserta courtesy of Captain Galante."

"I can see some connection there," I said. "But I don't see how it all hangs together, and where it's going. I keep thinking we have to go back to the beginning, that there's something we got wrong from the start."

"Like what?" Kaz asked.

"Wish I knew, buddy, wish I knew." We stood in silence, feet up on the rail, watching the activity on the wharf. It was a nice day, maybe mid-fifties, a hazy sky and calm waters. A good day for watching a parade. A bad day for solving mysteries.

"Look," said Kaz, as he pointed to a column of blue uniforms advancing along the wharf. Carabinieri. About a hundred, maybe more, marching in good order, packs on their backs and rifles slung over their shoulders. They halted before the Liberty ship next to us and began to file aboard, their boots clanging against the metal gangplank. Lieutenant Luca Amatori brought up the rear, giving his boss, Captain Trevisi, a snappy salute before he followed his men up. It was hard to make out at that distance, but I got the impression Trevisi was as glad to stay on shore as Luca was to leave him there. At the top of the gangplank, Trevisi saluted again, and leaned on the deck, just as we were doing, watching the massive preparations.

"I didn't have a chance to ask you about Luca and the concentration camp," I said. "What did you find out?"

"I spoke to a friend on the staff of British Army Intelligence, a fellow Pole. He had a file on Lieutenant Amatori. Our friend Luca was posted to the island of Rab, in the Adriatic, off the coast of Yugoslavia. The Fourteenth Carabinieri Battalion was charged with guarding a concentration camp there, mainly for Yugoslav civilians suspected of partisan activities. Mostly Slovenes and Croatians, often entire families if they were thought to have helped the partisans."

"He did say something about partisan activities," I said, reluctant to change my opinion about the likable Luca.

"Yes, but the Italian and German antipartisan sweeps were particularly brutal, and more than a thousand died of starvation in the camp itself. It held more than fifteen thousand prisoners, many housed only in tents, even in winter. Men, women, and children, including about three thousand Jews."

"What happened to them?"

"The story is not quite clear. There are references to complaints made to Rome by the commander of the Fourteenth Carabinieri Battalion, protesting the treatment of Yugoslavs. The Jews, all Yugoslavian, were treated much better than the partisan prisoners. Apparently the Jews, having not been part of the partisan movement, were viewed as being in protective custody."

"But in a concentration camp."

"Yes, the Fascist government did put them in the camps, in Italy as well as Yugoslavia. Some were worse than others, depending on the whim or politics of the commander. When Mussolini fell, the new government ordered the Jews released, but gave them the option of staying in the camps, in case they feared being rounded up by the Germans."

"That's a hell of a choice."

"Indeed. A few hundred joined the partisans to fight, others fled to partisan-held territory. But about two hundred were too old or sick to be moved. The Germans took over the camp and transported them to another camp in Poland. Auschwitz, I think it was."

"Auschwitz? Diana mentioned Auschwitz, and another camp in Poland, Belzec."

"The Germans seem to prefer Poland as their killing ground," Kaz said. "Belzec was the first camp set up, but Auschwitz has grown into a huge operation. I wrote a paper detailing what is known about it while I was in London with the Polish government-in-exile. Three main camps, over twenty-five satellite camps. Inmates are put to work on war industries, and often worked to death."

"It may be worse than that," I said. The

warm sea breeze on my face felt odd, as if nothing of beauty or any pleasant sensation should intrude upon these words. I told Kaz everything Diana had told me, and watched his face harden with disbelief, horror, anger, and all the emotions I had gone through. It couldn't be true, that was the first response of any sane person.

"Oh my God," Kaz said. "Witold Pilecki."

"Who?"

"Captain Witold Pilecki, of the Polish Army. In 1940, he volunteered as part of a Polish resistance operation to be imprisoned in Auschwitz."

"That's one brave guy, or a fool."

"Many people thought the latter, especially after his reports were smuggled out. The underground delivered them to London. He talked about the mass killings, and requested arms and assistance to free the prisoners. His request was never granted. He was thought to be exaggerating, either deliberately or as a result of conditions in the camp. His report stated that two million people had been killed there, during a three-year period. He simply was written off since no one believed the numbers he was reporting."

"What happened to him?"

"He escaped, last April. I think he must

be with the Home Army, the Polish underground."

"Three years in hell, and no one believes him."

"Does anyone believe Diana?"

"I do. But I don't think Kim Philby did. Or he didn't want to. Or couldn't."

I watched Luca Amatori on the deck of the Liberty ship next to us. He was enjoying the sun and the breeze, maybe feeling he was part of some grand plan, helping to liberate another piece of his homeland. Did he ever think about the two hundred sick and elderly Jews he left behind on Rab? Did they ever disturb his sleep? What else did he do, hunting partisans in the mountains of Yugoslavia, that might haunt him at night?

There was so much evil in this war. Maybe Luca was a good man, maybe not. Maybe he had been a good man once, before the shooting started. Before the hard choices. That's how evil made its way in this world. Not with a devil's face, as the nuns taught us. It slithered between the cracks, caught decent people off guard, dragged them along until they were in too far. Then it made them into something they never thought they could ever be.

Had our killer, our Caligula, once been innocent? Had evil snuck up on him, or was it an old friend? Death was everywhere. Soldiers and civilians, the grim and the meek, they were all drawn into this killing machine that sucked in souls from the front lines, the air, the water, from quiet homes far from the fighting. Why should some fool be allowed to feed the machine more than it demanded? That trumped evil in my book.

A column of GIs passed below us, and I saw Danny's face, glasses on his freckled nose under a helmet that looked way too large. I started to cry out, but it wasn't him. The kid didn't have his walk, and the set of his shoulders wasn't right. Somebody else's kid brother.

I covered my face with my hands and prayed. Prayed for Danny, for his innocence, even harder than I had prayed for his life. It seemed so precious.

When I looked up, Kaz was gone. Probably in search of better company. There was a flurry of salutes on the deck below, and I figured it had to be senior brass coming aboard. It was Major General John Lucas, commander of VI Corps and this whole damned invasion. He pulled himself up the steel stairs — ladders, I think the Navy insisted on calling them — huffing a bit as he made it to the upper deck. He turned and addressed the crowd on the lower deck, mostly correspondents and headquarters types. I saw Phil Einsmann waving and I waved back, but he was trying to ask the general a question, not flag down a drinking buddy. He got the general's attention and shouted above all the others.

"General Lucas, any comment on where we're headed?"

"It's top secret," Lucas said, and then waited a beat. "But no one told the street vendors, I hear, so I'll tell you what you already know. It's Anzio."

That got a laugh among the reporters, and a halfhearted cheer from the officers. General Lucas looked amused, like a banker at a Rotary Club luncheon who just told a joke. He had a stout banker's body and gray hair. He didn't look like much, but I'd heard he'd been a cavalry officer on Pershing's Punitive Expedition into Mexico, and then wounded in the Great War. There had to be some fire left in the man, but he was keeping it tamped down, as far as I could see.

"Are you headed for Rome once you're ashore?"

"Are you going to attack the Germans from the north?"

"What strength do you have?"

These and a dozen other questions were shouted out while Lucas signaled for quiet.

"Now that you're all on board and under armed guard," he said, to another round of polite laughter, "I can answer your questions. My orders are to secure a beachhead in the Anzio area and advance upon the Alban Hills. We expect the enemy to put up a stiff resistance and respond rapidly with reinforcements. Therefore, the primary mission of VI Corps is to seize and secure the beachhead. I have the British First Division, the U.S. Third Division, and other attached troops, including Rangers, paratroops, and British Commandos. We're going to give the Germans a surprise, I'll tell you that."

"What about after the beachhead?" Einsmann shouted. "Are you going to take the high ground?"

"The Alban Hills are nearly thirty miles from the beachhead. We're not going to rush into anything. We can't afford to stick our neck out and make a mad dash for the Alban Hills, or Rome, or anywhere else. Seize, secure, defend, and build up. That's what I aim to do. Thank you, gentlemen."

General Lucas ascended the ladder to the bridge deck, his corncob pipe stuck into a corner of his mouth. I wasn't exactly a fan of "Old Blood and Guts" George Patton, but it struck me that I'd rather have a general like him leading an invasion than this paunchy, grandfatherly figure.

"Billy, what are you doing here?" Phil Einsmann said, working his way to my corner of the deck. "I thought you'd still be in Caserta, tracking down the Red Heart Killer."

"Is that what you press boys are calling him?" I was sorry he'd been given such an interesting nickname. He didn't deserve it.

"It's catchy. I filed a story, but I doubt the censors will release it. Not good for morale back home. You didn't answer my question."

"Habit. I like reporters, I just don't like telling them anything."

"Hell, Billy, I already know about Major Arnold and how you found him stuffed in his own trunk. There hasn't been another killing since then, has there?"

"No. And I'm not taking this sea cruise for my health."

"So you think the killer is someone in the Third Division?"

"I didn't say that. Lots of other guys making this trip."

"Okay, okay. I'll tell you something, though. Lucas is not happy with his orders. He thinks he's being hung out to dry. He's got two-plus divisions and they're landing him on a flat plain with mountains almost thirty miles away. The orders from General Clark are pretty vague. Did you pick up on that? To 'advance upon the Alban Hills.' What does that mean — take them, or approach them?"

"Could be either."

"Exactly. If Lucas fails, Clark can blame him whichever way it goes, for not taking the hills or for advancing too rapidly. Lucas is between a rock and a hard place, without enough troops to do the job."

"Is that why you were asking him what his plans were?" "I was hoping to get him riled up, so he'd say something worth printing."

"I think it's been some time since he's been riled."

"That might be a damn good thing, Billy. A lack of rile could keep some of these boys alive."

"Where did you hear all this?"

"Not everybody clams up in front of reporters. It's easy to get stuff off the record. On the record and past the censors, that's another thing. So level with me, Billy, off the record. About the murders."

"I wish there was more to tell. Yeah, I think it's someone in the Third Division. Someone who knew the victims. Someone who had a reason to kill them. Did you ever meet a guy named Stefano Inzerillo? He ran a dive called Bar Raffaele in Acerra." I didn't mind trading information with Einsmann, especially since he'd probably not get word one past the censors.

"You used the past tense, Billy. I take it he didn't sell his business and move?"

"He's moved on to another location. Did you know him?"

"I know the joint."

"Not a spot for high rollers; not like the officer's club at the palace. What were you doing there?"

"Billy, I took you for a man of the world. What do you think? It wasn't for the fine wine. How did Inzerillo get it?"

"Someone beat him up pretty bad, so he barricaded himself in his bar. Some guy, a GI most likely, set the place on fire."

"Jesus. Anzio could be a rest cure after all this."

"Did you ever see Lieutenant Landry there?"

"The first victim? I don't know, never met him. Couldn't tell you. I did see Sergeant Cole there once though."

"I thought you said you didn't know him."

"I knew who he was. I only said I hadn't spoken with him since he got transferred to CID. Father Dare told me he helped get Doc Galante to wrangle a transfer for him.

Wait a minute — it would have been Major Arnold who did the paperwork on that. Was Cole's suicide part of this?"

"Off the record, I'd call it murder."

Chapter Twenty

There had been fireworks in the night, and I'd finally understood what "the rockets' red glare" meant. There were no bombs bursting in the air, but the shoreline took it on the chin. To the north, Anzio and Nettuno glowed a dull orange as smoke-wreathed fires spread. Kaz and I were on the beach, threading our way between craters, stacks of supplies, engineers spreading steel gratings over the sand for the heavy stuff to cross to the road, and noncoms yelling at GIs to move inland. We trudged up to the main road and watched as landing craft disgorged more and more men. After being crammed onboard ships for more than thirty hours with hundreds of men who had nothing better to do than play cards, sweat, puke, and pray, they looked excited, like kids on a trip to the shore. They laughed and gabbed, peppering their sergeants with insistent questions.

"Do you think I'll do all right?"
"Can I stick with you?"
"What will you do when we get to Rome?"
"No," a sergeant first class barked at them. "I think you'll piss your pants and run. And don't come near me if you can't keep your head and ass down, you'll just draw fire. You'll never make it as far as Rome, so don't worry about it. Now move your ASTP asses and prove me wrong!"

I watched the GIs following him, the smiles gone from their faces. I hoped the army had actually taught these kids something about warfare when they went to college.

"Hey Billy!" Phil Einsmann ran up the beach, his only armament a small portable typewriter in a wooden case and his war correspondent's patch on his shoulder. "Where are you fellas headed?"

"We're waiting for a jeep. Looking for a lift?"

"I have no idea where to go, but I'd rather not walk there."

"Here's Major Kearns," Kaz said, as a jeep fought its way against the flow of traffic. I'd gone over my suspicions with Kearns about all the connections with the Third Platoon, Cole, the rag doll, the WP grenade, Inzerillo, and the last murder. I left out the part about my kid brother, and my worry that he might cross paths with Red Heart. He might think I was being overprotective. Maybe so. Maybe it was only coincidence, but it all felt wrong. Someone in the Third Platoon had answers. Father Dare was on my list as well. Einsmann, too, for that matter. He seemed to know more than he'd let on, and cropped up at the damnedest times.

"Boyle, Kaz," Kearns said as he got out of the jeep. Not for the first time, I noticed how people liked Kaz immediately, taking to his nickname, responding to his suave continental charm, not to mention the unstated allure of the mysterious scar down his cheek. A surefire combination. "The outfit you're looking for is headed to Le Ferriere. Father Dare went along with them, since they didn't have a medic."

"Isn't that unusual?" Kaz said. "For a chaplain to go on a combat patrol?"

"From what I've heard, he stays close to the front lines and does a lot of work with the wounded. He's picked up some basic medical knowledge, so he's useful, especially on patrol."

"He's not your average holy Joe," I said. "How do we find them?"

"Go back down this road and turn right just before Nettuno. The road signs are still up. Take the Via Cisterna." Kearns opened a map that showed the village about halfway between the coastline and the Alban Hills.

"What is their mission?" Kaz asked.

"To reconnoiter the village, see if any Germans are there. Le Ferriere is a crossroads, just south of the canal. It'll be a key position if the Germans move in and put up a fight."

"You see any Germans yet, Major?" Einsmann asked.

"A few prisoners, a few corpses," Kearns said, eyeing Einsmann's correspondent's patch. "There was a small detachment in town, but no organized resistance. Might not be the same up the road. You might want to hang back."

"No organized resistance doesn't get the headlines, Major. I'll stick with these guys and stay out of the way."

"You do that. Boyle, get back to me tonight with a report. Corps HQ is a villa in the Piazza del Mercato in Nettuno. Can't miss it, just a couple of blocks in from the harbor."

"Yes sir," I said. "You need a lift back?"

"No, General Lucas is coming ashore, I'll go back with him. The general and a whole posse of colonels, so find this killer. Whatever you need, let me know. This is going to be hard enough without looking over our shoulder every ten seconds."

A snarling growl of engines rose from seaward, and we all turned to watch another formation of fighters head inland to hunt for German reinforcements. Four aircraft, flying low, turning in a graceful arc that would take them parallel to the beach, not across it.

"Take cover!" I wasn't the first to say it, but I yelled anyway. I grabbed Kaz and pulled him into a ditch with me, looking up at the planes, knowing I shouldn't. I couldn't help myself. It was one of those moments when everything happens fast but you see things with crystal-clear vision, small details blossoming out of a blur, deadly but hypnotic. Bright white lights twinkled from the nose. They looked oddly festive in that split second before the sound caught up and the chatter of cannon and machine-gun fire drove all thoughts but of survival from my mind. Geysers of water sprouted in the surf as the Messerschmitts went for the landing craft and the troops and vehicles piling out of them. They pulled up, split into two pairs, and sped away, ineffectual antiaircraft fire trailing them.

We stood up and dusted ourselves off as a gas tank exploded somewhere down the beach, leaving black smoke belching into the sea air. Yells, shrieks, and curses rose from the men on the beach, and I watched Major Kearns trot toward the landing craft, looking over his shoulder. He was going to have one helluva sore neck before this was over.

"Let's go," I said. Einsmann piled in back and Kaz navigated, holding the folded map in his lap as it flapped in the breeze. We drove through a cluster of pastel-colored buildings facing the water, the morning sun lighting them beautifully, giving even the blackened, smoldering hole in the roof of one of them a lazy, seaside quality.

"Where are all the people?" Einsmann asked as we slowed around a curve. "No one's here. You'd think by now the locals would be out to see all the excitement."

"Perhaps they are still hiding in the cellars," Kaz said.

"Maybe they're all die-hard Fascists," I said.

"Mussolini certainly was popular here," Kaz said. "He ordered the Pontine Marshes drained, and created farmland between the shore and the Alban Hills. His government built new towns and farmhouses, populating them with his supporters. I doubt many of the locals will be lining the streets cheering us on."

"That's good stuff," Einsmann said. "How do you know all this?"

"Kaz knows everything," I said, having found that to be true of most everything I needed to know. Ahead, I saw a cluster of GIs around a farmhouse, and pulled over as one waved me down. They were Rangers, and in the dusty courtyard between the house and the barn, the bodies of two German soldiers were laid out. One Ranger was going through their pockets, handing papers to an officer. The rest of them were gathered around six women, a couple of them young and very pretty, the others maybe their mothers and aunts. They were rubbing their wrists, strands of rope scattered on the ground at their feet.

"What's going on?" I asked. Two Rangers approached, surveying us with suspicious eyes. One American officer, one British officer, and one correspondent in his own ragtag version of a uniform. I didn't blame them for pointing their tommy guns in our general direction.

"We came up the road from Anzio, and found these two Krauts. First ones we saw," a corporal said, spitting out a stream of tobacco juice in their general direction. "Then we heard these ladies hollering inside the barn. From what we can make out, a German officer was bringing a detail this morning to execute them."

"What for?"

"Leaving a restricted area. Seems like anyone left in the coastal zone has to have papers to leave. They took a truck to Rome to buy food on the black market, and almost made it back. The Germans nabbed 'em and were going to shoot them in the morning, once they had an officer on hand."

"Good thing he was delayed. Kaz, ask them about Rome, and how many Germans are between here and there."

Kaz and Einsmann went over to the group, and were soon pulled into a swirl of kisses, embraces, and hands raised to heaven and back to ample breasts in thanks. It looked positively dangerous.

"We're looking for the road to Le Ferriere," I said to the corporal.

"Keep going, right around the bend," he said, pointing to a curve ahead. "Sign is still up. Looks like we caught the Krauts flat-footed. Be careful going up that road, though. By now they gotta have heavy stuff moving in."

"Or maybe that officer and a firing squad."

"Yeah, be nice to turn the tables on the bastards." He spit again, sending another splat of brown juice on the ground, as he looked at the women. "Looks like your Limey pal made out okay for himself."

Kaz returned to the jeep, a young girl on his arm, trailed by the other women, all talking at the same time, mostly to Einsmann.

"I told them he was a famous reporter, and would put their names in the newspaper for their relatives in America to see," Kaz said. "But Gina has something to tell us. *Di'al tenente quello che mi hai detto,*" he said, patting her on the arm.

"Ci sono pochissimi soldati tedeschi a Roma," Gina said proudly, smiling at Kaz and taking his hand.

"Very few German soldiers in Rome," he translated. "Mostly military police."

"They must have come through the German lines," I said.

"Hai visto i tedeschi fra qui e Roma?" Kaz asked her.

She shook her head no and unleashed a torrent of Italian, gesturing toward the two dead Germans.

"None," he said. "They drove to Rome and back and were only caught when three Germans left their post on the beach and came to the farm to look for food. They caught them unloading the truck, and tied them up in the barn. They told them when their officer came in the morning they would be shot. Then one of them drove off in the truck and these unfortunates stayed to guard their prisoners. Gina says the Germans moved most people out of the area, and let only those who were needed to work or farm stay. The penalty for travel without a permit is death."

"Seems like the locals are friendlier than you expected," I said, noticing how Gina had linked her arm with Kaz's.

"Yes, it appears that hunger trumps politics," Kaz said. He tipped his service cap to the women, and kissed Gina on the cheek, which raised a howl among the older ladies, who pulled Gina into their midst. I pulled out chocolate bars from a pack in the jeep, handed them around, and all was forgiven.

"That was a story," Einsmann said, writing in his notebook as the jeep rumbled along. "U.S. Army Rangers rescue Italian beauties from Nazi execution. My editor will love it, the readers will lap it up, and most importantly the army censors will like it. Maybe I can get it out tonight from headquarters."

"If what Gina said was true, that's the big story," I said. "No Germans between here and Rome. I wonder if General Lucas knows."

"You can't go by a story a pretty girl spins for you," Einsmann said. "Not without corroboration. You really think the Germans are dumb enough to leave this whole area undefended?"

"There's times I don't think too highly of our own brass," I said, turning right at an intersection where a faded white road sign pointed to Le Ferriere. "Don't see any reason why they should be any smarter on the other side."

The road was straight and narrow, with low-lying fields on both sides. Kaz pointed out the occasional farmhouse, a two-story stone structure, in the middle of a plowed field. At each one, I expected a machine to open up on us, but there was nothing but silence. We passed a farmer turning his field, and he looked at us with indifference. We were uniforms, and uniforms are bad for farmers. They mean crops churned up by tank treads, houses occupied, food stolen, and that was without the fighting. If General Lucas didn't move quickly, every one of these stone buildings would become a battleground.

I sped up, feeling giddy at how alone we seemed, how strange it was to be driving into enemy territory as if on holiday. On the side of the road ahead, I spotted a vehicle on its side in the ditch. It was a German *Kübelwagen,* a cross between a jeep and a command car, recognizable by the spare tire mounted on the sloped front hood. Kaz had the Thompson submachine gun out before I could even slow down. I pulled over about ten yards short and cut the motor, listening for any sign of movement. Nothing. Kaz and I exchanged glances, nodded, and got out. I motioned for Einsmann to stay put and he was eager to, scrunching down in the backseat, hugging his typewriter to his chest as if it were armor.

Kaz and I each approached a side of the vehicle. The canvas top was down. Bullet holes dotted the windshield and the hood. The driver was half out of his seat, his neck hanging at an odd angle. Another German, probably thrown from the passenger's seat, was on the ground next to him. He'd taken a slug or two in the throat, and the ground drank in his blood. We both made a circuit of the Kübelwagen, looking for evidence of another German. The two dead were enlisted men. Was this the detail heading to execute the women? If so, where was their officer?

Kaz stepped up on the mounded earth beside the drainage ditch that ran along the road. "Billy, come here," he said.

I followed, and saw two more bodies. One was a German officer. I could tell by his shiny boots and the gray-green visor cap lying in the mud. He was on his back, his neck arched up and his mouth wide open. His chest rose and fell with a wheezing sound, his eyes gazing at the sky overhead, as if searching for the way to heaven. One hand gripped a tuft of grass, desperately hanging onto this world. His boot heels had dug into the earth, leaving gouges where he'd flailed, as if running away from death. He had two bullet holes in his gut, powder burns prominent around each one. He'd been left to die slowly, and not that long ago.

"Hey, Fritz," I said, leaning over him. I didn't exactly feel sorry for him, since he probably was on his way to execute those women, but leaving him here to suffer didn't sit right either. His eyes widened, perhaps in fear.

"Er hat den Amerikaner getötet," the Kraut said, grabbing me with his free hand. *"Er hat gemacht!"* A thin pink bubble of blood appeared around his lips, and then burst as he gave a last gasp and died.

"What did he say?" I asked Kaz, as I unclenched his fingers from my sleeve.

"He killed the American. He did it."

"The Kraut? He was confessing?"

"No, those were his exact words. Someone else killed the American. Do you know him?"

I knew the American. He was immediately recognizable by his red hair and tall, lanky frame. Rusty Gates, platoon sergeant. He was laid out neatly, feet together, hands on his chest. A ground sheet covered his body, but the hair was unmistakable. I pulled the cover back and knew for certain. One dog tag was gone. One bullet hole to the heart, powder burns and all.

"Rusty," Einsmann said in a gasp, scaring the hell out of me. I hadn't heard him come up on us, and I swung my arm around, .45 automatic at the ready. "Jesus, don't shoot!" He threw his hands in front of his face.

"Yeah. Sergeant Rusty Gates, Third Platoon. You knew him?"

"Sure. Had a few drinks with him now and then. Met him back in Sicily. He was a solid guy. Think that Kraut officer got the drop on him?"

"Looks like it," I said, drawing the ground sheet back over him. Rusty had seemed like a solid guy. A leader. I'd felt good about Danny being in his platoon, but now, with former supply officer Lieutenant Evans in charge, I wasn't so sure.

"Maybe they shot each other," Einsmann said.

"Not likely," I said. "Probably the Kraut surprised Rusty as he came over the ditch. Dropped him with one shot, then somebody else shot the officer." But as I said it, I saw that things didn't add up. Rusty must have been shot at close range, three or four feet at the most, to leave gunpowder burns. He would have seen the German before he got that close. I looked at the dead officer again. His entry wounds were next to each other, straight on, at the same level you'd hold an M1 at the hip. Just above the belt buckle. *Bang bang,* you're dead, but not right away. "The Kraut must have shot Rusty at close range, then someone else killed him for it."

"Which makes sense," Kaz said. "If the German offered to surrender and instead pulled out his pistol and shot the sergeant."

"Yeah, if it happened that way. Strange, that's all. The guy makes it out of his vehicle after it's ambushed. He didn't run, didn't get more than a dozen yards away. Then he throws his life away to kill one American." I looked at his face. He wasn't young. Maybe thirty-five, forty. He wore a wedding ring. Regular army, not SS. A fanatic, never-surrender Nazi? Maybe. Maybe not.

"He was gut-shot," I said. "Sure to kill

him, but not right away. He suffered."

"For his sins, most likely," Kaz said.

I wasn't so sure. We'd heard the story of the Italian women who were to be shot, but I doubted Gates and his men had. Why leave him alive, in pain like that? Who killed the American? Another Kraut? A GI?

"His pistol is gone," Einsmann said. That was obvious. No GI could resist a souvenir, especially with so few Germans around. We went back to the vehicle and searched it, but that had already been done. Two Schmeisser submachine guns had been smashed, and the pockets of the dead searched. We got back in the jeep and started out again, more slowly this time, as I tried to work out in my mind what had happened back there, and what Danny might have seen or done. I didn't like anything I came up with.

A mile or so later, a signpost let us know we were in, then out, of the village of Cossira. It was hard to tell the difference. We came to a fork in the road, and Kaz traced the route we'd taken with his finger, looking around for a landmark or a sign. Drainage ditches, flat fields, and distant hills were all we saw. "This way," he said, pointing to the right fork.

"It's got to be a left," Einsmann said, leaning over Kaz's shoulder, tapping his finger on the map. "We want to be more north."

I looked at the map, and then up at the sun, as if that might give me a clue. "We'll go left," I said. "We can always turn around if it looks wrong."

Chapter Twenty-One

"The sign says Carano to the left," I said. "That's right where it should be."

"Sounds right to me," Einsmann said, turning the map around several times, viewing it from every possible angle. The jeep was idling at an intersection. Left was Carano, straight was Velletri, which I knew was up in the Alban Hills. To the right was nothing but emptiness, plowed fields, and damp gullies.

"We should turn around," Kaz said in an exasperated tone. "I said so back at the last turn."

"This feels right," I said, gunning the jeep and taking a hard left. I hoped it was. The road narrowed and became a hard-packed dirt surface. We came to a fork in the road, one weathered sign pointing left to Carano. We went right, on my theory that keeping Carano to our left was the wisest course. It *was* left of Le Ferriere on the map, so logic was on my side. Kaz didn't say a word, satisfying himself with switching off the safety on the Thompson. We drove farther and found another fork in the road. This time, the sign to Carano pointed back the way we'd come. Gianottola was to the left. I couldn't find it on the map, so I went right, for no particular reason, the road curving around a slight rise.

"We should turn around," Kaz said.

"Not yet," I said, unwilling to admit what I was beginning to suspect. That we were lost.

"No, I mean look behind us."

I pulled over and we craned our necks around. The view was stupendous. With all the twists and turns, I hadn't noticed we were slowly climbing. In the distance, the sea shimmered with sunlight. The flat plain of the drained Pontine Marshes was laid out before us, straight roads and canals dividing the ground, stone farmhouses dotting the landscape.

"Okay, we're lost," I said.

"How far have we driven?" Einsmann asked.

"Twenty miles or so, but not in a straight line."

"We haven't seen a single German," Kaz said. "I'm curious as to where they are."

"I'm not so curious I want to find any of them," I said. "Should we go back?"

"I think we should go on," Einsmann said. "Until we hit a main road or town, so we know where we are. Then you can bring back some intelligence."

"And you get an exclusive story, as the intrepid reporter behind the German lines."

"Billy, I don't think we're behind the German lines," Einsmann said. "I'd bet there's no Germans between us and Rome. This could be the biggest story of the war, an invasion that achieves total surprise. Hell, it is a big story, no doubt about it."

"He's right, Billy," Kaz said. "If I can make any sense of this map, we should come to Highway 7 soon."

"The road to Rome, through the Alban Hills?"

"Yes. From the height here, I'd say we are already in the Alban Hills."

"Okay, I'm in," I said, studying the map Kaz was holding. "Velletri, that's on Highway 7, and there was a signpost back a while ago." I waited for one of them to talk me out of it, but Einsmann had an eager grin and Kaz simply nodded, folding the map and cradling the tommy gun like a Chicago gangster. I turned at the intersection headed for Velletri, high up in the Alban Hills, armed with one automatic pistol, a Thompson, and a typewriter.

We saw Velletri, a cluster of buildings on top of a hill, and found a side road to get around it. I didn't want to get caught in a narrow roadway without a clear way out. We found a sign with the number seven, and in a few minutes were on a well-maintained double-lane road. Highway 7, the road to Rome. We were headed due west now, the wooded slopes of the Alban Hills above us and the view to the sea below. We passed small villages, seeing the occasional farm vehicle make its way slowly along the road. No one waved, or seemed to take notice. Perhaps they thought we were Germans and were deliberately ignoring us. Or maybe they knew we were heading into an ambush and couldn't bear to look.

There was no ambush, not at Montecanino, Fontanaccio, or Frattocchie. No traffic either, now that we'd left farm country. The miles were easy, as if we were out for a Sunday drive. I couldn't help but think about Diana, how tantalizingly close I was getting to her. Nothing but the German army somewhere between us.

"This is the old Appian Way," Kaz said. "It was the most important road of the Roman Republic. There are places where the original paving stones can be seen."

"Isn't that the road where the Romans crucified Spartacus?" I asked.

"Yes, and thousands of the slaves who revolted along with him," Kaz answered. "I didn't know you were acquainted with Roman history."

"I have a good memory for when the little guy takes it on the chin. Happens often enough."

"Thousands?" Einsmann said.

"Six thousand, if I remember correctly," Kaz said. "Look, Billy, pull over there." He pointed to a circular stone ruin, close to the road. "It is the tomb of Cecilia Mettela."

"Kaz, the history stuff is interesting, but we can't stop for a tour."

"What is noteworthy about this tomb is that it was built on the highest ground south of Rome. It is on a hill, and I've read that it provides a good view of the city."

I pulled over. The place was huge, a wide tower about thirty feet tall atop a rectangular base of stonework twenty feet high. I saw the possibilities, and grabbed the binoculars. We climbed the stairs and reached the top. One side of the circular wall was crumbling, pieces of stone scattered on the ground below. But the walkway was sturdy enough, and I saw that Kaz had been right. The tomb was on a hill, and from this height, I could see all around us, south to the Alban Hills, and north to Rome. Where Diana was.

I looked through the binoculars, steadying myself against the wall. I could make out buildings, but I wasn't sure what I was looking at. Then, beyond the sea of roofs, I spotted a white dome. St. Peter's, that had to be it. On a hill across the Tiber River. The Vatican, a tiny piece of neutral ground, and most likely home to Diana. I could be there in an hour.

"Vehicle coming down the road," Kaz said. I spotted a U.S. Army jeep, heading out of Rome. "It appears that we are not the first Allied tourists to visit the Eternal City."

"Two of them in the jeep," I said. "Let's flag them down."

We descended and stood in the street, each of us waving one hand and keeping the other on our weapon. The jeep slowed and stopped in front of us, and I could see that the lieutenant in the passenger's seat had his carbine at the ready.

"Who the hell are you?" He looked at us warily, and I realized that we did look like an unlikely unit: one Brit, one Yank, and one war correspondent.

"Lieutenant William Boyle," I answered.

"Did you just come from Rome?"

"Damn near. Lieutenant John Cummings, 36th Engineers," he said as he extended his hand. Everybody relaxed as it became apparent we were all on the same side. "What are you doing out here?"

"We got lost, and then decided to keep on going once we saw how close we were. Haven't seen a German between Anzio and here."

"There aren't any. We got close enough to see a few military vehicles crossing a bridge over the Tiber, but it wasn't much. A few trucks and staff cars."

"We should get this news back to HQ," I said, disappointed to hear that he had run across Germans. It would have been a swell surprise for Diana to see me show up for Mass at St. Peter's.

"I was ordered to reconnoiter towards Rome this morning, and we just kept going once we realized no one was in front of us. The Italians didn't even pay us any mind. I don't think word of the invasion has gotten up here. It's a total damn surprise. We've got to get back to report. Want to follow us?"

"That would be excellent," Kaz said. "Otherwise we might get lost and end up in Berlin."

We ate their dust all the way back to the beachhead. Einsmann commented on how quick the return trip was, compared to our back-road journey out. Kaz grinned, but kept his thoughts to himself as he swiveled in his seat, watching for phantom Krauts. It was hard to believe we had all this ground to ourselves.

We pulled into Corps HQ in Nettuno an hour later, parking the jeep in the courtyard of the seaside villa that VI Corps called home. The Piazza del Mercato was a pleasant little square with sycamore trees and a statue of Neptune dead center. Tattered posters of Mussolini fluttered in the breeze from the wall of a bank. A few civilians scuttled by, avoiding eye contact and getting clear of Americans as quickly as they could. I'd been in towns in Sicily and southern Italy where the locals cheered and threw flowers. Here, there was nothing but sullenness and the faded glory of Il Duce looking down at us.

We hadn't found the 3rd Platoon, but I figured we'd come up roses anyway. General Lucas himself would probably give up a colonel or two to find out there were no Germans between here and Rome. Einsmann left to type up his story and get it to the censor before he lost his exclusive. Cummings said he had to submit a report through his regiment, so he left to get it written up so it could work its way through the chain of command. It seemed like a slow process.

"Let's find Major Kearns," I said. "He can get us to Lucas right away."

We entered through heavy wood doors into a spacious home, with tall windows facing the Mediterranean. It was perched up on a hillside, with a view to the north of Anzio and to the south toward crystal-blue water. The polished wood floors were already scuffed and scraped by countless boots as GIs brought in desks, files, radio gear, and all the other hardware a headquarters can't do without, cases of Scotch included. The place was crawling with brass, and I thought we were about to be thrown out when I saw Kearns, heading down a staircase with General Lucas. The general gripped a corncob pipe in his mouth and held a cane in one hand. I had the uncomfortable thought that I was looking at a man not cut out for this work.

"Lieutenant Boyle," Kearns said, taking notice of me. He explained to Lucas that I was the officer in charge of the Red Heart investigation. "Have you anything to report?"

"Not on the investigation. But we got lost trying to find Le Ferriere, and we ended up right outside of Rome."

"Rome?" Lucas said. "You must really have been lost, Lieutenant. You couldn't have gotten anywhere near Rome."

"We were there, sir," Kaz said. "At the tomb of Cecilia Mettela, on the Appian Way. Highway 7."

"It's true, General. We didn't see a single live German the whole way. From the top of the tomb I could see the dome of St. Peter's."

"Impossible," Lucas said. "We're digging in for a counterattack right now. The old Hun is getting ready to have a go at me. It's a miracle you got back in one piece."

"General," Kearns said, choosing his words carefully. "We haven't seen much activity on our front. Maybe you have achieved total surprise."

"I'm not going to endanger my command because two young lieutenants got lost and managed to drive around the German defenses. I'm glad you fellows had a good ride, but it's hardly what I'd call credible intelligence. Now get some food, and then go out and find that killer. That's your job, not reconnaissance."

"General, we met up with Lieutenant

Cummings, 36th Engineers, and drove back with him. He went farther than we did, and he's writing up his report right now. Reconnaissance was his assignment."

"Fine. Then G-2 will evaluate and report to me. Keep up the good work, boys."

And with that, he turned his back on us, leaving a trail of tobacco smoke in his wake. Kearns followed him, and we were alone with the view. A light breeze stirred the curtains, a rich shade of burgundy. The color of blood.

Chapter Twenty-Two

After our Roman adventure, we decided to wait until the morning to try for Le Ferriere again. The sun was about to set, and I didn't want a repeat performance with the added bonus of being fired on by our own guys in the dark. So we drew gear and bedrolls from the beachhead supply depot, found a deserted house, and got ourselves a good night's sleep. At first light, we were drinking scalding hot coffee and eating powdered eggs, thanks to the cooks who'd set up their feeding operation overnight. Say whatever you want to say about army food, but when you've got no other choices and the chow is hot, it's a miracle of American ingenuity.

We followed a supply truck headed in our direction, and this time found Le Ferriere. It wasn't much of a place. The ground sloped up slightly from the farmland all around it, and a small church, a factory building, and a few scattered homes made up the whole town. No civilians were in sight, but a battalion headquarters was set up in the factory, and they showed us the Third Platoon position, set up on the right flank, on the low ground a couple of hundred yards out.

We left the jeep and walked, not wanting to draw any attention in case the Germans had gotten observers up in the hills. As we walked over plowed earth already tamped down into a path by GI boots, I grew nervous about seeing Danny. I was worried about him being at the front, but it was the possibility that he was in the same unit as a murderer that really troubled me.

Just as driving a jeep and sending up a cloud of dust could forewarn the Germans and point out our position, my questioning anyone in this platoon could give away too much of a warning. It hit me that this visit was a lousy idea; if the killer thought we were onto him, he might take it out on Danny.

"Kaz," I said as we neared the position. "We're not here to question anyone. It's just a visit, for me to see Danny. Follow my lead, okay?"

"You're the boss."

I scanned the group of men ahead, most

of them busy with entrenching tools. I saw Stump and Flint first, and gave them a wave.

"Hey, kid!" Flint yelled, beckoning to a figure knee-deep in a trench. "You got a visitor."

It was a face I'd recognize anywhere, even wearing a helmet that looked twice the size of his head, steel-rimmed army-issue spectacles, and holding a shovel instead of a book.

"Billy!" Danny ran up to me and looked like he was going to jump into my arms. Then he skidded to a halt, a confused look on his face. He started to raise his right hand in salute, but Flint grabbed him by the wrist.

"Remember what Rusty told you, kid? No salutes up here. Unless you want to point out an officer to a Kraut sniper."

"Sorry, Sarge. I just got confused. It's been so long since I saw my big brother, I forgot he was an officer."

"Let's keep him a live one, Danny boy. No salutes."

"Got it, Sarge," Danny said as Flint grinned and left us to our reunion. "Jeez, Billy, it's good to see you."

"Same here, Danny." I gave him a quick hug, nothing that would embarrass him, followed by a manly clap on the shoulder.

"You doing okay?"

"Sure. Don't worry about me. I really lucked out, this platoon is a swell bunch of guys. They told me they'd met you back in Caserta, investigating some officers getting bumped off. What are you doing here?"

"General Lucas couldn't get by without me, so he dragged me along. I heard you were out here, so I decided to pay a social call." I introduced Kaz around, giving his full title and lineage to impress Danny.

"So you're Kaz," he said. "Billy wrote us all about you. I never thought I'd get a chance to meet you in person. What are the odds, huh?"

"Indeed," Kaz said. "A long shot, yes?" Kaz gave me a look and drifted off, chatting with Flint and Stump.

"Danny," I said, draping my arm over his shoulder. "I can't believe you're here. I just heard about the ASTP program being broken up a few days ago."

"It all happened pretty fast," he said. "Mom wasn't too happy about it."

"What about Dad and Uncle Dan?"

"They wanted to cook something up like they did for you, but Mom told them to leave it alone, since it didn't keep you out of trouble. She said I should take my chances, that maybe I'd end up a clerk since

I was a college kid. So here I am, in a rifle squad, which is what I wanted in the first place."

"Listen, Danny. You've got to get your head out of the clouds before it gets shot off. This is for real. Keep your head down out here. It's not just a saying. Stay low. And don't panic."

"I won't," he said, moving out from under my grip. "I haven't yet, have I?"

"Okay, simmer down. Just some advice, don't blow a gasket."

"Sorry, big brother. I know you're trying to look out for me, but I'm not ten years old. I've been to college and I've made it through basic training, all without your help."

"This isn't the time to play grown-up, Danny. When the Krauts hit you, it's going to be with a ton of bricks, and they won't care how smart you are. They'll only care about killing you."

"What Krauts?" Danny gestured to the empty fields all around us. It was smart-alecky, the way only a kid brother can be. Half right and totally wrong.

"If you're so smart, tell me the last time in this war when the Germans retreated without a fight? It didn't happen in North Africa, Sicily, or anywhere else in Italy. It won't happen here. They're going to come down out of those hills with heavy stuff, dollars to doughnuts."

"Now you're the one blowing a gasket, Billy," Danny said, with a grin to show he didn't want to argue anymore. Which he often did when he started to lose an argument, but I let that pass. He was only a kid, after all. "I'll take any tips you can give me on digging foxholes. Take a look at this." He'd been digging a trench, and about two feet down, it was filled with water. "Did you know this used to be the Pontine Marshes, Billy? The water table is only a couple of feet deep."

"Yeah, Mussolini drained them after he made the trains run on time. Kaz told me all about it. Now I have two geniuses on my hands."

"How's them trenches coming along, kid?" Louie ambled over, cigar clenched in his mouth and Thompson at the ready.

"Louie Walla," I said. "Now where is it you're from? Can't recall."

"Funny, Lieutenant," Louie said. "Having a family reunion?" Louie seemed more serious out here. Wary.

"Yeah, came by to check on Danny. He in your squad?"

"Yep, him, Sticks, Wally, and Charlie over

there, and a couple of other replacements. I partnered the ASTP boys up with guys who've been around. A little while, at least."

"I'm with Charlie," Danny said. "He's an Apache, can you believe that? And Wally is with Sticks. He's got long legs, that's why they call him that."

"Listen, kid, this gabfest is swell, but get on that shovel. You'll be glad of a hole in the ground soon enough."

"Okay, Sarge," Danny said, frowning and halfheartedly digging into the muddy soil. "You coming back soon, Billy?"

"If I can. And Louie knows what he's talking about, so listen up. You're exposed out here, you need to dig deep, and sit knee-deep in mud if you have to. Got it?"

"Yeah, I got it. Listen, come back soon, we'll catch up, okay?"

"I will." I wanted to hug him again. I wanted to take him with me and find a nice safe job for him in Nettuno. But I didn't. I stuck out my hand, and we shook. I felt like my father, silent and full of knowledge that I wanted to share, but knowing that only experience could pass this lesson on. I turned away, leaving Danny to learn what he had to learn alone, or from strangers. I knew that the more I hung around, the more stubborn he'd get. And that the killer might start playing a new game, if he hadn't already.

"Seems like a good kid," Flint said as I passed his squad, all engaged in the same futile digging.

"That he is. Any sign of the Krauts yet?"

"Nothing. I thought I picked up some movement up in the hills, but it could have been anything." Flint turned his clear blue eyes on me, as if registering my presence for the first time. "What are you doing out here anyway?"

"Just paying a visit to Danny. Nothing much else happening. We had a joyride to Rome yesterday, but since then it's been quiet."

"Rome? Why don't we all go?"

"Good question. General Lucas wasn't impressed."

"You met the old man?"

"Yeah. We're temporarily attached to his headquarters. He thinks it was a fluke that we got through. May have been, since we'd gotten totally lost."

"Did I hear Rome?" Stump said as he joined us.

"Billy drove to Rome yesterday, nearly liberated it himself," Flint said.

"Well, there were three of us, so I have to share the glory. Kaz and Phil Einsmann were with me."

"Phil's here? I thought he was on his way back to London," Flint said.

"Yeah, looking for a story. I doubt the censors will let this one out though. If we get bogged down and it turns out that a reporter and two lieutenants made it to Rome on the first day of the invasion, heads will roll."

"Next time you see Grandpa, tell him we could use some tanks up front," Flint said. "Or at least some antitank guns."

"Is that what you call him?"

"Some guys call him Foxy Grandpa," Stump said.

"Wishful thinking," Flint said. "Listen, Billy, you could do us and Danny a big favor. Talk to Lucas, let him know how exposed we are. We oughta get up in those hills ourselves, or pull back. This is Indian country, and we ain't got a fort."

"I don't talk to him on a regular basis, but I will pass on the sentiment if I bump into him again."

"He's in Anzio?" Stump asked.

"Nettuno, in a nice waterfront villa. No mud."

"Ain't that the way of the world," Flint said, and they all went back to their shovels.

Fifty yards back I found Lieutenant Evans and Father Dare walking in from the village. The padre had a first-aid kit slung over his shoulder and carried a canvas sack full of wool socks. I tried to see him as the killer, dispensing dry socks and then strangling officers. Could a priest forgive himself?

"Lieutenant Boyle," Father Dare said. "I didn't expect to see you again. Still chasing that Red Heart Killer?"

"I wish I was close enough to give chase," I said. "I dropped by to see my kid brother. He's in Louie's squad."

"Yes, I've met him. I try to get to know all the replacements. Sometimes the men ignore them at first." What he was too kind to say was the experienced GIs waited to see if a new kid would live through the first few days. "He certainly looks up to you, doesn't he?"

"I don't know about that," I said.

"You should," Evans put in. "You're all he's talked about since he joined up."

"How'd you make the connection? Boyle isn't an uncommon name."

"I don't know," Father Dare said. "The same name, same Boston accent, someone probably just mentioned you."

"That was all Danny needed to hear," Evans said. "I think we all know your family story by now. Good thing Louie partnered him up with Charlie. He doesn't talk much, so they're a perfect pair."

"Is he really an Apache?" I asked.

"Yes," said Father Dare. "Private Charlie Colorado is a genuine White Mountain Apache. Interesting fellow. I asked him if he wanted any spiritual guidance, and he told me his shaman had taken care of that before he left. Apparently he's protected by Usen, which is what they call their God. The Giver of Life."

"Well, I hope he digs in deep anyway. Usen might be busy elsewhere," I said. "Are you the giver of socks?"

"I am," Father Dare said. "Lieutenant Evans asked me to scrounge some up. There's going to be a lot of wet feet soon, and we have to watch out for trench foot. Clean socks are worth their weight in gold out here."

"Far as I can see, it's our biggest threat so far," Evans said, watching Father Dare as he distributed socks to the men. "After losing Sergeant Gates, we can use a break."

"Yeah, I saw his body by the road yesterday. What happened?"

"Kraut officer got the drop on him. I guess he thought he was surrendering, but the bastard pulled a pistol and shot him in the heart."

"I didn't take Rusty for the careless type,

did you?"

"No," Evans said. "I depended on him, he was an old hand, know what I mean?"

"I do. Did you see it happen?"

"No. He had point, and all of a sudden there was a lot of shooting. The car crashed, and by the time I got there, Gates was dead."

"The German was still alive when I got there," I said. "Barely."

"Yeah, well, everyone was upset about Rusty. The Kraut was bawling about something, and no one really gave a damn. I told them to go on, that I was going to put him out of his misery. But I couldn't do it. I fired my pistol into the ground. I didn't want the men to know. I've never killed anyone, and I didn't want the first one to be some poor defenseless bastard. But now I wish I had. I can still hear him talking to me, crying and blubbering."

"You understand German?"

"No. Did he talk to you?"

"No, just curious about what he had to say," I said. No reason to let on that the Kraut was blaming someone else for killing Rusty. Maybe Evans had killed someone before, who knew?

"He did say *Amerikaner* over and over," Evans said. "Maybe he was saying he was sorry. All I know is that I can't get him out of my head."

As Evans spoke, I heard the sound of distant thunder, or at least what always sounded like thunder. Father Dare and I hit the ground. The shrill whistling sound of falling shells came next, and even a rookie like Evans knew what that meant. He went flat as the shells burst, bombarding the village of Le Ferriere. The artillery fire kept up, striking the village over and over. A fireball blossomed up, probably a hit on a fuel truck. Then the shelling widened, explosions reaching the fields all around Le Ferriere, churning up the freshly plowed dirt, sending mud skyward. The barrage crept toward us, and I prayed that Danny would keep his wits about him, dive into a trench and stay put.

The ground shuddered with each hit. I looked across the field to where the squads had been digging in. Shells fell around them, leaving smoking craters as the firing slackened, then stopped.

"Wait," I said as Evans began to get up. He looked at me quizzically until the whine of one last salvo announced itself, hitting Le Ferriere. It was an old trick, waiting to send the last shells over when everyone began sticking their heads out.

I was up, sprinting to the forward position, eyes peeled for Danny and Kaz. I spotted them, and thanked God, Usen, and all the saints I could remember. Next I saw Louie, then Flint and Stump checking on their men as they rose from the ground, wet and muddy.

Something was wrong. Kaz had Danny by the arm, helping him out of the trench. Danny's eyes were wide with terror, and I searched his mud-splattered uniform for signs of blood.

"Danny?" I spoke his name but looked to Kaz.

"He is not hurt, Billy. It is Malcomb, the other ASTP boy. He ran." Kaz pointed to a lifeless body twenty yards out, clothing, skin, blood, and bone shredded by the shrapnel-laced blast.

"I tried to stop him," Danny said. "I tried."

"You would have been killed too," I said. "He panicked. You were smart to stay put."

"I didn't. Charlie grabbed me and held me down," Danny said, his voice shaky as he glanced toward Charlie Colorado, sitting on the edge of the trench. A big guy, bronzed skinned, and quiet.

"Usen," I said.

"I am not the Giver of Life," Charlie said. I begged to differ.

Chapter Twenty-Three

"He was from Princeton," Danny said, as if the aura of the Ivy League should have protected Malcomb from shrapnel and fear. He looked away as Flint helped to roll the body onto a shelter half so it could be carried away. It was a messy, unnatural business. The nuns had taught us that the human form was a sacred vessel, but out here, where artillery fire descended from the heavens, it was a delicate, thin-skinned thing, ready to spill the secrets of life onto the ground. For a soldier on the front lines, nothing is sacred, nothing is hidden, nothing is guaranteed to be his alone. Blood, brains, heart, and muscle are ripped from him, put on display, like his possessions, and carefully searched for the illegal or embarrassing before being boxed up to be sent to loved ones. His gear is divvied up — ammo, socks, food, and cigarettes handed around to squad mates — until finally, with his pockets turned out, his shattered body is covered and carried away. He is useless now, unable to fight, devoid of possessions, weapons, and breath, wrapped in waterproof canvas. This kid was from Princeton. Now he was of Anzio.

"I'm going to get you out of here," I said to Danny, my voice low. I didn't want anyone to hear, not his pals or a suspect. I watched Father Dare rise from giving the last rites, his knees drenched with damp earth and blood.

"No," he said, scrunching his face like he always did when I told him it was time to come for supper. "Leave me alone, Billy. I can do this."

"You can get killed is what you mean. What if Charlie isn't around next time?"

"Billy, if you pull any strings and take me away from the platoon, I will never speak to you again. I mean it. Ever."

"It's only going to get worse, kid. This shelling was just a taste. Are you sure? You don't have to prove yourself to me." But I knew he had to. I wanted to take him by the arm and lead him away from here, but I knew neither of us could live with that.

"Yeah. I'm sure. I couldn't live with myself if I left these guys. It wouldn't be right."

"Okay. I'm just a lowly lieutenant anyway.

Probably couldn't pull it off." I jabbed him in the ribs to show there were no hard feelings, and thought about how I could make it happen so it didn't seem to be my doing.

"Thanks, Billy. Maybe the war will be over soon, now that we're so close to Rome. Then we can go back to Boston."

"Sure, Danny. Could happen."

Standing with his hands on his M1, in a muddy uniform and helmet, he looked like a child playing soldier, his wishful thinking nothing but a wistful dream of home. Who was I to burden him with the truth? He'd have more than enough of that in the days to come. It was time for a change of subject.

"Maybe we can get some leave together, paint the town. Have any of the guys mentioned a place in Acerra, name of Bar Raffaele?" I tried to sound like I was just making conversation, suggesting a hot joint.

"Yeah, all the time. Louie said he'd take me there when we got back. You been there, Billy? Is it true what they say, about the girls?"

"It probably is, but it went up in smoke. And if I ever catch you in one of those joints, I'll give you a whupping."

"Hey, I've been around. And even Lieutenant Landry went out with one of the girls there. It can't be that bad."

"Danny, she was a prostitute. He paid for her time, he didn't go out with her. And now he's dead."

"Yeah, I know," Danny said, trying to sound like a nonchalant man of the world. "But Charlie says she was going to give it all up, and wait for Landry. They loved each other. It's sad, kind of like Romeo and Juliet."

"How does Charlie know all this?" I asked, not commenting on Danny's naïve view of the world.

"He used to go all the time, when he was the lieutenant's radioman."

I felt like an idiot. I should have thought to talk to the radioman. He's the one GI in a platoon who spends a lot of time with the platoon leader. He'd hear things, have a sense of his officer that even the sergeants might not.

"Let's go," Louie shouted. "Someone at HQ finally used their noggin. We're goin' into the village, where they got dry cellars. Move out!"

"I gotta go, Billy," Danny said. "Will I see you again?"

"Sure. Maybe tomorrow."

Charlie appeared at Danny's side, moving silently for a big guy carrying two packs of gear. He didn't speak. Next thing I knew,

Danny was hugging me with more strength than I'd thought he had. We stayed that way for a moment, and the familiar feel of my brother's grip brought me back to Southie, baseball games on the corner lot, leaves burning in the cool autumn air, and the scent of home. I gripped him even harder, and then we broke off in silent agreement that too much memory might not be a good thing right now.

I watched him move out with Charlie, wondering what secrets the radioman might have been told and what he might have seen. And why had he lost that job? Not that anyone wanted to carry around a heavy radio, much less be a priority target for the enemy. And how much of a coincidence was it that my kid brother was assigned to Landry's platoon and buddied up with Charlie Colorado in the first place?

"You and the Limey officer staying in the village?" Louie asked as we walked along.

"He's Polish, actually, and no, we're leaving."

"No disrespect meant. Just wondering if you needed a place to bunk down."

"Thanks, Louie, but we have beachside accommodations. Too bad they don't have a Bar Raffaele here, eh? Some wine, women, and song would be good about now."

"You can sing all you want, Lieutenant, but the civilians were evacuated from Le Ferriere this morning. Bunch of Italian Carabinieri came in trucks and hauled them away. Guess they knew the place would get plastered."

"I wondered why they were part of all this. Good idea to bring in the local cops. Hey, too bad about Rusty," I said. "Hard to believe that German got the drop on him."

"Can't let your guard down, not for a second. Wasn't like him to, but everyone slips up now and then. That Kraut officer didn't even look like the type."

"What do you mean, the type?"

"You know, a combat officer. He looked soft, not the type to go down guns blazing."

"Must have thought he had a chance," I said. "Why else would he try it?"

"He musta thought he had no other choice. Or maybe he was loco."

"Speaking of strange, how did Danny end up with you? I mean, what are the chances?"

"Truck dumped him and that other ASTP kid off. I got 'em. Simple."

"Rusty assigned them to you?"

"Nothing that official. I was short compared to the other guys, so they were mine."

"You guys worked pretty well together, didn't you?"

"Yeah, with Rusty and Landry in charge, we were a good team. Now, we'll have to wait and see. If Evans don't get his head blown off, he might be all right."

"He got those replacements for you. At least he's looking out for the platoon," I said.

"Naw, they came from Major Arnold direct. Luck of the draw, I guess. But still, Evans ain't the worst we could draw for a second louie."

"Arnold? That your personnel officer?" I felt a twinge of guilt at not telling Louie that Arnold was dead, but I wanted to watch everyone for a reaction. The only guy here who would know Arnold was toes up was the guy who did it.

"Yeah. A souvenir hound, and a real jerk to boot. But at least he sent us a few new guys."

We were close to the village. Acrid black smoke hung in the air from the remnants of a burning truck. The buildings were made of concrete and stonework, and had absorbed the shelling fairly well. The church had taken a direct hit on its roof, and craters gouged out holes in the narrow streets.

"C'mon, double time!" Louie yelled to two men lagging behind us. "See ya, Billy. I want to find a nice deep basement."

I stood beneath a stone archway and watched as Stump and Louie ushered their men into buildings along the perimeter. Flint's squad entered next, and he paused to watch Kaz and Evans behind him, scanning the hills through binoculars, watching for movements or the telltale reflection of the sun off a pair of German binoculars.

"Have a nice chat with the kid brother, Billy?" Flint asked.

"Yeah. Never expected to run into him here," I said as I fell in with him.

"You just happened to be in the neighborhood?" Flint's eyes darted over his men, up to the hills, and to the nearest building. It was small but well built, and covered the entrance to the village. He signaled for his squad to enter.

"I took a little detour. I figured the army is one thing, family is another. You have any brothers?"

"Yeah. My older brother died at Pearl Harbor. I joined up the next day. Got a younger brother myself, he's training to be a fighter pilot."

"Sorry to hear it," I said. "That must have been tough."

"It was. Got everyone riled up, that's for sure. I didn't like leaving my mother and kid brother to run the ranch, but I had to get into the fight. Seemed the only thing to do."

"You're a cowboy?"

"You got to ride a horse to herd cattle, Billy. Guess you could say I am, West Texas born and bred."

"This is a long way from Texas," I said.

"You got that right. Flat like Texas, though. But cold and wet. Can't say I like it much."

I followed Flint into the building, which had been used for storing farm implements. A small engine, maybe from a tractor, was unassembled on a workbench. The place smelled of oil and sweat, but it was dry and had foot-thick walls. Evans glanced in and nodded at Flint, as if he approved.

"How's your new lieutenant coping since Rusty got it?" I asked.

"You heard, huh? Damn shame. I don't know about Evans. He hasn't done anything stupid yet, so we'll see." It wasn't exactly a ringing endorsement.

"Something happen to your radioman? I haven't seen one with Evans."

"We don't have a radio, and haven't been issued a new set. Charlie kicked in the last one, so we're short."

"Why'd he do that?"

"Charlie drinks. A lot. Not often, but

when he does, look out. You know how they say Indians can't hold their liquor? Well, no one ever told Charlie. He can drink more than any man I ever met. Stays pretty sober too, on the outside at least. Then he gets to a point where all his meanness comes out, and no matter who you are, best stay out of his way. He's big, strong, and a mean drunk. Took a swing at Landry once."

"And he wasn't court-martialed?"

"Nope. Besides being a mean drunk, Charlie's a damn good soldier. Landry had the MPs lock him up, and it took a pile of them to do it. After the booze wore off, he was all apologetic, and Landry let it pass. Next time, he smashed the radio instead of an officer. I guess Landry knew this little tea party was coming up, and didn't want to lose him."

"Lucky for Danny he didn't."

"Yeah. But if Charlie finds a wine cellar, he'll drink it dry, and then Danny boy better not be in the vicinity. Word of warning, pal." Flint unslung his musette bag and tossed it on the workbench. It fell with a heavy clunk, and the snout of a German pistol poked out where the strap wasn't secured.

"Souvenir?"

"Walther P38," Flint said. "I bought it off

Louie after he nailed that Kraut."

"This is the pistol Gates was killed with?"

"It is. It was Louie's by rights, but he didn't want it. I figure if I can get to the rear somebody'll give me good money for it. How about you, Lieutenant?"

"No thanks," I said, but I couldn't stop myself from taking the automatic and feeling the heft of it. The Walther was easy to hold, the reddish-brown grip molded to fit the hand. The peppery smell of gunpowder still lingered over the steel, and I wondered again how Rusty had been caught unawares. "Louie didn't say anything about shooting the German."

"He was pretty upset about the whole thing," Flint said. "We all were."

"Billy," Kaz said from the doorway. "They want us to take two of the wounded back to the aid station. The ambulance is full."

"Okay. Sarge, good luck with the pistol. Maybe try Major Arnold in personnel. I hear he pays top dollar," I said, watching Flint's eyes. No surprise, no flicker of awareness.

"If I get that far back to the rear, I'll have sold it already, but thanks."

The field ambulance had taken the badly wounded already, and the medics were bandaging the last two GIs when we got back to the jeep. Stump was being patched up as well, a medic winding gauze around his forearm.

"Shrapnel nicked me," he said. "Didn't even feel it until I saw the blood."

"Bad luck," I said. "A little worse and you might have been sent home."

"And miss this escorted tour of beautiful Italy? No way. You takin' those guys back? They ain't banged up too bad."

"Yeah. You're not going?"

"I'd be embarrassed with this scratch. Make sure they fix 'em up and get 'em right back to us. I got a feeling we're going to need every man pretty soon."

"It's a long way from Bar Raffaele, isn't it?"

"You got that right, Billy. Paying too much to drink rotgut wine in the sunshine has got it all over this. Them Krauts are gonna keep shelling us until we take those hills up there. All Inzerillo ever did was overcharge us."

"What about that fight, the one Landry and Flint had to pay damages for? What happened? I never heard the whole story."

"I dunno," Stump said, his voice low. "I got a dose of the clap there, you know what I mean? The docs gave me shots and I was out of circulation for a while. Don't spread it around, okay?"

"My lips are sealed," I said. "Any word about replacements?" I asked, thinking that venereal disease made a good motive, for roughing up Inzerillo, at least. Or a good excuse to pretend ignorance. Either way, I wasn't getting anywhere.

"Arnold wouldn't bother to tell us if he had a boatload. Not his style. He only comes around scrounging souvenirs, got a real sideline going for himself. Replacements either show up or they don't."

"That's good to know. I've got a nice SS dagger stashed away."

"Well, see Arnold, he's always buying. I hear he ships the stuff home, got a pal who sells it off. You think rear area guys pay top dollar? It's civilians and 4-Fs who shell out the real dough. Arnold's smart, I give him that. You see him, tell him we need some experienced men, or he might get a Tiger tank for a souvenir, complete with crew."

"Lieutenant?" a medic called to me. "These guys are ready to go."

I wished Stump well and promised him I'd deliver the message to Arnold if I saw him, which I knew was one helluva long shot. The two wounded managed to stay upright as we drove them to battalion aid, where they joined a long line of the walking wounded. German artillery had had a busy day. So had we.

Chapter Twenty-Four

It was easy to get back to the twin towns of Anzio and Nettuno. All we had to do was follow the pillars of smoke. The Luftwaffe had been back, going after transports anchored offshore and the buildup of supplies off the beach. Anzio had been hit hard, first by our own bombardment and now by German bombs. There was even more destruction now than when we'd driven off the beach. I maneuvered the jeep around rubble and burning vehicles, waiting as ambulances barreled by. Everyone seemed to be glancing up, watching for the next wave of attacking aircraft. Near the center of town, a row of houses had been hit, leaving nothing standing but the front facades, doors and windows opening to piles of stone, timber, smashed furniture, and debris. Three women sat at the edge of the ruins, each of them nursing a baby. A few salvaged possessions lay about them. Their clothes and hair were caked with dust, nothing but breast and child, clean and pink.

"Is not war terrible?" Kaz said. "That we should think them the lucky ones?"

I didn't answer.

Back in Nettuno, General Lucas's villa had been renovated, courtesy of the Luftwaffe. There was a gaping hole in the roof, but no sign of an explosion. A GI told us it was from an unexploded bomb, and that Corps staff had moved into a nearby wine cellar for protection. We found Major Kearns in a deep stone basement filled with giant wooden wine casks and thick spiderwebs. A sour smell rose from a dank earthen floor. The place was a full-fledged winery, but had been unused for years. GIs carried desks, tables, map boards, radios, and other gear down a rickety flight of wooden steps.

"Driven underground already, and the casks are empty," Kearns said by way of greeting. "Not the best start for an invasion. What did you find out?"

"Mainly that my kid brother was transferred into Landry's old platoon."

"Life is full of coincidences," Kearns said. "Does it mean anything?"

"I don't believe in coincidence," I said. Dad had always said people mistook cause and effect for coincidence. "If the killer is in that platoon, then he's managed to get one up on me. It's like handing him a hostage. Danny was part of an ASTP group that just landed at Naples. Major Arnold was sending them out to platoons just before he was killed. Now maybe that's a coincidence too, but I doubt it. Everyone knows Arnold was in the souvenir business. It would have been easy to ask him for a favor — like transferring one particular replacement into a certain platoon — in return for a Nazi flag or a pile of soldbuchs." Cause and effect.

"And then kill him?" Kearns said, with a touch of sarcasm.

"It does fit," Kaz said. "Otherwise, Arnold might make a connection, were anything to happen to Billy's brother. And he was the right rank for the killer's next target. It was the perfect opportunity."

"All right," Kearns said. "I'll get Danny transferred out. The division is pushing off in the morning, across the Mussolini Canal. It'll have to wait until after that."

"But sir, he's only a kid," I said, not liking the idea of Danny under fire out on that exposed field.

"There are a lot of kids out there, Boyle. I buy it that it will be better all around to get him out of the platoon, but there's no time to get the paperwork going. Besides, all you need to do is not make a move until after tomorrow morning. That way we won't tip our hand. After the attack, I'll send up the proper paperwork, and it will look completely normal. Now, tell me what else you've got."

"Not much. I spoke to all of them about Major Arnold, but none of them seemed to know he was dead."

"They wouldn't. They were all aboard ship by the time you found him. What else?"

"We confirmed that Lieutenant Landry did have a girl at Inzerillo's place. Seems he wanted her to go straight, but there's no way to confirm that now."

"Boyle, you're not exactly cracking this case wide open," Kearns said.

"I know," I said, not wanting to admit that I was taking time to protect my kid brother. "I just need a little more time to get Danny out so I can press these guys harder."

"So you went easy on them today? Let me guess, you said it was just a social call, to see your brother. Picked up a little gossip, then headed back here to get the kid transferred. Am I close?"

"I had to feel them out, Major. I couldn't even interrogate them properly, since we were under artillery fire for most of the time. They had dead and wounded to deal with too."

"All right, all right. But press them hard next time. Find this guy, before he finds his next victim. I want him brought to justice, and I want it to happen before some Kraut blows his head off. Anything else?"

"Only that Lieutenant Evans is worried about Sergeant Walla," Kaz said. He hadn't mentioned it to me, but between ferrying the wounded and driving through bombed-out ruins, we hadn't had time for much conversation. "He says he's changed since they've come ashore, as if something is worrying him."

"He should be worried," I said, stating the obvious. "Any sane man would be."

"But remember Signora Salvalaggio telling us that Galante and Father Dare dined together, and that they discussed the sergeant?"

"This is Louie Walla from Walla Walla?" Kearns asked. "Seemed like a happy-go-lucky guy to me."

"Yeah, that's him. He did seem different to me today. Less cheery, none of that Walla Walla stuff. I figured he was all business out here, that's all."

"He bears watching," Kearns said, sorting through a pile of maps.

"Louie was the one who plugged that German officer who killed Rusty," I said.

"Rusty Gates got it? Damn, he was a good man," Kearns said as he gave up looking through the maps and rubbed his temples. He looked tired, the exhaustion of too little sleep and too much death.

"I thought so too. Not the kind to let a Kraut fool him either. Apparently the guy was going to surrender but pulled his pistol and shot Rusty. Louie plugged him."

"Listen," said Kearns. "I've been in combat with Rusty. If a Kraut had a pistol in his hands, he would have shot him dead. If it was in his holster and he went for it, Rusty would've put two rounds in his chest before he cleared it. There's no way he would let his guard down."

"Unless the weapon wasn't in the German's hand," Kaz said. "And the German was shot to inflict maximum pain and suffering. Two in the stomach."

"You're saying the Kraut didn't kill Rusty? But why would Louie, even if he is Red Heart?" I said. "What's in it for him, especially in the middle of combat? Eliminating a veteran platoon sergeant increases everyone's chance of getting killed." I needed to question Louie about that. And to see if Evans really had offered to finish off the Kraut.

"It doesn't make sense," Kearns said. "I think we're getting carried away. Focus on what you know. Hopefully the attack tomorrow will keep everyone busy, including the Germans."

It was a hell of a way to run an investigation, right in the middle of an invasion, my kid brother dead center, and hoping that the Germans left our killer alive long enough for us to catch him. It made about as much sense as anything else did.

"Yes sir," I said. "We'll pick up tomorrow, after the attack."

"Good. There's one piece of good news, anyway. Sam Harding is here."

"Colonel Harding?" Kaz asked. "He was still in London when I left."

"He flew in to give a briefing on the situation in Rome and among the Italian partisans. And, I suppose, to check up on your investigation. Sounds like Ike is worried about one of our own bumping off the brass. It's one thing when Jerry does it, but it makes people nervous when they have to keep looking over their shoulder at every GI."

"Where is Harding now?" I asked.

"He's finishing up with Corps G-2. They're located in an old Italian barracks in the Piazza del Mercato, just down the street.

Tell him to meet me here when you're done. I'm hoping he brought his usual Irish whiskey."

Kaz and I found the barracks, a thick-walled concrete building that made up in sturdiness what it lacked in looks. A 20-mm antiaircraft gun was set up in front, and I could see two machine guns on the roof, their barrels pointed skyward. Everyone was going to ground, setting up defenses, protecting themselves. Here, anyway. Up front, Danny's outfit would be attacking in the morning, heading out in the open. It didn't feel right. If headquarters expected the attack to be a success, why weren't they moving up, too? Why go underground just a few hundred yards from the beach? Maybe they had their reasons, but it didn't add up. Like Louie killing Rusty Gates. Like a lot of things.

"Boyle!" The voice was unmistakable. Colonel Sam Harding, my boss. Who worked directly for Uncle Ike, maintaining liaison with the intelligence services of governments-in-exile and our own Office of Strategic Services.

"Sir," I said, standing at a semblance of attention. This wasn't exactly the front lines, but it wasn't good form to point out superior officers to snipers by giving a ramrod-straight salute. It was the kind of thing Harding would appreciate. "It's a surprise to see you here."

"Let's get some chow and you both can update me on your progress." Pure Harding, no nonsense, no time wasted on pleasantries. I could tell he was in a good mood, though. He wasn't wearing a dress uniform, and he was within the sound of enemy shells, with an M1 carbine slung over his shoulder. For a deskbound West Pointer and veteran of the last war, it was close to heaven.

We followed him to the kitchen and had our mess kits filled. The cooks already had their portable stoves in operation, cooking fresh bread, roast beef, and canned vegetables. Danny and his pals were still eating K rations, but Corps HQ was already feeding on the A-ration diet, the same grub you could get at any base back in the States. We were all wearing helmets and carrying weapons, but that was no reason not to eat well.

"Kearns tells me we're up to the queen of hearts," Harding said as soon as we sat at the end of a trestle table, far from the others.

"Major Arnold, personnel officer," I said. I told Harding about Danny and my suspicions about his being placed in Landry's old platoon, and asking Kearns to arrange a transfer. Harding grunted, meaning he didn't disagree but wasn't going to go to bat for me either.

"What have you found out about Landry and Galante?"

"Landry was well liked by his men. He had a soft spot for a prostitute at a joint called Bar Raffaele in Acerra. There was some sort of fracas there and Landry and one of his sergeants, name of Flint, paid off the owner for damages. The owner, Stefano Inzerillo, claimed Landry never paid him anything. But he'd already been beaten to within an inch of his life, and was hiding something from us. We went back to question him again, but someone got there ahead of us and took care of that last inch. Inzerillo burned alive inside his own club."

"No playing card?" Harding asked in between mouthfuls of roast beef. I looked at Kaz, hoping he'd take up the slack so I could eat something, but he shoveled in a forkful of peas and shrugged.

"No. If it's the same guy, he's got one method for officers and another for everyone else." I told him the story of Sergeant Cole, from the incident in Campozillone to the shot to the head in Caserta, not leaving out the rag doll I'd found.

"Pearls?" Harding said in disbelief. Thankfully, Kaz chimed in with the story of Signora Salvalaggio, probably with a bit more history of the Italian monarchy than was necessary, but I didn't mind because it gave me a chance to eat.

"Galante knew about the pearls, and he knew Cole," Harding said. "Perhaps he asked him to look for them."

"That's likely," I said. "He had the run of the palace. But I think the killer knew about the pearls, too, from the way Cole acted. Maybe he was being forced to hand them over."

"Are you certain the murderer is part of Third Platoon?"

"Not certain, but everything points to it. Landry was platoon leader. Cole had been in the platoon; Galante got him transferred out. Arnold sent Danny and another ASTP kid in. They all hung out at Bar Raffaele."

"Sounds reasonable. Do you think this guy has some sort of grudge against officers?" Harding asked.

"It seems he has a grudge against anyone who gets in his way," Kaz said. "But the playing cards are something special. A calling card, so to speak."

"It's interesting that the first body wasn't

hidden," I said. "Landry was left in plain view. Behind a tent, but still where anyone could see him. Galante and Arnold were both hidden."

"Are you sure Landry was killed first?" Harding said. I was about to say of course he was, but stopped myself. Why assume that? Not because the killer put the ten of hearts in Landry's pocket and the jack in Galante's.

"Not at all," I said, drawing out the words and thinking it through. "Arnold's body had to be hidden, to give the killer time to get clear of the scene. But the same logic doesn't apply with the first two. If Galante was the first, then the killer had to place his body out of sight —"

"To give him time to murder Landry," Kaz finished for me.

"Right. Which means Landry must have known that the killer was going to see Galante, and had to be silenced."

"Going to see him about the pearls?" Harding offered.

"There's no indication Landry knew about the pearls. There had to be some other reason."

"Simple," Harding said. "He ordered him to." I was about to say that was too simple, but for the second time, I saw something that was so obvious I'd missed it.

"He ordered him to," I repeated, letting it sink in. "But why? For what reason?"

"Doctor Galante specialized in combat fatigue," Kaz said.

"But Galante wasn't seeing anyone from Third Platoon. We checked his records."

"Off the books?" Harding suggested.

"That would work," I said. "The platoon was short on experienced men. If Landry didn't want to lose a veteran soldier, he might ask Galante to talk to him on the QT."

"So, Landry sends a combat fatigue case to Galante. The guy goes off his rocker, kills Galante, then hotfoots it back to the bivouac area to kill Landry," Harding said. "He comes up with the straight flush idea to confuse things, so it isn't obvious that Galante was the real target. It puts Galante in among a group of victims, so we don't see him as the primary victim."

"Then he didn't go off his rocker," I said.

"What?" Kaz and Harding said at the same time.

"It doesn't fit. Who goes off his rocker and then executes a plan like that?"

"Someone crazy enough to murder people," Harding said.

"That's a tough one, Colonel. It sounds

logical, but if someone is really crazy, as the law defines it, then he's not responsible for his actions. But these are very well-thought-out actions, up to and including getting Danny in as part of the platoon."

Kaz shook his head. "Then what happened with Galante?"

"Something that was a threat. A serious threat that had to be stopped in its tracks, and covered up with this card business. It has to be related to what happened at Bar Raffaele, which is why Inzerillo had to go."

"Perhaps the killer wanted to be sent home, and Galante refused to give him the diagnosis he needed," Kaz said. "He gets angry, and before he knows it, Galante is dead. Then he has to kill Landry, to keep it all a secret."

"Or maybe it wasn't combat fatigue at all," I said. "Maybe Landry was helping out somebody who had the clap, asking Galante to treat him so it wouldn't go on his record."

"Venereal disease isn't exactly rare," Harding said.

"No, but perhaps a married man would not want it to be known," Kaz said.

"Or a priest," I said, fairly certain that Saint Peter was putting a black mark next to my name for even suggesting it.

"I'm heading over to see Kearns," Harding

said. "What's next for you two?"

"I want to find the Carabinieri who came along on this joyride. They may know more than they're telling us about Bar Raffaele."

"Why do you think that?"

"A hunch is all," I said. I didn't want to complicate things by bringing up Luca Amatori's stint at a Fascist concentration camp. That was my leverage, and I needed to keep it to myself. For now.

"Okay," Harding said, rising from the table with his mess kit. "I'll be back tomorrow at 1100 hours. Report to me then. I need to send Ike an update on the situation. You'll find me with Kearns."

That worked fine for me, since I planned an early morning visit to Le Ferriere. I wasn't going to let Danny face the Germans alone, not with an American killer at his back. I knew Harding and Kearns wouldn't be happy with my protecting Danny, or tipping off the killer. But it was my kid brother, so colonels and majors be damned.

Chapter Twenty-Five

We found Tenente Luca Amatori at the Anzio Carabinieri headquarters, set up in a seaside casino pockmarked with bullet holes from the initial assault.

"Billy, Kaz," he said, rising from his desk, which had originally been a croupier's table. "I am glad to see you both. Is this a social call, or can I be of assistance?"

"We could use your help," I said as I took a seat. Luca's desk was filled with papers, lists of names and addresses from what I could see. An ornate white-and-gold telephone on his desk rang, and he ignored it, nodding to an officer across the room who picked up the call on another phone.

"Has it to do with the killings? The murders in Caserta?"

"Yes. We need some more information on the connection between Bar Raffaele and Lieutenant Landry."

"But I already told you the little I know,"

Luca said. "And we are quite busy, trying to provide for civil order."

"How many men do you have here?" Kaz asked.

"One hundred and fifty."

"Might not some of them know of Stefano Inzerillo and his bar?" Kaz asked. "Surely some of them visited it for personal reasons, while not on duty, of course."

"I could ask, yes. But as you know, the American military police have jurisdiction in such matters." Luca spread his hands and shrugged, to show how little there was he could do.

"We don't need help with jurisdiction," I said. "I want to know more about the prostitute Landry was involved with, and what happened to her."

"Billy, how can I find a prostitute in Acerra while I am in Anzio?"

"Listen, I know cops, and cops talk about things that are out of the ordinary. Like an American lieutenant trying to talk a prostitute into going straight. It's the kind of naïve thing any veteran cop would get a laugh out of, you know what I mean?"

"Yes, of course. But you must understand, the times are not normal. There are so many Americans, and so many prostitutes. My men come from all over Italy, it is not as if they are all from the area and know everything that goes on. Believe it or not, some of them do not even frequent houses of ill repute."

"It sounds as if you're making excuses," I said. "Is there a reason you don't want to help us?"

"No, not at all. As I told you before, I have only been in the area two months myself. Some of my men even less."

"Maybe you were taking bribes from Inzerillo," I said. "It wouldn't take two months to set that up."

"You have no right to make such an accusation! Are you mad?"

"What, cops in Italy don't take bribes?"

"Why are we even having this discussion?" Luca asked.

"Because we find it hard to believe that an experienced Carabinieri officer would have difficulty with such a simple request," Kaz said.

"Nothing in war is simple," Luca said. "And *I* do not take bribes." He left the implication hanging like a fastball right over the plate.

"But Capitano Renzo Trevisi does?" Kaz said.

"The Capitano grew up outside of Caserta," Luca said. "He knows many people."

"People in Acerra," I said.

"Yes."

"Stefano Inzerillo, for one?"

"I would rather not say. He is my superior officer."

"Luca, I took you for a rookie when we first met. A guy who got a fast promotion, maybe due to the war, but a rookie nonetheless," I said.

"A rook-ee?" he asked, sounding out the word.

"Someone new to the game. I thought the same thing when you came with us to Acerra, to interrogate Inzerillo, since you spilled the beans about Landry being dead."

"Beans?" He looked puzzled.

"Yeah. Don't you watch gangster movies in Italy? That was a rookie move, tipping Inzerillo off, getting him even more nervous than he was. But now I wonder, were you in on it with your capitano? Were you feeding information to Inzerillo and keeping watch on us at the same time?"

"This is ridiculous! You and your American words, they make as much sense as your accusation." He was right, I was making it up as I went along. I didn't think Luca was in cahoots with Trevisi, but I had the feeling he was holding back, and pressure was the best way to find out what.

"Why did a Carabiniere in Acerra call you a Fascist? He said you were a friend of the Nazis."

"I have no idea," Luca said, waving his hand in the air as he looked down at the empty green surface of the croupier's table.

"Was it because of what you did at Rab? At the concentration camp?"

His hand fell from the air, as if a puppet master's string had been cut. "I am not a Fascist," he said, sighing in a way that let us know he'd said it many times before. "I am also not a friend of the Tedeschi. What do you think this has to do with a bordello in Acerra?"

"I think it has something to do with your capitano. He has you under his thumb, and you feel you have to protect him. I'd say Inzerillo was paying him off, and you knew it. You tried to warn Inzerillo that Landry's killer would be coming for him; that's why you blurted out that Landry was dead."

"If it is as you say, then you are wasting your time with me," Luca said. He lit a cigarette, keeping his eyes on the pack, the matches, the ashtray, everything but me.

"No, I don't think so. You don't strike me as a man who likes working for a crooked cop," I said, leaning forward until he had to look me in the eye. "I think you're ashamed of something, and you know that protecting Trevisi is only going to lead to more shame and disgrace. Am I right, Luca?"

Some guys aren't made for lying. Some are. Luca was in between. He put a good face on things, and I'm sure he could lie to a crook or a killer if it meant getting a confession. But something was eating at him, and I knew he wanted to tell all.

"Yes, you are right," he said finally. He took a drag on his cigarette, leaned back and blew smoke at the ceiling. "Capitano Trevisi had business dealings with Inzerillo."

"What kind of dealings?" Kaz asked. Luca only shook his head. It was the same the world over. No cop wants to give up another cop, no matter how dirty. The blue wall of silence.

"That's why he was so glad to offer your services, so you could keep an eye on things?" I said, not asking him a direct question about corruption.

"Yes. He was worried about Inzerillo. He thought there was trouble brewing, even before you came to Caserta."

"Why?"

The truth came easier now. The dam had been broken, and it spilled out. "There was trouble, first with Lieutenant Landry. He threatened to bring in the military police if Inzerillo didn't let one of the girls go."

"I thought Inzerillo didn't run the girls himself."

"He didn't. It was what Ileana told him."

"Ileana? The prostitute Landry fell for?"

"Yes. She told him she needed money to buy her freedom from Inzerillo, that he would not let her go free. Trevisi said it was all a lie, to extort money from the lieutenant who loved her."

"So you lied to us when you said it would be impossible to find her," I said.

"She is gone, that much is true. She fled when she became frightened."

"Frightened by what?"

"One of the soldiers. He threatened to kill her."

"That couldn't have been Landry," I said.

"No, he saw himself as her defender, and she as his Dulcinea." I must have looked puzzled, since he explained. "From *Don Quixote.*"

"A simple peasant girl who becomes Don Quixote's idealized woman," Kaz added.

"Oh yeah," I said. I knew that was an old book, but not much more. "So who threatened her?"

"I only know it was a *sergente.* The same one who gave Inzerillo the beating."

"Was it Sergeant Stumpf?" He came down with venereal disease after partaking of the pleasures at Bar Raffaele. That might be a motive for attacking Inzerillo and the girl.

"I do not know. I would tell you if I did."

"Why didn't you tell us before? Why keep this a secret? You knew we were investigating a murder."

"The murder is another matter entirely. I can only say that this sergente asked for Ileana, even knowing Landry was smitten with her. Perhaps there was some problem between them, but I can only guess at that."

"Why did the sergeant threaten her?"

"Because she laughed at him," Luca said, a bitter laugh escaping his lips. "At his failure in lovemaking. He struck her violently and promised to kill her if she breathed a word. Inzerillo heard her screams and tried to intervene, and was beaten for it. I believe the sergeant came back again to hurt him some more."

"And then a third visit, to kill him."

"If it was the same man. All I know is what I heard from Inzerillo himself. A sergeant, and the second time he came with another man, but he would not say who."

"Inzerillo told you it was a sergeant?"

"Yes, but he would say no more. He and Capitano Trevisi both wanted it kept quiet so there would be no trouble with the military police."

"Do you know where the girl is now?"

"No, truly I do not. Trevisi had her taken away to a farm where she could heal. Not that he is kind, but so she can return to work as soon as possible. In another location, of course." Luca ground out his cigarette and stared at the ashes. Finally he looked at us. "I am sorry for lying to you."

"What does Trevisi have on you?" I asked. "Was it something that happened on Rab? What did you do there?"

"I did nothing," Luca said.

Chapter Twenty-Six

Luca had clammed up tight after that. He'd looked past us, out to sea where the sun was setting and casting a red glow across the horizon. I wondered if he was thinking of the view from the island of Rab, and if he preferred looking out over water to what he'd seen on solid ground.

I'd gotten Kaz on a PT boat shuttling brass between Naples and Anzio, leaving it up to him and his Webley revolver to talk to Trevisi and find Ileana. We needed to know who had beaten her and Inzerillo. That had to be our killer, fixing up loose ends. Maybe Landry was the real target after all, but if so, I couldn't figure out all the red heart stuff. It seemed overly complicated. I was stumped, and our only hope seemed to be that the killer would slip up and leave a clue or two next time. Not the best investigative technique, I'll admit.

Ileana was the key to finding out everything. If she hadn't run off, if she'd talk, and if she wasn't under lock and key in some Naples whorehouse, we had a chance of catching this murderer before he struck again.

But I had another reason for sending Kaz back to Naples. I didn't want him talking me out of heading back to the front in the morning. Someone had to watch over Danny. I might find a clue, but probably not. What I was more likely to find was a lot of lead in the air and bodies on the ground. But I might be able to make sure one of them wasn't Danny's.

Which is why the next morning I was on the road before dawn, driving without lights to Le Ferriere. Grenades in my pockets, extra clips in my ammo belt, Thompson on the seat. The road was packed with vehicles — trucks and ambulances, jeeps crammed with GIs, towed artillery, all strung out on the narrow straight road. If the Luftwaffe paid us a visit after the sun came up, it'd be a shooting gallery. Some of the traffic peeled off onto side roads, but most flowed to the front. Artillery thundered up ahead; outgoing stuff, thank God.

I was half a mile out of Le Ferriere when I noticed that the GIs marching on foot were making better time than I was. And that it was getting light. I didn't want to be a stationary target, so I pulled off the main road, crossing a short bridge over the wide drainage ditch that ran alongside the roadway, and drove down a dirt road until I found a dry spot to pull over. The road was packed with men and vehicles, but out here everything was still. The fields were empty, stubble showing where plants had last been harvested. A few hundred yards away was one of the stone farmhouses that dotted the fields around here, built according to Mussolini's plan. A woman came out of the house and began to hang laundry. White sheets fluttered in the early morning breeze, and the image of domesticity held me for a moment, before I turned to join the column of heavily armed soldiers heading into Le Ferriere.

"Here you go, fellas," a sergeant shouted from the back of an open truck as he tossed out small bundles to each man passing by. "Stick 'em in your pack, they don't weigh much."

"What are these?" I asked as I caught a tightly bound pack of folded white cotton material.

"Mattress cover," he shouted back, not missing a beat as he tossed them to the oncoming men.

"They got mattresses up front?" a skinny kid asked as he stuck the bundle into his pack. Laugher rippled around him, and a corporal by his side shook his head wearily. There were no mattresses waiting in Le Ferriere or beyond, I knew. The Graves Registration Units used them as shrouds for the dead. Usually they carried them to collection points where bodies were left, but they must have been expecting heavy casualties. Some officer who thought less about morale than efficiency probably figured this would save time. A couple of guys tossed the covers by the side of the road, but most kept them, either not knowing what they were for, not caring, or figuring they might get lucky and find some hay to stuff inside. Hell, maybe even a mattress.

As I approached the entrance to the stone wall that encircled the village, a sudden sound pierced my ears, rising above the clatter, clank, and chatter of GIs, the revving of engines, and the crunch of tires on gravel: the shriek of artillery shells. Not the thunderous, sharp sound of our own fire, but the piercing screech of artillery rounds falling toward us. Toward me.

"Incoming!" I yelled at the same moment a few other guys did, and I wasted no time running off the road and leaping face-first onto the flat ground, holding my helmet in place, bracing for the blast that I knew was coming.

The sound shattered the air as the explosions shook the ground and the concussion swept over me, peppering my body with dirt, debris, and who knows what else. The shelling kept on, hitting the village and the roadway precisely. The Germans had this area zeroed in. They knew the column was here, even though we'd come up in the dark and the approach was shielded from their lines by the walled village. I didn't spend much time thinking about that, though. I mainly tried to melt into the ground, praying that I was far enough off the damn road to survive. The ear-splitting crash of each explosion drove everything else from my mind, until there was nothing but the trembling earth beneath and my prayers sent up to the saints.

As quickly as it began, it ended. I moved my limbs, shaking off dirt and making sure everything worked. I was grateful for the silence, until it began to be filled with the groans and cries of the wounded. Smoke roiled from within the village, and wrecks of vehicles littered the road. Men rose from the fields, gazing at those who didn't. A few yards away an arm lay by itself, a gold wedding ring gleaming bright on the still hand. Medics began running out of the village, seeking the wounded, finding plenty. Most of the dead had been caught in the road, slow to react. The words to a prayer ran through my mind: *from thence he shall come to judge the quick and the dead.* I had to get into the village and find Danny, make sure he was still among the quick. As I got to the road, I saw the Graves Registration sergeant, dead, mattress covers smoldering at his feet.

My ears were ringing as I stumbled into Le Ferriere. Rubble spilled out into the street where buildings had taken hits. GIs began to file out of the standing structures, eyes cast to the skies, ears tilted to hear the incoming rounds. Officers formed them up and got them moving, toward the German lines. I passed one building that took a direct hit, the sign for 2nd Battalion HQ blackened but readable.

"Third Platoon, Easy Company?" I asked one lieutenant. "Know where they are?"

"Easy pushed off before dawn. They're out there somewhere," he said, pointing with his thumb to the open fields that led to a wooded rise across the Mussolini Canal. "You might be able to see the advance from the third floor of that factory over there. It's full of brass who came to watch the show."

"I'll give it a try anyway," I said.

"Good luck." He returned to his men, probably knowing that everyone's luck ran out, sooner or later. I climbed the metal steps up the outside wall of the factory, a short, squat concrete building that had a few chunks blown out of it, but was still in one piece. The third floor looked out over the town wall, to the northeast and the waiting Krauts. Inside, a gaggle of officers stood at the far wall, their binoculars trained on the advance. Their helmets and jackets were covered in dust shaken loose from the bombardment, but otherwise they were in good shape. No getting caught out on the open road for them. On a table near the door were thermoses of coffee and a couple bottles of bourbon. A man gets thirsty watching a battle, after all.

A lieutenant turned, probably checking to be sure I wouldn't swipe the booze. It was easy to tell he was an aide to a senior officer. Clean boots, a good shave, and a West Point ring on his finger. He was along to carry the booze and get points for being at the front, so his benefactors in the West Point Protective Association could promote him as soon as possible.

"Can I help you?" he asked.

"Where's Easy Company headed?"

"Battalion HQ could help you. They're down the street."

"They're in pieces. Who's running the show here?"

"Boyle?" It was Harding. He and Kearns detached themselves from the scrum of officers and gave a nod to the aide to let him know I was allowed access to the high and mighty. Ring knockers, we called them, for those big academy graduation rings they flashed around. "What happened to Battalion HQ?"

"Direct hit. If anyone's alive in there, they aren't up to running this attack. You didn't know?"

Neither of them answered, but Kearns was off, taking the aide with him. Maybe the kid would get his boots dirty.

"What are you doing here?" Harding asked.

"Checking on my kid brother," I said. I saw no reason to lie. Harding knew me pretty well, and I thought I had his number. He was a straight shooter, and he responded best to the truth, even when it went against regulations.

"Easy Company, Third Platoon, right?"

"Yes sir. How are they doing?"

He handed me binoculars and eased a major out of the way at the window. "See that track, across the canal?" I did. It was bigger than a path, smaller than a road. Drainage ditches had been dug on both sides, and the piled earth gave a few inches of cover. Small trees and shrubs grew along the ditches, giving some visual cover too. "They headed up there. Two companies on either side, spread out in the fields. The objective is that wooded rise beyond them."

I could make out men crawling in the road and across the fields. Others lay still, dead, or scared out of their wits. Explosions hit the wooded rise, but through the binoculars I could see the deadly sparkle of machine guns sending controlled bursts down into the advancing GIs. It was terrible, that ripping chainsaw sound of the MG42, a machine gun they called the Bonesaw. It spewed out 1200 rounds per minute, so fast that you couldn't hear the individual shots, just a blur of noise that sounded like heavy fabric tearing. Against that fire I could make out the almost leisurely *rat-tat-tat* of our machine guns, no match for the dug-in German firepower.

"They need smoke, and air cover," I said. "Do you have a radio here?"

"No," Harding said. "The communications gear was in the headquarters building, and the cloud cover is too low for air support. Hell, we're just here to escort the visiting brass, and to observe." He nearly spit out that last word as he grabbed my arm. "Come on, Boyle. I'll find a way to call in smoke and get more artillery on that hill. You find your brother and his platoon and help them out, then get word back to me. That's what you wanted, right?"

"Yes sir. I'll send a runner back and let you know how far they've gotten." I sprinted down the street, heading for the north gate that opened to the fields and the storm of steel and death my kid brother had plunged into. Danny, who used to follow me everywhere, who got bullied when I wasn't around, who was smarter than I was though I never admitted it, who I'd punched in the arm, hard, more times than I could count — Danny, out there, alone. Meaning with no one he could count on. No family, no Irish, no veteran platoon leader. I jumped smoking craters and debris until I was clear of Le Ferriere. As I descended the slope, I could barely make out the tiny shapes of crawling men amidst the smoke and dust of battle. In the distance, three Sherman tanks made their way along a narrow road across the canal, the first good news of the morning. Bad news caught up with the lead Sherman as it blew up, black smoke churning out of every hatch. The other two tanks reversed, not wanting to roll over another Teller mine or into the sights of a hidden antitank gun. They retreated, I went forward, and I couldn't help thinking they knew what they were doing.

Chapter Twenty-Seven

I came across the litter bearers first, hustling the wounded back to aid stations along the canal. Mortar rounds were landing near the closest bridge, so I went into the water, scrambling up the embankment into chaos. Two jeeps, pulling trailers stacked with dead, careened across the field, evading enemy fire so vigorously that the bodies leapt with every jolt, arms and legs bouncing as if they'd come alive. Machine-gun rounds chewed up the fields and zinged over my head, the odd thrum like a hornet buzzing by my ear. White phosphorous rounds began to land to our front, and I knew Harding had managed to get the coordinates to the artillery. Thick white smoke blossomed in the morning air, and I ran until I found the dirt track.

It was crowded with men, prone and pressed tight on either side, up against the cover of the ditch wall. The fields on either side had a gentle rise to them, like a lazy wave about to crest. It was less than a foot high, but when everything else is dead flat, a foot is damn good cover. That's where the advance on the flanks of the road had stopped. Men had scraped shallow depressions in the soil and rolled into them, protected at least from machine-gun fire. To their rear, a trail of bodies stretched back to the canal.

"Is this Easy Company?" I asked. "Who's in charge?"

"This here's Fox Company, and you better get your damn head down," a corporal snapped at me. "If you got further use for it, that is." That got a laugh.

"Where is Easy Company?" I stood up, straight as I could. It was crazy, I knew. I'd seen Harding do it a couple of times, taking a chance on stopping a bullet in order to show men he wasn't afraid and they shouldn't be either. I didn't give a damn about morale; I just wanted a straight answer fast. This at least got the corporal's attention.

"Down that way, Lieutenant," he said. "We were supposed to follow them, but we got pinned down. There was supposed to be a smoke screen a long time ago."

"Pinned down, my ass! Where's your officer?"

"Captain's right there," he said, pointing to a medic hunched over a body, bloody compresses scattered on the ground.

"Jesus," I said, and wished that hadn't popped out so loud. I was going to have to do something about morale whether I liked it or not. No one else was left standing. "Lieutenants? Platoon sergeants?"

"Dead. Mortar round caught them in a huddle, havin' themselves a powwow. Captain took us this far, then he took one in the chest. The boys and I took a look and figured this was a good place to hunker down."

"I'm in command now, Corporal. Get up, we're heading up to support Easy Company. You," I said, pointing to a PFC who looked only half scared to death. "You're my runner. Hightail it back to the village and find Colonel Harding. He's either at Battalion HQ or in that factory building on the same street. Tell him the advance is stalled and that I'm taking Fox Company forward to locate Easy. You got that?"

"Harding," he repeated. "The advance is stalled at this point. Fox going forward to find Easy. Who are you?"

"Boyle. Now run there and run back here,

fast as you can. Go." I waited for a few long seconds as he stared up at me. If he refused to go, that was it. If I couldn't get one GI to head back, I sure as hell wasn't going to get fifty of them to move up.

"Yes sir," he said, and was off like a jack-rabbit.

"Corporal, if you're the ranking noncom, then get your men moving. Follow me."

I didn't look back, and I didn't try to rouse the men. That was his job, and I had no idea if he was up to it. I crouched low, to show them that I wasn't completely insane. I heard the rustle of gear, curses, and the sound of boots on the ground. I broke into a trot, and the sound of men following me into the swirling smoke was the sweetest, most terrible sound of my life. Each death would be on my head.

The sound of mortar fire lessened. The German machine guns slowed their rate of fire, too, sending short bursts into the smoke, hoping for a hit. The *crump* of explosions ahead of us told me Harding had zeroed in on the hill, which would also make the Krauts keep their heads down. I picked up the pace, figuring the less time upright the better my chances were. Visibility was low, but the track was even and easy to follow.

It was then that I tripped. A dead GI lay half in the ditch, half on the track. I went sprawling and fell onto another body, but this one was alive. I lifted myself up and called for a medic. There were none with us.

"Water," he gasped in a raspy voice. I looked closer, and saw he must have been hit by shrapnel. His jacket was shredded and bloody, and one side of his face was torn and blackened. "Water, please."

I unscrewed my canteen and only then did I look at his face; not his wounds, but his face. Steel-rimmed spectacles lay bent and broken by his head. He was a kid, with the same color hair. My hand shook, and I reached for my canteen.

"Danny?"

"Water," the voice said, fainter.

"Danny!" I poured the water on his face, washing away the blood. His eyes bore into mine, beseeching me.

"Water."

It wasn't Danny. I rose and ran, as fast as I could. I couldn't face that wounded kid, I couldn't admit to my fear, to how I felt in my heart at that moment of mistaken identity. It was a cowardly thing to do, to leave him like that, I knew. I told myself someone else would give him water, somebody would be glad for the excuse to hang back. But it was all a lie. I was afraid, that's all. Afraid for Danny and maybe even more afraid for myself. If he died out here, I'd carry that guilt forever.

Now I knew. Now I understood my father. Now I was my father. He'd drummed it into me a million times. *Family comes first.* The Boyles, then the Boston PD, then Ireland. But family first. That's what leaving a dead brother on the battlefield does. That's what finding his brother Frank dead in the trenches of the last war did to him. I felt it in my heart, and it pained me, for all of us.

If I had been alone, I would have wept. But I wasn't, so I barked orders to cover my fears. We were too bunched up, so I got the men spread out, advancing straight down the track and on the flanks. I strained for the sound of our own weapons ahead, but there was too much racket. Not being able to see, it seemed as if the noise was on all sides, surrounding us, echoing in the empty air. They had to be dead ahead, I thought, then wished I'd used a different choice of words.

I felt a breeze at my back. It became a gust, and I could see the smoke drifting past me, coils of misty white churning at my feet, drifting off my shoulders, making for that wooded rise where the enemy waited: their eyes squinted along gun barrels, desperate for a glimpse of us. The cloud cover above had turned dark and swollen, and a salt smell came in with the wind. A storm was brewing, and it was blowing in from behind us, stripping us of the only cover we had.

"Run!" I yelled. "Run!" I prayed they'd heard me, and knew which way. I looked behind me, and could see far enough to know that whatever was left of Fox Company was still with me, and that the smoke wasn't. It blew past me, leaving a clear view to the rear, and at a run I could barely keep up with it. If we didn't find cover or Easy Company, it was going to be a turkey shoot. The guys around me understood, and we all picked up the pace, eyes darting across the revealed landscape, legs pumping, weapons at the ready.

The disappearing smoke revealed a streambed, fifty yards up. GIs waved us by while they watched the smoke roll on, cresting against the wooded rise, breaking like waves on the shore. Thirty yards to go, then twenty, and I could make out the shape of trees. Ten yards, then three long strides and I leapt into the streambed as the MG42s opened up, shredding the air with their terrible mechanical constancy.

"Where the hell have you been?" Evans demanded as I rolled out of the foot-deep water and threw myself against the bank. Bullets clipped the ground above us and zinged overhead, sending clumps of earth flying in the fields where we had been. I knew Evans didn't mean me especially; I wasn't even sure he recognized me.

"Evans, it's me, Billy Boyle. Where's your company commander?" I ached to ask about Danny but I had to focus on the jam we were in.

"Dead. Same with the other two platoon leaders. If this stream wasn't here we'd all be dead. What the hell happened to our support? Why are you here, anyway?"

"Doesn't matter," I said, answering his last question first and giving him points for even thinking of it right now. "HQ took a direct hit in that barrage, got knocked out. There was no one coordinating the attack or calling in artillery."

"We're supposed to have tank support," he said.

"I saw them hit a minefield and take off. I sent a runner back with our position. Maybe he can make it back with orders. You have a radio?"

"No, not even a walkie-talkie. Your brother's okay, last I saw anyway."

"Thanks," I said, letting the relief settle in, then pushing it aside. We all still had to get out of this alive. "Listen, there's something I wanted to ask you —"

"Jesus, Boyle, there's a time and place for everything. Just tell me where the Fox Company CO is."

"Dead, or near so last I saw. Highest rank left seems to be a corporal."

"Jesus Christ."

"No kidding. You're in charge, Evans. What's the situation?"

"We've got good cover right here, couple of hundred yards in either direction. Except for when they drop mortar rounds on us, but they might be running low on ammo. We haven't been hit too hard for a while. Their big stuff sails right over. With the men you brought, we probably have eighty or so effectives, not counting the walking wounded and litter cases. Father Dare and a medic are set up down a ways, with Louie's squad." As if on cue, artillery shells whistled overhead, detonating to our rear, showering us with dirt that rained on our helmets and hunched shoulders.

"Where does this stream lead?" I asked. It wasn't much of a stream, at least not this time of year. Damp gravel fell from the banks, littered in places with torn and bloody bandages. But it was deep enough for cover, and for that it was our Garden of Eden.

"To the left it loops around the woods. To the right to turns south, back to our lines. But we'd be exposed for about three hundred yards. They'd chew us up. And with this wind, more smoke wouldn't last long enough to give us cover."

"Okay, watch for the runner. I'm going to check on the wounded." We both knew I meant Danny. I duckwalked in the cold water until I found Father Dare. He'd found a bit of flat, dry ground next to the bank, and he and a medic were patching guys up as best they could.

"Lieutenant Boyle, was that you who brought the cavalry?" Father Dare asked, as he wound a bandage around the thigh of a GI who grimaced as he did. Once again, I had to wonder, could a murderer soothe the wounded and then kill the living?

"Jeez, Father, can't you give me some morphine? The pain is killing me," the GI said through clenched teeth.

"I could, but then when we get out of here, it might take two fellows to carry you. You'll have to hang on, son. I'm sure the lieutenant here is bringing good news, aren't you, Boyle?"

"Sure. Fox Company's here and we're back in contact with headquarters. They'll be in touch soon. Hang in there," I said, patting the wounded man on the shoulder.

"Easy for you to say," he gasped, but I saw relief flicker across his face. I hoped I wasn't talking through my helmet.

"Shrapnel," Father Dare whispered as we turned away. "Too deep, otherwise I'd cut it out myself. How bad are things, really?"

I told him what happened to headquarters and about Harding taking over, and the losses Fox Company had taken trying to get to them.

"If we'd made this push yesterday, we might have had a chance. But now the Germans are dug in on every piece of high ground within a mile," he said.

"Yeah, and they seemed to know we were coming. They dropped artillery right on the village and the approach road this morning, caught everyone with their pants down."

"It's a real FUBAR situation," Father Dare said, then pointed. "He's down that way, Boyle. Hasn't done anything stupid, so he may be all right."

I thanked him, and went down on my hands and knees until I ran into Louie, leaning against the bank and smoking a cigar, his feet in the water.

"Hey, Louie," I said.

"It's Louie Walla from Walla Walla," he said, with a smile.

"Having fun out here, Louie?"

"Walla from Walla Walla," he finished for me.

"Exactly."

"Well, why not? I'm down to my last stogie, the Krauts got the high ground, what am I gonna do, cry? Not me. I figure this here cigar will drive 'em crazy. Krauts got lousy tobacco, you know? This is my secret weapon." He blew a plume of smoke straight up, letting the stiff breeze take it straight to the Germans.

"We got them right where we want them, Louie Walla from Walla Walla. Where's Danny?"

"Right behind that clump of bushes. Kid ain't half bad for a college boy." He went on puffing, oddly serene, especially compared to how sullen he'd been the last time I saw him.

"Billy!" Danny said, nearly jumping up when he saw me. Charlie Colorado put a stop to that with one hand on his shoulder.

"How's it going, kid?"

"Charlie says he's been in worse spots," Danny said. He leaned against the gravelly bank, loose sand and stones giving way and tumbling down to his boots. His hands gripped his M1, knuckles turning white. He looked away from me, digging his helmet into the earth as if he wanted to burrow into it.

"Don't worry, Danny," I said. "Everyone's scared. But we'll get out of this, believe me."

"I'm not scared. Well, maybe I am, who wouldn't be?"

"Right," I said, sensing that I was missing something.

"Danny is a good shot. He is a warrior today," Charlie said.

"I killed a man, Billy."

I put my hand on his shoulder. There were no words for this moment. Sure, that was what we were here for. Kill or be killed and all that. But when it was your little brother bearing the burden of death, words seemed useless. But I felt I had to come up with something. "The real test is not living or dying, kid. It's killing and living."

"It felt strange," Danny said. "Like I should have felt worse about it. But then I felt bad that I didn't."

"It was his time to die, not yours," Charlie said. "Usen gave you good eyes and a steady hand. He would not want you to turn away from his gifts."

"When did this happen?" I liked it that

Usen was watching out for Danny, but I needed to know what was going on in the here and now.

"Not long ago," Danny said. "Flint found a gully that leads up to the hill. We crawled up it and got an angle on the machine gun crew. They were firing into the smoke and didn't see us. I lined up a shot and took it. I got the gunner, saw his helmet fly off. Then they started throwing grenades, and we had to get back."

"Why Flint? Louie's your squad leader."

"Louie is dead," Charlie said.

"No he isn't, I just talked to him."

"Louie is dead," he repeated. "He knows it is his time, and he is waiting. He is dead."

"He is acting strange," Danny said. "Like he doesn't have a care in the world."

"He knows he is free of this earth," Charlie said.

"But why —" I didn't get a chance to finish. Stump crawled up to us, hugging the embankment.

"Sorry to interrupt the reunion, boys. Billy, that runner you sent made it back."

"How'd he get through?"

"He said a Colonel Harding turned him right around, sent him up the streambed in the other direction. Come on."

Danny and I shook hands, putting on a

good show for everyone watching, saying "See ya later" like we'd meet up at Kirby's for a beer. I followed Stump. The odd shot rang out from above, but it had turned quiet. I figured the Krauts knew they had us pinned good. If I were in their shoes, I'd hustle up some reinforcements before nightfall, when we had a better chance of pulling out in the dark. Until then, I'd conserve my ammo, just like they were doing.

The PFC was with Evans and Flint, and they were all checking watches. Flint gave a curt nod as he set his watch, all business.

"Boyle," Evans said. "We're moving out in fifteen."

"What's your name?" I asked the PFC. Evans was doing all right, but I wanted to hear exactly what Harding had planned, and this kid was the only one with a clue.

"Kawulicz, Lieutenant. Robert Kawulicz. But they call me Bobby K, on account of the Polack name."

"Okay, Bobby K, I'm going to tell Colonel Harding it's time for corporal's stripes as soon as we get back. Now tell me what he said to you."

"He told me that if I could get to you, I could bring you back. He pointed me down that streambed, and sent a few smoke rounds in. The wind didn't take it like it did above ground. I stayed low, had to crawl in a few places, but they never saw me."

"Good work, Bobby K. You ready to lead us back?"

"Sure as hell don't want to stay here," he said.

"Okay, the smoke is going to hit all over, but mainly on the streambed," Evans said. "So the Germans won't know what we're up to. Stump, go tell Father Dare to get the wounded up front. We don't have much time."

"That's why the wounded should be at the tail of the column," I said, hating how easily the words came.

"No, we have to take care of the wounded, especially the litter cases," Evans said. "That's an order. I'm in command here, not you, Boyle."

"Billy's right," Flint said. Stump nodded his agreement. "The wounded will go as fast as they can, which is slower than the rest of us. Put them up front and you slow down eighty or so men. Say someone drops a litter, and everyone has to wait. The wind could kick up even worse, and suck the smoke right out of that streambed. Then we're all dead men."

"Put the wounded in the rear, they'll make it out almost as quick," Stump said. "Without endangering everyone else."

Evans was silent. He was new to the mathematics of war.

"Time's wasting," Flint said.

"Okay, Okay. Bobby, you're our scout. Flint, take him up front. Have Louie's squad close behind you. Keep an eye on him. Boyle, will you help the medic and Father Dare with the wounded?"

"Yeah, no problem." Evans was learning fast. Why risk one of your own men as tail-end Charlie?

"Send Louie up front, okay?" Flint said. I nodded and crawled off.

"We going back already?" Louie asked when I told him the plan. "I ain't finished my cigar."

"Train's leaving the station, Louie Walla from Walla Walla. Take care of my kid brother, okay?"

"My days of takin' care of people are over," Louie said.

"That's a sergeant's job, isn't it?"

"In this war, a sergeant's job is to get killed or go crazy. Rusty took care of all of us, and look what happened to him. I'm next, I know it."

"Hey, you're not dead yet, are you?" I said, trying to snap him out of it. He looked at me like I was crazy, which didn't surprise me. "You're still breathing, so get your squad up front, and keep them low and quiet."

I told the same thing to Danny and Charlie. Sticks was with them, the tall kid from the squad. I wished them luck. Father Dare and the medic had two litter cases and half a dozen walking wounded. Other men who'd been wounded slightly were already with their squads. The main problem was that we weren't walking, we were crawling.

The wounded guys didn't need much encouragement, not even the GI with shrapnel in his leg. No one wanted to be captured and have to depend on POW medical care. Carrying the litters was tough. We shanghaied one GI to help the medic, and Father Dare and I took the other. We had to duckwalk, holding the litter up to clear the ground. It was easy for the first few awkward steps, then near impossible, until finally spasms of pain were shooting through my arms and thighs.

"You were right, Boyle," Evans said as we halted next to him. "About the wounded."

"You would've figured it out," I said. "We ready?"

"As we can be. Two minutes until the artillery hits the hill and they lay smoke." Eighty men hugged the edge of the bank, all facing the same direction, waiting for the signal. "Good luck," Evans said, and was off, bent low, checking the men. There was going to be no safe place; it was either going to work or it wasn't. I spent the two minutes catching my breath, rubbing my sore thighs, not thinking about Danny in the lead.

The screech of incoming shells was followed instantly by multiple explosions on the wooded hill. The firing continued, keeping the Germans occupied, I hoped. Muted explosions to our rear were followed by plumes of churning white smoke concentrated along our escape route. The line ahead of me shuffled forward, slowly, like a long line of cars when the light changes. We moved, stopped, moved, stopped. I wanted to scream, to tell them to hurry up, but I bit my lip. Low and quiet, I told myself.

Finally we were moving, into the smoke. It was thick enough for us to run bent over, keeping our heads just below the surface. The smoke swirled in places and settled into thick pools in others. The artillery fire on the hill stopped, and for a moment there was nothing but an eerie, empty silence. The small sounds of leather, metal, and gear, boots on muddy soil, and hurried whispers quickly filled the void. Bursts of white phosphorous smoke landed behind us, and for the first time I thought we had a chance.

Machine-gun fire ripped through the air, probing the ditch we'd just left. I felt the air vibrate above me as the rounds searched farther afield, stitching the earth, hoping for flesh.

The line halted. Father Dare, at the front of the litter, nearly collided with the medic. An awful groaning sound rose up ahead of us, and I knew someone had been hit. A stray bullet, I hoped for the rest of us. For the man hit, it made no difference. We laid down the litters and Father Dare gave the other wounded men water. We waited while impatient murmurs ran up and down the line. I was the last man, and felt nothing but the white emptiness of death behind me. I fought the urge to leap out of the streambed and run for it, taking my chances with speed and leaving this ghostly, slow retreat behind.

Minutes passed, and we began shuffling along again. I lost track of time, hunched over, carrying the burden of a badly wounded man, able to see nothing beyond a yard away. The machine-gun fire rose in intensity, and this time it was aimed at us. The Krauts had figured it out, and were spraying the general vicinity with all they had. Clods of dirt kicked up along the bank as we bent further down, our arms heavy with the weight we carried. I had to tilt my head back to see anything, and I could barely make out Father Dare.

The air thrummed with bullets, hundreds of rounds slicing above us, looking for the right angle, the perfect trajectory of bullet and bone.

They found it. Screams tore loose from throats ahead of us, the sounds of men dying. It was like a dam breaking — no more low and quiet, but a footrace as the column sprinted, trying to outrun the Bonesaw, fear taking over where caution had been in control. The bursts kept coming, and I heard Stump coming down the line, telling us to hustle, we were almost there. He stayed with us as we passed bodies being carried out, including Flint with Louie draped over his shoulders, fireman style. Other GIs were carrying wounded between them, and I was too exhausted to even look for Danny. We ran until the streambed curved and brought us out into a field, behind a stone farmhouse. Medics were waiting, and in the swirl of smoke I saw Harding, standing next to a couple of Carabinieri. What were they doing here? We set down the litter, and I collapsed against the wall, my chest heaving, my lungs choking on the smoke, my mind as clouded as the air.

Chapter Twenty-Eight

Somebody gave me a canteen and I drank half of its contents down and poured the rest over my head. The damned gray haze was everywhere, and now smoke grenades were tossed out to cover the jeeps coming up for the wounded. I managed to stand, and Harding materialized out of the swirling clouds.

"You okay, Boyle?"

"Yeah, I'm fine. Thanks for getting us out, Colonel."

"I wasn't entirely sure that runner would make it."

"I told him you'd make him a corporal once we got back."

"I'll see to it. Your kid brother okay?"

"I'm pretty sure, but I need to find him."

"Get a move on then. We have a report of Kraut tanks on the other side of that hill. If they decide to hit us now, things could get worse real fast."

Clutching a pair of binoculars, Harding was off to observe the German lines while I went in search of Danny. It was a mass of confusion, the badly wounded waiting for evacuation, the lightly wounded being treated behind the stone farmhouse, as smoke eddied and curled around the building and along the ground. I found Evans trying to sort out his squads from the crowd. He hadn't seen Danny. Dead bodies were laid out, about half a dozen, but I didn't want to look there yet. Flint walked by me, glassy-eyed, working the thousand-yard stare, so I didn't ask him how Louie was doing.

Father Dare was with the medics, looking about ready to pass out himself. He'd seen Stump and his squad, and thought he'd seen Danny and Charlie head down the road to Le Ferriere. I went in that direction as the Krauts lobbed a few mortar shells at us. It was halfhearted, as if they knew we'd pulled a fast one and were only going through the motions, but I jumped into a shell hole until it was over anyway.

When the shelling stopped, I looked up to see I was sharing the hole with Phil Einsmann.

"Hey Billy, helluva mess, isn't it?"

"What are you doing up here, Phil?"

"I was with a party of brass who came up to observe the advance. I snuck away for a closer look and nearly got my head blown off. Were you out there?"

"Yeah. Most of us made it back. Watch out for yourself, Phil. The Krauts aren't going to be looking for that war correspondent's patch on your shoulder."

"I hope I don't get that close. But if I do, look what I won in a poker game last night." He opened his jacket to show me his .45 automatic in a shoulder holster.

"Nice," I said. "For a noncombatant. Ditch that if you're captured."

"Not planning on that either. You going back to the village?"

"After I find my kid brother. Good luck," I said, climbing out the shell hole. I wandered down the road, looking at small clusters of GIs sharing canteens or a smoke, laughing as if they hadn't nearly been killed. Or because.

"Billy!" It was Danny and his pal, leaning against a tree by the side of the road, eating K rations. Canned cheese and biscuits. It actually looked good. I sat down next to him and we just grinned at each other. He gave me a biscuit with cheese and for some reason it seemed like the funniest thing in the world. We both started laughing, and

Charlie even joined in, understanding how good it felt to be alive and in the company of someone you cared about.

"I saw Flint carrying Louie out," I said. "Is it bad?"

"Louie is dead," Charlie said.

"I know, but how is he?"

"Billy, Louie is really dead. Sticks too. They both got it in the head," Danny said.

"Jesus," I said. "What a waste." Another round of mortar fire came in, closer this time, leaving no time for mourning. Jeeps with wounded laid out on litters zipped down the road, making for the safety of Le Ferriere. "They're getting closer."

"We had to get out of the smoke," Danny said. "Charlie doesn't like it. He got lost for a while, but I found him."

"It is not a good place to die," Charlie said. "A man's soul would be lost as sure as I was. Louie should have waited for a better place."

Danny raised an eyebrow, not in a mocking way, but in sympathy. It sort of made sense, considering the riverbed was underground and smoke still drifted out of it. It was hard enough for the living to get out, never mind the recently departed.

"The smoke did save our lives," I offered.

"True. But it did not save Louie."

"Hard to argue —" A sharp *crack* cut me off, followed a second later by a massive explosion that engulfed the farmhouse and blew out the back wall where the wounded had been moments ago. Another retort echoed and the roof blew up, sending debris sky high. The force of the blasts was so great that the concussion instantly evaporated the smoke. This wasn't mortar fire, it was high-velocity cannon fire.

"Get back to Le Ferriere," I said to Danny as I ran to the farmhouse. As usual, he didn't listen to me, lieutenant or not. I closed in on the scene with him and Charlie on my heels. A section of roof collapsed, and granite stones fell from the weakened rear wall like tears.

"Tigers!" someone yelled, and others took up the call. Every GI thought every German tank was a Tiger tank, but today they had it nailed. Four Tigers, their 88-mm guns pointed straight at us, were trundling across the fields, infantry spread out behind them. Harding had been right: we were sitting ducks, a mass of disorganized men with practically no cover. We had to get back to the village.

"Fall back, fall back!" I yelled, and few needed the encouragement. I saw one Tiger halt, and knew what that meant. "Get down!"

Another shell slammed into the farmhouse, this one bringing down the roof completely, starting a fire inside. Behind the gutted ruin, two GIs were struggling to get up, blood and dust caked on their faces.

"Help these two get to the village," I said, pointing out the wounded men to Danny and Charlie. I searched for Evans, not finding him anywhere, the flames and smoke making it hard to see. The heat drove me back and I stumbled over someone. I knelt and shook the man to check if he was alive. It was Louie. I'd stumbled across the dead, already laid out for Graves Registration. I could see the hit he'd taken, right at the base of the skull. It wasn't pretty. I saw something else, too. Gunshot residue on his neck. Powder burns from a weapon held close to his head.

"Billy, help!" It was Flint, half carrying Evans, whose arm hung limp and dripped blood. Evans looked to be in shock, his mouth half open and eyes wide. "Back there, Stump's hurt."

I stumbled in the direction Flint had indicated, moving against the flow of the last of the dazed GIs making their way to Le Ferriere, my mind reeling. Who had shot

Louie at close range, and why? Is that why Louie thought his time was up? Did he see it coming? And did this confirm Louie wasn't the killer? Or did someone take revenge on him? All I knew was that another GI was dead, robbed of his chance for survival. It was a slim chance, but it was all he had in the world.

Two more explosions wracked the earth, and I hit the dirt, feeling debris rain down on me. The clanking of tank treads grew louder, and I rose, shaking off the dust and confusion, willing my body to move faster, to get the hell out before the place was swarming with Krauts, or those tanks got close enough to use their machine guns.

I heard a hacking, choking sound and crawled toward it. I saw two bodies, off to the side of what had been the farmhouse. One was still, the other on his knees, struggling with something wound around his neck, dust and dirt coating his hair and face. I got closer and saw it was Harding. He was pulling at the leather straps of his binoculars, and my mind struggled to understand what I was seeing, to figure out what he was doing. His mouth was open, gasping for air, getting damn little, and I saw the tightly wound straps digging into the skin of his neck. I drew my knife and cut at the leather, knowing we had only seconds before he lost consciousness, the tanks were on us, or both.

The binoculars fell and Harding drew in a wheezing lungful of air. Deep red welts rose on his neck where the strap had gouged his skin. He motioned to Stump, unable to speak. I felt Stump's neck and found a pulse. He had a nasty gash over one eye, and there was a lot of blood, but other than that I didn't see another wound. But what I did see was a king of hearts, crumpled in his clenched fist. I opened his hand and showed it to Harding, although he already had a pretty good idea.

Harding and I draped Stump over our shoulders and dragged him away, the sound of tank treads and German war cries not far behind. We met up with Danny and Charlie outside of Le Ferriere, as our artillery began to pound the area around the farmhouse, ground we had held and given up. They took Stump and we entered the village through the gate where the attack had begun early that morning, and I wondered if the brass had stuck around to watch the retreat of the survivors. Probably not.

An antitank gun was wheeled up and positioned at the gate. All I cared about was getting some peace and quiet to think things through, which was a bit difficult with an artillery barrage sailing over my head and Tiger tanks a half mile down the road. We headed to the aid station, which was doing brisk business. Most of the wounded were being treated outside, with only the most serious cases going inside the small building, one of the few structures in Le Ferriere that had escaped damage. Ambulances pulled up and medics loaded wounded aboard, then returned to the line of men with bloody bandages and dazed looks.

We laid Stump down and Danny began to clean his head wound, washing away blood with water from his canteen and applying sulfa powder. Harding sat on the ground, still not looking all that well. I gave him my canteen and he drank thirstily.

"Can you talk, Colonel?"

"Get . . . his . . . weapon," he managed to croak out. I took Stump's .45 from his holster as Danny looked at me strangely. I checked the magazine as I sat down next to Harding. There were six rounds, and one in the chamber, meaning one had been fired. I sniffed the barrel. Recently.

"Louie, Danny's squad sergeant, was shot in the back of the head, close range," I said. "Probably when we came under fire in the streambed. With the smoke and the noise, no one would have noticed one more guy going down. Can you tell me what happened to you?"

"Thought I saw vehicles. Used binoculars," Harding said, choking out each word. "Next thing, someone's twisting the strap around my neck. Forced me to the ground. Almost had me, then that Tiger opened up. I blacked out, then you were cutting the strap."

"I found Stump about ten feet from where you were. Did you see who attacked you?" Harding shook his head no, and drank more water. I went over to Stump and checked him again. The cut on his forehead was bad, but that seemed to be his only injury. He was probably hit by a piece of wood or masonry. If it had been shrapnel, he'd have been dead. I went through his pockets as Danny stood back. Nothing unusual.

"What's going on, Billy?" Danny asked. I took the card from my pocket and showed Danny. He whistled. I stowed it away and put my finger to my lips, signaling him to keep quiet about it. Then I brought him over to Harding, who'd managed to stand up.

"Colonel Harding, this is my brother Danny." I was glad Danny didn't play the rookie and try to salute. Harding nodded and stuck out his hand, and they shook.

"Billy has told us a lot about you, Colonel."

"I can only imagine," Harding said, his voice returning but still sounding harsh. "He's mentioned you as well. You hold up all right out there?"

"I think so, sir."

"He did, Colonel, I can vouch for that," I said.

"Good to meet you, son. Take care of yourself. Stay low out there," Harding growled.

"I will, sir. That's just what Billy tells me."

"Danny, see if you can find Lieutenant Evans. Flint probably brought him here."

"Okay, Billy," he said, and he and Charlie began searching the wounded.

"Do we have our killer?" Harding asked.

"Sure looks like it. He had you lined up to be part of his royal flush."

"I was in the wrong place at the right time, for him anyway. I never was so glad to almost be killed by a German 88."

"I don't think he's going anywhere soon, but can you keep an eye on him? I want to find Father Dare." I handed Harding Stump's .45.

"Not a problem," Harding said. "I hear the padre does good work as a medic."

"He does," I said, thinking about the .45 that he carried. Plenty of guys who weren't officially issued automatic pistols, like Father Dare, got them one way or the other. How many of those weapons were out there today, in the smoke? A fair number, but most wouldn't have been fired at all. This fighting hadn't been at close quarters. I stared at Stump's face, cleaned of blood and grime, and wondered why. Why did the killings start, and why did they have to go on?

I asked around and a medic told me he saw Father Dare enter the village church, a few buildings down. I climbed the steps and opened the carved wooden doors, feeling the weight of centuries behind them. The small church had been hit by a shell on the roof, and thick, heavy timbers had fallen in, crushing rows of pews. Father Dare knelt at the altar, his helmet on the floor, his head bowed. He swayed, and it seemed as if he were so lost in prayer that he might lose his balance. I stepped closer, not wanting to interrupt his prayers, but unwilling to let him crack his head against the marble altar. I went to steady him, and only then noticed the pool of blood spreading under his left leg.

"Father," I said, kneeling at his side. Even though he was a rough-and-tumble padre, and we'd dodged bullets together, here in God's house I felt ill at ease, like the altar boy I'd been, unsure of the ways of adults and especially priests. "Are you all right?"

"I am praying, Billy. Praying for God himself to come down and save us. I told him to leave Jesus home, that this was no place for children." He folded his hands in prayer once again, and fell into my arms.

"Shrapnel in his calf," the medic told me after I'd carried Father Dare back. "He must have been bleeding into his boot, and when he knelt down, it all came out."

"Is he going to be okay?"

"He won't be dancing anytime soon, but it should heal up. It's mostly shock that concerns me, losing all that blood. It would have been a lot worse if you hadn't gotten him back here." With that, he went back to tending to the last of the wounded, the less serious cases who'd had to wait.

Danny had found Evans, on a litter, waiting for the next ambulance. His arm and shoulder were heavily bandaged, and an IV drip had been set up on a rifle set in the ground by its bayonet. He looked as white as a sheet.

"Doc said he lost a lot of blood," Danny told me. "Flint saved his life getting here."

"How you doing, Evans?" I asked as I

squatted down next to him.

"They gave me enough morphine that I think I'm okay," he said lazily. "But I don't think I am."

"That's a million-dollar wound you got, Lieutenant," Flint said, appearing at Evans's side. "Doc told me himself. You'll live, but you'll do your living back in the States."

"I'm sorry," Evans said. "Sorry to leave you guys so soon. Did we lose many men?"

"It would have been worse without you, Lieutenant," Flint said. "You did real good for your first time out, you can be proud of that."

"Thanks. Tell Louie and Stump so long, okay?"

"Sure," Flint said, barely missing a beat. "Soon as I see them." He walked away, giving me a secretive wink as he passed. No need to burden Evans with the bad news. Danny and Charlie said their good-byes, and I sat next to Evans.

"What was it you wanted to ask me back there?" Evans said, his eyes closing.

"When you were assigned to the supply depot in Acerra, did you ever go the Bar Raffaele?"

"Sure, lots of guys did. But I never . . . you know."

"Never paid for a whore?"

"Right."

"You talked with the girls though," I said.

"Couldn't avoid it," Evans said. His eyes were fully closed now.

"Ever meet a girl named Ileana?"

"Oh yeah, Ileana. A looker." His head nodded off as the morphine took effect. He mumbled something under his breath. ". . . one of the guys . . . wanted . . ."

"What? Who?" But there was no waking him, the drug had taken him far away from this ruined village and the jagged steel buried in his shoulder.

Chapter Twenty-Nine

The jeep careened around an antiaircraft emplacement, hitting forty as the driver gunned the engine and sped by a fuel dump, jerrycans stacked ten high for a hundred yards. He was trying to outrun a stick of bombs dropped by a Ju 88, exploding in a ragged line behind us. I held my breath, waiting to be blown to kingdom come if one came close to all that gasoline.

"Listen," I said, grabbing the driver's shoulder from the backseat. "I want to get to the hospital, not be admitted to it. Slow down."

"Not the way it's done, sir," he said, downshifting as he cleared the burning wreckage of a truck and towed artillery piece. "This hospital is set up next to an airfield, ammo dump, supply depot, and most of the ack-ack in the beachhead. It ain't a healthy place to linger, wounded or healthy."

"Why the hell did they put it there?"

"On account of there's nowhere else. You mighta noticed real estate is at a premium around here. I've been ferrying wounded from the aid stations for two days straight, and I've brought guys here and seen 'em hitching a ride back to the line on my next trip. They say it's too damn dangerous."

He slowed as we drove through a gap in the five-foot-high sandbag wall surrounding the field hospital. Rows and rows of tents marked with giant red crosses were set up, the ground between them churned into mud. Engineers were excavating one area, digging in tents so only the canvas roofs were above ground. A field hospital was supposed to be behind the lines, far from enemy fire. This was not a good sign. If the walking wounded started walking away from a field hospital for the relative safety of their foxholes on the front line, something was seriously wrong.

The driver backed up the jeep to an open tent as medical personnel scurried out. Stump was still unconscious, strapped to a litter across the rear of the jeep. By the time the orderlies got Stump off and I had one foot on the ground, the driver had hit twenty, one hand waving good-bye.

"Welcome to Hell's Half Acre, Lieutenant," said a nurse clad in fatigues several sizes too large and GI boots caked in mud. "We'll take good care of your pal, don't worry."

"He's not my pal," I said, pointing to his wrists, tied tight. "He's my prisoner."

"He's my patient, and the rope comes off. I don't care what regulations he broke, he gets treated just like everyone else. Now get out of my way."

"Okay, okay. But I'll be watching. And give me his clothes, I need to search them."

"What'd he do, swipe General Lucas's pipe?"

"He's murdered at least six people." Landry, Galante, Cole, Inzerillo, Arnold. Probably Louie Walla from Walla Walla. Cole was by proxy, but he was a victim just the same.

"You mean six on our side? Who'd want to kill his own kind in this hellhole?"

"Good question," I said. I watched as she checked his eyes and another nurse cut away his clothes, looking for wounds. She called for a doctor as I gathered up Stump's uniform and sat on a cot to check its contents. Like a lot of GIs, Stump fought out of his pockets, not wanting to carry a pack and risk losing it. The medics had made sure to empty out ammo and grenades, but they didn't bother with personal effects.

Cigarettes, a lighter, packs of toilet paper. Chewing gum. A letter from his mother, asking if he'd gotten the mittens she'd knitted him, and reminding him to keep clean and change his socks. It sounded like he was at summer camp, not war. He'd started a letter back to her, saying how swell Naples was, and how their barracks were warm and dry. Odd that a six-time murderer would fib to his mother so she wouldn't worry about him at the front.

Other than a half-eaten Hershey's bar, that was it. No clues. No deck of cards missing the ten through king of hearts.

All I knew was that I was hungry. I ate the rest of the chocolate, and waited.

"Lieutenant," a voice said, from somewhere off in the distance. "Lieutenant?"

"Yeah," I said, waking up with a start. At some point the cot must have reached up and grabbed me, since I was laid out flat.

"The doctor can fill you in now," the nurse said, pointing to a guy in a white operating gown, removing his cotton mask. But I would have recognized him anyway, with that blond hair.

"Doctor Cassidy, right?"

"Boyle! I guess we were both headed to

the same place. Did you find that murderer back in Caserta?"

"I think I found him here. The sergeant you just treated."

"No kidding? Did you give him that whack on the head? Nearly did him in."

"No, that was courtesy of a German 88, or at least a piece of a farmhouse that was hit by it."

"He did have some small bits of shrapnel in his legs, but nothing serious," Cassidy said, leading me to another tent that served as the post-op ward. "He's got a pretty severe concussion, but that's it. Not from shrapnel, most likely flying debris, like you said. His helmet must have absorbed most of the blow, otherwise he'd have been a goner."

"Can he be moved?"

"No, we need to watch him for a day or so, in case there's any other damage. We'll know within twenty-four hours."

"Is he awake?"

"In and out. He's got one helluva headache, and is a bit disoriented. Is he really the killer?"

"I found him next to a colonel he was trying to strangle, with this in his hand." I showed Cassidy the crumpled king of hearts.

"A colonel? So he got his major?"

"Yeah, Major Arnold, just before we pulled out."

"Arnold, now he was a piece of work." Cassidy shook his head, his grief at the loss of Arnold easily kept at bay.

"What do you mean by that?" I asked as he opened a canvas flap and we entered a long tent, with wood plank flooring and rows of cots along each side, filled with the wounded, who were bandaged in every possible place.

"Like I told you, he and Schleck didn't believe in combat fatigue. Or I should say, Arnold believed whatever Schleck told him to. And he was a souvenir hound of the worst kind."

"Hey, everyone wants a Luger or an SS dagger," I said, interested in what Cassidy thought the worst kind was.

"Yeah, but with Arnold it was business. He took loot from homes, and collected soldbuchs — you know what they are?"

"Sure. German pay books, with a photo of the soldier."

"Something macabre about that, don't you think? Collecting pictures of dead Krauts? And all that other stuff — caps, medals — he didn't exactly pay top dollar for them. I heard he took them for favors.

Not right for an officer. Well, it doesn't matter now. Here's Sergeant Stumpf."

Stump had a thick bandage around his neck, and several on his legs. His eyelids flickered open, then shut. I knelt by his cot.

"Stump, can you hear me?"

"What . . . happened?" His voice was weak and raspy.

"Remember the Tigers at the farmhouse?"

"Yeah. My squad?"

"I don't know," I said. "Can you open your eyes?" He did, and I held up the king of hearts. "Tell me about this."

I watched his eyes blink and his brow furrow, as if he couldn't understand what I was showing him. Then came the sound of artillery, the metal-on-metal screeching sound like hitting the brakes at high speed with pads worn clean away. Every doctor and nurse in the tent instantly covered the wounded with their bodies, leaning over the bandaged men and cradling heads with their arms. I did the same with Stump, just as the first rounds landed — *whump, whump, whump* — close enough to shower the canvas tent with debris that sounded like hail. I felt something burning my back and stood up, swatting at myself.

"Shrapnel," Cassidy said, pulling off my jacket. I noticed small tears in the tent, and one patient dousing his blanket with water. "From that far away, it has lost most of its momentum, but it's red hot." He shook the jacket and a sharp, jagged piece of metal fell out. Another round of artillery echoed across the sky, but was a good distance away. No one paid it any mind, except for one GI, both arms swathed in bandages, who rolled out of his cot and began scratching at the floor, trying to dig into it with damaged hands. Two nurses took his arms as Cassidy raced over with a syringe, jabbing the screaming soldier in the thigh. He went limp, moaning as the nurses lifted him back onto his cot.

"Thanks," Stump said, then pointed to the card I still held. I showed it to him again.

"Some colonel dead?"

"No, no thanks to you. This was in your hands when that German shell knocked you out, as you were strangling Colonel Harding."

"Who? God, my head hurts." He tried to raise his head and check out the rest of his body.

"Bad concussion, a bit of shrapnel in the legs. Nothing to worry about," I said. "It's over, Stump. We got you dead to rights. Found you next to Harding, with that card in your hand. You were trying to strangle him with his binocular strap. Almost had him, too. Then one of the Tigers blasted the farmhouse, and you got hit on the side of the head."

"Harding? The colonel who got us out when we were pinned down?"

"The same."

"Why the hell would I do that? You think I'm Red Heart?" He winced, the effort of speaking painful.

"Why would you have this in your hand?" I held up the king again.

"Dunno. Someone put it there?" His voice was weaker, and his eyes closed.

"That's what they all say, Stump," I said, leaning closer. "Tell me the truth. Why did you kill all those people? What did you have against them? What did you have against Louie?"

"Louie? Jesus, he was my pal. What happened?"

"Bullet in the back of the head, close range. You fire your automatic out there?"

"Of course not, we were never close enough to the Krauts for that."

"It was fired. One round gone. I checked it when I found you."

"Can't be. Louie, who'd want to kill Louie?" he said, struggling to keep his eyes open. "Was a major killed? Who?"

"Yeah. Arnold, the day we left Caserta. You know that."

"No. You mentioned him, said he was alive."

"I just didn't say he was dead. How'd you do it, Stump? Get him alone like that?"

"I didn't," he said. "Why would I?"

"That's what I want to know. Why strangle Harding after he saved our bacon? Why any of them?"

"You said Harding was choked by his binocular straps?"

"Yes. Do you remember?"

"And that you found me holding that card?"

"Yes."

"Lieutenant, my head is scrambled, but even I know you'd need two hands free to strangle a guy. You'd grab and twist those leather straps real tight. Hard to do with a playing card in your hand. That one's a little worn, but it would be badly crumpled if I'd done that. You'd keep it in your pocket until the deed was done. Now leave me alone."

Maybe that made sense. Maybe I should have thought of it. But I wasn't taking any chances. I found an MP and had him cuff Stump to the cot. If he was going anywhere, he'd be dragging an army cot along with him.

I wandered outside, wondering what to do next. I could go back to HQ and see if there was any message from Kaz. I could also check with Kearns about Danny's transfer and see about getting him out of the platoon. It was a dangerous place, with death dealt from both sides of the table. But first I needed some chow. I spotted Cassidy checking charts and asked him where the mess was. He ditched his bloodstained operating gown and said he was buying.

"It's not much on taste, but there's plenty of it," Cassidy said as we filled our mess tins with corned-beef hash and lima beans. The coffee was hot, and there was even sugar, so I couldn't complain.

"Do you get many cases like that fellow who tried to dig a hole in the floor?" I asked after I got most of the grub down.

"We're starting to see them. The artillery bombardment has been getting worse real fast. Most of the wounds we treat are shrapnel. It's the kind of thing that wears on a man."

"But the Third Division is a veteran outfit. Shouldn't it take longer for them to be affected?"

"That's just it, Billy. The Third has been at the sharp end since North Africa. Then Sicily, then the landing at Salerno, where they took a lot of casualties. After that, the Volturno River, and then Cassino. They only had a few weeks' rest before this landing, and now we've got Germans on the high ground shelling us constantly. The replacements don't know what to expect, the veterans do, and I can't tell you which is worse."

"What do you do for them?"

"The GI you saw will be evacuated as soon as a transport is available. He's got a million-dollar wound, both arms riddled with shrapnel, so he's going home. It's the ones without physical wounds I worry about. A short time in a safe rear area is a big help, but there is no safe haven here. Last I heard, the beachhead was only seven miles wide. The Germans can shell us anywhere they want, day or night."

"How do you doctors decide which wounds are the million-dollar variety?"

"It's not an official term, Billy. It's any wound bad enough to get you sent home but not bad enough to be permanently crippling. That guy had severe muscle damage. No way he could heal up well enough to handle a rifle in combat, but with physical therapy he should be okay. Might take a while, so he fits the bill."

"What do you think about these murders?

Does a killer like that have to be crazy?"

"Crazy isn't an official term either. Well, to a normal person, yes, someone who commits multiple murders is crazy, since they operate outside the norms of society. But these killings were well thought out, and had a distinctive pattern. The killer eluded capture, until now. These are all signs of intelligent planning. Is that crazy?"

"You sound like a lawyer."

"Goes to show, there are no easy answers when it comes to crazy."

"Take a look at this, and tell me if this sounds like a lunatic murderer," I said, handing Cassidy Stump's unfinished letter to his mother. Cassidy read the letter, nodding a few times. He handed it back.

"I can't say he's not a murderer, based on this. There are many reasons for murder, and plenty of them wouldn't preclude telling your mother a little white lie. He obviously wants her to think he's safe behind the lines, in Naples, since the Anzio landing will be in the news."

"What about the lunatic part?"

"That's harder, Billy. This letter shows genuine concern for another person. I'm just theorizing now, but cold-blooded murders as you've described them demonstrate a total disregard for others. No remorse at all. This letter shows the opposite. He could have not written her, or he could have written her the truth, but instead he took a different tack, making up a story to ease her mind."

"So Stump is normal?"

"Billy, one of the things you learn on a psychiatric ward is that words like normal and insane are essentially worthless. It's what I find fascinating about the human mind."

"That's swell, Doc, but I need answers and I need them now. I've got a lunatic on the loose."

"Well, 'lunatic' is not a precise term, but 'psychopath' is. I think that may be what you're looking for."

"Like I said, crazy."

"A psychotic is crazy, in the conventional sense; they're the ones who hear voices, that sort of thing. But a psychopath is different. You could talk with one and you'd never know it. A true psychopath could write that letter, only if it served a specific purpose and was to his benefit. They're emotional mimics. They don't feel real emotion, but they are great observers, and know when to act normal. But a psychopath wouldn't care about his mother's feelings. He wouldn't even understand what that meant."

"So how can you spot one?"

"It's easy, once they're caught. They're great deniers, sometimes telling such outright lies about their guilt that it's easy to see through them. They usually have a grandiose sense of their own self-worth and capabilities. But otherwise, they can act just like you and me."

"Except that it wouldn't bother them to kill half a dozen people."

"No, it may even be a source of satisfaction for them. Think about it. No conscience, no empathy or understanding of others. They're not good at long-term planning, so they find it easy to act on impulse, and they are highly manipulative, so they can often get away with things."

"But you said this whole thing took planning."

"Yes, but if we're dealing with a psychopath, I doubt he planned everything out first. I'd bet it was an impulse that started the ball rolling. Then the grandiose thinking might kick in. In his own world, he might derive pleasure watching those around him react to his escalating crimes. The more he gets away with, the more powerful he feels."

"It doesn't sound like he'd be a candidate for combat fatigue."

"No. He'd have a sense of self-preservation, but he wouldn't suffer any effects from killing, or seeing his comrades killed. Other than enjoying the spectacle of it all, maybe. Want some more joe?"

"Yeah, thanks," I said, and thought about what Cassidy had said while he refilled our cups. Impulse. The sequence of the first two killings always had bothered me. Now I was sure Landry hadn't been killed first. The playing cards were a trick, a manipulation, to cover up an impulse killing to divert suspicion. Galante had been an immediate threat, and had to be dealt with on the spot. On impulse. I'd bet dollars to doughnuts that Landry knew the killer and Galante were together, so he had to go. Then that grandiose imagination kicks in. Make it look like a guy with a grudge against the chain of command. Get everyone in a tizzy, and watch the fun.

"Would a psychopath enjoy army life?" I asked when Cassidy returned with the coffees.

"Well, you'd have to be crazy to," he said, grinning at his own joke.

"So what would happen if someone told this nutcase he was going to pull him off the line? Send him to a hospital, cure him?"

"You mean a psychiatric hospital? No way. Our hypothetical guy would kill to stay out of one of those."

"He'd prefer to stay in combat? Now that's crazy."

"I'd say in some ways it could be the perfect environment, since there are clear rules and procedures. He could figure out how to manipulate the system easily. But on the other hand, the peacetime army would be too boring. Psychopaths crave stimulation."

"Combat is stimulating."

"Yeah, I see what you mean. I've always said that if you keep men in combat long enough, ninety-eight percent will break down from combat fatigue. The other two percent will be psychopaths."

Chapter Thirty

"We're short on men, Boyle," Kearns said. "I'm sorry, but Second Battalion has been pulled back into reserve, and that'll have to do. No transfers, not for anybody."

"But sir —"

"Can it, Boyle. If I could I would — we really owe you one. But orders are orders."

"Okay," I said, not liking it one bit, and not certain that I was owed a damn thing yet.

"The provost marshal is taking charge of Sergeant Stumpf as soon as he's discharged from the hospital. Meanwhile we have MPs standing guard. You going back with him?"

"I have to talk to Colonel Harding first, Major. There are a few loose ends I'd like to tie up."

"Be my guest. I'm sure you'll want to visit with your brother for a while."

"Yes sir."

"Well done, Boyle," he said, rising from

his desk in the underground wine cellar and extending his hand.

"Thanks. But remember, Stump still denies he's the killer, and we're short on proof."

"I wouldn't expect a mad killer to admit his guilt. And that card and the marks around Sam's neck are proof enough. Not to mention a couple of dozen colonels and generals who aren't asking for bodyguards."

Explosions shook the ground above us, loosening dust from the rafters and coating everything in the room with gray grit. Men wore their helmets even here, deep underground. The German bombardment was becoming more intense, as the Krauts brought more and more heavy stuff up into the Alban Hills.

I'd stayed with Stump for hours after my talk with Cassidy, just watching, talking a bit, trying to size him up. He was sure of his innocence, but worried about the military justice system taking him in and spitting him out. It seemed like a sane way to look at things. They finally gave him something to help him sleep and kicked me out. I'd been dog-tired, and went back to the house where Kaz and I had bunked, only to find everyone sleeping in the cellar. Between a snoring captain and a couple of artillery barrages, I didn't get much sleep.

This morning I'd hoped to get Danny's transfer in the works, but Kearns had put the kibosh on that. At least Danny's outfit had been pulled off the line and put into reserve, which meant a couple of miles between them and the front. Still in artillery range, but then what wasn't?

There were no messages from Kaz, and I couldn't check with him since I didn't know exactly where he was. So I drove back to the field hospital, looking for Lieutenant Evans and Father Dare. I wanted to find out what Evans had been trying to say about Ileana at Bar Raffaele, and I was still curious about the pistol-packing padre. I'd known my share of priests, and while some liked a good game of poker, none of them carried a .45 automatic. Being a man of the cloth could be a good cover for the kind of maniac I was hunting. Like the army, the church gave you a nice set of rules to follow, and it had been my experience that rules were good things to hide behind. Then another talk with Stump. I wanted to look in his eyes and see — what? All that I saw last time we talked was derision at the idea he was the killer. His only proof he wasn't was an uncrumpled playing card. If he wasn't lying, then the real killer was bound to strike again. How sure was I?

Then I'd visit Danny and Flint, and question anyone in the platoon who might have seen a GI with an automatic in his hand during the retreat. What about Flint? If I was right about the killer being in the 3rd Platoon, then he had to be on the list of suspects. But I'd seen him helping Evans out of the smoke. Could he have gone after Harding, then left the job half-finished? Why? If the object was to frame Stump, a dead Harding would have been even better. Could the 88 have interrupted him? But Flint had looked fine, as fine as anyone who'd been through that attack and retreat. If the Tiger had stopped him, he would have shown some effect from the explosion. It didn't make sense.

"Father Dare? He left early this morning," a nurse told me. "Said he had to get back to his unit and be of some use. We wanted to keep him another day or so, but his leg will be all right if he keeps it clean."

"How was he? Was he upset about anything?"

"He just said he didn't want to become a permanent resident of Hell's Half Acre. Can't say I blame him." She consulted a chart and led me to the tent where Evans was resting, a cast encasing his shoulder and arm, bandages wrapped around his head.

"Flint saved my life," Evans said. "I took a load of shrapnel in my shoulder. They told me I would've bled to death if he hadn't pulled me out. There was so much smoke, I'm damn lucky he found me."

"He's the senior noncom now. He's probably in command of the platoon."

"What happened to Louie and Stump? Are they wounded?"

I filled him in on Louie being shot in the head, and Stump being in custody as the Red Heart Killer.

"It's hard to believe. Stump? And why kill Louie? They were buddies. It doesn't add up."

"He's killed whomever he needed to, not just officers. There had to be a reason, I don't think he killed randomly. Is there anything you can think of? Something Louie said or saw that he shouldn't have?"

"Louie spoke to me about believing his time was up," Evans said. "But that was about the war, not these killings. That's how I took it, anyway."

"Were he and Gates close?"

"Yeah, they went back to North Africa. He took Gates's death hard, kept saying he wished he'd been with him, maybe he could have gotten the drop on that officer. Caught out there yesterday, I think he'd given up all hope."

The snarl of aircraft approaching interrupted us, and the crash of bombs down by the sea, a few hundred yards away, signaled the approach of the Luftwaffe, hard at work hitting the ships supplying the beachhead. Our antiaircraft batteries opened up, and the pounding of the guns combined with explosions was deafening. The medical staff grabbed helmets and stood by their patients.

"Can you make it to a shelter?" I asked Evans, yelling into his ear.

"No, takes too long. Best to ride it out. You go."

Now, I had a burning desire to make it home from this war in one piece, and normally at the sound of air-raid sirens I dive headfirst into the nearest bomb shelter. But with those nurses, doctors, and orderlies staying put, I felt embarrassed to skedaddle. Dumb, I know. I held my helmet in place with my hands and sat on the floor, pulling my knees up to protect myself. If a bomb hit close by, it would be meaningless, but it gave me something to do.

I felt the vibrations from the bomb hits in the wood flooring, and then a tremendous crash, the cots and me bouncing a couple of times. That was real close, and I was glad that no one tried to dig a tunnel out of there. I would have been tempted to join in.

"Now I know why they call it Hell's Half Acre," I said as the explosions receded.

"I won't miss the place," Evans said. "They say I'll be shipped out to Naples in a few days." He shifted in his cot, trying to get comfortable. His arm was set up, a brace in the cast supporting it.

"Does it hurt?"

"Yeah," he said. "Still got some shrapnel in there. The doc said it would take a few operations to get it all out."

"Hey, a million-dollar wound, congratulations," I said, meaning it. Evans had done all right. But I still had questions for him. "Do you remember when we were talking about Bar Raffaele, right after you were wounded? About the girl, Ileana?"

"I remember Ileana, but I don't recall talking with you about her. They gave me morphine out there, so everything's kind of hazy.

"You started to say something about one of the guys and her, but then you faded away."

"There was a lieutenant who was sweet on her. It was kind of sad, really."

"Could that have been Landry?"

"No idea. I guess so. I didn't know the

guy, maybe saw him there a few times. It was just something you talked about, you know? Was she playing him for a sap, or was she going to give up the business? Either way, it'd be tough for him."

"You got that right. Rest up, and enjoy Naples."

"Thanks. You find that killer and end this, okay? There's enough dead bodies here for a lifetime."

I couldn't argue.

Outside, I buttoned my jacket up against the cold wind coming off the sea. The sky was leaden gray, the ground damp, and I felt the chill creep up through my boots. I decided a cup of joe was in order, and headed for the mess tent. I saw that the dug-in tents were finished, set four feet underground and reinforced with sandbags. Litters were being carried down the steps into what looked like an operating room. Not the fanciest hospital, but likely the best north of Naples.

In the mess tent, I spotted Bobby K, wearing his new corporal's stripes.

"Those look good on you, Bobby K," I said, sitting across from him with my coffee. We were at the end of a long trestle table, and I set my Thompson down next to the coffee.

"Thanks, Lieutenant," he said. "I lost sight of you yesterday. Glad you're okay."

"I am. What are you doing here?"

"I was escorting some Kraut prisoners when we got caught in the bombing and had to bring a few of them in to be treated. Soon as they're patched up they're getting loaded on a transport and shipped out. How lucky, huh?"

"No kidding. You're not hurt, right?"

"Nope, just enjoying the privileges of rank. I got three privates watching the wounded prisoners while I sit here. So thanks again. Colonel Harding came through, like you said he would."

"You deserve it, Bobby. You're in reserve with Second Battalion, right?"

"Yeah, we're digging in deep. They've been shelling us pretty bad. We had the POWs in a holding pen but we had to bring them into our shelters. Some of the guys wanted to leave them out there for a taste of their own medicine, but that didn't seem right. Anyway, our captain ordered us to, so that was that."

"So when did they get hit?"

"After it was over. The Kraut observers must have seen the trucks coming in to load them up, 'cause all of a sudden we got plastered. Couple of POWs got killed, but the rest were minor wounds. Minor-when-it-ain't-you kind of minor."

"They seem to be able to zero in pretty well. Spotting a few trucks from up in those hills is a neat trick," I said. I noticed Corporal Kawulicz eyeing my Thompson. He had a carbine leaning against the bench by his leg. "Looking for a Thompson?"

"I tried to get one, but they're hard to come by."

"Why do you want one? That M1 carbine is more accurate."

"Yeah, but it's not like we're target shooting. And they're only .30 caliber rounds. The Thompson has better stopping power with that .45 slug. Corporals are supposed to be issued one, you know."

"Tell you what," I said. "We'll swap." I pushed the submachine toward him and undid my web belt with the extra magazines.

"Really? You sure, Lieutenant?"

"I'm sure." He didn't need much encouragement.

A few minutes later, we walked out of the mess tent, the new corporal proudly sporting his new Thompson submachine gun. I carried the lighter M1 carbine, glad of the reduced weight but still feeling a burden settle onto my shoulders. I was worried about Danny going through the barrages

Bob described. How were the Germans hitting us so accurately, so far from the front lines?

We stopped at a tent with a bored private standing guard, and Bobby K stuck his head inside to ask if the prisoners were bandaged up and ready to go.

"Perhaps you can explain this, Corporal," I heard a familiar voice say, and saw Doctor Cassidy emerge from the tent with Bobby in tow. "Billy, didn't expect to see you here again. Are you in charge of this prisoner detail?"

"No, I was just having coffee with the corporal. We're old pals. What's up?"

"Follow me," he said. He took us to another tent and opened the flaps. A sickly smell wafted out and I guessed this was the morgue, or where they stashed the dead if 'morgue' was too fancy a term for a dirt-floor army tent. Several bodies were on the ground, already zipped up in mattress covers. One had only a sheet covering him. "Care to tell me how this happened, Corporal?" He pulled the sheet away to reveal a German officer. His tunic collar was undone, and he wore the distinctive paratrooper's smock.

"Fallschirmjäger," I said. His right trouser leg was torn open and his leg swathed in a

dirty bandage.

"Right, but he didn't die of his wounds, did he, Corporal?" Cassidy said.

"I don't know, he was limping but seemed okay. Then after the shelling he was out cold. I couldn't find any other wounds, so I brought him here. What's wrong with him?"

"This," I said, pointing to the bruises around his neck.

"And these," Cassidy said, showing the trademark red splotches in the eyes and across the face. "He was strangled, Corporal. What do you know about this?"

"Nothing, sir, honest. We protected these guys from the barrage, brought them into our own shelters. Then we got hit again after the all clear. It was all confused, and we had to make sure no one got away. I loaded this guy in with the wounded and brought him here. That's all I know."

I got a sinking feeling in my stomach. On the paratrooper's sleeve was the camouflage insignia of an *oberst.* German for colonel, two green leaves with three bars underneath. I reached into his tunic pocket, knowing what I would find there.

"The corporal didn't do anything wrong," I said, showing Cassidy the king of hearts. "Take the handcuffs off Stump."

Chapter Thirty-One

"A Kraut? He's killed a Kraut?" Heads turned as Major Kearns raised his voice. His worried tone did sound odd, since killing Krauts was our stock-in-trade. Several heads turned among the Corps HQ staff laboring underground.

"Quiet down, Major," Harding said, hustling us off to a far corner of the wine cellar where clerks worked their Smith Coronas. Harding told them to take a break and we sat at the narrow table, typewriters in front of us, army forms and carbon paper scattered about. I'd brought Cassidy along because I thought an expert might explain things better than I could. I still didn't quite get whether this murderer was crazy or not.

"Now calmly and quietly, tell us what happened," Harding said. "I thought you had the killer in custody. Case closed."

"I thought I had," I said, laying the king of hearts found in Stump's hand on the table. The edges were crumpled, but it lay flat. "Until Stump pointed out something I should have picked up. Colonel, you said your assailant used both hands?"

"Yes. He grabbed the binoculars with one and twisted the straps with the other. He pulled back on either side of my neck, so the straps dug into my throat."

"Both hands would have been clenched shut, like this?" I stuck out both hands, mimicking the movement as Harding had described it. When he nodded, I opened my hands and a playing card fell out. It sat crushed next to the king of hearts, folded in on itself from the pressure of my grip.

"Somebody put that card into Sergeant Stump's hand," Kearns said.

"Yes. I wasn't sure until we found the German colonel. It was by accident, really. A bunch of POWs were wounded in the bombing, and their guards brought in the *Herr Oberst* as well, thinking he might still be alive."

"His tunic hid the bruises," Cassidy said. "When I opened it up, they were clear as day, as well as the petechiae."

"Speak English, Doc," I said.

"Small red marks, burst blood vessels in the eyes and on the face."

"That couldn't be caused by concussion

from a bomb blast?" Harding asked.

"No, and a concussion wouldn't leave bruises shaped like thumbs and fingers on his throat. That man was strangled, no doubt about it. He had a leg wound, fairly severe. It would have caused him pain, made it hard to walk, but it wouldn't have killed him."

"Maybe he was unpopular with his men," Kearns suggested.

"He was the only paratrooper in with the bunch," I said. "The others were regular *Wehrmacht.* He couldn't have made enemies that fast."

"So our killer is still on the loose," Harding said. "But it sounds like he may have shot his wad. He failed with me, and now he's reduced to murdering a wounded POW. Hard to see how he could move onto a general after that."

"No, not at all," said Cassidy, shaking his head, as eager as a schoolboy with the right answer. He took one look at Harding's frown and remembered to add "sir."

"Colonel, please listen to Doctor Cassidy. He's studied cases like this, and he has a theory." Harding eased up on the frown and I nodded to Cassidy to continue.

"We are most likely dealing with a genuine psychopath here. Someone who totally lacks empathy for another human being. For him, a person is either a target or a tool, nothing in between. He has a self-centered view of the world, an overblown grandiose imagining of his own importance. For whatever reason, Red Heart has set up this card game, with the goal of filling his royal flush."

"I'd hardly call it a game," Kearns said.

"That's because you're not a psychopath. To him, it *is* a game. High stakes, since it's all about him, but still a game. I know it's hard to grasp, but this is a man who places no value on human life, except as it exists to benefit him."

"So what's your theory?" Harding asked.

"It's important to understand a few things. Psychopaths generally have a need for high levels of stimulation. They are also very clever, manipulative, and versatile. Don't imagine this guy as a drooling sadist; he's a lot smarter than that and very good at covering up what he is. He can observe and copy emotional reactions, but he can never *feel* those emotions. He enjoys humiliating people who trust him. It's one of the behaviors that stimulates him."

"Is that what this whole card game is about?" Harding asked. "Stimulation? Showing us how smart he is?"

"Yes, exactly. And you were onto something when you talked about his failure to kill you. I thought it might knock him off course. Sticking to a long-term plan is not a psychopath's strength. But he rebounded. He found a way, after being thwarted, to kill his colonel."

"And that means what?" Harding said.

"That previously he was following a script. The victims he left his calling card with were all American officers. But now, he's gone from almost being derailed to one card away from filling a royal flush. He probably sees himself as invincible. And he's upped the ante, adding a German to his victims. So I'd bet he'll go after a general for sure, and as soon as possible. Not an American, he's broken that pattern."

"A British general?" Kearns said.

"Unless you got any others around here," Cassidy said. "Italian, French, it wouldn't matter to him. What matters is upping the stakes. I think the POW murder was a desperation move, but one that may have reinvigorated him."

"Wait a minute," Harding said, holding up his hand. "Didn't you just say that sticking to a plan is not what these nutcases do? He's got one helluva plan here."

"I think I know why, sir," I said. "From what the doc told me, being in combat might be a psychopath's dream. Lots of opportunity for killing, legit and otherwise. Arms and ammo. Rules and rank to hide behind."

"As a professional army man, I might take offense at that, Boyle."

"No, it's not the army he likes. It's war. War gives him everything. Death. Stimulation. Belief in his own power. I think something happened in Caserta that put Galante onto him. I was bothered by the order of the murders, but if you think about Galante being the first victim, it makes more sense. The cards were a cover, to confuse us. I think Galante wanted to help this guy. Maybe he told Red Heart he could get him into a hospital, heal him, something like that."

"That would have instantly turned Galante into a target," Cassidy said. "The last thing Red Heart would want to give up would be his freedom to kill."

"So he planted the jack on Galante, then killed Landry? So Landry must have been the one to send him to Galante."

"Exactly. Maybe he noticed something, and sent Red Heart to Galante to be evaluated."

"Why not stop there?" Harding asked.

"Because he'd created a new pattern,"

Cassidy said. "Remember, this isn't a normal, logical mind at work. He may be addicted. Perhaps killing in combat no longer satisfies him."

"But he also had a reason for each murder. You, Colonel, because you're here to oversee the investigation. Arnold —" I stopped myself. I hadn't thought about Arnold, but there was only one reason I could see. "Arnold, because he paid him off to have my brother transferred into the platoon."

"Are you sure Major Arnold was the type to be bought off?" Harding asked.

"It wouldn't surprise me," Kearns said. "Rumor was he was in the souvenir racket, big time. No one paid it much mind, but I think it was more about loot than souvenirs with him. What do you think the killer's motive was to get your brother in the platoon?"

"Simple," I said. "To use him against me if I got too close. Insurance."

"I don't know if I buy all this," Harding said. "Seems long on theory and short on facts."

"Colonel," Cassidy said. "I observed psychopaths when I was a resident. They're chilling. Some of their stories of cruelty gave me nightmares. Training and arming a psychopath, and giving him permission to kill, well, that's the biggest nightmare of all.

Because no matter how many people he kills, it's never enough. He'll never sicken of it. Nothing can ever fill that black hole he has inside. That's why I think he's going to strike again. There's no alternative for him, no going back."

Everyone was silent. These men knew how to fight the enemy, but not how to combat this particular terror. "What about Danny?" I said. "Will you transfer him now?"

"Let's do it another way, Boyle," Harding said. "Let's keep this under our hats. Ship Sergeant Stumpf out and let people think we've got the killer. That will lull this Red Heart character into thinking he's pulled one over on us. You go spend time with your brother. Tell him we're staying a few more days and you're having a reunion. As long as the Germans don't attack, the battalion can stay in reserve. That will give you a chance to watch things."

"What do you have in mind, Colonel?"

"I'm already working on finding a general to use as bait. We'll offer Red Heart a tempting target. We should have somebody here soon."

"Who?" I asked.

"Never mind, just get over there. Bring an entrenching tool, they're digging in deep."

I wondered if the bait was me and my

brother. Generals were hard to come by, and the only one I'd seen around here was deep underground, smoking his corncob pipe. I had Kearns sign a supply requisition, and drove my jeep to the quartermaster's tent, where I stocked up on what GIs digging in out in the open really needed. Pickaxes, shovels, blankets, a few cans of meat and vegetable stew, tins of coffee, and a carton of smokes. At least I'd be popular with everyone, with the exception of one lunatic, a lunatic I thought I'd had in custody.

I'd been fooled, and by an expert. In the midst of strangling Harding, a German shell sent them both flying. A near miss that could have killed him. Most guys would have been stunned, groggy, disoriented. Not Red Heart. He quickly found a guy to throw suspicion on, and clocked him one. So who was Red Heart?

I could rule out Evans, not that I'd ever thought him a likely suspect. He'd been in the general area of the first murders, but I doubted he could have attacked Harding with shrapnel in his shoulder, and he was tucked away in Hell's Half Acre when the Kraut paratrooper bought it.

Flint? The last surviving sergeant. But he'd been busy rescuing Evans, under fire, after he brought out Louie's body. It didn't seem to be the kind of thing a psychopath would bother with. Father Dare, with blood in his boot? Maybe he'd gone to that church to pray for forgiveness. Charlie Colorado, lost in the smoke, the radioman I'd already overlooked? Phil Einsmann? Maybe he thought he'd get away clean after the first two, only to have his agency send him right back to Italy. Did he have a nose for news, or murder?

Or Bobby K, who I'd just met, or any of the other guys in the platoon, company, or whole damn VI Corps who I hadn't met yet. Anyone could be Red Heart, but one thing my heart told me was that he was close to Danny. Too close.

Chapter Thirty-Two

The battalion was in reserve in an open field. A pine grove bordered it on the south side, and to the north a paved road cut across it, the roadbed built up about six feet above the soggy ground. GIs were digging in the woods, or along the embankment, carving out caves in the sloped earth. A convoy of trucks carrying replacements and supplies made its way along a dirt track, skirting the customary stone farmhouse in the center of the field. In the midst of these martial preparations, a woman hung her white sheets on a clothesline, domestic chores once again uninterrupted by war.

I saw Charlie Colorado walking along the edge of the embankment, a burlap sack over one shoulder and an M1 over the other. I slowed and asked if he wanted a lift.

"Thanks, Lieutenant," he said, setting the sack down between his legs, the dull clinks signaling full bottles of something alcoholic.

"Having a party?"

"Toasting the dead," he said. "I traded C rations for wine at that farmhouse."

"Hope they like Spam," I said.

"They seemed nervous," Charlie said, glancing back at the woman in the yard. "Maybe they thought I was coming to shoot them. The daughter spoke a little English, and said they hated the Fascists and the Germans."

"Of course."

"It would be foolish to say otherwise to an American soldier with a rifle and C rations to trade."

"Good point," I said, noting that Charlie was pretty sharp. "I heard you were Landry's radioman."

"Yes."

"You went to Bar Raffaele with him?"

"Sometimes. But the owner didn't like me there. Said I drank too much and caused trouble. He was right."

"Did you know Ileana?"

"Everyone knew Ileana," he said, a touch of weariness in his voice.

"Landry fell for her, right?"

"He did. I think she liked him too. She hated working there, most of the girls did. But they had to feed their families, even if it brought them shame."

"She told you that?"

"I could see it, when they thought no one was looking. But there were worse places to work."

"I can imagine. Inzerillo said he had his own doctor for the girls."

"And a priest," Charlie said. "For their shame."

"An Italian?"

"No. Someone who wanted to keep watch on his own sinners."

He clammed up after that, probably thinking he'd said too much. But then again, Charlie Colorado impressed me as a guy who didn't waste a single word.

Ahead of us, trucks disgorged their passengers and handed down supplies to waiting lines of troops. I scanned the sky for enemy aircraft, not wanting to be caught in a line of vehicles during an air raid. Charlie pointed to a section of embankment and I pulled over.

Entrances to the hillside had been scraped out, with shelter halves strung up over the holes, some reinforced with thin wooden planks from ammo and ration cartons. It had a distinctly hobo look about it.

"Billy," Danny said, walking up to the jeep. "You're just in time. Flint's been made Platoon Sergeant. Charlie went to scrounge some vino for a celebration." He looked at the sack Charlie held up and whistled. "You did okay!"

I studied my little brother. He'd already lost that permanently startled look that replacements had. He was at ease, feeling part of the platoon if only because so many had died since he'd joined. Being a survivor meant he was a veteran of sorts, which gave him confidence. The fact that the odds were against him living many more days didn't seem to bother him. For now, he was surrounded by his buddies, toasting their remaining sergeant, celebrating a promotion made necessary by three departed sergeants — two dead, one prisoner.

"Acting Platoon Sergeant," Flint said. "How you doing, Billy? Is it true what they're saying about Stump? He's the Red Heart Killer?"

"Yep. Caught in the act. Denies it, of course, but they all do."

"What's going to happen to him?" Danny asked.

"He's going back to Caserta in irons. Court martial, then firing squad would be my guess."

"Hard to believe," Flint said, shaking his head. "Stump always seemed to be a regular guy."

"Yeah," I said. "The way the doc explained it, that's what guys like him are good at. Anyway, I brought you some decent tools and grub, plus some smokes. Thought I'd spend some more time with Danny before I ship out tomorrow."

"Real shovels," Danny said, obviously tired of digging with a folding entrenching tool.

"Okay," Flint said. "Charlie, stow that vino in my dugout. No one touches it until we give these tools a workout and dig in good and proper. Then we eat and drink."

They unloaded the jeep and got to work, digging wider and deeper. Father Dare came by, and took charge of the extra rations. The meat stew was a new addition, and I figured it would be a welcome relief after meat hash, Spam, ham, and lima beans every day.

"I have a cooking pot I found in the rubble," Father Dare said. "I'll get this heated up for the boys." He took an empty can, punched holes in the bottom with his can opener, and dropped in a couple of heating tabs. Smokeless, the tabs ignited easily and burned hot, long enough to heat a meal. Unfortunately, one pot was going to be enough for this platoon, since it had suffered so many losses.

"Hey, Billy," a voice called from inside a dugout. It was Phil Einsmann, sitting cross-legged in his little cave, pecking away at his portable typewriter set up on a ration box. Above the opening was a wood plank with "Waldorf Hysteria" painted on it.

"That's funny, Phil," I said, pointing to the sign. "What are you up to?"

"Well, I tried to get a story about your killer past the censors, but they wouldn't go for it. Injurious to morale, they said. Ruined my goddamn morale, that's for sure. So I'm doing a piece on the lost company."

"What lost company?"

"Easy Company. I don't want to call it a retreat, since that might not go over well with the censors. But the rescue of a company in a forward position, slipping away from the clutches of the enemy, using the *fossi* to escape, that'll get through and sell papers."

"Fossi?" I was there and I was having trouble following Einsmann's story.

"Italian for ditches. The English call them wadis. Either sounds better than a daring escape through a smoky ditch."

"No argument there. Did you talk to my brother? Make sure you spell his name right."

"Sure did. And that Apache, Charlie.

Great stuff. What do you have to say about it, Billy?"

"Talk to this guy," I said, when I noticed Bobby K swinging a pickax not far away. "He ran through enemy fire twice to get messages through, and led everyone out. Earned a battlefield promotion."

"No kidding? He wasn't here an hour ago when I made the rounds."

I walked over to Bobby K and stood with my back to Einsmann. "Bobby K, I'll fill you in later, but have you told anyone about that colonel in the hospital?"

"No, I haven't had a chance. The CO sent me over here, said Third Platoon needed a noncom."

"Keep it between us, all right?"

"Whatever you say."

"Now follow me and I'll make you famous."

I left Bobby K with Einsmann, glad I had a chance to get to him before he spilled the beans about the German colonel. I hadn't expected him to show up in Easy Company, but with the losses in noncoms, it made sense that somebody would be sent to fill in. I wandered over to Father Dare and took a seat on a carton of K rations.

"Do you have your own dugout, Padre? I trust the Lord myself, but I'd rather do it underground."

"God helps those who help themselves, Billy. I've got my own foxhole right over there," he said, pointing behind him with his thumb. "I prefer to dig straight down, not into the side of a hill. Saw two fellows buried alive in Sicily when a shell sent a few tons of dirt sliding over their dugout."

I didn't need to mention that I'd seen what was left of a man in a foxhole at Salerno who took a direct hit from a mortar round. To each his own. "How's your leg?"

"Okay. I got the bandage changed this morning and the nurse said it was fine. I was a little dizzy yesterday, I didn't realize how much blood I'd lost." He dumped a couple of large cans of meat stew into the pot.

"Padre, would you happen to know any chaplains who visited Bar Raffaele in Acerra?"

"Are you asking me to inform on my brethren, Billy?"

"I didn't say they went there for the hookers. Maybe someone thought the men might need some guidance in such a sinful place?"

"Billy, if a chaplain showed up at a joint like that, the men would simply move on to the next disreputable establishment. I told you when we first met, we would not be welcome at such a place."

"What if someone needed help? One of the girls, maybe? Or Lieutenant Landry?"

"Landry was brought up Protestant."

"Interesting, but not an answer."

"I am the chaplain for this unit," Father Dare said. He stirred the pot, staring into the stew as wisps of steam began to drift up. I could tell he was working on a way to explain something to me. "For all the men, Catholics, Protestants, Jews, and even those who do not believe. I've noticed that atheists enjoy talking about religion in a way that believers don't."

"I've noticed that cops and criminals sometimes sound a lot alike. More so than cops and grocers or accountants."

"Exactly. We share a common interest, but one viewed from differing perspectives. That's why Landry and I were friends. He was an agnostic. He believed the unknowable was . . . unknowable. I call it a lack of faith, but that's another matter. We often talked of life and death. He wanted the men to have spiritual solace, but he couldn't partake of it himself. That's why when he asked me to help, I was only too glad."

"Help for him and Ileana."

"Yes. He wanted me to help get permission for them to marry. To testify to her good character."

"To lie for him."

"Can't a woman sin and still be a good woman at heart? Ileana lost her father in the Allied bombing, her brother was killed in Africa, and her mother has succumbed to grief. There are two younger sisters at home, and Ileana did what she had to do to keep them off the streets. There is so much misery in this war, how could I not help alleviate some small part of it?"

"So you didn't think it a lie?"

"What does it matter? They turned Landry down, and now he's dead. I wonder if it's even worth trying to help anymore. What help can I provide against all this killing? It's monstrous, too much for any man to overcome. A priest on a battlefield, I used to think it made sense, great sense. Now it seems pathetic. Anyway, I didn't think Landry and Ileana had anything to do with these killings, and I saw no reason for the authorities to delve into what on paper would sound sordid. Landry's family doesn't need to hear the army's version of what went on between them. Call the boys, will you, the stew's ready," he said, putting a lid on the pot and the conversation.

I stood, heaving a sigh and wondering what would become of Ileana. I put my fingers between my teeth and whistled, signaling that chow was ready. In the distance, two trucks raced toward the stone farmhouse, slamming on their brakes close to the door. Blue-jacketed men spilled out, circling the building. Carabinieri.

"What's going on?" Flint said, pointing to the farmhouse. Just then the shrieking sound of incoming artillery tore at the sky, and men dove in every direction, heading for dugouts, foxholes, any cover at all. I tripped on a shovel and felt myself being pulled underground, strong hands gripping my shoulders. At least a dozen explosions rippled the ground all around us, spraying debris against the soles of my boots as I slithered into the dugout with Flint.

Artillery blasts thundered around us, and I wondered if the GIs caught out in the field had had time to get to cover. Green replacements and trucks filled with ammunition were not a good combination in a barrage. I couldn't think about it long. The shelling kept up, shaking my bones every time a salvo hit close by. Dirt cascaded from above, and my thoughts went to those guys Father Dare knew, buried alive in a dugout like this one. Then I tried not thinking at all, and closed in on myself, knees to my chest, hands on my helmet. The damp, freshly dug soil jumped up at me with every blast, as I felt the impact of each explosion, the concussion traveling through the earth and air, enveloping me, reaching into our hole where the shrapnel couldn't, letting me know that life and death had come down to mere chance, the weight and trajectory of shells alone determining who would walk away and who would remain.

The shelling stopped abruptly and I was left with ringing in my ears and dirt in my mouth. I looked at Flint, and he was already at the entrance, looking out over the open field.

"Jesus," I said as I crawled next to him, neither of us ready to stick our necks out any farther.

"Yeah," he said. "Hell must look like this."

Trucks were wrecked and overturned. Gasoline burned in bright yellow-red plumes, tires in thick, acrid black smoke. Blackened shell holes were strewn in lines across the field, a half dozen in each group, testimony to the accuracy of the German fire. The ground smoldered, an odd smell drifting up, of burnt vegetation, burning rubber and human flesh. Too many men had been caught out in the field, replacements who hadn't learned how to react without thinking or asking questions.

"They had the field zeroed in," Flint said. He crawled out of the dugout and stood. Other men followed his cue. Danny and Charlie, Father Dare, Einsmann, Bobby K, all safe. "Look at the shell holes. This wasn't a random barrage. There were several batteries firing, all hitting within this field."

It didn't make sense. We were in the rear, such as it was. The Germans couldn't have an observation post that could see us, especially behind the roadway embankment. The farmhouse. Carabinieri still surrounded it, and not a single shell had come close. The white sheets still hung on the line.

"You're right," I said. "Just like Le Ferriere. There was a farmhouse there, and a woman hung white sheets on the line. A few minutes later, the shelling hit a column on the road. We were in a blind spot, the Germans shouldn't have been able to see us."

I took off at a run, toward the farmhouse, away from the carnage and the cries of the wounded. I should have stayed and helped, but I told myself I wasn't a medic. I knew I was a coward. I couldn't face the torn bodies, the pleas for help, for mercy, for mother. I ran, glad of the excuse, my palm on the butt of my .45, itching to deliver revenge, or at least blot out the screams for a moment.

Flint was at my heels, and as we closed in on the farmhouse I recognized Luca directing the Carabinieri, who were holding the farmer's wife back as she screamed at him, hands outstretched to heaven one second, beating at her breasts the next. A small girl clung to her skirts, and an older one stood behind her, sullen.

"Dove la radio è?" Luca demanded.

"It's the sheets, isn't it?" I said, breathless. The other Carabinieri had turned toward us, weapons at the ready, uncertain if we were a threat or a nuisance. Luca acted as if he expected us.

"Yes, the sheets, the bright white sheets which can be seen at a distance. The signal for the German observers to tune to the frequency assigned to their radio. *Fascisti,*" he spat.

"There are others," I said. "I know of one outside Le Ferriere."

"There are many," Luca said. "And we already have visited that farmhouse. Whenever they have a target to report, the wash goes out. We found out about it yesterday, when a neighbor of one family reported them, suspicious of all the laundry being hung. He said they were filthy pigs and doubted they washed once a month, much less every day."

"Have you found their radio?"

"No, and if we do not, we may have to let them go. It could be a coincidence, after all."

"Can we look around?" Flint asked.

Luca gave commands in Italian and one of his men led us inside, where other Carabinieri were ransacking the joint. In the kitchen, two officers had the farmer seated at his kitchen table. He had a stern face, his thick black hair peppered with gray. He wore a work shirt and vest; his hands were rough and callused. On the wall, a rectangular patch of dark wallpaper showed where Mussolini's portrait had probably hung until the invasion.

The Carabinieri were throwing rapid-fire questions at him, to which he shook his head repeatedly. They seemed frustrated. He looked calm and haughty, as if he knew his secret was safe. He was a good actor, but then Mussolini and his bunch were pretty theatrical.

Flint moved closer, edging the officers out of the way. He reached into his pocket, and the farmer flinched. But he pulled out a pack of cigarettes, and the fellow relaxed. Flint offered one, and lit it for him.

"Nome?" Flint asked, smiling as he clicked his Zippo shut.

"Frederico Pazzini," he said, giving a slight bow of his head, before taking a deep drag on his Lucky.

Before he could exhale, Flint struck him on the cheekbone with the butt of his .45, hard. Blood spurted onto the table, and Frederico choked on smoke and blood as Flint shook off the two Carabinieri who tried to pull him away. He grabbed Frederico's arm and held it to the table, the muzzle of his automatic pressed into the palm of one callused hand. He thumbed back the hammer, and spoke one word.

"Radio?"

Frederico shook his head, but with fear in his eyes this time. The two officers stepped back, apparently liking what they saw, or at least the fact that someone else was doing it for them. I wondered how far Flint was going to take it. Myself, I was ready to shoot the other hand, images of the dead and wounded still fresh in my mind.

But Flint didn't shoot. He released Frederico, smiled, and shrugged his shoulders. Then he pointed outside, and simply said, "Signora Pazzini." We hadn't taken two steps when Frederico began bawling and pointed to a cupboard near the sink. The officers got down on their knees and pulled out cans of olive oil, tins of flour, and some large bowls. Then they pried up the floorboards, and lifted out a radio. Under one of the dials was the word *Frequenzeinstellung.*

That told us all we needed to know. Flint hit him again, on the other cheekbone, then wiped his .45 with a dishrag, and left. Under the floor, where the radio had been hidden, was the portrait of Il Duce.

The Pazzini family was hauled away in a truck, their little girl in tears at the sight of her father's face. I felt bad for her. I felt bad for the little girls back in the States who'd be crying when they heard their fathers were dead, killed in a field outside Anzio. I felt bad all around.

"What will happen to them?" I asked Luca as he halfheartedly searched through the house.

"They will be sent back to Naples. A trial for the father, perhaps a displaced persons camp for the woman and children."

"He must have been a die-hard Fascist."

"Many of these people are. You know Mussolini settled this area with them. They hate you, and they hate us more for fighting with you." He tossed a pile of books off a chair and sat.

"Must be hard," I said, taking a chair myself.

"At first I looked forward to this assignment. I thought we would be bringing law and justice here. But instead, now that General Lucas is not moving inland, we have received orders to remove all civilians."

"Everyone?"

"Yes. First we have to track down the remaining Fascist spies and make sure they do not escape. Then all nonessential civilians will be shipped back to Naples. The entire Anzio-Nettuno area, evacuated. For their safety, the general said. Because of the bombing."

"He's right, you know. Especially now that the Germans won't have observers in our midst. The shelling is not going to be as accurate. Good news for us, bad news for civilians."

"Yes, yes. But I did not expect to spend this war putting civilians in camps, for both sides, no less."

"It's not quite the same, Luca."

"No, but neither is it combat, where a man can be tested. What shall I tell my children? That I helped run a concentration camp, then worked for a capitano who was corrupt, before evicting thousands of Italians from their homes?"

"What happened, Luca? On Rab?"

"You have to understand, when the camp was first set up, it was to house partisan prisoners. Tito's Yugoslav Partisans fought us and the Germans everywhere. The Nazis and the Fascists treated the Yugoslavian people horribly, shooting civilians without provocation. It quickly descended into bloodthirsty reprisals. The decision was made to remove many of the local Croats and Slovenes and bring in Italians, to repopulate the area. So the camp expanded, with thousands of local civilians, whole families, brought in. Soon we had over fifteen thousand, living in tents. Many grew sick and starved. When the commander of our battalion complained, saying that this mistreatment only drove more people to support the partisans, conditions improved, somewhat." He grew quiet, surveying the wreckage of the living room, one of many he must have seen in his strange career.

"But then?"

"Then the order came for all Yugoslavian Jews to be interned. About three thousand were brought into the camp."

"To be killed?"

"No, no, not at all. We followed the orders of our government, but the army insisted that the Jews be well treated, not as a hostile force. They weren't fighting us; they were only peaceful people who'd been swept up in this madness. So they were put in a separate part of the camp, and provided with what comfort we could give. My commander told me it was the only way to preserve a shred of honor. We had to obey the German commands and the orders from Il Duce, but we could at least do so with some dignity."

"I didn't know, Luca."

"No, and not all camps were the same. In some, Jews were treated terribly. But on Rab, we did what little we could. We were sick of fighting the partisans and all the hatred. It felt good to do something halfway decent."

"What happened?"

"After the fall of Mussolini, orders came from the government that the Jews were to be released. For their own safety, they could remain in the camp voluntarily under our protection. Several hundred left to join the partisans, and many others were taken to partisan-controlled territory. At this point, we had an uneasy truce with the Yugoslavs, and worried more about our former German allies."

"All the Jews got out?" I knew this story wasn't going to have a happy ending.

"No. There were two hundred elderly and sick left in the camp. My battalion was ordered back to Italy after the armistice, and I was in charge of a detachment, which was to close the camp. The last of the Slovene and Croat prisoners were released, and I was trying to find medical care for those Jews who could not travel."

We sat in silence, and I could hear the low murmur of other Carabinieri in the yard and smell their cigarette smoke as they waited for Luca.

"There was none. No transport, no fuel. A German column approached the camp, several hundred men in armored vehicles. We were but a few dozen, with nothing more than rifles. I gave the order. We ran. We ran away, leaving two hundred innocents behind. The Germans took them. I heard later they were sent to a camp in Poland. I expect they are all dead, don't you?"

"Yes, I do." I didn't expect they were dead, I knew it. From Zyklon B, probably in a place called Auschwitz. It had all been hard to believe when Diana told me Kurt Gerstein's story in Switzerland, which seemed like another world, another time. But here it was, half a continent away. How large was this killing machine, that it would send an armored column to a little island in the Adriatic, and ship two hundred old and sick Jews to Poland? It made no sense. Of course, in a world where people were killed with assembly-line precision, nothing *could* make sense.

"Now you know my shame. I did nothing."

"Once the Germans came, there was nothing you could do. Except die. And then you wouldn't have been a witness. Believe me, I'm a cop, and sooner or later the law appreciates a good witness."

"Perhaps. When the war is over, do you think anyone will care? The graveyards will be full. Who will want to hear the truth? Who will care?"

"The dead," I said. I left Luca in the room staring at the wall. It wasn't my job to absolve him. It wasn't my job to explain that the methodical extermination of Jews and other undesirables could not be stopped by a single Carabiniere, that perhaps it was a small blessing that it was at least remembered. I began to feel the fervor with which Diana had told the story, her need to reveal the secret that burdened her.

I walked back to where the platoon was camped. Graves Registration wandered the field, carrying sacks of mattress covers, stacking the dead like cordwood. Medics treated the lightly wounded as the last of the ambulances trundled off over uneven ground to Hell's Half Acre. The wind stiffened and I felt a cold chill rising from the damp earth.

"Billy, you won't believe this," Danny said as I approached the group. "The meat stew made it. It's still warm. Have some, it's not bad." Danny had indeed passed over a threshold. On a field littered with the dead and injured, he still had his appetite, and celebrated what passed for the luck of the Irish at war: an intact pot of hot stew.

Father Dare ladled some into my mess tin, and I sat on a crate next to Danny. Everyone gathered around the pot and its feeble warmth. Charlie passed a bottle of wine, and it tasted good, sharp on my tongue, warm in my stomach. The living have to take what pleasures they can, from each other and whatever comes their way.

Phil Einsmann had a newspaper and was sharing pages around. "Only two weeks old," he said. "The *Chicago Tribune*."

"Says here Charlie Chaplin is demanding a Second Front now," Flint read.

"They can give him this one," Charlie said, and everyone laughed. Except him. He was serious.

"Coal miners are on strike for more money and decent working conditions," Danny read from another section. "Sure feel bad for them, burrowing underground and all." That got a laugh, and I drank some more wine, happy to be with Danny, happy to be alive.

I flipped through the paper as it was passed around. Nightclub owners in Miami were protesting having to close at midnight to conserve electricity. Business was good. In Michigan, thirteen legislators were arrested on bribery and corruption charges. Business was good there too, until you got caught.

I walked over to Einsmann, and gave him back the paper. "Phil, what do you know about what the Nazis are doing to the Jews?"

"What everybody knows, I guess. They take their property, send them to camps, shoot a lot of them. Why?"

"You ought to talk to Luca Amatori, a lieutenant with the Carabinieri here. He knows what went on in one of the Italian concentration camps."

"No thanks. Not worth my time. The Italians are our allies now. No one wants to air dirty laundry, not when we need them fighting the Germans."

"You've been told that?"

"Not in so many words. But you get the sense of things after enough stories have been squashed. Italian concentration camps? Not what the reading public wants to hear about."

"Ask Luca about clean laundry then. Might be worth your time."

"What's that mean?"

"You're the reporter, you find out," I said as I got up and went back to my seat. Maybe if he got the story about the spies from Luca, he'd ask him about the camp. Maybe not. Maybe Einsmann was busy planning his next murder. Maybe not. Maybe I'd live to see the dawn.

We drank some more. Guys smoked and chatted. No one was trying to kill us. We had warm food and good wine, and deep holes to jump into. Anything beyond those immediate needs was insignificant.

"You sure keep that weapon mighty clean, Padre," Flint said as he opened a letter. Father Dare had his automatic in pieces, cleaning each with a toothbrush.

"Cleanliness is next to Godliness, they say. Letter from home?"

"Yeah," Flint said. "Mail truck had this for me, and a couple for Louie and Rusty. That's it. Sorry, fellas." He looked around at the others, then scanned the single page, before tucking the letter back in the envelope and stowing it away. He shook a cigarette loose from a crumpled pack. "Anyone got a light?"

"I never saw a padre carry a pistol," Bobby K said, tossing Flint a lighter while eyeing Father Dare.

"There's a first time for everything, son," Father Dare said, as he rubbed gun oil on the metal. He cleaned the pieces slowly, handling each like holy relics. When he had it all put back together, he held it between his palms, as if it gave off warmth. "Especially at war, there are many first times."

He sounded weary, and I wondered if the pistol was a temptation, a way out for a man who, in his mind, had failed at whatever good he had tried to do. Or did he worship the weapon, aware of the power it bestowed, so much more immediate than penance? Or maybe the vino had gone to my head.

Einsmann took out his .45 and began cleaning it as well. He had a little trouble taking it apart, not being as adept as Father Dare.

"Geez," Bobby K said. "Watch out, you could shoot someone with that thing." Everybody thought that was hilarious.

"Flint," a captain called as his jeep pulled up. "Your replacements never made it out of the truck. Take a vehicle down to the docks and see what you can find." He scribbled out an order and gave it to Flint.

"Right now, sir?"

"Right now. They won't last long." With that, he was off.

"Okay, let's see what we can find. Danny, you come with me. We'll show these new boys it doesn't take long to become a grizzled veteran. Billy, sorry, but duty calls. Good luck back in Naples." Flint smiled, shook my hand, and walked away, giving Danny and me a minute.

"Be careful," I said, wishing I could take Danny with me.

"I will be. I'm in good hands, Billy. And remember, you were the one who taught me how to fight." We shook hands, even though I wanted to give him a bear hug, which would have embarrassed him. I stopped myself from reminding him that knowing how to bob and weave in the ring was not going to help at Anzio.

I watched Danny and Flint depart, taking a truck that was parked near my jeep. I said my good-byes to the others, reinforcing the story that I was leaving in the morning with Stump in custody. On the way to my jeep, I saw a crumpled envelope on the ground. It was Flint's letter. Had he thrown it away, or had it fallen from his pocket? I was about to give it to Father Dare to hold, when I thought it would be a good excuse to follow Danny down to the docks and see him again, maybe throw some weight around and get some decent replacements for the platoon.

Always looking out for my kid brother, I thought, as I laid my carbine down on the passenger seat and drove off toward the fog that was rolling in from the sea.

Chapter Thirty-Three

After an hour of looking, I'd given up trying to pick out Danny from among the hundreds of helmeted GIs swarming over the docks. LSTs were arrayed along the waterfront, like openmouthed whales disgorging modern-day Jonahs. It looked like a major resupply effort, and I figured Stump would be heading back with the wounded on one of these LSTs riding high in the water.

It was almost dark, and I decided to talk with Doc Cassidy again before checking in at headquarters to see if Harding had come up with a general and if Kaz was back yet. Driving to the hospital area, I had to pull over as a line of ambulances came screaming down the road, horns blaring.

Hell's Half Acre was in chaos. The wounded were everywhere, pulled out of ambulances and set in rows, where doctors and nurses checked them, yelling instructions to move this one, leave that one, prep for surgery, all amidst the groans of morphine-addled pain.

"They're all Rangers," I said to a young kid standing next to me.

"Yeah, they tried to infiltrate into Cisterna last night. The Krauts must have known they were coming."

"Looks like they got hit hard pulling out," I said.

"This is the relief force. Two battalions of Rangers made it into Cisterna. Six men made it out," he said in a soft Texas drawl. "Eight hundred good men, half killed, half prisoner, they's saying."

"Jesus," I said, and thought of Father Dare praying to God for help, but asking Him to leave Jesus home. This was no place for kids, but as I looked at this scrawny sergeant, I thought he ought to be still in high school. "How old are you, Sergeant?"

"Nineteen, sir. I mean twenty, twenty years old."

"Don't sweat it, kid. If you're dumb enough to lie about your age to get in the army, I'm not going to get you in hot water. How'd you make sergeant so fast?"

"Guess because sergeants get killed so fast. I've been here since North Africa."

"Looks like the army is robbing the cradle."

"Listen, Lieutenant, just because I look young don't mean you have to insult me," he said. If it weren't for the sweat popping out on his forehead and his fluttering eyelids, I would've bet he was thinking about decking a superior officer.

"Sorry, Sergeant," I said, steadying him before he fell flat on his face. "What are you in for, anyway?"

"Malaria," he croaked. "Give me a hand, will ya?" I helped him back to his tent, and got him off his feet.

"You all right?" I asked as his head hit the pillow.

"Yeah, I'll be out of here soon. Damn malaria hits me now and then. Picked it up in Sicily."

"Want anything?"

"No thanks, Lieutenant. Sorry I mouthed off out there."

"Forget it, kid. The name's Billy Boyle, by the way. From Boston." I gave him my hand.

"Audie Murphy, from Farmersville, Texas. Take care of yourself, Lieutenant." I left him in bed, wondering how he ever got this far, a thin little whip of a kid with a strain of malaria, which I knew had sent stronger men home on a Red Cross ship.

I went back out and looked for Cassidy. The scene had calmed down, and most of the stretcher cases were gone. A few were draped with blankets, those who had died on the way in. A nearby tent was filled with other stretchers, and I watched a medic give a morphine syrette to a Ranger with blood-soaked compresses on his chest. He threw down the empty syrette and ran his fingers through his hair, shaking his head. This was the tent for the not-yet-dead. I walked on.

"Wait for me in the mess tent," Cassidy said when I finally found him. "I have a leg to amputate."

I waited, drinking coffee with sugar, not tasting a thing.

An hour later, Cassidy came in, looking drawn and exhausted. His blond hair was dirty, and there were dark bags under his eyes. "I'm hungry," was all he said. I followed him through the line, accepting frankfurters and beans in my kit, topped off with fresh-baked bread.

"I know I shouldn't be able to eat after all that," Cassidy said as we sat down. "Some guys drink. I eat. Can't help it."

"Those guys were shot up pretty bad," I said.

"They went through hell trying to get to their buddies. Lots of multiple wounds. Two battalions lost, and a third ripped apart trying to rescue them. We only get the worst cases here, you know what I mean? The aid stations and casualty clearing stations take care of the light wounds. And you know what? Most of them want to get up and go right back out there."

He raised a fork to his mouth, his hand trembling. He set it down and gritted his teeth.

"Fuck," he said. "Fuck!" Louder this time, but no one looked. Not uncommon, I guessed. He cupped his hands on the table and took a deep breath. "Too many of them. We were overwhelmed. I shouldn't have had to cut off that leg, but by the time we got him on the table . . ." He shook his head and uncupped his hands. He tried the fork again, and this time his hand was steady, but he still didn't eat. Combat fatigue comes in all forms, I guess.

"Sorry to bother you, Doc," I said, after giving him some time. "Bad timing, but I have a few more questions."

"It's never a good time here," he said. "Ask."

"I need to know what to look for if this guy we're after really is a psychopath. Everything you said points to someone who can act normal, so how can I spot him? I need something to look for, some sign. There's got to be something."

"I'm not sure. The few I knew of were spotted by experts, usually after some violent event that left no doubt. But I'd say the key is what you said about acting normal. It's all an act, so watch for something that takes him by surprise."

"To see how he reacts, like flying off the handle over some little thing."

"That could describe half the guys here. Constant exposure to death can make anyone overreact. Watch for the opposite. Some event that would draw an emotional response from any normal person."

"That's not much to go on, Doc."

"Okay, I'll make it easy on you. Just look for someone without a soul."

"I know a priest who might be able to help with that."

"Father Dare? The padre who was in here with a leg wound?"

"That's him."

"Strange fellow. Didn't want to be separated from his Colt. But he's got a good reputation with the medics and stretcher bearers. He stays up front, helps the wounded."

"He says he keeps the automatic to protect the wounded."

"Could be," Cassidy said. "But how much protection would a pistol really provide against machine guns, mortars, tanks and artillery?"

It was a really good question, but what I needed were some really good answers.

The sun had set, and the going was slow back to headquarters. As I drew close, air-raid sirens began to wail, and the street filled with men running for the shelters. Searchlights blinked on near the harbor and began stabbing at the sky, probing for the shape of German bombers. Flares blossomed in the inky darkness, floating to earth on parachutes, illuminating the town and harbor, creating day from night. Bombs were not going to be far behind. I pulled the jeep over and jumped out, making for a shelter dug out of the earth and covered with a corrugated tin roof. It wouldn't withstand a direct hit, but it would have to do.

There were already about twenty guys crammed inside. I sat near the door, listening to the antiaircraft batteries open up and the *crump* of exploding bombs creeping closer. I hoped Danny was well away from the docks by now; no reason why he shouldn't be. Someone lit a candle, and it gave off a flickering light. I leaned back, settling in for a long wait. I noticed Flint's letter sticking out of my front jacket pocket.

I took it out and looked at the return address. American Red Cross. Why would they be writing to him, from the States? I removed the letter, looking around guiltily, as if anyone in the shelter would know I was reading someone else's mail.

> We regret to inform you that your mother, Abigail Flint, died on December 25, 1943, of injuries sustained from an unknown assailant. Police are investigating and we will provide you with further information as it becomes available. Please accept our sincere condolences.

A chill went through me. Flint's mother had been murdered on Christmas Day, and all he'd done was ask for a light. He'd read the news with no visible emotion. Or if Cassidy was right, with no emotion at all.

Chapter Thirty-Four

"I know who the killer is," I said. Harding looked up without a trace of surprise. As soon as the all clear sounded I'd gone straight to headquarters and found him with Kearns. "Sir," I added, having been well trained.

"Sergeant Amos Flint," he said. "We're already looking for him."

"How . . . ?"

"Lieutenant Kazimierz has returned from Naples," Harding said. "Good to know you both agree. He's over there, with our general and his driver." He pointed to a far corner of the wine cellar, where Kaz, Big Mike, and Major Charles Cosgrove were huddled around a desk.

It was an unlikely crew. Staff Sergeant Mike Miecznikowski was Polish, like Kaz, but there the resemblance ended. He was over six feet tall, and so broad in the shoulders that he split seams on his uniform regularly. The nickname came naturally. Big Mike was a former Detroit cop who'd become part of our unit after helping us out in Sicily. He got into so much hot water because of it that Harding had to bail him out and take him in.

Major Charles Cosgrove was another story. We'd started off badly when I first came to London, which is a nice way of saying we'd hated each other. Long story. By now, we had both mellowed a bit, and there was a grudging respect between us, which is something for an Irish lad to say about a British intelligence officer from MI5.

"Billy," Kaz said excitedly. "I know who the Red Heart Killer is."

"Amos Flint?"

"I told you he'd figure it out," Big Mike said. "How you doing, Billy?"

"Glad you're here, Big Mike," I said as we shook hands. "When did you get in?"

"A couple of hours ago. First thing I do is pick up Kaz down at the docks off a PT boat from Naples, and he announces the identity of the killer. Looks like the major and I spent twenty-four hours in a Catalina for nothing."

"How are you, Major Cosgrove, or is it General Cosgrove?"

"General Bernard Paget, Commander in

Chief, Middle East Command, if you don't mind. Got to bait the hook well, don't we? Paget recently took over as CIC, so it lends a bit of realism to the charade."

"You look the part, General," I said. Cosgrove was kitted out in a nicely tailored dress uniform, with the red lapel patches of a general officer. I wondered when Harding had begun to cook up this scheme, or if maybe Cosgrove had a whole closet full of disguises. "But is this really MI5 territory?" MI5 was charged with counterespionage, catching German spies, not GI killers.

"Personal requests from Winston tend to blur lines of jurisdiction. Colonel Harding asked General Eisenhower, who asked the prime minister, who said by all means. Anything to help get this invasion moving. Winston is not pleased with the progress, or lack thereof, and doesn't wish things to get any worse if this maniac gets close to a real general. So here I am, the sacrificial lamb."

"Don't worry," Big Mike said. "I ain't leaving your side until we got this guy."

"Very good. You make a larger target than even I do," Cosgrove said. Which wasn't the case with most men. Cosgrove had fought in the Boer War and the Great War, but his days of fighting trim were long gone. He was thick-waisted, with a full gray mustache and a limp. Without Big Mike as a bodyguard, he'd be a sitting duck.

"So what did you find out about Flint?" I asked Kaz.

"I found Ileana," he said.

"How?"

"Well, I probably should not return to the Naples area for a while. An officer matching my description is wanted for the theft of penicillin from the hospital at Caserta. I knew I needed something to bargain with, and nothing will make the owner of a bordello talk more than a supply of penicillin for his girls."

"It's practically a public service," Big Mike said.

"Sure it is. So you got someone to talk."

"Yes. Ileana was recovering south of Naples, at a farm. She had been badly beaten. As it turns out, she and Landry really were in love. She rejected him at first, fearing that he would cast her aside. But he persisted, and she came to love him. They had a plan for him to take her away, but they kept up the story of her milking him for money, so Inzerillo would not be suspicious."

"Let me guess," I said. "Landry told Flint."

"Yes. He asked for his help. Instead, Flint

went to Bar Raffaele and paid for Ileana's services. He intended to humiliate Landry, to ruin their love. But he could not perform, and Ileana made the mistake of laughing at him. He nearly killed her. He threatened Inzerillo with the same if he said anything, and told Ileana he would kill Landry if she revealed what had happened."

"Then what happened to Inzerillo?"

"Flint's game was not over. He told Landry that Inzerillo had beaten Ileana, so they both went to confront him." "That was the story about going to pay for damages," I said.

"Yes. Landry demanded to see Ileana, but Inzerillo had already sent her off. Ileana later found out what had happened from one of the girls who had visited her. There was a fight, and that is when Flint beat Inzerillo and threatened to kill him. Apparently Landry managed to stop Flint, who had flown into a bloody rage. Inzerillo escaped, and Ileana's friend heard Landry tell Flint that he would get him help, because he was a good friend and a good soldier. But that he needed help to control himself."

"That was his death sentence," I said. "Landry got Galante to talk with Flint, to treat him off the books, as a favor. Landry knew something big was about to happen, and I'm sure he didn't want to lose a good squad leader."

"Good?" Cosgrove said. "Hardly seems like a good solider."

"An armed man with no remorse. No hesitation, no second thoughts. No soul. He'll never suffer shell shock, combat fatigue, whatever you call it. And a master manipulator to boot. Makes for an effective killer. Landry just didn't understand who he was dealing with. He probably thought Galante could treat him with some pills and sack time."

"But why would Flint care what Galante said? He hadn't murdered anyone yet, and the MPs wouldn't get too worked up over a pimp with a bloody nose," Big Mike said.

"Because Galante understood what Flint really was, and wanted to treat him for it," I guessed. "With all good intentions, he was going to take away the one thing that Flint valued above all else. War. He's like an alkie, or a kleptomaniac, except that instead of booze or theft, he's addicted to killing."

"So he kills this chap Galante, then the lieutenant, if I understand the sequence," Cosgrove said. "But he uses the ruse of the playing cards to reverse the order, to throw off the investigation?"

"Yes, and according to Doc Cassidy, this scheme then took on a life of its own in his mind. Since he failed to kill Harding, switching to a German opened things up for him. Best bet is that he's going to try for an international royal flush."

"Everybody up to speed?" Harding asked as he joined the group.

"I think so, except for how we're going to pick up Flint."

"You know where his unit is?" Big Mike asked. "Let's go put the cuffs on him."

"Hold on," Harding said. "Boyle, you were with them this afternoon, and they're not going anywhere tonight. I don't want to risk approaching him in the dark. Some trigger-happy GI is likely to think we're enemy infiltrators. Let him be, and we'll go in at dawn, with a couple of supply trucks. It will look completely normal."

"Perhaps we could put this uniform to good use," Cosgrove said. "Why not proceed with the plan? You said you already alerted division headquarters. What could be more normal than carrying on with the inspection? I imagine you'd like some actual proof, wouldn't you?"

"Listen, my kid brother is in Flint's platoon. I don't want to take any chances."

"I think Major Cosgrove is right," Kaz

said. "You may put Danny in greater danger by going after Flint directly. If he thinks he is about to be taken, he could try to harm Danny. But if we tempt him with our general, he might be vulnerable."

"That makes sense, Boyle," Harding said. "If he has time to react when he sees you, he could take Danny and others down with him. But if he thinks he's stalking a general, he might go at it alone."

"Why don't I walk over and plug him?" Big Mike said. "He don't know me from Adam. I'm just saying."

"All the same, my good man, I think we should proceed with some attempt at legal proceedings," Cosgrove said. "Which will be more productive if we catch him in the act. All we can charge him with now, with any hope of conviction, is assault on this Ileana girl. There's no evidence against him otherwise."

"Okay," Harding said. "General Paget will inspect the battalion in the reserve area at 0700 hours. I'll pass the word along so Flint will hear about it tonight. Boyle, you need to sit this one out. You'll only spook him."

"I guess so. Sir."

"I still say I should plug him, Sam," Big Mike said.

"Thanks, Big Mike, but I'd rather see you

keep those stripes," Harding said. "I had the personnel section pull the files on Landry's platoon, so you and Major Cosgrove can check Flint's photograph, along with others." Harding shoved a pile of folders toward Big Mike, leaving a stack behind. The dead.

"Hey," Big Mike said, opening Flint's file and looking at the army photograph. "This is Flint?"

"Yes," Harding said. "Memorize the face."

"I don't have to. I saw this guy down at the docks, when I was waiting for Kaz. He stood out because he ducked behind a truck, like he'd spotted someone he didn't want to see."

"Was this guy with him?" I pulled Danny's photograph from his file.

"Didn't see him."

"They were both sent down to the docks to pick up replacements. Danny should have been with him."

"Billy, there were hundreds of guys milling around. I could have missed him easy," Big Mike said. He was right. It probably meant nothing. My gut told me otherwise.

CHAPTER THIRTY-FIVE

I watched the small column leave at 0600, Big Mike at the wheel of a staff car and Cosgrove in back, the red stripe on his service cap proclaiming his general's rank at a glance. A jeep full of MPs provided escort, nothing out of the ordinary for a VIP. Soon after that, Harding, Kearns, and Kaz drove out, an MP sergeant at the wheel. The plan was for them to hang back and observe, waiting for Flint to make his move.

It was a good plan, and it made sense to leave me out of it. Still, I wished I could be there to keep Danny out of trouble. But if all went as planned, I'd have another shot at getting him transferred out, and I had to settle for that.

Military police had set up shop in a municipal building near headquarters. They had coffee brewing and a good cellar in case of an air raid, so I waited there for news from Harding. The MPs had a radio in their vehicle, and would call in as soon as something happened.

The Germans were shelling around the clock, not always a massive barrage, but enough to keep everyone awake and jumpy. Last night had been no exception, and between air-raid sirens, antiaircraft fire, and the Kraut artillery, I hadn't slept much. I was pouring my second cup of joe when a clerk from HQ came in looking for me. I had mail. From Boston. It was over six weeks old, but I was amazed it had even caught up with me.

It was from my mother, of course. Dad might scribble a line or two at the end, but it was always Mom who wrote. She caught me up on family news, cousins getting married, a new baby born to the neighbors, the onset of winter. Then she got to Danny. She had just heard about the ASTP program being cancelled, and was worried about him being sent overseas. Could I ask Uncle Ike about him? See that he got a job in London, perhaps? Stay safe, and watch out for your brother, she said. Both were tall orders in Anzio. Dad wrote about lots of overtime waiting for me at Boston PD, and I thought about all the cash I'd have if the army paid time and a half.

I folded the letter and put it in my shirt

pocket. As soon as I had Danny squared away, I'd write. I'd tell her he was safe and sound, doing some boring job at headquarters, sleeping inside under blankets. I hoped it would be true.

I relaxed, listening to the familiar chatter of law enforcement. Gripes, complaints, calls coming in, cops going out. It was early, and with the Carabinieri policing the local populace, there wasn't a lot going on. Until a major burst in to report his jeep stolen. He'd had a .30-caliber machine gun mounted on it, and he wanted it back, now. Never mind that it was pinched yesterday and he'd been too busy to report it, he wanted action now. A pudgy, red-faced guy, he was with the Quartermaster unit that off-loaded supplies in the harbor, and he cursed and hollered until he got an officer to listen to him. I watched the MPs as they turned away, rolling their eyes at the posturing of a supply officer who needed a machine gun on his jeep. I knew the type, and would bet dollars to doughnuts that he'd have a photograph of himself at the wheel, looking as if he were ready for a raid behind enemy lines. It struck me as strange that even while he was doing important work, in constant danger from German shells and bombs, a guy like him had to throw his weight around and try too hard to impress people.

A couple of MPs donned their white helmets and followed the major out while another radioed units with a description and serial number of the jeep. Good luck with that one, boys, I thought. With a day's head start, it could be anywhere, and I doubted any MP worth his salt would search front-line units for a stolen jeep, especially for this loudmouthed major.

An hour passed, and then another. I asked the radioman for the tenth time if there were any messages, and he suggested I get some fresh air. He was a corporal, so he said it nicely, but I got the hint. I walked down to the water and watched landing craft ferry in supplies from Liberty Ships anchored in the bay. Antiaircraft guns pointed their barrels at the sky, swiveling back and forth as they searched for targets. A quiet morning at war, almost peaceful, if you didn't think about all the weapons and rubble about. The water lapping at the rocks along the shore reminded me of Boston, down by the inner harbor. It could be peaceful there, too, until you spotted a dead body bobbing in the swell.

I waited as long as I could, then decided that one of the benefits of being an officer was bothering radiomen whenever you wanted. As I walked up from the seafront, Big Mike pulled up in the staff car, followed by Harding and Kaz.

"He wasn't there, Billy," Big Mike said. He sounded worried, more worried than he should've been. "He's been gone since yesterday."

"Danny as well," Kaz said, as he got out of the jeep. "Neither of them returned to the unit yesterday afternoon, after they drove to the harbor to get replacements."

I felt them all looking at me, waiting for a reaction. I didn't know what to say, or, worse yet, what to do. Flint, loose somewhere in the Anzio beachhead, the sea at his back, the Germans all around, and Danny at his side. I tried not to think about the memory of that floater in Boston harbor as I tried to calculate what Flint's game was.

"Billy," Kaz said, resting his hand on my shoulder. "What should we do?"

"I wish I knew," I said. We trooped inside, and the MPs stood to attention when Cosgrove entered in his general's getup. He quickly waved them off. Harding spread out a map of the beachhead on a table, and marked the front lines with a red pencil.

"The British are on our left flank," he said, drawing an arc from the coast up to Compleone, a northward bulge showing where the British had been attacking toward Rome. In the center, the front was a wavy line from Corano to Sessano, south of Cisterna where the Rangers had been cut to pieces. "This is all Third Division, with supporting elements from the 504th Parachute Regiment."

"Who's holding the right flank?" I asked, pointing to where the Mussolini Canal flowed south to the sea.

"The First Special Service Force," Harding said. "It's a joint U.S.-Canadian volunteer outfit. A commando brigade."

"That's a long stretch of canal for three regiments to cover," Big Mike said.

"German activity is sparse on that flank," Kearns said. "They're covering the approaches to Rome on the north. Besides, these Force men are damn aggressive. The Krauts pulled back a mile or more on the other side to avoid their patrols."

"Is there a general in command?" Kaz asked.

"Yes, Brigadier General Robert Frederick, recently promoted. I doubt anyone could get the drop on him," Kearns said. "Even without hundreds of his men around him, he'd be tough to take. A real fighting general."

"Boyle, what do you suggest?" Harding said.

"Let's have the MPs check the hospitals, in case they got caught in the bombing last night. And send out a bulletin with their names and description to every checkpoint. And to the Carabinieri as well."

"Billy, Flint may have got himself aboard one of the ships. He could be halfway to Naples by now," Big Mike said.

"Danny would never desert," I said. "And if he hasn't turned up, he's still with Flint."

"Sure," Big Mike said, turning his attention to the map, not saying what we all thought. Danny could be dead anywhere, his body hidden under rubble or weighed down and tossed in the harbor.

"Okay, Boyle, I'll get the MPs looking for two men, traveling by truck. I'll contact Naples, and have MPs waiting there. If Flint gets off one of those ships, they'll grab him," Harding said. "Then we'll organize another tour for our general."

"I'm sure it would be possible to board a ship in all the confusion at the docks," Cosgrove said. "But staying hidden, and getting off safely in Naples? I doubt it."

"I agree," Kaz said. "We need to think like this madman. What would he do?"

"And why?" I said. "What does he want?"

"To win the game," Kaz said. "To get his general, fill the royal flush, and beat you, Billy."

"He has Danny," I said. "I'm counting on him keeping him alive until he finds a general to take. Which means he has to have a story, something that would convince Danny to go along with him."

"So boarding a ship to Naples is out. But how many places are there to go within the beachhead?" Kaz said.

"I don't think he'd head for the British sector. A couple of Yanks would stand out. Back to the Third Division front? They'd be nabbed and sent back to their unit," I said. "It doesn't make sense, there's nowhere to go. What does he hope to accomplish?"

"Okay, we gotta slow down and think like detectives," Big Mike said. That wasn't hard for Big Mike; blue flowed in his veins. He still carried his shield from the Detroit Police Department wherever he went. "When's the last time you saw Danny and Flint?"

"Yesterday, mid-afternoon. I brought some supplies out to them; I was supposed to be leaving since we'd found the killer. We took some artillery fire, watched the Carabinieri haul off some Italians, had some chow, and then the company CO told Flint to go down to the docks to grab replacements. The ones for his platoon had been killed in the shelling. It was probably five o'clock by the time they got there."

"How was Flint acting? Like something tipped him off, maybe?" Big Mike said.

"No, he played it cool. He's not a guy who rattles easily."

"So something happened between there and the docks. Something that caused him to skip town with Danny."

"That was about the time I came ashore," Kaz said. "Could he have seen me?"

"What if he did? It wouldn't mean anything to him," Big Mike said.

"Oh no," I said, the sequence of events becoming clear in my mind. "I think I know what it was. Stump. The guy we supposedly had in custody as the killer. Doc Cassidy was going to transfer him to Naples with the wounded. Damn! I'll check with Cassidy, but I bet Stump got on a ship yesterday afternoon."

"And Flint saw him, and knew the jig was up," Big Mike said. "Then he comes up with a story that Danny will buy, and takes off to parts unknown."

"But there are no parts unknown here," Kaz said, pointing at the map. "The beachhead is nothing more than an open-air prison, with the Germans guarding all sides."

"Maybe he's planning a jailbreak," Big Mike said. I stared at the map, trying to put myself in Flint's shoes. "From what Cassidy said, he's pretty committed to going through with this plan. But he also said psychopaths can be impulsive, so it makes sense that he changed course so quickly."

"If he's like most hoodlums, he'll have a new set of wheels in no time," Big Mike said.

"There was a major from the Quartermaster Corps in here earlier. His jeep was stolen yesterday, down by the docks," I said. It fit perfectly. "Big Mike, check with the officer in charge, and find out the time it was taken. If it was around 1600 hours, it was probably Flint. Tell them to approach with caution, that we want the driver and passenger taken alive. There's a mounted .30-caliber machine gun on that jeep, and I don't want any itchy trigger fingers with Danny on board."

"Sure thing, Billy."

"What should we do next?" Kaz asked. I gazed at the map. The right flank, lightly guarded, lightly defended. A wide gap between the Germans and the First Special Service Force. That had to be it.

"We have to tempt him," I said, looking at Cosgrove. "We have to let him think he has a chance to pull it all off. And we have to take him before he does any of it." Once, I might not have cared if Cosgrove got himself killed, but familiarity had bred admiration, so I wanted to be reasonably certain he didn't end up being a victim. Most of all, I wanted Danny out of Flint's clutches. Trouble was, Flint knew that, and would use it against me.

"Billy, the time checks out," Big Mike said, returning to the table. "The jeep was last seen at 1530 hours. That major left it there for his corporal to pick up, but when the corporal got there, he thought the major had kept it. That's why it wasn't reported right away."

"Okay. They sending it out?"

"Yep, radioing it now to all units, and sending a message to the Carabinieri like you asked. And here's the good news. The major gave them the serial number, VI-37Q-DP-4. The Q identifies it as a Quartermaster vehicle, and the DP means from the Depot Company. It ought to be pretty easy to spot a Quartermaster's jeep with a .30 mounted on it."

"Good work. Now let's catch up with Harding and get this thing rolling." The army believed in doing things big, so each vehicle had its serial number stenciled in white paint on the front bumper. If the MPs kept their eyes open, and Flint stayed on the roads, it was only a matter of time. Big if.

Cosgrove was not going to be very popular. Harding agreed to inform First Special Service Force HQ that a senior general was coming through on an inspection tour, to determine if the unit should be disbanded. It was precisely the kind of news that would spread like wildfire throughout the brigade. If Flint came within earshot of even a single private, odds were he'd hear about it. If I'd guessed right about his plan.

"You sure you want to go through with this, Cosgrove?" Harding asked as our phony general eased himself into the backseat of the staff car. "The Force men are a rough bunch. Between Flint, the Krauts, and them, you won't have a friend within miles."

"Don't worry, Sam," Big Mike said. "I got my .45 automatic, a Winchester Model 12 trench gun, and a .38 police special for backup." Harding permitted a causal familiarity from Big Mike, which no one else would ever dare to try to get away with. Big Mike did it so naturally, I don't think

Harding could take offense. Plus, Big Mike knew when to call him 'sir.'

"Where the hell did you get a shotgun?" Harding asked.

"It's not hard when you've got a supply officer desperate to get his fancy jeep back," Big Mike said. "Automatic at my hip, shotgun by my side, revolver in my pocket, and walkie-talkie on the seat. If Major Cosgrove gets killed, you can fire me."

"That's General Paget to you, Sergeant," Cosgrove said. "And if he does get me killed, Harding, break him to private and keep him in the army for life."

"In that case, you're safe as a baby with me," Big Mike said, settling in behind the wheel.

"Remember, the SCR-536 has a range of only a mile. We'll stay close, but don't wander off, or we'll lose you. Check in every thirty minutes."

"Will do." With that they were off.

Their first stop would be Valmontorio, on the coast where the Mussolini Canal ran into the sea. It was the far end of the line that the Force held, and the plan was for Cosgrove to kick up a big stink, so word would spread ahead of him. Kearns had already radioed General Frederick, who agreed to go along with the plan, and let word slip to his staff about an inspection by a British general who thought highly trained units like the FSSF were a waste of resources.

The unit held the canal north up to Sessano, and that was where Luca and his Carabinieri came in. He was there with a truckload of men, supposedly searching for spies. If we needed help, we'd send a radio message and then have reinforcements from another direction. It was a good plan, especially since GIs were used to seeing the blue-uniformed Carabinieri, and tended to ignore them.

The dull *crump* of distant artillery rolled in from the north, and I had the usual thought: glad it's them, not me. We went in the MP office for one last check. No one had reported seeing the missing jeep, no sign of Flint or Danny. By the time we left, the artillery was louder. Closer.

"Why'd you switch to that peashooter?" Harding said as we got into the jeep. He was carrying a Thompson submachine gun. Kaz was armed only with his Webley revolver, but he was pretty good with it and didn't like carrying anything else. Ruined the cut of his uniform, he claimed.

"Traded with a guy who got us out of a scrape," I said. "Besides, it's light, and more accurate than the Thompson."

"Just make sure you shoot him more than once with that," Harding said. "I've seen Krauts take a couple of those slugs and keep running." He was right; compared to the M1 rifle, or the Thompson, the M1 carbine round was small and less powerful. Still, it had its uses.

I drove, Kaz at my side, Harding in the back. We went along the coast road, and watched destroyers cut circles in the bay, smoke pots churning on their fantails, disappearing into the white clouds that they created. All that smoke was camouflage for an incoming convoy, and the German gunners registered their disapproval by sending a few shells after the destroyers, not even getting close but sending up great geysers of blue-and-white foam. The wind kicked up, and dark clouds drifted in from the sea, blowing the smoke in our direction. The water, air, and sky became the same uniform gray, the heavy weather covering the land with an opaque, damp, shivering chill. I steered the jeep around the occasional bomb crater not yet filled in by the engineers, who had round-the-clock work keeping roads, bridges, and airfields functioning.

Where was Danny? What would I do if he were killed out here, not by the Germans, but by a man I'd been sent to track down? How could I tell my mother, or confess my failing to my father? I ached to find Danny, and I prayed as I drove, bargaining with God, offering everything I could think of, frightened that it wasn't God who held Danny's future in his hands, but a homicidal maniac. I'd bargain with him too, if I knew what he wanted, and if it were mine to give.

Chapter Thirty-Six

"Look out," Kaz said, leaning forward in his seat. "Slow down, there are shell holes all around."

"Good reason to go faster," Harding said from the backseat, where he'd just finished checking in with Big Mike on the walkie-talkie. I maintained my speed, weaving between the blackened holes, aware of the burned-out wrecks of vehicles on either side of the road. "Looks like the Germans have this area zeroed in. Narrow road, nowhere to go. We'd be sitting ducks if it wasn't for this fog."

The wind had died down, leaving the coast shrouded in mist, making it hard to see where I was going. But if I couldn't see, the Germans up in the hills sure as hell couldn't either, and I was glad not to have a ton of explosive steel raining down on us.

"Stop!" Harding yelled. I braked, and he jumped out, running to an overturned truck, where a body lay sprawled on the ground. All I could think was, please let it not be Danny.

It wasn't. There were bloody compresses on his chest, where medics had worked on him. Other medical debris was scattered around him. There may have been other wounded, so the medics left the corpse behind for Graves Registration.

"False alarm," Harding said.

"Perhaps not," Kaz said, holding the dead man's dog tag. "This says Amos Flint."

"Search him," I said. "We need to find out what name Flint is using." Kaz and I went through his pockets, but Flint must have beaten us to it.

"Nothing," Kaz said. "The man is clever, I must say."

"Save the compliments," Harding said. "The fog is clearing, let's go."

We crossed a wooden bridge and took the road into Valmontorio, a cluster of cinder-block buildings scattered about on either side of the road as it bent north, along the bank of the Mussolini Canal. Every building had been hit. Roofs were gone; the contents of homes tumbled out into the street or were left charred inside gutted structures. It looked like a ghost town.

"Get that goddamn jeep out of sight!"

barked a GI who appeared from nowhere. Suddenly men appeared in doorways and at windows. One of them waved us into a spot between two houses and beckoned us to follow inside. "What are you boys doing here?" he said, as if we'd been caught trespassing. At the far end of the room, two GIs were eating their rations, glancing occasionally at the foggy view of the shoreline and canal. A radio sat on a table, along with binoculars and a map of the coast. A rather casual observation post.

"Your rank, soldier?" Harding said, stepping forward so his insignia could be seen.

"Lieutenant George Bodine, First Special Service Force. What can I do for you, Colonel?" He made it sound like a chore to even answer the question.

"Why did you pull us in? Are there Germans close by?"

"No, Colonel, there ain't a live Kraut within a mile of here," Bodine said as the other two men chuckled. "But the fog is about to blow off, and in five minutes you'd be dead if you went up that road. German gunners have been waiting for hours now to spot something."

"It doesn't look like it's clearing," Kaz said, peering out through the glassless window.

"It is. You wait."

"Lieutenant," I said. "We're looking for a sergeant and a private, traveling by jeep most likely, one with a mounted .30 caliber. You see anybody like that?"

"Only visitor here was some loudmouth British general, about an hour ago. Asked a lot of stupid questions and said units like ours were a waste of resources. On some kind of inspection tour or some such bullshit."

"What'd you say to that?" Harding asked.

"Offered to take him out on patrol tonight so he could see what the Krauts' opinion was. He didn't take us up on the offer. You know what they call us out here? Black devils. That's what *they* think of us."

"Why black devils?"

"Because we blacken our faces when we patrol at night. And we leave these calling cards behind, pasted to the foreheads of dead Krauts." He handed Harding a red-and-white sticker, with the arrowhead insignia of the Force, and the words *Das dicke Ende kommt noch.*

"What does that mean?" Harding asked.

"The worst is yet to come," Bodine said, with a smile. "That's why there aren't any Krauts within a mile or so. They began to pull back once we started going out after dark. Now we have to walk farther each night to find any."

"Is this your right flank?"

"Hell no, Colonel. This is the rear area. Most of our guys are across the canal, set up in Sabotino and other towns over there. Nice and snug, not all blown up like this dump. This is where we bring the wounded for transport back to Anzio, and pick up supplies."

"Does HQ know about this?"

"Maybe," Bodine shrugged. "It's a fluid situation."

"Meaning you like being on your own."

"Yes sir. Less interference from the brass, the better. Meaning no offense."

"None taken. You're sure about not seeing our two men pass through?"

"Yeah. Maybe they got hit back at the bridge. The Krauts like to shell that area."

"So I noticed," I said, then heard the shrill whistle that was becoming too familiar. I flinched, and noticed Bodine smiling.

"That's the bridge again," he said. "Must be another supply run. You boys might want to get a move on while the Germans are busy."

We took his advice, heading north along the canal, and damned if the fog didn't clear a few minutes later.

"I guess he knew what he was talking about," I said.

"They recruited a lot of outdoorsmen for that outfit," Harding said. "Lumberjacks, game wardens, fishermen, guys who are used to living rough. They have a sixth sense about the weather."

"Did you believe him about not seeing Flint and Danny?"

Harding shrugged. "Why shouldn't I?"

I glanced at Kaz, wondering if he'd picked up on it. He looked perplexed, and I gave him a minute as I drove down a tree-lined road, hoping the branches gave us some cover from the German observers, or that they wouldn't want to waste all those shells on a single jeep.

"He didn't ask why we were looking for them!" Kaz said, snapping his fingers. "That would be a natural question to ask."

"Yep. Good catch, Kaz. You'll be a detective yet."

"Why didn't you press him then?" Harding said, growling with irritation, at either my lack of follow-up or the fact that he hadn't noticed it. I nodded at Kaz, giving him the go-ahead.

"Because there was only one direction for Flint to go, the same one we are taking. And, assuming Lieutenant Bodine is an honest man, Flint must have fed him some story that made him sympathetic. Something that would appeal to a solider slightly contemptuous of authority."

"Slightly?" Harding said, as he picked up the walkie-talkie for the routine check. "Big Mike, come in. Big Mike, come in."

Big Mike reported in. He and Cosgrove were in Santa Maria, which he said was nothing more than a cluster of farmhouses and chicken coops. Cosgrove was going through his routine, making enemies. Something he seemed to have a flair for. No sign of trouble.

We drove on, slowly, not wanting to overtake them. It began to mist, a fine drizzle that seemed to float in the air rather than fall. I scanned the few buildings that dotted the road, most of them shelled by the Germans, denying us observation posts and a dry place to sleep.

"There, Billy," Kaz said, pointing to a stone farmhouse ahead and to our left. Whenever possible, vehicles anywhere in the beachhead were parked behind buildings to block the view of German observers in the hills. There, tucked in the lee of the farmhouse, was a jeep with a mounted machine gun. The house, set too far back to be an observation post, had not been hit by artillery. It was intact, with a full view over open fields in every direction. A perfect hideout. Kaz was still pointing, and I pressed his arm down.

"Don't," I said, as I carefully maintained my speed. "If Flint is looking, I don't want him to notice anything out of the ordinary." We had him. Now came the hard part. I continued on until a grove of trees masked a turn in the road, and pulled over. "We have to approach on foot," I said. "Very carefully. There's a few rows of trees we can use as cover."

"But this way we don't catch Flint in the act," Kaz said.

"But we get Danny out safely," I said, looking to Harding. He nodded, and we checked weapons, crossed the road, and ducked low as we ran through rows of turnips toward the line of trees. Lemon trees, but my mind wasn't on fruit. It was on getting in and getting Danny out. We needed to go in hard and fast. I was most worried about being in the open, where Flint could see us. That would give him an edge, since he'd have Danny for cover and we'd be exposed. We got near the end of the trees and hunched down.

"I'll take the back door," I said. "Kaz, you follow me. I'll check the jeep. If it's ours, you stay outside and guard it. Make sure Flint doesn't escape if he gets past me. Colonel, wait until you hear me hit the door, then go in the front. Okay?"

"Okay," Harding said. "Low and quiet until we go in."

"And make sure —"

"Yes, we know, Billy. We'll be careful not to shoot Danny."

"Or let Flint get near him. Let's go."

We scuttled to the building, watching the windows for any sign of movement. This was dangerous, too; I wouldn't shoot at a shadow for fear of hitting Danny, but a shadow might not worry about shooting me. We went flat against the rough stone, Harding ready by the door. Kaz and I crouched and went to the rear of the building, hiding behind the jeep. It was splattered with muck, the identification on the bumper hidden by caked-on mud. Flint was a smart one, all right, but his luck was about to run out. I wiped the mud away and saw VI-37Q. It was enough. I nodded to Kaz, gripped my carbine, and made for the door. When I pressed my back against the wall and went for the latch, I noticed the door hadn't been fully closed. I pushed at it with the barrel of my rifle, just a touch, to get a look inside. I needed to signal Harding, and a silent entry wasn't going to do that. Once I got a peek, I'd kick the door and go in like gangbusters.

I didn't get a peek. Instead, I got the muzzle of an M1 Garand in my face.

CHAPTER THIRTY-SEVEN

Two Force men pinned me to the wall as two others advanced on Kaz, Thompsons aimed at his head. He wisely laid his revolver on the seat of the jeep. They dragged us both inside, where Harding was seated in the kitchen, disarmed. His colonel's eagle insignia seemed to be buying him a bit more respect than my lieutenant's bars were. A sergeant stood behind him, arms folded, holding a .45 pointed at the floor.

"Who the hell are you?" the sergeant said, to none of us in particular. *"Sprechen Zie Deutsch?"*

"Sergeant, I am Colonel Samuel Harding, of General Eisenhower's staff. These two work for me."

"Yeah, right. Ike's in London last I heard. You tellin' me he sent you down here to sneak up on us? You with that British general snoopin' around? Or have we caught ourselves some Kraut spies?"

"General Eisenhower did send me," I said. "To catch a murderer. Sergeant Amos Flint, last seen driving that jeep outside." I saw the men exchange glances.

"Murder? Who'd he kill?"

"His own lieutenant. A doctor, a captain, a major, a POW, and at least one sergeant from his own platoon. He stole that jeep and we think he's headed into enemy territory. What line did he feed you?"

"Big tall guy? With a skinny kid tagging along?"

"Yeah, that's him," I said. "Hey, if you're sure we're not Germans, how about giving us our weapons back?"

Harding stood and held out his hand. The sergeant gave him his .45 back. Our other weapons were laid on the table.

"They were here earlier this morning. Gave us a story about bein' on the lam from the MPs for slugging some desk jockey who got a bunch of his men killed for nothin'. Seemed believable."

"He's a practiced liar," I said. "Damn good at it, so don't feel bad. He let you have the jeep?"

"We swapped. Had an old Italian ambulance, a Fiat truck, that we used for transporting wounded. Most times, the Krauts don't shell ambulances on their own. But we liked the jeep and that .30 caliber, so we suggested a trade. Thought it might help him blend in."

"Did he say where they were headed?"

"Back to his outfit, he claimed, in Le Ferriere. Said they'd lie low for another day or so until the dust settled, then show up to get the lay of the land."

"How well is the line defended along here?"

"Well, you got the Hermann Goering Panzer Division over there, but they pulled back pretty far. You can cross the canal any time you want and get nothing more than wet feet. It's more of a big drainage ditch than any canal I ever saw."

"You have outposts along the canal?"

"Colonel, our outposts are way across the canal. That's why the Krauts pulled back. They don't like waking up in the morning to find sentries with their throats slit."

"Das dicke Ende kommt noch," Kaz said.

I was sure the calling card that the Force men left behind would appeal to Flint. "Did you give him any of your stickers?"

"Yeah, a souvenir, sorta. He didn't like hearing about that Limey any more than we did. No offense, lieutenant," he said to Kaz. "Seeing as you're Polish."

Kaz, who wore the red shoulder flash that

proclaimed Poland on his British uniform, nodded in acceptance.

"We have to get to Big Mike," I said. "Fast."

We hotfooted it out of there, all of us worried about Big Mike and Cosgrove now, not to mention Danny. Flint had a new vehicle, one that gave him an edge. The red cross on the Italian ambulance was like a free pass. GIs would wave him on, the Germans would hold their fire, and Big Mike wouldn't know what hit him.

"Big Mike, come in," Harding said into the walkie-talkie, holding down the press-to-talk switch. "Big Mike, come in." He released the switch. Nothing.

"Keep trying, maybe they're out of range," I said as I started the jeep and pulled out into the road. We were clear of the trees in a few seconds, and I prayed that whatever German up in the hills had his binoculars trained on us couldn't be bothered to call in fire on one measly jeep.

For the second time today, I was wrong. Really wrong. I heard the whistle of incoming shells, and stepped on it. For the third time today, wrong again. The salvo hit just ahead of us, and if I'd pulled over I could have avoided going through it. Bright flashes shuddered against the ground, sending dirt and smoke everywhere, blinding me as I lifted one arm to shield my eyes, holding onto the steering wheel with the other.

The next thing I knew, I had a mouthful of mud. I was in a ditch by the side of the road, a thin rivulet of water soaking me. I tried to get up and clear my head. I saw a blurry figure standing over me, got up on one knee, and blinked my eyes until I could make him out.

"You all right, Colonel?"

"Leg's banged up a little, but I'm fine," he said, taking my arm and helping me up.

"Where's Kaz? What happened?"

"He's looking for the walkie-talkie. We hit a shell hole and rolled the jeep. We're lucky it didn't come down on top of us."

The barrage had stopped, but I heard shelling farther up the road. "That could be Big Mike and Cosgrove getting hit," I said. "Or Flint and Danny."

"The radio is useless," Kaz said, pointing to the jeep on its side in the ditch. The pieces of the walkie-talkie were pinned underneath.

"See if you can get some help to right the jeep," I said, grabbing my carbine. "I'm going up there." I started to run, hearing Harding and Kaz yelling at me to stop, but I couldn't. I couldn't wait by the side of the road like a stranded motorist. I had to move, to get to Danny before everything went wrong. If it hadn't already.

The first thing that went was my helmet. Too damn heavy. Then the canteen from my web belt. I wasn't wearing the ammo bandolier, so all I had was the fifteen rounds loaded in the carbine and my .45 automatic. If that wasn't enough, I was in bigger trouble than I thought. My Parsons jacket went next, and then I settled into a run, remembering track team in high school. Danny used to come watch me practice. I did the hurdles and the long jump. Not all that well, but it had been a hell of a lot easier without combat boots, an automatic flapping on my hip, and an M1 carbine at port arms.

I could see puffs of explosions in the distance, rising above the shrubs and trees that lined the canal. If there were Force men hidden along the canal, they didn't show themselves. From what the GIs we'd met told us, most were on the other side, hiding out until nightfall. I ran, focusing on lifting my legs, getting the most out of each stride, keeping my breathing regular and my eyes on the horizon. Get into the rhythm, Coach used to say. Don't stare at the ground in front of you, it's all the same. Look ahead, to where you want to be.

I ran.

Chapter Thirty-Eight

The explosions ahead had ended. The road was deserted. I kept running, my legs aching and my lungs burning. I wondered if a German observer was tracking me through his binoculars, figuring another dogface had gone nuts. Shell-shocked, battle-fatigued, crazy. I ran, remembering Coach's words: *Just because you feel pain, you don't have to stop.* My boots beat a rhythm on the road, and I imagined Danny waiting for me, although all I could see in my mind was a kid in short pants, running through the backyards of our neighborhood.

I stumbled, one boot catching on the pavement, and went head over heels, tucking my chin and rolling until I came up again, running. I was bleeding somewhere on my arm, and one knee felt wobbly, but I focused on picking up my feet and kept going, watching the road ahead.

Then I heard shots. *Pop pop pop,* followed

by a *rat-tat-tat,* then a chorus of mayhem as automatic weapons and rifles spat fire, and I picked up the pace, ignoring the searing pain in my lungs, trying to figure out where the fight was. On the right, by the canal. Small explosions thudded, grenades maybe. I was closer to the fight now, and slowed so I could catch my breath and be ready, watching for movement along the canal. I got off the road, double-timing it across a field and into the trees and shrubs lining the bank of the canal, hoping for cover before I was spotted. I worked my way into a patch of dense brush, and stopped, kneeling as I waited for my breathing to get under control. Gasping for air, I parted the bushes and scanned the canal, both directions. Nothing. Then I saw a head pop up across the bank, about fifty yards upstream. More rifle fire sounded, then a submachine gun, probably a Schmeisser MP40.

What was this? A German raid? The Force men said they'd pushed across the canal, but they had a lot of ground to cover, and maybe the Krauts had infiltrated for prisoners. Or revenge, for all those dead sentries. I took a deep breath, the cool air easing the burning in my lungs, and made my way along the riverbank, carbine at the ready, wishing I had my Thompson and a whole lot more ammo.

I heard splashes behind me, and ducked under cover. Footsteps came up the path and I heard snatches of whispered German. Two figures darted past me, and I recognized the camouflage smocks of the Hermann Goering Division. I stepped out onto the path and squeezed off two shots into the back of one of them, then fired two more at the other guy, but I must've missed, because the next thing I saw was a potato-masher grenade sailing through the air in my direction. I ran back down the path, until I heard the explosion behind me, then worked my way into the underbrush and crawled forward. Shouts and cries intermingled with firing, and all I could tell was that up ahead someone was putting up a helluva fight.

I took a chance and crawled out of the underbrush and into the field, running at a crouch along the edge of the farmland, hoping the Germans were too busy with the opposition ahead to worry about where I'd gotten to. I saw the outline of burned-out buildings through the vegetation. The firing was centered on the buildings, and it seemed as if the Germans were trying to flank whoever was inside. I ran faster, closing in on the tree line and the clearing in front of the buildings.

I heard two blasts, and recognized the distinctive booming sound of a shotgun. That had to be Big Mike. Were he and Cosgrove fighting off the Krauts? I scooted forward, staying as low as I could, watching for the familiar helmets and camouflage of Goering's Luftwaffe troopers.

A single German stood up from the undergrowth not ten yards ahead, ready to throw a grenade at one of the houses. I fired my carbine — three, four shots — wanting to be sure he didn't make the throw. He spun around and for a second he looked at me, his mouth open wide in surprise. Then he fell backward, the grenade still in his hand. First came the explosion, then the shrieks. There were others with him, probably hurt but still alive.

I dove into the greenery again, as bullets clipped the leaves over my head. I had their attention now, and I expected another grenade at any moment. I wished I had some of my own. How many times had I fired? Seven, eight? I crawled toward the canal this time, stopping to listen for the telltale rustling of leaves and branches as Germans searched for me. I was near the path, and as I drew myself up into a crouch, I heard a voice.

"Willi?"

"Ja," I answered in a rough whisper. I was rewarded with a hand thrust through branches, clearing a path. I shot him twice, then fired once more in case there was somebody behind him. I backtracked. Four, maybe five shots left.

It grew quiet. Splashes again, but they sounded as if they were heading back across the canal. I went back out into the field, and circled around to the buildings. The first thing I saw was the staff car, then Big Mike on the ground. I froze. Who had been firing? Three dead Germans lay in the clearing, one more at the blown-out door to the ruined home. Shotgun shells were scattered on the ground. I made my way to Big Mike, as silently as I could. His hair was matted with blood, but he hadn't been shot. Maybe grazed, but he was still breathing. I shook him. No response.

Chapter Thirty-Nine

I heard a noise in the bushes, rose, and aimed my carbine over the hood of the staff car. I expected Germans, and my mind took a second, maybe two, to understand what my eyes were seeing. It was Danny, pulling at a leather strap twisted tight at his neck. Flint was behind him, shoving him forward, grinning so wide I could see his white teeth gleaming against pink gums. Then I realized what the strap was: the sling of Big Mike's shotgun. The barrel was against Danny's head. Flint's victims ran through my head, and I struggled not to cry out as I calculated my chances. And Danny's. The odds were against both of us, and I felt my stomach drop and my skin go clammy. I aimed at Flint's head, which was mostly hidden behind Danny's. I really didn't know what to do.

"Thank you, Lieutenant Boyle," Flint said, pushing Danny ahead of him. Danny dug in his heels and grabbed at the strap gouging his throat, getting a finger underneath. "You saved our lives. I guess I owe you something."

"Let Danny go," I said. "Then we'll be even."

"Even? No, not after all the trouble you've caused. What the hell did I ever do to deserve meddling lieutenants, huh? First Landry, now you."

"Landry just wanted to help you," I said, knowing that meant nothing to Flint. But I figured he'd kept his grand scheme bottled up so long that he might want to talk. And if he talked, he might make a mistake while he was jabbering.

"Landry was pathetic. Falling for that whore. Can you imagine living with a woman who sold her body to other men? It's disgusting. I did him a favor, and look what he did to me."

"You beat up Inzerillo, and Ileana too. He sent you to Galante, on the QT, to keep you out of trouble. It's my bet Galante wanted to put you in a loony bin, that's why you killed him." I kept my eyes fixed on Danny's, hoping he wouldn't do anything stupid.

"You're smart, too smart for your own good. Yeah, Galante wanted to get me into a psychiatric hospital. Made it sound like going to college. We'd work together and learn new things about the human mind, he told me." Flint's mouth twisted in disdain for the foolishness of Galante's efforts. "I didn't kill him until I had to. He was going to submit paperwork to have me discharged. He shouldn't have done that. It was his own fault."

"Sure, it was all his fault," I said. "Then you cooked up the crazy card scheme to confuse things, right?"

"Crazy? It worked, didn't it?" We were less than ten feet apart. Danny had stopped struggling, his hand limp where he held the strap. "It would have worked perfectly if it wasn't for you getting in the way."

"Like Louie?"

"It was too bad about Louie. I told you that I bought the Walther off him after he shot the Kraut officer. But it was me. I shot Rusty and the Kraut." He said it proudly, his vanity too strong to resist the impulse to brag. Danny struggled, and Flint twisted the strap tighter. I had to keep Flint talking to me to keep his attention off Danny.

"But why Rusty?"

"He irritated me," Flint said. He relaxed his grip on Danny, who gulped air. Danny's eyes widened, as if asking me what I was going to do. I had no idea.

"That's it? What about Louie? I thought you got along with him."

"Louie was okay, but I knew a smart-ass like you would start asking questions about the pistol, so he had to go. Too bad, because you were sniffing around him, figuring him for the killer. I liked that. You screwed up, Boyle. If you'd left things alone, Louie would be alive. Or dead. This *is* war, after all."

"Cole?"

"The bastard killed himself! What, are you going to blame me for every nutcase who takes a nosedive off a building?" Flint shoved Danny closer, his voice rising, his face red with sudden anger. I needed to calm him down.

"Pretty smart, the way you drove him to it, with the doll, always reminding him about that cellar."

"You found the doll, huh? I didn't know your skills extended to rummaging through garbage. Yeah, I had something I wanted and Cole was the guy to find it."

"So Galante told you about the pearls, and you figured out how to find them?" I tried to keep my voice steady, just another guy in awe of his intellect.

"Galante told me they were hidden in the palace. He was big on museums and Italian history. I think he liked the idea of educating me. He even said I could lead a normal life one day. Normal! Can you imagine that? Being one of you faceless creatures, one of the nameless? Not for me."

"Pearls," I said, desperate to keep him talking. "The pearls were for you, right?"

"Bingo! They'd been stolen, Galante said, and hidden in the palace. No one ever found them. I gave Cole all the dope I got from Galante as he figured things out, based on what that old Italian broad told him. Cole and I were going to split the take if he found the pearls."

"He did," I said, doubting he would have lived to collect. "He gave them to me right before he jumped."

"That crooked bastard! He held out on me. Goes to show, you can't trust anyone." He shrugged, as if it made no difference.

"Don't you want the pearls? I could get them for you."

"The pearls! I don't want the goddamn pearls anymore, they're no good to me."

"What, were they for your girl back home, and she dumped you?"

"Drop the rifle, Boyle. Your sidearm too. Then let's go inside, I have a surprise for you."

"Your mother," I said, remembering the

letter. "They were for your mother. Then she died, and spoiled all your plans. You were going to bring them home to mother, weren't you?"

Flint's face contorted into a twisted, teeth-crunching snarl. His cheeks went red and he began to tremble. I prayed I hadn't gone too far and was about to speak when I saw movement in the bushes they had just come out of. A flash of camouflage, and then I made out a German, limping on one bloody leg, making for the canal. He turned, Schmeisser in hand, and I fired once, and missed; again, and hit him. He staggered, but he was still up. Then a third shot to the head, and he went down, firing into the ground as his finger involuntarily twitched on the trigger.

I swung the carbine back to Flint, and his face was calm, as if the previous exchange had never happened. How many bullets did I have left? Two? None?

"Thank you again," Flint said, his politeness a knife in my gut.

"Why go through all this, Flint? What's the point, in the middle of a war, for Christ's sake! Why?" I wasn't stalling now, I wanted to know. If he killed Danny, I needed to know.

"Why? Because I can. Because I'm not

one of the sheep," Flint said, the last word hissing out between his teeth. "I'm not a man who depends on what's sewn on his sleeve to tell him who he is and what he can do. Or who needs a uniform to run his own world. Your rules, your ranks, your salutes, they mean nothing to me. A street sweeper is the same as a bishop or a general to me. You all play roles and kiss the ass of the player above you, and thank him for the privilege. Why? Because you all make me sick. I'd kill the whole fucking world if I could."

"You're a powerful man, Flint, I can see that," I struggled to keep my words even, to not react to Flint's venom. "So how about a favor, for a kid who doesn't even know what his role is yet? Let Danny go."

"I don't think so. Now, let's go inside, like gentlemen," he said. "I have a card to play." Flint herded us into the house, me first, Danny between us, the shotgun at Danny's head. I held onto the carbine, not sure how many rounds were left. The first thing I saw was a chair. Communications wire lay on floor, some of it still tied to the armrests. Cosgrove. He'd had Cosgrove tied up in here, but he'd gotten away. Blood stained one of the armrests. Not much, but enough to tell me Cosgrove was hurt.

"Big surprise," I said. Explosions erupted outside, sending a blast of dirt and smoke into the ruined house. We each instinctively went into a crouch, Flint still pressing the shotgun against Danny. "Mortars."

"Just the Krauts covering their retreat," Flint said. "No heavy stuff."

"Let me go, Sarge," Danny managed to croak. Another series of explosions hit, closer to the canal.

"No can do, kid. As a matter of fact, if your brother doesn't find that old Limey general and drag him back in here, I'm gonna redecorate the place with your brains." He looked at me with a smile and raised his eyebrows, daring me to call his bluff. I had my carbine, but there was no chance to get a shot off, and he knew it.

More explosions hit the far end of the house, shaking dust and grit loose from the ceiling and showering us all. We covered our heads, the instinct of the battlefield taking over. A flash of movement caught my eye, and I saw Cosgrove, moving faster than I thought possible, a tire iron in his grasp, which he brought down on the kneeling Flint, smashing into his wrist and breaking his grip on the shotgun, not to mention bones. Flint howled, but kept a firm grip on Danny with his other hand, pulling him up and out of the house, the shotgun wrapped around his neck but hanging free. Another mortar round hit the house square above us, sending timbers crashing down around Cosgrove and me. Cosgrove's face was gray with dust and streaked with bright red, but I could see he was more angry than injured.

"Go," he said, working at a section of roof that had pinned one leg.

Mortar rounds churned the water in the canal, but Flint was headed straight for it, Danny in tow. He was ahead of Danny, keeping him as a shield. In seconds they were in the canal, Flint making his way through the waist-deep water. I heard a German machine gun open up, close by. There were still plenty of them out there. Then, a burst stitched across the water, driving me back. Flint and Danny were up on the other bank now, Danny fighting, punching at Flint with one hand and trying to get a grip on the shotgun with the other. Flint had only one good hand, and he needed it to hold onto Danny, to keep him between us. He kicked Danny twice, and that put an end to his fight.

Rifle fire picked up. Something was happening, but I couldn't focus on it. Flint stood with Danny on the opposite bank, his good arm around his neck. He yelled something, but with more mortar rounds dropping all over, it was lost. I knelt, and braced my arm on my knee, aiming at Flint. I could see his white teeth, his mouth wide, speaking to Danny, his eyes on me all the time. I watched Danny, wondering if Flint would take him, or find a way to kill him. And if Danny got away, how long until a bullet or a bomb caught up to him? How long until he'd be a corpse or a combat fatigue case, unable to control the shakes, his dreams and waking nightmares, his life? I didn't want him serving beefsteak to the brass and diving for cover every time a plate dropped. I didn't want Danny to become one of the faceless crowd of casualties in this war.

I tried to count the number of shots I'd fired. Flint was too far away for the pistol, so it had to be the carbine. Gunfire echoed up and down the canal, louder now, and more explosions hit behind me, the Germans working their mortars overtime. I steadied myself, let out a breath, lined up the target in the sights.

Flint shouted one last time, then pushed Danny down the bank. He stood alone for a moment, silhouetted against the sky. Danny faced away from me, trying to free the shotgun, its strap still twisted around his neck. I had my target. I fired.

And shot my brother.

I waited, watching for Flint, but he was gone. So was the machine-gun fire. I tossed the carbine away and ran to Danny, my legs heavy in the brackish water. His right shoulder was bloody, and his eyes dazed. He blinked, as if he thought I might not be real.

"What happened?" He clutched at my arm, wincing in pain. It tore me apart, and I held back the tears I knew would give me away.

"You've been hit. Take it easy, I got you." I took the shotgun from around his neck and hung it from my shoulder. I picked up Danny like I'd done so many times, carrying him in from the backseat of the car, sound asleep, cradled in my arms. His weight was nothing as he rested his head on my chest, grabbing at my shirt with his good arm, his face contorted in pain.

"Am I going to make it, Billy?"

"Don't talk stupid, Danny. You caught some shrapnel in your shoulder, that's all. You'll be fine." I sloshed through the water, watching Cosgrove turn over Big Mike, wadding his jacket under his head for a pillow.

"Flint?" Danny said.

"Yeah," I said. "He got away."

"Why didn't you shoot?"

"I did. I only had one round left, and I missed. What did he say to you?" I laid Danny down, leaning him against the fender of the car, next to Big Mike.

"He said the joker would be waiting for you, downriver."

"That's all?"

"Yeah. He told me that he was granting you a favor, like you asked. Since I hadn't disappointed him."

"You have any idea what that meant?" I pulled open his uniform, sprinkling sulfa on the wound, and applied a compress from the first-aid pack that Cosgrove had retrieved from the car.

"No. I have no idea what anything means." Danny gritted his teeth, grimacing with pain. The bullet was still in there, nestled in a mix of shattered bone and muscle. He needed a hospital, and so did Big Mike.

"How is he?" I asked Cosgrove, who was trying to clean Big Mike's wound with water from a canteen.

"Breathing, is all I can say."

"Thanks for getting the drop on Flint. That was just in time."

"Old trick I learned in Cairo. Tighten your

muscles when you're being tied up. When you relax them, you've got a bit of wiggle room. Unfortunate, Flint getting away like that. Jerry should have no trouble bagging him, though, out alone with a broken wrist."

"Yeah," I said, not certain what he'd seen.

"But your brother, he's safe now, isn't he? Banged up, but he's seen the elephant and will live to tell the tale. Not every man here will be able to say the same."

I had nothing to say, nothing left. I felt a tremendous weariness settle in my body. I slumped down next to Danny, as I heard the sound of vehicles pulling to a halt and boots stomping on the ground. Jeeps, an ambulance, even a truck full of Carabinieri. I put my arm around Danny and held him close, his blood sticky and thick. I watched Big Mike, willing him to wake up and shake off the pounding he'd taken. All this suffering, and Flint had gotten away. But I had Danny, and I prayed I'd made the right choice. And that I could live with myself.

Harding, Kaz, and Luca hovered over me, but I couldn't speak, couldn't answer their questions or look into their eyes. Medics pushed them away and took Danny from me. Others picked up Big Mike and put him on a stretcher. Graves Registration men wandered around with the mattress covers, searching for the dead. Finally, someone came for me.

Chapter Forty

"Your sergeant has a subdural hematoma," Doc Cassidy said. "We're prepping him for surgery right now."

We were back at the hospital, in a small tent that had been set aside for our banged-up group. Danny's shoulder was encased in bandages. Cosgrove sported a bandage over his right temple, and for some reason I was on a cot, too. Harding and Kaz sat at a small table by the open flaps.

"Will he be okay?" I asked.

"If he got here fast enough," Cassidy said. "I'll let you know as soon as I can."

"Can I see him?" I asked, sitting up and getting my feet on the floor.

"You stay put, doctor's orders. You were disoriented, in shock when you came in. I want to watch you for another day."

"How long have I been here?" I asked, not remembering the journey here or anything since lights out back at the canal.

"A couple of hours. You don't remember?" Cassidy pushed me back down on the cot and peered into my eyes.

"No, I don't think so. How's Danny?"

"I'm fine, Billy," he said from his cot, a sloppy grin on his face. "Listen to the doctor and lie down."

"Is he?" I asked Cassidy in a whisper. "Is he really fine?"

"He's feeling no pain right now, due to the morphine we gave him. We got the bullet out, but he'll need another operation in Naples. That's a million-dollar wound he's got there."

That was all I needed to hear. I closed my eyes.

Time passed. I must've slept, because I know I dreamed. Of home. Danny, Mom and Dad. Uncle Dan telling stories at the tavern. Walking the beat, playing baseball and mumblety-peg. Sunday dinners. It was all nice until I lost Danny, and I was just a little kid myself, alone in a strange city, and my hands were smeared with blood.

"Billy, what is it, what's wrong?" It was Kaz, seated by my cot.

"Huh?"

"You cried out in your sleep."

"Bad dream, I guess. Where's Danny? How's Big Mike? How long . . . ?"

Kaz answered me, but I fell back asleep, the thought that Doc Cassidy had given me something bubbling up from the tiredness inside me.

It was light outside when I awoke again. I was alone in the tent. I must have slept through the night, I thought, then saw I was wearing pajamas. When the hell did I put these on? I struggled to get up, felt a little dizzy, then lay down for a minute.

"Boyle? Boyle, can you hear me?" It was Doc Cassidy, shaking my arm. I must've dozed off. I opened my eyes, and a lantern was the only light in the tent. How could it be night already?

"Yeah, I hear you. What's going on? Where's Danny?"

"In Naples by now. How are you feeling?"

"Thirsty. Hungry."

"Good," he said, helping me sit up and giving me a glass of water. "I was worried about you."

"I must've been tired. How long have I been out?"

"Forty-eight hours."

"Impossible," I said, although I knew it wasn't.

"I gave you a mild sedative when you came in here. You seemed agitated, in a state of shock. But it shouldn't have knocked you out for two days."

"Big Mike?"

"I don't know. We relieved the pressure on his brain, and Harding got him on a hospital ship headed to Naples, where he can be treated by a specialist."

"What kind of specialist?"

"A brain surgeon. Billy, he didn't wake up. But that doesn't mean he hasn't by now. Your Colonel Harding didn't want to take any chances."

"Danny's doing all right, isn't he?" *Please.*

"That shoulder is going to bother him whenever it rains. After a few months of physical therapy, he'll have at least ninety percent use of it. Could have been worse."

"Yeah. So he's going home?"

"Definitely. He's a lucky kid. He told me about Flint, and how he let him go. And being wounded by shrapnel. Yep, one lucky kid."

"Can I get out of here now?"

"Can you stand?" I got my legs off the cot and stood. Wobbled a bit, but stayed vertical. I looked at Cassidy. "If you can stay upright, you can go," he said.

"What was wrong with me?" I asked as I shuffled around, testing my legs.

"Shock, or to be more accurate, acute stress reaction. Pressure. Exhaustion. Moral dilemma. Guilt."

"What do you mean?"

"Nothing at all. Just words from my psychiatric residency. Here. I saved a souvenir for you." He pressed a small hunk of metal into my hand. "Keep your head down, Boyle."

I waited until he left. I opened my palm and saw the misshapen but unmistakable shape of a .30 slug from an M1 carbine.

Harding and Kaz walked on either side of me as we made our way to the mess tent in Hell's Half Acre. I guess they wanted to be sure I didn't fall facedown in the mud.

"We're on a PT boat out of here at 0600 tomorrow," Harding said as we each sat with our mess kits full of hot chow.

"Not soon enough," I said. "I'm sorry Flint got away, Colonel."

"Well, at least he didn't fill his royal flush. We've sent his name to the International Red Cross, in case it shows up on a POW list. Meanwhile, we're looking into anyone who was on that road and was reported missing. We'll figure out whose dog tags he grabbed."

"Any word on Big Mike?" I asked.

"Nothing yet. Your brother is shipping out

tomorrow from Naples. Sorry you'll miss him."

"As long as he's going home in one piece, I'm happy."

"Any idea what Flint meant?" Kaz asked. "About a joker downriver?"

"The joker must refer to a card. Maybe he had me tagged for a joker in my pocket. Downriver? No idea. Maybe he meant in the future. Who's to know? So what's next, Colonel?" I said. "After Naples."

"Cosgrove has set something up for us in Brindisi. Then back to London. I hope to God Big Mike is alive and kicking when we get back. How about you, Boyle? Are you all right? That was a helluva nap you took."

"Doc Cassidy said it was a reaction to the sedative he gave me. I guess seeing Danny almost get killed was more of a shock than I thought it was."

"It makes sense," Kaz said.

"Nothing makes sense," I said.

They exchanged looks, and Kaz shrugged, granting me the point. I lifted a cup of coffee, and saw ripples in the black steaming brew. My hand was shaking, so I set it down. Harding and Kaz stared at their food. I tried to look at mine, but all I saw was Danny and his ruined shoulder, Big Mike inert on the ground, the look of surprise on the face of the German with the grenade, and a blur of faceless uniforms, dappled camouflage drenched in blood. Flint, giving me his silhouette on the riverbank, daring me to shoot.

"Billy," Kaz said, his arm reaching toward mine. "Are you all right?"

"Leave me alone," I said, not wanting to lie to Kaz, or tell the truth to Harding. I settled for bitterness instead. I was hungry and I ate, which was simple, unlike everything else that had happened here. I went after my food, not caring what anyone thought, wanting only to fill my belly and get out of the Anzio Bitchhead, which was what the orderly who brought my clothes had called it. I couldn't argue.

■ ■ ■ ■

Part Four: Brindisi, Italy

■ ■ ■ ■

Chapter Forty-One

Never one to miss an opportunity to improve relations with our allies, even one that had recently been our enemy, Harding had come up with the idea of returning the pearls Cole had found to the Italian royal family. Me, I had sort of hoped everyone would forget about them, and Kaz and I could do a split once we were back in London, since I'd come to know some fellows there who might be in the market for hot jewels. But Kaz was already rich, so that plan didn't occur to him. Plus, being one of the European nobility, even if from a minor branch of that intertwined family, he felt it was the right thing to do.

The only thing I liked about the whole idea was that Signora Salvalaggio was the one who was going to give them back to the king and queen. It was only right, since she'd practically been accused of the theft, and her whole life had been changed by it.

Maybe the king would be so happy to get his mother's pearls back that he'd give her a reward, or a castle, or whatever kings these days had to give.

The only thing that worried me about the whole idea was that Signora Salvalaggio had insisted on bringing Ileana along. She'd taken her under her wing, and since neither had anyone else to take them in, it didn't seem like a bad match. But escorting a former prostitute to see a king just plain made me nervous.

We walked up the stone steps to the Swabian Castle in Brindisi, on the heel of the Italian boot. It was a medieval fortress overlooking the harbor, where King Victor Emmanuel III hung his hat. It would have been hard for him to find a suitable joint any farther from the fighting. Signora Salvalaggio was dressed in her finest black. Ileana wore a long white silk dress that the signora had helped her sew. It showed off her raven-black hair and dark eyes. I didn't comment on the fact that it looked like parachute silk. Shopping was hard in war-torn Italy, after all.

"Remember," Harding had lectured us. "There are over twenty thousand Italian soldiers fighting the Germans right now, and acquitting themselves well. We want more to join them, and we want King Emmanuel to encourage it. He's been supportive, and any little thing we can do to show our appreciation will be good for the war effort. So best behavior, Boyle."

I wanted to ask why he singled me out, but instead I just said, "Yes sir."

The beachhead seemed very far away as we trooped through the ornate rooms of the castle. I'd cleaned myself up, gotten a new dress uniform, and was currently trying to fool myself into believing everything was going to be fine. Danny was on his way home, and he'd have stories to tell. He'd proved himself in combat, and would live to tell his kids about it. Flint was hopefully in a POW cage where he wouldn't be associating with generals, and where, with the help of the International Red Cross, we might find him. What could go wrong?

Nothing. Except that everything already had gone wrong. I was living in a world where shooting your own brother was the logical thing to do. I had known I was going to do it, if the opportunity presented itself, for quite a while. I just hadn't admitted it to myself, even though I knew exactly why I'd swapped for that damn carbine. Now I was having dreams of shooting shadowy men in Luftwaffe camouflage, and as they fell and their faces turned in surprise, they became Danny. All of them. I was no longer afraid for Danny; I was afraid for myself. Would I be able to pull the trigger next time? Be fast enough, quick enough, to act without thinking?

This world had gone mad, and I was part of it. One of the faceless crowd. Flint had been right about that.

I felt a hand on my arm. It was Kaz, and we were already standing in front of the king. How did we get here? I tried to focus, but it was all a lot of Italian mumbo-jumbo. King Victor was a bit short in the legs, and I could barely see the top of his head over Signora Salvalaggio's bent form. Harding had a translator who gave a cleaned-up version of how the pearls were found, and then introduced the signora. She bowed, spoke for a minute, and then motioned to Ileana, who opened her purse, drew out the coiled pearls, and presented them to the king. He said something in a low voice, and nodded to one of his aides, who came and retrieved them. I knew enough Italian to hear him thank Signora Salvalaggio before he turned his back and walked away.

"That was underwhelming," I said. Even Harding didn't disagree, as our small group was left alone in the large room with portraits of long-dead rulers staring down at us.

"I am sure the king will make some gesture," Kaz said once we were outside. Harding and Cosgrove had gone to get the staff car while we waited with the ladies. "Once he understands the value of the necklace."

"His mother draped herself in them," Signora Salvalaggio said. "That family knows the value of pearls like a pig knows mud. I don't want his money. If anyone who is left alive knows of the theft, now they know I and my officer did not do it, God rest his soul. That spineless shrimp can go to hell. His father would be ashamed of what he's done to Italy."

"But it is not fair," said Kaz. "You should have something for all this time under suspicion, not to mention for returning the pearls."

"You are a good man, Baron," she said. "Truly noble, in the real sense of the word. I do not want you to worry about an old woman, or a young one, either." She patted Ileana's arm, who smiled at her with a gentle grace. "So I will tell you a secret." Her fingers worked at the top buttons of her dress, and with a girlish smile showed us a short strand of pearls, which quickly disappeared beneath the folds of black. Ileana giggled as she took the old woman by the arm, guiding her to the car that Harding had just driven to the curb. I laughed, and winked at her as she waited for the door to be opened.

"Kaz," I said, draping my arm around his shoulder, "I don't believe I've felt this good in quite some time. Let's ditch Harding and Cosgrove and find ourselves a bar."

"And toast that grand lady," he said. We were already walking away when a British Army motorcycle skidded to a halt in front of us. The rider approached Cosgrove, who had helped the ladies into the car. He handed him a note, saluted, and roared off. Cosgrove read the note, then handed it to Harding. They both looked at me.

"What?"

"Message from SOE headquarters here in Brindisi. I'd asked them to keep me posted," Cosgrove said. I didn't have to ask about what. Diana worked for the Special Operations Executive, and her mission to Rome had been planned here. She had even adopted an accent from the Brindisi area as part of her cover story.

"Tell me," I said, balanced on a knife edge between two worlds, one with Diana alive, the other too terrible to imagine.

"Miss Seaton has been taken," Cosgrove said, his voice quavering. "The Germans have her."

Epilogue

Pain stabbed at his wrist where the old man had struck. He tucked the useless hand into his shirt, and waited his turn. That bastard had surprised him all right, but not as much as Boyle had. He didn't think Boyle would shoot him in cold blood, not once he'd let Danny go. But shooting his own brother, that took some steel in the spine. He hadn't expected that. It was fun giving him a moment's temptation, and the bonus was watching the shot hit bone, seeing the puff of dust from the hit, sensing Danny's blood in the air.

He hoped Danny had given his brother the message. He couldn't find fault with the kid. He'd fought hard, saved his skin, and hadn't done anything stupid. It pleased him to grant the favor, like a great lord would do for a faithful servant.

Sooner or later, though, they all disappointed him. Rusty Gates, Cole, Landry, they were all the same. Pretending to be pals, then becoming insistent, tedious, demanding, deserving of death. Danny was too young, too new for that. Besides, his plans had to wait. He didn't get his general or Boyle. He still had the ace of hearts and the joker to play. A man had to plan things carefully, not kill everything in sight. Unless the army wanted you to. Downriver, he knew he'd come across a general somewhere. And if he was lucky, Boyle would follow once again. This time, the joker would not get away. The Ace of Hearts would taunt him, remind him of what he'd lost, and of what Flint knew about him. Draw him in deeper. Cain and Abel, in Italy.

The river was everything to Flint. It flowed to the killing sea, and he drifted in it, taking what he needed. Downriver, there would always be more. Downriver, Boyle waited.

"Kommt!" The guard poked at Flint with his rifle. There were six of them in the room, seated on a bench, guards at either end. There had been seven, but one had gone into the adjacent office and not come out. Flint wasn't worried. He knew they did it to scare them. He let the guard prod him along into the next room. *"Sitzen!"*

He sat in the wooden chair facing a German officer seated at a small wooden table, a stack of papers in front of him. His cap lay on the table next to an ashtray full of cigarettes.

American cigarettes. He didn't offer one from the pack of Luckies, but lit one for himself.

"We don't get many prisoners from among the criminals on the canal," the German said. He spoke English well, but carefully, drawing out each syllable, pronouncing prisoners as priz-sun-ers. It took Flint a moment to understand he was referring to the First Special Service Force.

"Those guys make me nervous," Flint said with a smile. "Can't imagine how you feel."

"Amusing," the German said, consulting his paperwork. "Sergeant Peter Miller. You are now a guest of the Third Reich, as will be many others from Anzio. How long have you been there?"

"Listen to me," Flint said, leaning forward, focusing his gaze on the German's eyes, getting him to see this was more than another of his endless encounters with grubby Americans. "I can tell you a whole lot more than how long I've been dodging artillery shells in the beachhead. But first, I need a doctor for my arm. I think my wrist is broken. One of those Force men did it, the bastard."

"And why did he do that, Sergeant?"

"We got into an argument. I mentioned my family name had been Mueller, and that they had changed it to Miller during the last war, on account of my dad getting beat up for being German. He said he'd deserved it, and one thing led to another."

"Commendable that you defended your father's honor. But foolish that you had your wrist broken."

"The other guy was more foolish. I broke his damn neck. That's why I took off across the canal." Flint knew he needed a story. He'd been captured minutes after he went across, and this officer probably knew that. Still, it could work to his advantage if he didn't go overboard with the Kraut stuff.

"You killed a comrade?"

"He was no comrade of mine. Those guys think they run everything. I risk my life every day bringing stuff from Nettuno and returning their reports to HQ. You'd think they'd say thanks, but no —"

"Headquarters? What headquarters?"

"General Lucas's headquarters. In Nettuno. Every day I make the trip, and let me tell you, it ain't easy with all that firepower you're throwing at us."

"Tell me about your work at headquarters, Sergeant Miller."

"Here's the deal. I'll spill plenty, once you take care of my arm, and find some officer's uniform for me. I don't want to go to an enlisted man's POW camp. I want medical attention and a promotion. Then we sit and talk, one good German boy to another. Ja?"

"I have another idea. I will have you taken out and shot."

"Hey, suit yourself. Go ahead, and lose the services of a sympathetic German-American who's seen General Lucas every day since he landed." Flint could see the man's eyes flicker, as he calculated what he might gain if the story were true. He knew he could spin tales of HQ long into the night, made up from bits and pieces of gossip, scuttlebutt, and even a bit of truth. Like most GIs he knew which units were where along the line in the beachhead. It might not be news to the Krauts, but it would make the rest of what he told them sound real.

"Very well, Herr Mueller. We will attend to your arm, and find a more suitable identity for you. I take it you do not care how we do so?"

"God's honest truth, I don't give a damn."

AUTHOR'S NOTE

Kurt Gerstein, as described by Diana Seaton in Chapter Two, is a real historical figure. As a witness to the gassing at Belzec, he alerted as many religious leaders and foreign diplomats as he could, unfortunately to little effect. Gerstein surrendered to the Allies at the end of the war in 1945, and was initially treated well by his French captors, who allowed him to reside in a hotel in order to write up what became known as the Gerstein Report, documenting his wartime activities. However, he was subsequently transferred to a prison in France and treated as a war criminal. In July 1945, he was found dead in his cell. Whether it was suicide or murder by members of the SS to keep him quiet has never been determined.

Witold Pilecki, whom Kaz describes in Chapter Nineteen, was also a real person. A Polish Army officer, Pilecki deliberately allowed himself to be picked up in a Nazi roundup, knowing he would be sent to Auschwitz. In 1940, he began to smuggle out reports to the Polish Underground. Finally, in 1943, he escaped from Auschwitz and wrote a detailed report on the exterminations being carried out. The report was sent to London by the Underground, which requested arms and assistance for an assault on Auschwitz. The report was either disbelieved or ignored, and nothing was done. After the war, Witold Pilecki resisted the Soviets with as much fervor as he did the Nazis. He began to collect information on Soviet atrocities and executions of former Underground members. In 1948, he was arrested, and after a show trial by the Communist government of Poland, executed.

It was during World War II that the term "thousand-yard stare" was coined. It referred to the unfocused gaze of a battle-weary soldier, who appeared to be looking through the observer to some distant image. During World War II, 1.3 million soldiers were treated for what was then known as battle or combat fatigue, and it is estimated that up to 40 percent of medical discharges were for psychiatric reasons.

Although much had been learned about

shell shock — as it was called — during the First World War, the U.S. Army forgot many of those lessons and had to relearn them in the Second World War. In the Mediterranean Theater of Operations, it was not until March 1944 (after the events described in this book) that a psychiatrist was added to the medical staff of each combat division. The term "exhaustion" was used to describe conditions that came to be known as combat or battle fatigue, or later, combat stress reaction, and now post-traumatic stress disorder.

Old Sergeant's Syndrome, as described in this novel, is an actual condition defined by the U.S. Army Medical Department during the Second World War. The syndrome was described in 1949 by Major Raymond Sobel, U.S. Army Medical Corps, in his article *Anxiety-Depressive Reactions After Prolonged Combat Experience — the "Old Sergeant Syndrome"* (*U.S. Army Medical Dept. Bulletin,* 1949, Nov. 9, Suppl.: 137–146).

In a study of men who had broken down in combat, the authors stated that the "question was not, 'Why did they break?', but 'Why did they continue to endure?' " It was in this study that the calculation was made that if left in combat for prolonged periods, 98 percent of soldiers would suffer from symptoms of combat fatigue. The remaining 2 percent would undoubtedly be sociopaths. For details, see: Swank, R. L., and Marchand, W. E. (1946). *Combat Neuroses: Development of Combat Exhaustion. Archives of Neurology and Psychology.*

Audie Murphy makes a brief cameo appearance in this story. Murphy, at seventeen, lied about his age to join the service, and became the most decorated American soldier of the war. Murphy was at Anzio, where he suffered a recurrence of malaria, which is what brought him to Hell's Half Acre. After the war, Murphy suffered from severe depression and insomnia, stating that he remembered the war "as I do a nightmare. A demon seemed to have entered my body."

Murphy became addicted to sleeping pills, which he took to overcome his insomnia. To break himself from their grip, he locked himself in a motel room for a week. After that, he broke what had been a taboo about public discussion of combat fatigue, and became a dedicated spokesperson for veterans, urging the government to provide greater support and to increase the understanding of the emotional impact of combat experiences.

The battle for the Anzio Beachhead is still a matter of debate among military historians. Winston Churchill famously remarked that he "had hoped that we were hurling a wildcat onto the shore, but all we got was a stranded whale." General John Lucas was relieved of his command after a month, and it was not until three months later that Allied divisions finally broke out of the encircled beachhead. What could Lucas have done differently? He knew his forces were inadequate and his orders muddled at best. This was a recipe for disaster, but Lucas went along with an operation he felt was doomed, even as his forces were diminished from the original planned allocations. To be fair to his reputation, many veterans of Anzio say they owe their lives to his caution, and that a more aggressive general might have gambled all and lost.

ACKNOWLEDGMENTS

Thanks are due to Edie Lasner for once again graciously reviewing my use of the Italian language. Any errors are certainly due to my transcription in spite of her expertise. My wife, Deborah Mandel, provides constant support and vital feedback in the creation of these stories. My debt to her is profound.

The employees of Thorndike Press hope you have enjoyed this Large Print book. All our Thorndike, Wheeler, and Kennebec Large Print titles are designed for easy reading, and all our books are made to last. Other Thorndike Press Large Print books are available at your library, through selected bookstores, or directly from us.

For information about titles, please call:
(800) 223-1244

or visit our Web site at:
http://gale.cengage.com/thorndike

To share your comments, please write:
Publisher
Thorndike Press
10 Water St., Suite 310
Waterville, ME 04901

Ron Diamond

GWYNNE DYER has worked as a freelance journalist, columnist, broadcaster, and lecturer on international affairs for more than twenty years. Born in Newfoundland, he originally trained as an historian and served in three navies before taking up academic positions at the Royal Military Academy, Sandhurst, and at Oxford University. In 1973, he gave up his day job and turned to writing and documentary filmmaking. Since then, his major activity has been his twice-weekly column on international affairs, which is published by 175 papers in some forty-five countries and is translated into more than a dozen languages.

Dyer's first television series, the seven-part documentary *War*, aired in the mid-1980s and one episode, "The Profession of Arms," was nominated for an Academy Award. The accompanying book, also titled *War*, won the Columbia University School of Journalism Award in 1986. His more recent documentaries include the 1994 series *The Human Race* and a series on peacekeepers in Bosnia, *Protection Force*, which aired in 1995. He has also made documentaries for radio, including *The Gorbachev Revolution* and *Millennium*, on the emerging global culture. Dyer's books include *The Defence of Canada: In the Arms of the Empire* (1990), which he co-authored with Tina Viljoen, and the 2003 best-seller *Ignorant Armies: Sliding into War in Iraq*. Gwynne Dyer lives with his family in London, England.

FUTURE: TENSE

BY GWYNNE DYER

War (1985, new edition 2004)
The Defence of Canada (1990)
Ignorant Armies (2003)

FUTURE: TENSE

THE COMING WORLD ORDER

GWYNNE DYER

Library and Archives Canada Cataloguing in Publication

Dyer, Gwynne
Future: tense : the coming world order / Gwynne Dyer.

ISBN 0-7710-2978-0

1. International relations. 2. World politics – 1989-.
3. Human rights. 4. Security, International. I. Title.

JZ1308.D89 2004 327 C2004-904763-9

We acknowledge the financial support of the Government of Canada through the Book Publishing Industry Development Program and that of the Government of Ontario through the Ontario Media Development Corporation's Ontario Book Initiative. We further acknowledge the support of the Canada Council for the Arts and the Ontario Arts Council for our publishing program.

Typeset in Minion by M&S, Toronto
Printed and bound in Canada

This book is printed on acid-free paper that is 100% recycled, ancient-forest friendly (100% post-consumer recycled).

McClelland & Stewart Ltd.
The Canadian Publishers
481 University Avenue
Toronto, Ontario
M5G 2E9
www.mcclelland.com

1 2 3 4 5 08 07 06 05 04

To Emilia, Jack, Ruby, Jacques, Natasha, Mike,
Catherine, and Isaac, whose future it will be

*

"Terrorism" is what we call the violence of the weak, and we condemn it; "war" is what we call the violence of the strong, and we glorify it.

– Sydney J. Harris, "Nations Should Submit to the Rule of the Law," *Clearing the Ground* (1986)

CONTENTS

INTRODUCTION

It was never about Iraq. It is not really about terrorism any more either, though the terrorists are still there. Suddenly, to the vast surprise of practically everybody, it is about the whole way we run the world.

There is a classic scene, lovingly replicated in a hundred cartoons, in which Our Hero removes just one brick from a wall – and one after another, in an endless, slo-mo domino sequence, every structure in sight collapses into rubble. Osama bin Laden is a bit like that hero. With one spectacular act of terrorism, he has undermined the United Nations (UN), the international rule of law, the whole multilateral system of collaboration and compromise that keeps the world safe – half a century of slow and painful progress all suddenly at risk. It's likely, of course, that bin Laden doesn't even understand how much his actions have destabilized the entire international system, for his frame of reference is radically different – but if he did, he wouldn't mind a bit.

He had help: the Bush administration was his "objective ally," as the Marxists used to put it. Its world-changing ambitions might never have got off the ground without the opportunity that bin Laden handed it on September 11, 2001, but three years later, American troops have plunged deep into the Middle East and Central Asia, the UN is struggling to survive, and most of America's traditional allies and friends are in shock.

There is now a symbiotic relationship between the Islamist terrorists and the coalition of interests in Washington that has clambered aboard the "war on terror." Neither side wishes the other to triumph, but both thrive on the confrontation – and they have grown far beyond the original small groups of determined people who dragged the rest of us into this mess. In fact, neither the death of Osama bin Laden nor the fall of the neoconservatives would necessarily bring a return to normality. The rhetoric of jihads and crusades has grown more familiar, and the number of people whose emotions or career interests have committed them to an apocalyptic confrontation has grown greatly.

It is the far side of bizarre, for both the Islamist and the American projects as originally conceived are doomed to fail. The notion that Islamist revolutionaries will sweep to power all across the Muslim world, Talibanize it, and then wage a victorious jihad against the West is as implausible as the idea that the United States can permanently assume the role of global policeman (or, rather, global vigilante), that other countries will acquiesce in this unilateral declaration of hegemony, and that U.S. voters will be willing to pay the cost in American lives and money over the long term. It's not going to happen: the danger is not that extremists from the margins will dominate the global future, but that they will do enormous damage to our future before they go under.

What is really at risk here is the global project to abolish war and replace the rule of force in the world with the rule of law, the project whose centrepiece is the United Nations. It was mainly an American initiative at the start, almost sixty years ago, and today it still commands the support of almost every government on the planet (although the Bush administration has been an exception). It is a hundred-year project at the least, for it is trying to change international habits that had at least five thousand years to take root. The slowness of change causes immense frustration, especially given the urgency of change in an era of nuclear weapons, and yet the project continues to enjoy majority popular support in almost every country, including the United States. But it is now under serious threat.

The core rule of the UN is that war, except in immediate self-defence or in obedience to Security Council resolutions, is illegal. The new American strategic policy, post-9/11, asserts that the United States has the right to use military force wherever and whenever it judges necessary. Of course, the United States has used military force against foreigners without Security Council approval before, but this time is different.

The UN is a hundred-year project because it will take at least that long for the great powers to stop yielding to the temptation, from time to time, to impose their will on weaker countries by force. The great powers do understand that a world under the rule of law, where the resort to force has become almost unthinkable by long habit, is also in their own long-term self-interest, because they, too, are vulnerable to destruction if war gets out of hand – but every so often they simply cannot resist "solving" a problem by using their own superior force.

The UN system recognized from the start that the great powers were the problem: they were given vetoes precisely so that the Security Council would never find itself in the hopelessly compromised position of trying to enforce the law against them. All hope of progress therefore lies with the gradual habituation of the great powers to obeying the new international law that forbids a unilateral resort to force – and since that is ultimately in their interest too, they have generally at least tried to cloak their actions in legal justifications acceptable to the UN. But current American strategic doctrine *requires* the destruction of the international law embedded in the United Nations Charter.

To believe that this huge shift of doctrine is really driven solely by the "terrorist threat" is about as sensible as believing in fairies. According to the U.S. government's own figures, only 625 people, the vast majority of them non-American, were killed by "international terrorism" in 2003, down from 726 people worldwide in 2002: about two people a day, far fewer than die from dog bites. It truly is not about terrorism.

Iraq is much more relevant, although the U.S. invasion of Iraq has been discussed and debated mainly in terms of what are frankly secondary issues. For critics of the war, the key questions have been who cooked the intelligence that gave the

U.S., British, and Australian governments cover for the attack, and who in those governments knew it was dodgy and when did they know it? For supporters of the war, the justifications have shifted over time from "weapons of mass destruction" and imaginary links between Saddam Hussein and al-Qaeda terrorists to the current one of liberating the Iraqi people from an evil tyrant and creating a beacon of democracy in the Arab world. None of that will matter ten years from now – but the invasion of Iraq may still be seen as a turning point in world history.

If the present U.S. strategy of undermining international law and asserting American military hegemony around the planet is quickly abandoned under the pressure of events in Iraq, then normal service will soon be restored internationally and we will get our global project back with only a few dents in it. If the U.S. adventure in unilateralism continues for another five years, other great powers will start taking steps to protect their interests and the UN will start to die. No other major power wants to abandon the project to outlaw war and start back down the road to alliances, arms races, and all the other old baggage, but if the world's greatest power becomes a rogue state they won't have much choice.

If that happens, we have lost a lot.

CHAPTER I

THE STAKES

"In all of American public life, there is hardly a single prominent figure who finds fault with the notion of the United States remaining the world's sole military superpower until the end of time."

– Professor Andrew Bacevich, Boston University

The United States needs to lose the war in Iraq as soon as possible. Even more urgently, the whole world needs the United States to lose the war in Iraq. It would be nice if Iraq doesn't lose too, but that is a lesser consideration. What is at stake now is the way we run the world for the next generation or more, and really bad things will happen if we get it wrong.

The temptation to take charge of the world was bound to be great when the United States emerged from the Cold War as the only superpower, for it seemed like a goal within easy reach. It was nevertheless resisted, by Republican and Democratic administrations alike, for almost a decade. Then a random event – for 9/11 might easily *not* have happened – unleashed forces in Washington that were itching to make a takeover bid, and now we live in the middle of a train wreck.

The idea that the United States can remain "the world's sole military superpower until the end of time" is comically over-ambitious, but there it is, embedded in a thirty-four-page document submitted to Congress in September 2002 entitled *The National Security Strategy of the United States*. "The United

States will not hesitate to strike preemptively against its enemies, and will never again allow its military supremacy to be challenged." Never again allow its military supremacy to be challenged? The United States has 4 per cent of the world's population and a larger but declining share (currently about 20 per cent) of the world's economy. It had a budget deficit of more than half a trillion dollars in 2004, and a foreign trade deficit of about the same size. How is it going to do that?

Obviously, it can't. As it becomes clear what the project to turn the United States into the world's policeman (or, more precisely, its judge, jury, and executioner) will cost in American lives and in higher taxes, American voters themselves will pull the plug on it sooner or later. Or maybe the world will pull the plug on the project first, by refusing to go on holding dollars as the gradual collapse in the value of the U.S. currency deepens. The risk is that it will all take too long. If an American defeat in Iraq takes another four or five years, huge and maybe irreparable damage will have been done to the international institutions that are our fragile first line of defence against a return to the great-power wars that could destroy us all. We need the United States back as a leading architect of global order, not a hyperactive vigilante, and we need it back now.

"*The French plan, which would somehow transfer sovereignty to an unelected group of people, just isn't workable.*"

– U.S. national security adviser
Condoleezza Rice, September 2003

In September 2003, when French president Jacques Chirac urged a high-speed handover of power to Iraqis as the best way of clearing up the huge mess created by the illegal American invasion of Iraq, the U.S. government rejected the idea out of hand. The Coalition Provisional Authority (CPA) that ran the occupation regime under pro-consul Paul Bremer would stay in power as long as necessary to ensure the creation of an Iraqi constitution and the election of an Iraqi government that was (a) democratic and (b) pro-American.

Coming up with an Iraqi government that matched both of those criteria was a very tall order, given U.S. closeness to Israel and Washington's determination to open the entire Iraqi economy up to foreign companies. In fact, Bremer's predecessor, retired general Jay Garner, had been fired in April 2003 after only a month in the job because he had publicly called for early elections in Iraq; his superiors wanted to privatize the Iraqi economy first, in accordance with a plan that had been drawn up in late 2001. It was a crucial opportunity squandered, but it didn't seem urgent to the new rulers of Iraq at the time.

There had been scattered outbreaks of guerilla resistance ever since the war officially ended in May, but Bremer's initial response was bluster: "We are going to fight them and impose our will on them and we will capture them or, if necessary, kill them until we have imposed law and order on this country. . . . We dominate the scene and we will continue to impose our will upon this country." Nobody in Washington panicked, and

Deputy Defense Secretary Paul Wolfowitz, ever the uncon-cious ironist, declared: "I think all foreigners should stop interfering in the internal affairs of Iraq." Even the big car bombs in Baghdad in August didn't shake the Bush administration's confidence that the CPA was firmly in the saddle and there was no need to rush.

"I think we have to recognize that as time goes on, being occupied becomes a problem."

– Paul Bremer, October 2003

Two months later, there was a rush. By mid-November 2003, the Iraqi resistance had grown from small beginnings – "Bring 'em on," President Bush had confidently said when its attacks began to build up in July – to the point where it was killing an average of three American soldiers a day. Bremer was hastily summoned back to Washington and the policy switched to high-speed "Iraqization": getting Iraqi soldiers and policemen out front as sandbags to protect American troops, which in turn required coming up with a more or less credible Iraqi government that they would be willing to die for. So all of a sudden, handing over "sovereignty" to an unelected group of people stopped being a problem: then Washington announced that sovereignty would be handed over to just such a group on June 30, 2004.

They could have been an elected group, of course. Six months was ample time to organize elections in Iraq, and the problem of an out-of-date voters' roll could have been mostly solved by using identity cards and rationing cards. Lots of post-conflict elections have been held in far worse circumstances, and the security situation in Iraq was still manageable in early 2004. But democracy is a messy and unpredictable business. An Iraqi government with a genuine popular mandate would be an unmanageable entity: it certainly would be no friend of Israel, it would probably reverse the privatization process, and it might just order U.S. troops to leave. So it would have to be an appointed government, at least until after the U.S. election in November 2004 was safely past.

In December 2003, that still seemed to be a viable proposition. In fact, it still seemed reasonable for chief political adviser Karl Rove to plan a triumphant return visit to Baghdad by President George W. Bush. The president's surprise visit to U.S. troops in Iraq at Thanksgiving in November 2003 had been a great media success (although he never left Baghdad airport), and the man who had masterminded Bush's political strategy since Texas days immediately started planning a victory lap for the president in Baghdad at the start of the 2004 presidential campaign.

On June 30, 2004, the Liberator of Iraq would land at Baghdad airport and drive into the city past cheering crowds of grateful Iraqis. He would mount a podium in Firdous Square, where one of Saddam Hussein's ubiquitous statues had been toppled in a staged-for-the-cameras event seen round the world on the day Baghdad fell to U.S. troops in April 2003. His speech would wish the newly appointed Iraqi government every success as it took "sovereign control" of Iraq, and gracefully grant its request that American troops stay in the fourteen "enduring bases" that were already under construction in the country to help ensure the stability of the region. He would congratulate it on its commitment to a future Iraqi democracy and to good relations with Israel. God bless Iraq. God bless America. The crowds in Iraq would cheer, the audience in the United States would feel a warm glow of satisfaction, and whatever sacrificial lamb the Democrats had found to run against Bush would change his name and move to Mexico.

At the end of 2003, the game plan still seemed plausible if you lived in Washington, not in Baghdad, for the first crisis of the occupation was past. The pace of the attacks on American troops and on Iraqis who worked for the occupation regime had dropped off after the capture of Saddam Hussein in December, and both the Pentagon and the local occupation authorities in Iraq insisted that they were only the work of scattered Baath Party "dead-enders" and "foreign terrorists" who had infiltrated into the country. By next summer the resistance would be a thing of the past. So Rove pulled the appropriate strings, and in December 2003 the North Atlantic Treaty Organization (NATO) summit that had originally been scheduled for Istanbul in May 2004 was abruptly postponed to the end of June, which happily coincided with the recently announced date for the "handover" of sovereignty in Iraq. If the president were already in Istanbul, only ninety minutes' flying time from Baghdad, on the day before the scheduled handover on June 30, then a surprise visit would work perfectly once again. But it didn't play out quite as Karl Rove intended.

At first, the confident assurances of Donald Rumsfeld at the Pentagon and of Paul Bremer in Baghdad seemed to have some basis in reality. In February and March, Bremer won a major confrontation with the senior religious authority in the Shia community, seventy-three-year-old Grand Ayatollah Ali al-Sistani, who was objecting to the indefinite postponement of elections as a trick devised to cheat Shias out of the democratically elected majority government that was their due. (Shias are 60 per cent of Iraq's population, but have traditionally been dominated by Sunnis.) But Sistani's only weapon was a threat to declare a Shia uprising, which entailed the risk of influence flowing away from him to younger and more radical Shia clerics, so he really had no weapon at all. Eventually, he accepted the U.S. plan to hand over "sovereignty" to an appointed body of Iraqis in June in return for the promise of elections in 2005. Attacks by the Iraqi resistance were rapidly building up again, however, and the CPA seemed to have not a clue as to who was behind them. Then, in April 2004, Iraq exploded again.

There were two triggers, and they were both pulled by Bremer. The first was his complicity in the U.S. military's decision (possibly driven from the Pentagon or even the White House) to besiege the city of Fallujah, whose 300,000 inhabitants were the most defiant supporters of the resistance in the whole of the "Sunni triangle" west and north of Baghdad. On March 31, four U.S. "contractors" (paramilitary security personnel) were killed in their car by members of the resistance in Fallujah. It was not all that uncommon an event in Iraq by the spring of 2004, but a mob of local citizens screaming hatred of the United States then set the dead men's bodies afire and kicked their heads off while others videotaped them. Two of the bodies – headless, handless, and footless – were hung above the stream of traffic crossing the Euphrates bridge and left there for hours. It was a ghastly display, but the reaction of the U.S. forces in Iraq was foolish beyond belief. They besieged Fallujah, and announced that they would seize and occupy it unless the residents handed over those guilty of the atrocity against the contractors.

Sir Jeremy Greenstock, a career diplomat who served as British envoy to the CPA for a time in early 2004 before resigning in despair, said that Paul Bremer should have had a sign on his desk that read: "Security and jobs, stupid." The U.S. military in Iraq should have had one that read: "Hearts and minds, stupid," but instead they gave the resistance more than it could ever have hoped for: a full-scale military siege of an Iraqi city full of young men who were eager to fight, and of old people, women, and children who would inevitably do most of the dying.

"What is coming is the destruction of anti-coalition forces in Fallujah," said Lieutenant-Colonel Brennan Byrne, commander of the 1st Battalion, 5th Marine Regiment. "They have two choices: submit or die." It was never imaginable that the Iraqi militants would hand over the people who had abused the Americans' bodies (if they were even in Fallujah any more), so the U.S. forces were effectively committed to the street-by-street conquest of a middle-sized Iraqi city. That would involve significant American casualties, and a huge toll of deaths and injuries among the civilian population.

The other trigger Bremer pulled, apparently as a free choice, was his decision to close a small-circulation weekly newspaper (less than 10,000 copies) that supported radical Shia cleric Moqtada al-Sadr and to issue a warrant for his arrest. The paper inveighed against the American occupation and printed truth, rumours, and flat lies with a fine lack of discrimination, but in that it differed little from dozens of other weekly party papers that had sprung up in post-Saddam Baghdad. Sheikh Moqtada al-Sadr himself was a more serious proposition: young, radical, and relatively poorly educated in Islamic law, but able to trade on his renown as the son of a revered grand ayatollah who had been murdered by Saddam Hussein – and in charge of a private militia called the al-Mahdi army that drew its recruits from the overwhelmingly Shia slums of eastern Baghdad. Faced with the threat of disappearing into Abu Ghraib or some other part of the U.S. prison system, he mobilized his militia and took over the Shia holy cities of Najaf and Karbala south of Baghdad. If the United States wanted to arrest him, it would have to fight its way into those cities and violate the holy shrines.

American firepower meant that it was possible to capture both Fallujah and the rebel Shia cities without suffering large U.S. casualties, but it could not be done without inflicting huge Iraqi casualties. For a week or so, the offensive against Fallujah was pursued vigorously on the ground, killing at least six hundred residents, most of them civilians. But a large proportion of the local men joined the active resistance, and it became clear even to the U.S. planners that the full subjugation of the city would involve killing thousands of Iraqis and losing a considerable number of their own soldiers. (Twenty- or fifty-to-one kill ratios are quite normal when highly trained soldiers backed by modern artillery and air power take on untrained and poorly armed volunteers fighting amid their own homes, but 138 U.S. soldiers still died in Iraq in April 2004, more than during the war itself.)

The kill ratio was even more one-sided in the Shia cities, where hundreds of members of the Mahdi militia, mostly poor young men from east Baghdad, were killed by American forces on the outskirts of Karbala, Najaf, and neighbouring Kufa with almost no American casualties, mostly by air strikes. U.S. troops never tried to penetrate to the centre of the holy cities for fear of damaging the sacred mosques and completely alienating the Shias of Iraq, who had hitherto been less active in the resistance. Even so, the images being disseminated across the Muslim world were disastrously bad for the United States, as they were almost identical to the images of Israeli troops suppressing resistance in occupied Palestinian towns and cities. Eventually, Washington realized that it would have to back away from both confrontations, and negotiations began to allow it a face-saving way out.

Even worse images began to appear in late April, as the photographs of Iraqis under torture taken by American soldiers at Abu Ghraib prison began to leak out to the media and the public. The obsession with the sexual humiliation of naked Arab males seemed calculated to confirm all the worst imaginable stereotypes that Muslims hold about American behaviour and values, which might just have been an unfortunate coincidence – or it might have been an intrinsic part of the process, for humiliating prisoners and photographing the results is a standard part of the package of measures for putting pressure on captives that is generally known as "torture lite." How much of this behaviour towards the thousands of Iraqis held without charge in U.S.–run prisons was authorized by American military authorities, and how high the blame went, will probably not be admitted for years, but in a sense it does not matter. The result was to blacken the already poor reputation of the United States virtually beyond repair, at least for this generation, in the Arab world.

In the midst of these events, various Iraqi resistance groups began to employ the new tactic of kidnapping and killing civilian foreigners, tens of thousands of whom had arrived in Iraq to work for the many foreign companies that had been granted contracts for the "reconstruction" of the country. A number of these captives were beheaded, their murders videotaped by their killers, and the tapes made available to Arab satellite TV stations or posted on the Web. This led to a general exodus of foreign "carpetbaggers" (to borrow the phrase used during America's own episode of Reconstruction after the Civil War), which caused further major delays in the restoration of basic services like electricity, water, and sewage that had been severely damaged during the American invasion and the subsequent orgy of looting.

The events of April were as much a psychological turning point in the Iraq War as the Tet Offensive of 1968 had been in the Vietnam War. By mid-May, when the worst of the uprisings had abated, the inability of the United States to control the situation by force had become clear to Iraqis and to the world. The U.S. Marines besieging Fallujah were withdrawn and the city was handed over to the nominal control of a Saddam-era Iraqi general who recruited a "Fallujah Brigade" of troops locally, mostly from among the men who had been fighting the Marines – and the city effectively became a no-go zone for foreign forces. Very occasional high-speed drive-throughs by American troop convoys, negotiated well in advance, were permitted by the Sunni resistance forces, but Fallujah became their safe haven and provisional capital.

Farther south in the Shia-majority part of Iraq, Najaf and Karbala also became American-free cities apart from a couple of negotiated patrol routes. Not only had U.S. forces failed to "kill or capture Moqtada al-Sadr" as Lieutenant General Ricardo Sanchez, America's most senior general in Iraq, had loudly vowed to do, but the radical young cleric had gained enormously in prestige and become a serious rival to the more moderate Grand Ayatollah Ali al-Sistani. A CPA opinion poll conducted in May revealed the full extent of the damage: only 2 per cent of Arab Iraqis still saw the Americans as liberators, while 92 per cent saw them as occupiers. A year previously,

Iraqi opinion had been almost evenly divided. And a CNN–*USA Today* poll of 3,500 Iraqis at about the same time found that 57 per cent wanted U.S. and British forces to leave immediately. (Since the 38 per cent who wanted them to stay longer presumably included most Iraqi Kurds, who dream of an independent Kurdistan and therefore prefer a weak and dependent government in Baghdad, the majority opposing the U.S. presence among Iraqi Arabs was probably close to 4 to 1.)

Over May and June, several more cities in the Sunni triangle gained a significant degree of freedom from American forces after ferocious clashes. Ambushes and roadside bombs took a steady toll of American troops while car bombs and kidnappings spread fear among civilians, and it became quite clear that Rove's dream of kicking off President Bush's re-election campaign with a television extravaganza in Baghdad marking a "handover of sovereignty" to a group of unelected Iraqis would have to be cancelled. Even choosing that group of Iraqis became a troubled issue. In mid-May, Ezzedine Salim, the chairman of the existing, virtually powerless Iraqi Governing Council that had been appointed by Bremer the previous year, was killed by a car bomb at the entrance to the Green Zone, the vast American military and civil headquarters area in central Baghdad. Hussein al-Shahristani, the non-partisan scientist selected to be prime minister by United Nations envoy Lakhdar Brahimi, who had been brought in to lend a veneer of legality to the proceedings, either refused to work for the Americans or was rejected by them. (Accounts differ, but Brahimi was heard to mutter, "I'm sure he doesn't mind me saying that Bremer is the dictator of Iraq. He has the money. He has the signatures. Nothing happens without his agreement in this country.")

The man who was eventually selected as prime minister, Iyad Allawi, was a former exile and long-standing CIA "asset" who openly admitted having taken money from fourteen foreign intelligence agencies – all in the cause of overthrowing Saddam Hussein, he insisted, and it may well have been true, but it was not exactly the CV you would choose for a man who had to win the support of a country that was drifting towards a general revolt against its American occupiers. Allawi picked more than half the members of his new cabinet from the former, U.S.–nominated Iraqi Governing Council (on which sixteen of the twenty-five members were returning exiles), but the "handover" (minus President Bush) didn't even take place on June 30 as planned. The resistance forces staged an extravaganza of their own on June 25, carrying out simultaneous attacks on police stations and army barracks in five cities that killed 85 people and injured 320 – so the occupation authorities secretly moved the date for the "transfer of sovereignty" up by two days to avoid the similar round of attacks they feared was being planned for the scheduled date. The actual ceremony was held in a featureless room in the heart of the Green Zone, behind four rings of checkpoints, on the morning of June 28. Most of the witnesses were foreign journalists and American troops.

And nothing changed. There were still 138,000 U.S. troops in Iraq, and it was still true that Iyad Allawi would be dead in a day without their protection. The resistance forces kept attacking, and they were still overwhelmingly Iraqi despite American propaganda: only 2 per cent of the 8,500 "security detainees" arrested by U.S. troops and held in jails at Abu Ghraib or elsewhere were non-Iraqis, and half of those were Syrians from clans that straddle and habitually ignore the border between the two countries. American troops and the Iraqi soldiers and police who had been recruited to help them kept on getting killed at about the same rate as before: American military deaths in Iraq passed the thousand mark in late summer. Iraqi civilians kept dying from car bombs, crime, and American firepower alike: recorded deaths from gunfire in Baghdad were up ninety-fold from Saddam's time, and many more were unrecorded.

The third major upsurge of the resistance in Iraq, after the peaks of November 2003 and April 2004, came in August, when the militia of the radical Shia cleric Moqtada al-Sadr again took control of the Shia holy cities of Karbala, Najaf, and Kufa. American forces spent most of a month killing the poorly armed Shia militiamen, eventually penetrating within a hundred feet of the Imam Ali shrine in the centre of Najaf, but again they finally drew back from attacking the mosque itself. Al-Sadr's surviving militiamen marched out, still armed, after mediation by Grand Ayatollah Ali al-Sistani. At least a thousand militiamen and civilians had been killed, but Najaf and Kufa became no-go zones for foreign military forces, al-Sadr emerged from the confrontation stronger, and the U.S.–approved government of Iyad Allawi emerged weaker.

Meanwhile, most of the cities of the "Sunni triangle" slid inexorably into the grip of the resistance: not just Fallujah, but

Ramadi, the whole of Anbar province, and cities like Samarra. The "Fallujah Brigade" fell apart, the National Guard battalions that had originally been allowed to operate in those cities were decapitated (sometimes literally), and U.S. forces retreated to fortified encampments on the edge of the desert. It wasn't exactly like South Vietnam in 1964, just before President Lyndon Johnson began the escalation that eventually put a half-million American troops on the ground in that country, but it was close.

There were already more American troops in Iraq in July 2004 than there had been in South Vietnam in 1964. The guerrillas and "terrorists" – a distinction without a difference; all guerrillas use terrorist methods – were less united than the Viet Cong had been in South Vietnam. They did not have a sympathetic North Vietnam to back them up, but they were managing to co-operate effectively against the occupiers, and they had the sympathy of the whole Arab world. The government the United States had installed in Baghdad was probably less corrupt than the one President Kennedy had put in place in Saigon after he ordered the overthrow of President Ngo Dinh Diem in 1963, but it also had far less to work with, because Paul Bremer had disbanded the entire Iraqi army and fired most senior government employees the previous year in his first decisions as pro-consul.

In reality, President Bush didn't have the option of following President Johnson's example and flooding Iraq with troops. By scraping the bottom of the barrel, Bush would have been able to find around another 20,000 troops for Iraq, for a total of 160,000 – but after that, he would have had to bring back the draft, which would have been political suicide. Besides, escalating the war hadn't solved the problem for Lyndon Johnson: even with 550,000 American soldiers and 450,000 South Vietnamese troops available, the United States had been unable to defeat the guerrillas in a country with a smaller population than Iraq. What the United States was up against in both countries, behind the screen of ideological cant about Communism or Islamism, was nationalism, and once a majority of local nationalists had decided that America's motives for being in their country were not good – whether they were or not – then the game was hopeless. That point had already passed in South Vietnam by 1964, although the U.S. military involvement there lasted another nine years, and it had already passed in Iraq by the summer of 2004.

"*Television brought the brutality of war into the comfort of the living room. Vietnam was lost in the living rooms of America – not on the battlefields of Vietnam.*"

– Marshall McLuhan, 1975

In anti-colonial guerrilla wars, the locals always win. The Dutch learned that lesson in Indonesia, the French in Vietnam and Algeria, the British in Kenya and Cyprus, and the Portuguese in Angola and Mozambique. The United States went through the same learning process in Vietnam, and the Russians in Afghanistan. It's all about how much time and how many lives the two sides are willing to spend on the issue. The fighting may go on for years, the better-equipped foreigners will win almost all the battles, and ten or twenty guerrillas may die for each foreign soldier, but there is an endless supply of locals and very little patience for a long war with high casualties back in the foreigners' home country. In the end the foreigners invariably succumb to the temptation to cut their losses and go home, because otherwise there will be no end: the guerrillas are never going to quit and go home, because they already are home. And it makes no difference how noble the foreigners think their motives are; only the opinion of the locals counts.

Almost all of America's friends and allies in the world understand this, which is why they have been trying to make it easy for the United States to get out of Iraq quickly without losing too much face. That was the real purpose of the Security Council resolution in June 2004 that retrospectively cast a cloak of legitimacy over the U.S. presence in Iraq and the puppet regime it was installing there. French president Jacques Chirac, as blunt as ever, called it "an exit strategy from a crisis," but he supported it too.

Nobody was willing to send more troops into the Iraqi cauldron or to bless the occupation as a UN operation – the whole point of the exercise was to get the U.S. troops out – but they were all willing to indulge in a little hypocrisy if it would speed American troops on their way. They were well aware that chaos might reign in Iraq afterwards, but Iraq was in chaos already. The priority for the whole world was to get the U.S. defeat in Iraq over with and forgotten as soon as possible and with the least possible damage to American self-esteem, rather than submit to the inevitability of a long, bitter, losing guerrilla war that would set the United States against the rest of the world, feed Islamist extremism, and undermine the whole project for great-power collaboration in the service of peace.

It is not clear, however, that President Bush understood where the rest of the world wanted him to go, or gave a damn about what they wanted anyway. It is equally unclear whether many senior figures in the Democratic Party had fully grasped the fact that the Iraq adventure has irredeemably failed, and that the only sensible course of action that remains is to declare a victory and leave as soon as possible. Pride, and the myth of American military strength, bulk large in the calculations of the political elite, for whom "failure is not an option." The belief that American ingenuity and determination can overcome any obstacle was the reason that the Vietnam War went on long after rational decision-makers would have cut their losses and left, and the same fatal flaw may now be at work in Iraq.

Neither George W. Bush nor John Kerry would face insuperable obstacles in pulling out of Iraq rapidly after a November election victory. Bush would obviously have to dump and scapegoat some of the prominent neo-conservatives who led the United States into the mess, but cabinets are often reshuffled drastically at the start of a second term anyway. Even the most flawed of elections in Iraq in January would give a victorious President Bush the opportunity of pulling U.S. troops out and enjoying a "decent interval" of a year or two (as

Henry Kissinger put it when pulling U.S. troops out of South Vietnam in 1973) before the roof fell in on the government that Washington left in charge in Baghdad. Few people in America would object if he did that; certainly nobody would in the rest of the world. And what was true for Bush would be doubly true for a John Kerry presidency. Pulling out of Iraq would be easy for Kerry, and it wouldn't necessarily even be bad for Iraq.

Iraq is an ethnically complex country that has suffered under a succession of bad governments, and the dominant political tradition at the top since the overthrow of its British-imposed monarchy in 1958 has been brutally simple: losers die. However, all the other countries in the vicinity are ethnically complex too: Turkey is almost a quarter Kurdish, Syria has Sunni Arabs and Alawites and Druze and Kurds, Lebanon omits the Kurds but adds several varieties of Christian Arabs to the mix – and Iran has Persians and big minorities of Kurds, Azeri Turks, Arabs, Turcomans, and Baluchis. Most of these countries also have turbulent and frequently violent political histories, and all of them have seen clashes between ethnic groups in the past century. But only one of them, Lebanon, has tumbled into a full-scale civil war. There is no particular reason to believe that Iraq would do so if American forces left. It didn't during eight decades of independence before the United States invaded.

There is not even any good reason to despair of a democratic future for Iraq, provided that American troops do not stay so long that power automatically devolves to the men with the guns who finally drive them out. If Turkey is a fully democratic country and Iranians keep trying to turn their country into one, why can't Iraqis do the same?

Yet there is reason for pessimism about the likelihood of an early U.S. exit from Iraq. The Islamist radicals associated with the al-Qaeda network will certainly do their best to prevent it. Ever since 9/11, the Bush administration has been doing exactly what they want, invading Muslim countries and serving as an unpaid but highly effective recruiting agent for the extremists across the whole of the Muslim world. Back in 2001, popular support for the Islamists was in decline almost everywhere except Saudi Arabia and perhaps Pakistan. Even in Afghanistan, where the Taliban were actually in power, the incessant meddling of the Islamists in the details of private life was making them almost as unpopular as the Communists had been, for much the same reasons. The U.S. invasions of Afghanistan and Iraq have given the Islamists an enormous boost in the Muslim countries that are their main targets (just as the planners of 9/11 intended), and they will try to keep American troops mired in the Middle East for as long as possible. At the moment, however, they don't have to put a lot of effort into it.

It is hardly surprising that there has not been a single act of terrorism sponsored by Islamists on U.S. territory between September 12, 2001, and the time when I write this in late August 2004. Apart from one bumbling British convert to Islam, Richard Reid (who dropped the matches while trying to light the explosive soles of his shoes on a flight from Paris to New York), there has not been even one serious attempt to attack Americans on or near home soil – if indeed the mentally disturbed Reid was operating under direct orders from al-Qaeda. This absence of attacks may, of course, be thanks to the eagle-eyed efficiency of the CIA, the FBI, the DIA, the NSA, MI5, MI6, GCHQ, CSIS, and all the other intelligence services, or to the sheer lack of Islamist sleepers already in place in North America who could carry out further attacks, but a likelier explanation is that such attacks have not yet been ordered. The Bush administration was already doing what al-Qaeda wanted; why risk discrediting it by making further terrorist attacks in the United States?

This logic argues that there should be no terrorist attacks in the United States during the 2004 election campaign either – unless President Bush's numbers started to slide, in which case a modest attack might be ordered. Not a large attack that killed thousands of Americans (supposing that al-Qaeda retains the resources for something so ambitious, which it probably does not), for a massacre might discredit Bush's whole claim to have kept the United States safe and lose him the election decisively. But if they really feared that Bush was going to lose anyway, then whoever is now in charge of North American operations might well authorize a small attack designed to frighten a few million swing voters back into Bush's arms – a truck bomb in some heartland city like Cincinnati or St. Louis, for example. By the time you read this, you will know what happened, if anything.

On the other hand, if Bush, safely back in office for a second term, then showed serious signs of intending to pull out of

Iraq, al-Qaeda would promptly stage the largest attack it could manage on U.S. soil in an attempt to seal the exit shut. But would Bush actually do that? That depends on how much he believes his own administration's propaganda.

If he truly believes all the nonsense that was peddled about links between Iraq and al-Qaeda to provide a pretext for the invasion of Iraq in the first place, and all the lies that have been told since then about the huge "foreign influence" over the "terrorist attacks" in Iraq, then this is his Stalingrad and he will not retreat. That's perfectly possible; after all, Lyndon Johnson truly believed that he was making a stand against the world Communist conspiracy in Vietnam. If Bush just says that stuff because it plays well in Peoria, but he actually knows better, then like Richard Nixon he might just turn around and leave – except that in practice, even though Nixon desperately wanted to get out of Vietnam and American casualties were soaring (two-thirds of the 55,000 Americans killed in Vietnam died *after* his inauguration in early 1969), it took Nixon more than four years to get out of Vietnam.

It took him so long because he was trying to find a way to do it that would not constitute an admission of defeat or do damage to American prestige. No such way was available. In practice, that four-year delay just made the defeat more dramatic and the damage to America's prestige far worse – and it also rendered the U.S. army virtually unusable for the next ten years. Would George W. Bush be wiser? Would the neoconservative ideologues around him be able to abandon the rose-tinted spectacles through which they have read every report on the deteriorating situation in Iraq so far, swallow their own words, and just walk away from a project they have been nurturing for at least a decade? It is doubtful, especially since some of them, at least, must realize that if they did try to pull American troops out of Iraq, al-Qaeda would go flat out to thwart them, using terrorist attacks as its main argument. There was a good deal of speculation in mid-2004 that Bush had already decided to pull out of Iraq and was just waiting for the election to be past, but it may have been just wishful thinking.

The expectation that President John Kerry would promptly pull U.S. troops out of Iraq may also have been wishful thinking, however. Professor Andrew Bacevich's lethally perceptive comment about there being no prominent figure in American public life "who finds fault with the notion of the United States remaining the world's sole military superpower until the end of time" certainly applies to Kerry, who consciously played up to the militaristic strand in American public discourse during the campaign with his endless references to his heroism in combat. His anti-war supporters assumed that he would promptly pull U.S. troops out of Iraq after being elected, and was only saying otherwise during the election campaign to avoid being vilified by the Republican machine for failing to support American soldiers in action overseas, but it is possible that he actually meant what he said. And what he said was that he would stay in Iraq indefinitely.

"[Iraqi] extremists appear to be gaining confidence and have vowed to drive our troops from the country," Kerry said in a radio address in the midst of the April uprising. "We cannot and will not let that happen. It would be unthinkable for us to retreat in disarray and leave behind a society deep in strife and dominated by radicals." Two weeks later, speaking in Fulton, Missouri (where Winston Churchill made his famous "Iron Curtain" speech), Kerry declared: "If our commanders need more American troops, they should say so and they should get them. . . . But more and more American soldiers cannot be the only solution. . . . The coalition should organize an expanded international security force, preferably with NATO, but clearly under U.S. command." And how was the United States going to persuade those laggard Europeans to send their troops into the Iraqi meat-grinder? "For the Europeans, Iraq's failure could endanger the security of their oil supplies, further radicalize their large Muslim populations, threaten destabilizing refugee flows, and seed a huge new source of terrorism."

Even supposing that the Europeans believed that these threats would be smaller if American troops stayed in Iraq rather than leaving promptly (which most of them do not), didn't Kerry realize how impudent his remarks were? He was arguing that countries that had opposed the U.S. invasion of Iraq precisely because it would unleash the dangers he listed should now go and pull America's chestnuts out of the fire because its invasion had indeed unleashed them. It was the same tone that Lyndon Johnson and Richard Nixon used to adopt when demanding that the NATO allies in Europe send troops to Vietnam, and it was just as likely to get a warm response. "Our goal," said Kerry, "should be an alliance commitment to deploy a major portion of the peacekeeping force that will be needed in Iraq for a long time to come." This is a man who said in mid-August that he would have voted to authorize President Bush to invade Iraq even if he had known that Saddam Hussein had no weapons of mass destruction. Perhaps he was lying to his audience or perhaps he was lying to himself, but he certainly didn't sound like a man laying the groundwork for an early pullout.

But why would any American *want* to stay in Iraq? There were no weapons of mass destruction in Iraq, Saddam's regime had no links with al-Qaeda or any other Islamist extremists, and Iraq had never posed any danger to the United States. There are doubtless a few foreign Islamist terrorists in Iraq now, attracted there by the opportunity created by the overthrow of Saddam and the presence of so many American targets, but there is no reason to think that they would end up in power if U.S. troops went home. What can explain this strange desire to stay?

Well, there's oil, of course, and things are getting a little tense now that Saudi Arabia seems about to slide off a cliff. But the United States doesn't need troops on the ground to buy oil from Iraq, no matter what regime is ruling there, any more than it needs troops in Iran to buy oil from there. Anybody who is seriously considering American military intervention to stifle a revolution in Saudi Arabia is certifiably crazy. What *logical* reasons could there be for keeping U.S. troops in Iraq?

"Let us be clear what is happening in Iraq. It is the battle of seminal importance for the early twenty-first century. It will define relations between the Muslim world and the West. . . . Who is trying to bomb the UN *and Red Cross out of Baghdad? Or killing Iraqi civilians in terrorist attacks? Or sabotaging the work on electrical cables or oil installations? Not America. Not Britain. Not the coalition. But Saddam's small rump of supporters, aided and abetted by foreign terrorists.*

"And why are they doing it? Because they agree with me about this battle's importance. They know that if we give Iraq democracy, set it on a path to prosperity, leave it in the sole charge and sovereignty of the Iraqi people . . . it means . . . the death of the poisonous propaganda monster about America these extremists have created in the minds of much of the world."

– British prime minister Tony Blair, November 10, 2003

Like his nineteenth-century predecessor William Ewart Gladstone, Tony Blair can "convince most people of most things, and himself of almost anything," but the notion that the future domestic political arrangements in Iraq are of great moment to the rest of the world is just fantasy. Nevertheless, the invasion of Iraq, and how long the occupation lasts, *is* of great moment, because Iraq is the linchpin of a far larger enterprise. The point where things began to go badly wrong in the world was not 9/11, which was the sort of isolated tragedy that happens from time to time, with a death toll on the same scale as a small battle, a medium earthquake, or a minor flu outbreak. The real turning point was January 29, 2002, when President George W. Bush gazed earnestly into the teleprompter and told us all in his State of the Union message that he was declaring war on the "axis of evil." Suddenly he was Ronald Reagan, and it was the Cold War again.

Even the old vocabulary came back: Bush constantly referred to the "Free World" in his public statements, as if it were still 1984. The "war on terror" was another global crusade against evil, with everybody expected to fall in behind American leadership, and it would go on indefinitely: permanent low-level war, worldwide, just like in the Good Old Days. We were all caught up in a fantasy rerun of America's Finest Hour, and the question is: Why?

"On 16 September 1985, when the Commerce Department announced that the United States had become a debtor nation, the American Empire died."

– Gore Vidal, 1987

Most of the full-blown conspiracy theories have as their point of departure the extreme vulnerability of the American economy. U.S. foreign trade went into deficit in the 1970s and never recovered; in recent years, the American trade deficit has ballooned to half a trillion dollars a year. To make matters worse, the U.S. federal government has been running enormous deficits most of the time since the Republicans discovered fiscal irresponsibility under President Reagan in the 1980s. There was a successful attempt to move back to balanced budgets under Bill Clinton in the mid-to-late 1990s, but under George W. Bush the annual budget deficit attained a new record of more than half a trillion dollars within two years.

Normally, huge budget deficits cause roaring inflation, which forces central banks to raise interest rates and rein in the rampant government borrowing (at the expense of killing growth in the rest of the economy as well). Normally, too, an enormous foreign trade deficit will cause the external value of the currency to drop like a rock, forcing the guilty government to slash imports – and, once again, to jack up the local interest rate in an attempt to attract foreign funds and stabilize the currency. But in the United States, none of these things has happened. The entire economy is sustained by an inflow of foreign capital so enormous that it covers the entire trade deficit and also, one way and another, the budget deficit.

It is the Indian Rope Trick conducted on a national scale. Well-to-do Americans reward themselves with massive tax cuts, the government goes on spending like there is no tomorrow – and the party will never have to end so long as foreigners, almost all of them in Europe or east Asia, are willing to keep pouring their money into the United States. Why do they do that, and is there any risk that they might stop?

They do not do it for the allegedly higher returns available in the U.S. stock market: a third of the inflow of foreign capital goes straight into relatively low-yielding bonds, and most of the rest into blue chips. They do it because they see the United States as the safest place to park their money. It is the centre of the world economy, after all, and the dollar is the world's reserve currency. But there is a dangerous circularity to this argument: the foreigners go on investing because the U.S.

economy is strong, and it remains strong only because they continue to invest. What if one day the huge budget deficit caused the confidence of the foreign investors to falter? It would suddenly become clear that the emperor is wearing no clothes – and the sky would fall.

In mid-2004, the total amount of foreign money invested in the United States in forms that could be sold off fairly quickly was $8 trillion. If those investments started to move out, the U.S. dollar would fall so fast that the dollars that moved on Day Two of the panic might be worth only half as much in euros or yen as the dollars that moved on Day One. Nobody would win in such a panic, neither Americans nor foreigners, so the latter have almost as great an interest in pretending that the emperor is fully clothed as the former. Nevertheless, the markets have a way of discovering the truth sooner or later: the U.S. dollar's steady fall since the beginning of 2003 has already inflicted such losses on exporters who denominate their prices in dollars (like the oil producers) that its continued status as the world's main reserve currency, used for most international transactions, is becoming doubtful.

The U.S. economy is a confidence trick based on everybody else's perception that the United States is centrally important for the world's security and that its economy is equally central in the global economy. Both those propositions were true in 1945; neither is actually true any more.

The post–Second World War recovery of the European economies and the subsequent extraordinary growth of the East Asian economies have shifted the centre of gravity of the global economy back to Eurasia, now home to about three-quarters of the world's gross domestic product (GDP). The United States still has the biggest single economy, but it is separated by wide oceans from all the others and there is no non-historical reason why it should still be seen as central.

The political and strategic centrality of the United States lasted longer, because until the mid-1980s the core of Eurasia was controlled by Communist powers that were fundamentally hostile to both democracy and the capitalist system: the Free World really did face a mortal threat, and depended on America's military strength (above all its nuclear weapons) for protection. But China has been a capitalist country for most practical purposes for about twenty years now, and Russia hasn't even been Communist for almost fifteen years, so where's the threat? Why does everybody else need the United States any more? They don't – but if the party is to continue, they must be persuaded that they do.

This is where the conspiracy theories kick in. The earliest to gain wide currency in the United States was the hypothesis that Saddam Hussein had been promoted to Target Number One because he was threatening to re-denominate Iraqi oil exports in euros rather than dollars, a move that might cause other oil producers to follow suit and trigger the collapse of the dollar. A much more elaborate and sophisticated version, now pretty much the industry standard, was offered by Emmanuel Todd in his book *After the Empire: The Breakdown of the American Order*, first published in France as *Après l'empire* in 2002: "There is a hidden logic behind the drunken sailor appearance of American diplomacy. The real America is too weak to take on anyone except military midgets. . . . These conflicts [Afghanistan, Iraq] that represent little or no military risk allow the United States to be 'present' throughout the world. The United States works to maintain the illusory fiction of the world as a dangerous place in need of America's protection."

In Todd's view, President Bush's declaration of an open-ended "war on terror" of indefinite duration after 9/11, and his subsequent nomination of an axis of evil that must be expunged by American-led coalitions, were actually intended to be a way of reviving the old American global leadership role of the Cold War even though there was no longer a global military threat. America's economic vulnerability could only be disguised by emphasizing its global strategic role, and in the absence of the Soviet Union and the threat of the Third World War, terrorism would just have to fill the bill.

Todd believes that this is essentially a bipartisan policy, pointing out that the United States first began to fixate on "rogue states" and to pump up both the dangers they allegedly posed and its own defence budget under the Clinton administration in the later 1990s. Since U.S. military strength is quite limited in ground forces, and since the American public has a very low tolerance for military casualties, the designated enemies that are first to be inflated as bogeymen and then crushed to demonstrate the indispensability of American military power must be small, weak states that will crumble quickly. This is the phenomenon for which Todd invented the now-famous phrase "theatrical micro-militarism" – and its primary political purpose, he argues, is to make it appear that the United States is shouldering the burden of defending the world from chaos. This applies just as much to Bill Clinton's no-American-casualty, air-attacks-only little wars against Iraq in 1998 (Desert Fox) and Kosovo in 1999, in Todd's view, as it does to Bush's wars post-2001. It was Clinton's secretary of state, Madeleine Albright, who told the *New Republic* in 1998: "If we have to use force, it is because we are America. We are the indispensable nation." And so long as everybody else believes that, the party will continue.

If such a bipartisan and Machiavellian approach to America's difficulties really did exist, then we would all be in very deep trouble, but the evidence for it is less than convincing. First, there is no other way that America *can* fight now: it is politically unimaginable that the United States would ever commit its forces to combat against a first-rate military opponent on the ground, so the pattern of recent American wars proves nothing. Second, the multiple failures of planning, foresight, and strategic calculation that litter the history of both the Clinton and the younger Bush administrations make it very hard to believe that behind it all was a subtle master plan for restoring America's geostrategic position in order to ward off an impending economic crisis that almost nobody in official Washington admits is coming. But we do need to know how long the present foreign policy will last, and how hard the landing will be when the United States finally has to face strategic and economic realities.

Here the argument gets more worrisome, because it no longer depends on a conscious conspiracy. People in positions of power in the United States, faced with the reality of America's declining political importance and its precarious economic situation, have been and will be forced to respond to the problems arising from America's relative decline in strategic importance and economic power in one way or another even if they only dimly understand them – and the course of least resistance, if they are not prepared to make a rigorous analysis and tough choices, will be to drift back towards solutions that served the United States well in the past. The default choice is to recreate the world of the Cold War, or at least a pale facsimile of it, because that was when the United States really was the indispensable nation, with a genuine and legitimate role at the centre of both politics and economics. The orgy of nostalgia that accompanied the death of Ronald Reagan in the summer of 2004 illustrated just how powerful is the longing throughout the U.S. political elite for a return to the halcyon days of the Cold War – and it is a bipartisan longing, because it comes out of the shared historical experience of the present adult generation, regardless of their political ideology.

That means that American administrations of either party will instinctively tend to go for a massive, Cold War–style confrontation as the "solution" to any significant threat that comes along, like terrorism, particularly because that approach will resonate well with an electorate that is more uncomfortable than most with nuance and complexity. But that still does not explain the unprovoked American invasion of Iraq, which had no credible links to anti-U.S. terrorism.

This is where the lesser conspiracy theory comes in. This quite widespread theory argues that the neo-conservatives in the Bush administration simply seized on the opportunity presented by 9/11 to launch their cherished project for *Pax Americana* and put America back in charge of the world where it belongs. They had total confidence in the supremacy of U.S. military power and they hadn't a clue about the vulnerability of what they saw as the American economic miracle. The strongest evidence for this is the fact that the Bush administration pushed through the biggest tax cuts in history, despite the huge U.S. trade deficit and the extreme vulnerability of the U.S. dollar, as if they were oblivious to the linkage between the health of the U.S. economy and foreign investor confidence. "Reagan proved that budget deficits don't matter," snapped Vice-President Dick Cheney when Treasury Secretary Paul O'Neill protested against the massive tax cuts. (O'Neill later resigned over the issue.)

"The lunatics have taken over the asylum," as the *Financial Times* put it in May 2003, arguing that the "more extreme Republicans" were deliberately trying to engineer a fiscal catastrophe in order to be able to justify an assault on federal aid to the poor: "Proposing to slash federal spending, particularly on social programs, is a tricky electoral proposition, but a fiscal crisis offers the tantalizing prospect of forcing such cuts through the back door."

In this version of reality, the neo-conservatives were thoroughly self-deluded about America's economic strength, but they did have a coherent politico-military strategy and they were doing their best to put it into practice. They had seized upon terrorism as useful domestic cover under which they could get *Pax Americana* up and running – and the invasion of Iraq was their launch vehicle. The world just didn't co-operate, mainly because their assumptions are wrong. Shame about all the lives. That is not a pretty picture, but it would mean that the world's American problem is containable. The United States is not becoming a rogue nation; it just fell temporarily into the hands of a band of ideological adventurers who are not even representative of the older traditions of the Republican Party.

There is also another possibility, which is that the people controlling defence and foreign policy in the Bush administration just blundered into Iraq because they really believed their own propaganda about weapons of mass destruction and an Iraq–al-Qaeda link, even though people with no access whatever to secret intelligence and just a little common sense knew that it was patent nonsense. The invasion of Iraq was simply a mistake, and they'll try to do better next time. This is very much the option to be preferred, but it doesn't really have the ring of truth to it.

So there you have it. The more radical conspiracy theorists argue that there is a conscious and very sophisticated strategy, tacitly shared by both the Republican and the Democratic wings of what Gore Vidal calls the Property Party, to preserve American global hegemony and the illusion of U.S. economic indispensability in the much less favourable environment of the post–Cold War era. Iraq, in this strategy, would be seen by the mainstream political elites on both sides in Washington as a useful tool to that end. Others, reading the documents produced by the Project for a New American Century over the years, would narrow the focus and say that the Iraq adventure was really the opening move in a hare-brained plan for global domination hatched by a tight little band of neo-conservatives who staged a successful takeover of the traditional Republican Party. Or was it just an isolated, horrible mistake by a group of arrogant people who knew a great deal less than they thought they did?

As the British would say, Cock-up or conspiracy? The answer matters a great deal, because there is so much more at stake now than just the future of Iraq or the Middle East.

If American troops are home from Iraq a year from now and the idea of American global hegemony has lost favour in Washington, then we get the world of the late 1990s back relatively undamaged, and we can pick up from where we left off with the job of building the multilateral institutions that we need to see us through the international storms that are sure to come. This is still a world where almost all the bigger countries have nuclear weapons, and our task is to use the "holiday from history" that we have been granted since the beginning of the 1990s to strengthen the international rule of law and the habits of co-operation among the great powers now that they are not (at least for the moment) enemies. It could work, if we have enough time before climate change and the rise of new great powers and all the other pressures that we know are on the way overwhelm us.

It will not work if the United States stays in Iraq. If that happens, sooner or later most of the other great powers will give up on the United Nations and the rule of law in favour of getting together to counterbalance the weight of the rogue superpower, and the drift back into the bad old world of alliances and confrontations will have begun. Especially it will not work if the United States really is pursuing a coherent strategy of redefining the world in terms of a perpetual, global "war on terror" with itself as leader: that simply will not fly elsewhere, although it sells quite well in the United States at the moment.

Moreover, the isolation and loss of international confidence that the United States will suffer if it continues to pursue this course could easily lead to an early and extremely painful collapse of the dollar, not a gradual decline and a relatively soft landing. Jim Rogers, the Wall Street wizard who in 1973 in partnership with George Soros co-founded the Quantum Fund, one of the first and most successful hedge funds, recently told *The Guardian* that "The U.S. dollar is going the way that sterling went as it lost its place as the world's reserve currency. I suspect there will be exchange controls in the U.S. in the foreseeable future.... Whoever is elected president is going to have serious problems in 2005–06. We Americans are going to suffer." Most economists who are not on the payroll, so to speak, would agree that America's economic situation is grave. A sudden collapse would inflict such economic hardships on ordinary Americans that it could well lead to a further radicalization of U.S. domestic politics and foreign policy.

The stakes are much higher than they seem. The foundations of the First World War were laid by decisions that were made ten to twenty years before 1914, and after that it was very hard for anyone to turn back. There is a strong case for saying that we have arrived at a similar decision point now; what happens in the next year or so matters a lot, so we need some answers fast. Is the terrorist threat really worth worrying about? Is there a serious bipartisan project for restoring American global hegemony, or is it merely a bunch of neo-conservatives dreaming of lost glories – or is it just the usual cock-up on an unusually large scale?

CHAPTER II

THE ISLAMIST PROJECT

Summoning up every thread of experience and courage, I looked Khalid in the eye and asked: "Did you do it?" The reference to September 11 was implicit. Khalid responded with little fanfare: "I am the leader of the al-Qaida military committee," he began, "and Ramzi is the coordinator of the Holy Tuesday operation. And yes, we did it."

He went on: "About two and a half years before the holy raids on New York and Washington, the military committee held a meeting during which we decided to start planning for a martyrdom operation inside America. As we were discussing targets, we first thought of striking at a couple of nuclear facilities but decided against it for fear that it would go out of control."

I was dumbfounded. Nuclear targets? Could he be more specific?

"You do not need to know more than that at this stage, and anyway it was eventually decided to leave out nuclear targets for now."

"What do you mean 'for now'?"

"For now means 'for now,'" Khalid said, silencing me.

– Yosri Fouda, *Masterminds of Terror* (2003)

Let's start with whether there is really a terrorist threat worth worrying about – *really* worrying about, in the sense that we mobilize all our resources to fight it, change the way we live, invade foreign countries, generally turn our world upside down. The quoted interview (opposite), which took place in April 2002, is taken from a book by Yosri Fouda, chief investigative reporter for the Arabic-language satellite TV channel al-Jazeera; "Khalid" is Khalid Shaikh Mohammed, generally reckoned to be number three in the al-Qaeda organization, and Ramzi, co-ordinator of the Holy Tuesday operation, is Ramzi bin al-Shibh, also quite senior in the organization. Fouda called his book *Masterminds of Terror*, presumably because the marketing department insisted on it, and if you close your eyes you can just imagine these master terrorists in their secret underground lair. It's a bit lower-tech than the headquarters of the typical James Bond villain, but basically the same idea – and from these hidden headquarters, the orders go out to legions of terrorists obedient unto death all around the world.

Well, not quite. The interview actually took place in a safe house in Karachi where Khalid and Ramzi were still kicking their heels eight months after 9/11, having fled Afghanistan after the U.S.–led invasion. The "military committee" was scattered to the winds, and if Khalid was trying to organize further attacks he wasn't having much success: there had been no major Islamist attack since 9/11. Five months after the interview, Ramzi was wounded in a shootout and arrested. Six months after that, Khalid was picked up by the Pakistani police, asleep in a house in a Rawalpindi suburb. They also found his laptop and large numbers of notes littering the room, which gave them hundreds of names, addresses, and telephone numbers to chase. He had clearly not been paying attention back in terrorist school.

Not only are al-Qaeda's "masterminds of terror" not ten feet tall, they are sometimes seriously amateurish. They got very lucky once, on 9/11, because they came up with a way of committing mayhem that no security force in the world had thought to guard against: five-man teams of suicide airplane hijackers that included trained pilots. But that was a once-only surprise, and in all the attacks by al-Qaeda and similarly inclined Islamist groups since then – a nightclub in Bali, a synagogue in Tunisia, a hotel in Mombasa, trains in Madrid, and so on – they have not managed to kill as many people as on that single occasion. The attacks are absolutely standard low-tech terrorist stuff – car bombs, explosives stuffed in backpacks, and the like.

So why have we been hearing about nothing but terrorism for the past three years? Why have there been two wars, in Afghanistan and Iraq, that have killed at least five times as many people as the terrorists have? If the threat is that small, why are thousands of mostly innocent people in prison on suspicion of terrorism, without charge or prospect of release? Hasn't all this been blown up way out of proportion?

Yes, of course it has. It has been inflated mindlessly by the media, but also quite deliberately by powerful people with political agendas. One way of restoring a sense of proportion is to figure out who the terrorists of al-Qaeda and its various clones and affiliates really are, what their goals and strategy are, and how they fit into their own culture and society: Are they the coming thing in the Muslim world, or an isolated minority of fanatics, or something else entirely? Another way is simply to figure out the maximum amount of damage they might do.

If we are ever to get our sense of proportion back about terrorism, we need a logarithmic scale for disasters like the one they use for stars. Only the very brightest stars in the sky are First Magnitude; divide the brilliance by ten for Second Magnitude stars, by a hundred for Third Magnitude, and so on. Ranking human disasters by the same system, only those that could kill, say, half the population in question would be First Magnitude. For the twelve million Jews who lived in Europe in 1939, the Holocaust was a First Magnitude calamity: half of them were dead by 1945. At the global level, a First Magnitude disaster would be one that killed around three billion people: it is possible to imagine a return of the Black Death, for example, that would kill three billion people, and an all-out global nuclear war could reach the same casualty level.

Divide by ten, and a Second Magnitude global disaster is one that kills in the low hundreds of millions of people. A "clean" Third World War with relative restraint in the nuclear targeting of cities and no nuclear-winter effects would fall into this range. The AIDS epidemic may ultimately prove to be a Second Magnitude disaster, although a very slow-moving one. Divide by ten again, and we are down to Third Magnitude disasters like the First and Second World Wars and the Spanish influenza outbreak of 1918–19, which all killed 10 to 50 million people. An Indo-Pakistani nuclear war would be a Third Magnitude disaster, as would be an Israeli decision to unleash its nuclear arsenal on its Arab neighbours.

Divide by ten once more, and we are down to Fourth Magnitude events, only one-thousandth as big as First Magnitude ones. Big or long-lasting local wars like Korea 1950–53, Vietnam 1965–73, and Sudan 1983–2003 fall into this range, killing two or three million people. The slaughter in the Great Lakes region of Africa that began with the Rwanda genocide of 1994 and continues today in Eastern Congo probably qualifies by now as a Fourth Magnitude event. An out-of-control nuclear meltdown in a densely populated area or a megaton-range bomb exploded at the right height over a very large city could also cause deaths at a Fourth Magnitude level.

Divide by ten yet again, and we drop to the level of purely local catastrophes like the Lisbon earthquake of 1755, the Krakatoa explosion of 1883, the atomic bombing of Hiroshima in 1945, and the wars in former Yugoslavia in the 1990s, each of which killed in the quarter-million range. Potential Fifth

Magnitude calamities in the present include the Big One along the San Andreas fault in California, an average year's famine toll in Ethiopia, or a successful terrorist attack on a major city using a ground-burst nuclear weapon.

Another division by ten, and we drop to Sixth Magnitude events like the war in Iraq in 2003, the 2004 earthquake in Iran, and the Arab-Israeli War of 1967, all of which caused 20,000 to 50,000 fatal casualties. Worst-case scenarios for highly successful terrorist attacks using biological weapons very rarely rise above this level. And a final division by ten brings us down to Seventh Magnitude events like the IRA's war in Northern Ireland from 1969 to 1998, the Second Intifada in Israel/Palestine from 2000 to the present, and the 9/11 attacks on the United States in 2001, all of which have caused on the order of three thousand deaths. About as many Americans die each month from gunshot wounds as died in the Twin Towers, the Pentagon, and United Airlines Flight 93, and those losses, unlike the terrorist attacks, recur every month. So why is terrorism regarded by both the U.S. government and media as the world's number-one problem?

True, the 9/11 deaths all occurred on one day, which gave them an impact far greater than similar numbers of deaths spread over a longer period of time. The fact that the attacks were carried out by foreigners on U.S. soil was profoundly shocking to Americans, who had not experienced such a thing (except for Pearl Harbor) for almost two hundred years. The terrorists' choice of powerfully symbolic buildings reinforced the shock, and the fact that the buildings actually collapsed provided a visual image so striking that nobody who saw it will ever forget it. Nevertheless, it is extraordinary that a Seventh Magnitude event can hijack the entire international agenda for years.

The simple response is to blame the media, and God knows they deserve to be blamed. The greedy sensationalism with which the major Western media greet each new terrorist "outrage" has inflated the danger far beyond its true size in the public's mind, in just the same way as their melodramatic coverage of crime has caused popular anxiety about it to rise steeply in most Western countries even as the actual crime rate has fallen steadily in recent years. Public ignorance about the statistics of risk makes this media manipulation easy: there are heavy smokers who worry about terrorist attacks. But it is also true that terrorists always aim to manipulate the media.

Terrorism is the weapon of the weak. It is a technique that tries to maximize the political impact of relatively minor acts of violence – because that is generally all that such weak groups can manage – through the magnifying glass of media coverage. Indeed, terrorism scarcely existed as a discrete political strategy before the emergence of the popular mass media in the late nineteenth century; as a political technique in its own right, terrorism is overwhelmingly a modern phenomenon. And the most important thing about it is that it is relatively speaking a very *small* threat.

Even the biggest one-day terrorist atrocity ever committed, the attacks on the United States on September 11, 2001, is an event whose huge impact is entirely due to the careful choice of high-visibility targets and reflexive, relentless media promotion of the event. The lives of the other three thousand Americans who died violently that same month in gun-related murders, suicides, and accidents were just as valuable, and they would have been relatively cheap to save compared to the immense cost of the "war on terror." But gun deaths happen singly or in small groups, generally out of camera-shot, and as a routine monthly tragedy they are not newsworthy – so nobody called for a "war on guns" in September 2001. This is not to devalue the tragedy of the Twin Towers, but it *is* to say that the "terrorist threat" is not the major threat of our times.

Even the frantic speculation about terrorists getting their hands on weapons of mass destruction in the aftermath of 9/11 failed to impress people who remembered that we lived for forty years before 1990 with the entirely credible threat of thousands of nuclear weapons exploding simultaneously over every city in the entire industrialized world. That was a really serious threat: the weapons existed, their targets were known, and the buttons could be pushed at any time. If terrorists were someday to get their hands on a nuclear device and explode it in some unfortunate city, it would be a disaster, certainly – but a disaster a full three magnitudes smaller than a real nuclear war. And the terrorists will probably never even manage that.

The other truth that has been largely forgotten in the post-9/11 frenzy is that terrorism is a technique, not an ideology or a country. It is a technique that any group can pick up and use, without distinction of ideology, creed, or cause, and the people wielding it could as easily be fanatical anti-government

Americans, Trotskyist Germans, or separatist Tamils as Islamist Arabs. (Indeed, the world's leading suicide bombers are still the Tamil Tigers of Sri Lanka, not any Islamist group.) You don't even have to represent a lot of people or a very popular ideology to make an impact as a terrorist; a small number of people with not-very-popular ideas will do. When small groups of terrorists commit spectacular acts of destruction and get the public's attention, it doesn't mean that they have suddenly become large and powerful groups; just that what they did was widely publicized.

The U.S. government should recognize this, but prefers not to. It says that it has declared war on "terror," but to the extent that it is actually fighting terrorism at all, it is waging a struggle solely against the particular brand of Islamist terrorists who attack American targets. That is a very small enemy, though Washington does everything in its power to pump it up. So we return, therefore, to the original question: How did a relatively limited disaster like 9/11 lead to the huge, system-wide disruption we are now seeing? The best answer is that the terrorist project of the al-Qaeda jihadis has collided with and energized another, far more dangerous project for changing the world: that of the American neo-conservatives. The two groups of would-be world-changers do not collaborate or even communicate, and their goals are largely opposed, but they do feed off each other. Both their projects, as a result, are now up and running.

Why does al-Qaeda want to change the world, and why is there a certain sympathy in the Muslim world for its goals, if not for its methods? There is a back story that explains why Muslims almost everywhere perceive themselves as the chief victims of the past few centuries of world history and the West as the chief architect of their misery. There is also a much more recent narrative of disaster that explains why the Arabs in particular are so filled with rage and despair. What the Islamists bring to this stew of resentment and pessimism is a seductive religion-based analysis of why Muslims have been losing for so long, and a program of action to turn all that around.

"The indivisibility of any aspect of life from any other in Islam is a source of strength, but also of fragility. When all conduct, all custom, has a religious sanction and justification, any change is a threat to the whole system of belief. Certainty that their way of life is the right one thus coexists with fear that the whole edifice – intellectual and political – will come tumbling down if it is tampered with in any way. . . . And the problem is that so many Muslims want both stagnation and power; they want a return to the perfection of the 7th century and to dominate the 21st, as they believe is the birthright of their doctrine.

"If they were content to exist in a 7th-century backwater, secure in a quietest philosophy, there would be no problem for them or for us. Their problem, and ours, is that they want the power that free inquiry confers without either the free inquiry or the philosophy and institutions that guarantee that free inquiry. . . . [T]he tension between their desire for power and success in the modern world on the one hand, and the desire not to abandon their religion on the other, is resolvable for some only by exploding themselves as bombs."

– Theodore Dalrymple, *The Times*, April 15, 2004

The intense and sometimes obsessive quality of Islam's emotional relationship with what used to be called "Christendom" and is now "the West" has waxed and waned with time, but it is not just due to the natural hostility between rival religions that both inherited their God from the Jews. In some senses, Islam is the other half of "the West": certainly, the Arab world is the other heir of the classical Greco-Roman world that the two faiths divided between them long ago.

Between about A.D. 630 and 730, Arab invaders inspired by the new faith of Islam conquered almost half the territory of the former Roman Empire, which is to say around half of the then-Christian world. (Christianity had become the state religion of the Roman Empire about three hundred years before.) It took some generations to convert the conquered lands thoroughly, but with the exception of Spain, which remained mainly Christian despite eight centuries of Muslim occupation and eventually freed itself, the Christians in the new territories gradually dwindled away to a small minority: under 10 per cent in Egypt, Syria, and Iraq, and even less elsewhere.

The Muslim invasions were quite unlike the Germanic invasions that had already overrun Western Europe. The peoples who conquered Roman Germany, France, England, and Italy were mostly illiterate barbarians who brought a Dark Age in their train, although they were relatively easily converted to the far more sophisticated Christian religion. The Arab conquerors of the Fertile Crescent (what is now Israel and the occupied territories, Jordan, Syria, and Iraq), North Africa, and Spain had lots of fanatical desert horsemen in their armies, but the leaders were literate townspeople from the cities of Arabia, and it was their Muslim religion that prevailed in those lands.

There was no Dark Age in the lands conquered by the Muslims; instead the conquerors preserved many of the best elements of classical civilization and married them to the egalitarian spirit of Islam. And this set the pattern for a thousand years: chronic warfare in the borderlands between the worlds of Islam and Christendom, but in the Muslim heartlands a profound lack of interest in the chaotic affairs of the barbarian Europeans. Even the still-civilized Christian rump of the Roman Empire in the Balkans and Anatolia, latterly known as the Byzantine Empire, was not seen by the Arabs as a cultural equal – and besides, newly Islamized Turkish nomads broke into Anatolia in the late eleventh century and started carving Byzantium up into little Muslim-run principalities.

There was one great interruption to this story of Muslim triumph and Christian ruin, of course: the Crusades. The Christians of Western Europe, their Dark Age now past, decided to have a go at recapturing Jerusalem. It had been a Jewish city for a thousand years, a Christian-ruled city for three hundred years, and a Muslim-ruled city for another four hundred and fifty years. There was no law decreeing that the merry-go-round had to stop, and in 1099 the Crusaders took Jerusalem.

It took almost two hundred years of war for the Arabs of the Fertile Crescent and Egypt to destroy the Crusader kingdoms that sprang up along the eastern coastline of the Mediterranean, but after that they largely forgot about Europe again. (The current rhetorical obsession with Western "Crusaders" in Islamist circles is a deliberate revival for propaganda purposes of a long-dead bogeyman.) And then the advance of Islam resumed: in the fifteenth century, Turkish armies conquered Constantinople (now Istanbul), destroyed what remained of the Byzantine Empire, and surged up through the Balkans. By 1529 a Turkish army was besieging Vienna, right in the heart of Europe. The last Muslim kingdom in Spain had been destroyed about a generation before, but there was no obvious reason yet for anybody in the Muslim world to fear that the long high tide of Islam might be turning. A thousand years of Christian-Muslim relations in five paragraphs – but it helps to explain why Muslims were so deeply shocked when the tide did turn.

In the early sixteenth century, there were three very large and powerful civilizations on this planet that dwarfed all the others. They were all in Eurasia: the Christians of Europe in the west, China and its Confucian satellite cultures in the east, and between them, stretching eight thousand miles from Morocco to Java, Islamic civilization. (Hindu civilization in India, which might have made a fourth, had been largely subjugated by Muslim invaders.) Each of these great civilizations naturally assumed moral superiority over the other two, but in practical terms they were roughly equal in size, wealth, and power. They had been the dominant three for almost a thousand years, and there were no obvious signs that a great change was coming.

For educated Muslims in the Middle East, China was a place so far away that they knew little about it except for its art.

Europeans were a lot closer, of course, but those were the old, known neighbours, turbulent and uncultured, and they always lost in the end. They had nothing of value to offer the world, and no sensible person took much interest in them. The real world, where interesting and important things happened, was the Muslim world. And then things started going wrong.

It was quite slow at first – European ocean-going ships showing up off the Muslim-ruled coasts of the Indian Ocean and establishing trading posts backed by cannon-fire during the 1500s, the start of the long Turkish retreat down the Balkans in the late 1600s – but gradually it picked up speed. One by one, the Muslim kingdoms of Asia were extinguished or subordinated to European rule; then in the nineteenth century it was the turn of the Muslims of the Balkans and North Africa; by the early twentieth century all the Muslims of sub-Saharan Africa also found themselves living in European colonies. The roof finally fell in on the Arabic-speaking Middle East, the old heartland of Islam, at the end of the First World War. By 1918, all the wealth and power of the Muslim world were gone and 95 per cent of Muslims were living as the subjects of one foreign Christian empire or another. It was the greatest shock and the deepest humiliation that Muslims have ever experienced, and its echoes still influence behaviours and attitudes in the Muslim world today.

I'm not suggesting that Muslims in great numbers are wandering the streets of Jakarta, Karachi, or Istanbul muttering to themselves in fury over this history. Like other people, most Muslims have no detailed knowledge of the past, and anyway they have their own lives to live right now – but most Muslims are aware that something has gone desperately wrong with history, and that Muslims have suffered terribly as a result. They also know that it was mainly the Christian West that was responsible for this disaster.

There is no need for contemporary Westerners to flagellate themselves with guilt over this past. When Muslims held the whip hand, half of the then-Christian world was conquered and lost forever; it's just history, that's all. But Muslim historical grievances are a good deal fresher than Christian ones – and what hurts even more than the old history is the fact that, although the European empires all collapsed half a century ago, allowing the Muslim countries to regain their independence, Islamic civilization had lost its leading place in the world. There are now no rich, powerful, scientifically advanced, and universally feared and respected Muslim countries. This is probably a transient post-colonial phenomenon, but for Muslims of the present generation it remains a deep and open wound.

How much it hurts, however, depends very much on where you live within the Muslim world. In the big Asian countries where most of the world's Muslims live – Pakistan, India (home to 150 million Muslims), Bangladesh, Malaysia, and Indonesia – resentment about the history is mitigated by the fact that there is now some light showing at the end of the tunnel. Economic growth is promising, a better educated younger generation is rising to power, democracy is becoming the norm (except in Pakistan), and it seems likely that the future will be better than the present. Even in the Middle East, the non-Arab countries are no longer obsessed with the West: the younger generation in Iran are more concerned with getting rid of the dead hand of the 1979 "Islamic revolution" that stifles their lives, and Turkey is a modern, democratic, reasonably prosperous country that is in the queue to join the European Union. Only in the Arab world is the pain of military, political, and economic defeat still acute – because it is still going on.

The Arab world is a disaster area by almost every measure. Even the land itself is eroded, salinated, and worn out by ten thousand years of irrigation agriculture and free-range goats; it is barely able to support the three hundred million people who live on it now – half of whom are under twenty-one. The region's population has doubled since the 1970s, and its youthful profile guarantees many more years of high-speed growth. According to the UN's *Arab Development Report* of 2002, prepared by Arab intellectuals and partly sponsored by the Arab League, half of Arab women are illiterate, the maternal mortality rate is four times that of East Asia, and poverty is omnipresent. Living standards have been falling in most of the larger Arab countries for at least a generation now, as vigorous population growth outstrips feeble economic growth. Science and technology are comatose, research and development are practically non-existent, and, across the whole region, youth unemployment is 30 per cent, the highest in the world. All twenty-two Arab states combined, despite all the oil, have a

GDP smaller than Spain's, and the whole Arab world translates only 300 books annually from foreign languages. (Greece, population ten million, translates about 1,500 each year.)

The governments of the Arab states are almost uniformly dreadful: near-absolute monarchies or clapped-out military dictatorships that are oppressive, corrupt, and sometimes very cruel. A majority of them are also in thrall to foreign interests, principally those of the United States. Democracy, common enough in the rest of the Muslim world, is non-existent in the Arab world apart from a couple of timid experiments in power-sharing with elected parliaments by relatively benevolent monarchs in Morocco, Jordan, and a few of the smaller Gulf States. This is the oldest civilized region in the world, and yet across the whole range of measures from birth rates and literacy to economic growth and political freedom it comes in behind every other region except sub-Saharan Africa.

The Arabs themselves tend to blame these disasters on the twin curses of oil and Israel, and there is some truth in that. Possession of about half the world's oil reserves has only guaranteed that the Arab countries suffer endless interventions by more powerful foreigners: as they say only half in jest in Washington, "What is all of *our* oil doing under *their* sand?" The sense of helplessness that this has engendered partly explains the striking shortage of pro-democracy activists and civil society enthusiasts in the Arab world. Rightly or wrongly, people believe that the United States simply will not allow local political changes that would damage its interests. The rest of the explanation for the political paralysis of Arab society has mostly to do with the long fixation on Israel.

The creation of Israel in the very centre of the Arab world in 1948 was a political calamity for countries just gaining their independence after centuries of subjugation, first in the Turkish and then in the British or French empires. It was impossible for them to ignore the appeals of their Palestinian neighbours, but the poorly led and ill-disciplined Arab armies didn't have much chance of beating the highly motivated Israeli forces. It was the first of five successive lost wars for the Arabs, and the result has been a helpless obsession with the dwarf superpower in their midst that has fatally distracted them from their own urgent domestic priorities. Moreover, since Israel is a creation of the West, defended by the United States in particular no matter how it behaves, for many, perhaps most, Arabs the struggle with the West is not really over yet. The bitterness runs very deep, and the surprising thing is not that there are so many extremists in the Arab world willing to use violence against the West, but that there are so few.

An Arab bill of indictment against the West would start with the conquest of North Africa by the French and Italians between 1830 and 1911 and the gradual British takeover of Egypt (which was never reduced to outright colonial status) in the late nineteenth century, but that was just imperialist business as usual, no more outrageous than previous Muslim conquests of Christian lands. The real Arab sense of betrayal starts with the First World War, when the British promised that there would be an independent Arab state in the Fertile Crescent if only the Arabs revolted against their Ottoman Turkish overlords. The Arabs believed those promises, but the British and the French secretly agreed to divide up the territory between themselves in the Sykes-Picot Agreement of 1916, even as Colonel T.E. Lawrence ("of Arabia"), having given Britain's word to the Arabs, was helping to lead the Arab uprising. Lawrence spent the rest of his life consumed by guilt.

What the Arabs got as a reward for their assistance to the winning side in the First World War was not the promised independent state but an exchange of colonial masters. In the place of the Turks, who were at least Muslim, they got British or French overlords. They also got the balkanization of the eastern Arab world, as London and Paris carved the separate countries of Iraq, Syria, Palestine, and Jordan out of the former Ottoman lands. They then subdivided them even further: France separated Lebanon from Syria in 1920, with the intention of creating a loyal state dominated by Maronite Christians to control the Syrian coast. Britain was stuck with the pledge it had made to the Zionist movement in the Balfour Declaration of 1917 to create a "Jewish homeland" in Palestine, a pledge that would ultimately result in the partition of Palestine – although London was deeply reluctant to fulfill that pledge, which it knew would alienate not only its Arab subjects in Egypt, Sudan, Palestine, Iraq, and its Arab allies in the Gulf, but far more importantly the huge Muslim population of the Indian subcontinent.

This is not ancient history for Arabs; it is as vivid as today's news, and practically everybody knows about it. It is also the answer to the plaintive American question: Why do they hate us? Even though Americans had very little to do with the creation of Israel.

The original Balfour Declaration was a cynical deal between a British government, going broke in the middle of a world war, that desperately needed new loans and still believed in the old anti-Semitic stereotype that Jews controlled the world's finances, and Zionists who were willing to play up to that myth in order to extract the promise of a Jewish homeland in Palestine. Once the war was won, the British government did everything it could to renege on that promise too, as it had on its commitment to the Arabs, but it proved much harder to walk away from the Balfour Declaration – partly because there were many more Zionist Jews than Palestinian Arab nationalists in influential positions in the great powers of the West, but also because the looming shadow of the Holocaust, prefigured in the anti-Semitic outrages of the Nazi regime in Germany in 1933–39, made it impossible to dismiss the legitimate fears of European Jews that if they stayed where they were, they would be massacred.

The circle could have been squared, of course, if Britain, France, and countries like the United States and Canada had been willing to accept very large numbers of Jewish refugees, but they weren't. The British authorities vacillated, turning the tap of Jewish immigration to Palestine on and off repeatedly, and the local Arab population, foreseeing that they might one day become a minority in their own country – that indeed it was the stated Zionist ambition to make them a minority – fought back with riots and massacres. (Being effectively colonial subjects of Britain, they had no government or army of their own.) Jews in Palestine organized their own militias and terrorist groups to fight both the Arabs and the British, and the final showdown was only briefly postponed by the Second World War.

The discovery of the Nazi death camps in 1945 made the creation of Israel a certainty. The major Western countries that had failed to save the millions of European Jews who died in the camps simply had to grant the survivors the Jewish homeland they wanted – and that homeland was not to be in England or New England but in Palestine, so happily it would be the Arabs, not British or American voters, who paid the price. Jewish immigration into Palestine soared in 1945–47, and terrorist attacks on British troops by Zionist extremists like the Stern Gang and Irgun forced London to hand the whole problem over to the newly established United Nations and walk away. The UN, then still an overwhelmingly Western organization (as the rest of the world was mostly still colonies), duly decreed the partition of Palestine between the Jews and the Arabs – and then everybody stood back to watch the war as the surrounding Arab states, themselves only independent for a couple of years, attacked the new Jewish state.

Israel not only won the 1948 war but expanded its borders very considerably beyond those laid down in the UN partition plan. It also used the opportunity (as a new generation of

Israeli historians openly admits) to drive most of the remaining Palestinian population beyond the borders that were defined by the end of the fighting, thereby ensuring a large Jewish majority within the frontiers of the new state. And that was only the first of five wars that Israel has fought against its Arab neighbours.

In 1956 it conspired with Britain and France to invade Egypt, although in the end American intervention on Cairo's behalf forced the conspirators to withdraw from the Sinai Peninsula and the Suez Canal. In 1967 Israel launched a pre-emptive attack on Egypt, Jordan, and Syria that ended with the conquest of the old city of Jerusalem, the West Bank, the Gaza Strip, the Golan Heights, and the Sinai Peninsula. In 1973 it was struck by a surprise attack from Egypt and Syria that was designed to force it into territorial negotiations, and although it regained the upper hand militarily after a few days, it did subsequently respond by making peace with Egypt and giving back the Sinai Peninsula. And finally, in 1982, it invaded Lebanon in an attempt to destroy the Palestine Liberation Organization (PLO), which then had its headquarters in Beirut. The initial attack took Israeli forces all the way to Beirut, and they remained in southern Lebanon for another two decades.

There is nothing shocking or even surprising in this. A new country, set up in a region where it is not welcome, is almost bound to have to fight a few wars to persuade the neighbours that it is there to stay, and it scarcely matters who started which one. The wars, if Israel won them (which it did), were bound to cause great anger and bitterness among its defeated neighbours, so that was a given too. At some point, however, if the transplant is to take, the new country has to move on from wars and start making deals that cement its place in the region. That is bound to be tricky because of all the resentment that the wars have generated, but by the early 1990s Israel had reached that point, at least in the view of some of its leaders. What nobody had taken sufficiently into account was the psychological impact of all these defeats on the populations of the Arab countries.

Roll back the tape to the 1940s and 1950s. Arab states newly emerged from colonial rule are looking for some quick way to escape their backwardness and poverty. Overwhelmingly the larger countries – Egypt, Algeria, Syria, Iraq – opt for secular socialist regimes, mostly led by military men, which they hope will enable them to catch up with their former European oppressors as fast as the Soviet Union is catching up (or seems to be catching up) with its Western rivals. A generation of young Arab revolutionaries, most of whom rarely see the inside of a mosque, promise to build countries that can both make their people prosperous and take on Israel as an equal. They believe what they say, but it's nonsense: the system they have adopted isn't really even working very well in Eastern Europe, and in the Middle East they are starting from a lot farther back in terms of industrial plant, scientific resources, and educated people.

The overwhelming Israeli military victory of 1967 and the accompanying fourfold expansion of Israeli territory, accomplished without any British or French help, was a blow to the reputation of the secular "socialist" regimes of the Arab world from which they never recovered. They hadn't delivered the goods economically, and they couldn't beat Israel either. But the strange and crippling thing is that they didn't disappear beneath a wave of righteous public anger. They are all still there, almost forty years after their sell-by date, no longer really socialist but still very much in power: the Armée de libération nationale (ALN) generals in Algeria, so secretive that they don't even like their names to be known to the public; Hosni Mubarak in Egypt, third in a series of military officers who have monopolized power in Egypt for a full fifty years; the Assad clan in Syria, now in its second generation of presidents – and until very recently, Saddam Hussein and the Baath Party in Iraq.

What saved the military/socialist secular regimes of the Arab world was the Cold War. The Soviet Union had been an early supporter of Israel, racing with the United States to be the first to recognize its independence because it reckoned that the dominant socialist tradition within the Zionist movement would make the new state a natural ally. The United States, quite wisely, refused to be drawn into the Arab-Israeli military confrontation on either side; most Americans undoubtedly wished Israel well, but practical U.S. interests in the region were mostly in the oil-rich parts of the Arab world. Indeed, during the 1950s and the early 1960s Israel's principal military supplier was not the United States but France (which is even alleged to have helped Israel to develop its nuclear weapons).

At the end of the 1950s, however, Israel's Arab opponents, finding no Western country willing to sell them the arms they needed to fight Israel on equal terms, turned to the Soviet

Union. Moscow was receptive, having by now abandoned its earlier hope that Israel could be a reliable Middle Eastern base and ally, so it happily sold arms to Egypt, Syria, and Iraq – and suddenly the Cold War arrived in the Middle East. The United States took over as Israel's main arms supplier, and in return Israel became America's indispensable Middle Eastern ally and base.

The utter defeat and humiliation of the Arab states in the 1967 war should have destroyed the old military/socialist regimes, but they survived because by then the Soviet Union was functioning as a sort of external life-support system. As the Soviet Union's economic difficulties grew and it got less generous, the Egyptian regime switched to American life-support in the mid-1970s. (Egypt is now the second-largest recipient of American foreign aid – after Israel.) Saddam Hussein's Baathist regime in Iraq also switched its primary foreign alliance from the Soviet Union to the United States in the 1980s (because Saddam was then fighting Iran, an American enemy). Eventually, after the 1991 elections in Algeria had to be cancelled by the regime to prevent Islamists from winning, even the Algerian generals signed on. None of these Arab regimes was troubled by the fact that the United States was also Israel's principal military supplier and diplomatic supporter, for by then not even Egypt worried about having to fight Israel again. Indeed, Egypt formally made peace with Israel in 1979.

By the late 1970s it was recognized by all serious military observers that Israel's Arab neighbours could not attack it again with any hope of success. Israel's armed forces were by far the strongest in the region; it had an absolute monopoly of nuclear weapons and long-range delivery systems and could destroy any Arab city on short notice without fear of retaliation; and the United States backed it 110 per cent. No Arab attack could possibly succeed – and by the early 1980s Arab regimes stopped buying weapons of the types and in the quantities that would even put them in the same military league as the Israelis. A perfectly rational decision – but how did ordinary Arabs feel about it?

Terrible, of course, and deeply betrayed. Their dictators had promised development and promised victory over Israel. They had delivered on neither – but they were still there, comfortable in their palaces, and now they had given up even thinking about taking Israel on. It was in this post-1967 atmosphere of defeat and perceived betrayal that Arabs first turned to Islamist explanations of what was wrong and Islamist programs for fixing it.

The word *Islamist* is better than *fundamentalist* because Islamism is a political project based on a religious interpretation of what is happening in the world, whereas fundamentalism . . . well, actually, fundamentalism is a Christian concept, and in Islam it is virtually meaningless. The two religions draw so heavily on Judaism in their vision of God and their moral categories that they have sometimes been described as twin Jewish heresies, but in the matter of scripture there is a huge difference between them – and fundamentalism is all about scripture.

Both the old and the new testaments of the Bible were written by a number of different individuals, and the various prophets and evangelists don't always agree on the details. So Christians are free to believe the gospel of Luke, for example, which claims that a Roman census obliged Jesus's father, Joseph, to return to his birthplace to be counted, thus ensuring that Jesus was born at Bethlehem in Judea. Or they can observe that none of the other gospels mentions this story, that there is no other record of this alleged census, that the ultra-practical Romans were not likely to do something as pointless and crazy as insisting that everybody return to their birthplace to be counted – but that Luke's story conveniently deals with the awkward fact that Jesus grew up in Galilee, whereas prophecy stated clearly that the Messiah would be born in Judea. The very nature of Christian scripture encourages a diversity of interpretations, and so there is a special name for those who accept every word of the Bible literally (ignoring the numerous contradictions): fundamentalists.

The Quran is different, because it was not written by a number of men. In fact, Muslims believe that it was not written by a man at all: rather, it is the direct word of God as dictated to and written down by the prophet Muhammad. Because it has only one author, it is a far more unified text, containing no glaring contradictions of fact – and *all* Muslims are fundamentalists in the sense that they are bound to accept the Quran as literally the words of God. That does not mean that all Muslims are rigidly conservative in the way they interpret God's will in their daily lives; every religious community finds ways to contain and express the diversity of human personality and experience, and Islam does it as well as any. There are liberal Muslims; there are conservative Muslims, and there are some very radical Muslims indeed, but *fundamentalism* in the Christian sense has no meaning in Islam.

The reason that so many Western observers have given this label to radical Muslims is that, like Christian fundamentalists, they are both socially conservative and politically engaged. Both movements are in revolt against the increasing secularization of their societies, which they experience as destructive. They see themselves as last-ditch defenders of key values that are under attack – from the "liberal establishment" at home, in the case of Western fundamentalists, but also from the foreign and aggressive culture of the West, in the eyes of Islamist radicals. However violent and apparently aggressive their actions, they see themselves as acting defensively: most Islamists believe quite literally that the entire Muslim world is under attack by a "Crusader-Zionist conspiracy" that intends to destroy it. Most U.S. actions since 9/11, particularly the invasion of Iraq, are seen by Islamists as evidence that this is true – and this interpretation is gaining ground in the broader Muslim community as well.

The fact that the Islamists have turned themselves into a revolutionary political movement is not intrinsically wrong or sinful in Muslim eyes, because religious movements have often played that role in Muslim history. From its earliest days, Islam was the religion of conquerors and of the state itself, so it does not make the same distinction between sacred and secular power as Christianity, which spent its formative years as the religion of underdogs, outsiders, and slaves. Indeed, since the authority of the Muslim ruler came from God, anybody wanting to oppose or overthrow an existing Muslim government had to couch his criticisms in religious language, accusing the ruler of failing to respect and uphold true Islamic principles.

In politics, as in ecology, every niche is filled. From the beginning of the eighteenth century, Muslim governments that were scrambling to respond to the overwhelming challenge from the West by adopting Western technology and organization invariably faced domestic opponents who criticized them for neglecting Islamic traditions and values. Some of the critics were genuinely appalled at the idea that the perfect ordering of Islamic society ordained by God (in their understanding of His word) should be changed simply to counter the threat from the European empires; others had more personal motives for their opposition, but found the religious critique a useful stick to beat the regime with. And some of the reformist rulers – especially in the Ottoman Empire – did get overthrown and killed.

As the railways, telegraph lines, and steamship routes of the nineteenth-century European empires brought the far-flung parts of the Muslim world more directly into contact than ever before, something else began to take shape: a political concept that you could call *Islamist*, though the preferred term at the time was *pan-Islamic*. The chief purveyors of this idea were the rulers of the last surviving Muslim empire, the Turks, and their vehicle was the caliphate, once the centre of political and religious authority in the early Islamic empire. The Turks had unilaterally moved the seat of the more or less defunct caliphate from Cairo to Istanbul in the sixteenth century when they conquered Egypt and the Ottoman sultans had appropriated the title of caliph for themselves, but at that time it meant little. Even in the glory days of the eighth and ninth centuries the caliphate governed fewer than half of the world's Muslims, and it had long since lost all real authority. But in the last days of Ottoman decline, after the radical officers known as the Young Turks seized power in 1908 in a desperate attempt to save the empire, pan-Islamism became a central part of their strategy.

The idea was to turn the moribund caliphate into a meaningful symbol of Muslim unity. The sultan (and caliph) was now a mere puppet in the hands of the Young Turk officers, many of whom were not religious at all, but if he could serve as a focus of Muslim loyalty that rose above language and ethnicity and bound Arabs and Kurds to the Turkish-run empire, that would be quite useful. If he could also embody the spirit of Islamic unity and resistance to European conquest for the hundreds of millions of Muslims living under European rule, and perhaps inspire them to revolt against their Christian imperial masters, even better.

The pan-Islamic propaganda machine ran full blast for ten years, until the final collapse of the Ottoman Empire in 1918 – but nobody paid any attention. When the First World War broke out in 1914, Indian Muslims fought willingly for the

British Empire against the Turks, North African Muslims served France on the Western Front, Central Asian Muslims failed to revolt against their Russian rulers – and the Arabs did revolt against the Turks. The whole pan-Islamic idea failed so dramatically and comprehensively that it did not resurface in public again for fifty years.

It was Mustafa Kemal Atatürk, a member of the original Young Turk revolutionary group, who hammered the message home. He had consistently argued to his Young Turk colleagues that the pan-Islamic approach was doomed and that the only hope was to salvage a Turkish national state from the wreckage of the empire, and he proved to be spectacularly right. Turkey had lost the war and the empire by 1918, but Atatürk created a resistance movement and eventually an army that defeated the attempt of the victorious Entente powers to divide Turkey up among themselves. Once the Turkish republic was safe, he contemptuously abolished the caliphate in 1923.

Atatürk was a profoundly secular man, and his strategy for modernization was broadly followed by practically every other Muslim country that gained its freedom in the next half-century, though not always with the same success that he had in the Turkish republic. The formula was nationalism, a strong, secular state, and the wholesale adoption of Western models in every domain of public life from government and industry to education and civil law. Give or take a bit, Sukarno and Suharto followed the same course in Indonesia, as did Muhammad Ali Jinnah, Zulfikar Ali Bhutto, and Muhammad Ayub Khan in Pakistan, the Shah in Iran, the Baath Party in Iraq and Syria,

Gamal Abdel Nasser and his successors in Egypt, and the Front de Libération Nationale (FLN) in Algeria. In some places, it worked reasonably well. In the Arab world, it didn't.

After the stunning and completely unforeseen Arab defeat at the hands of Israel in 1967, Arab nationalism was deeply wounded and the pan-Arab movement was stone dead. The secular, socialist path to modernization was discredited, and a generation of desperate young Arabs was ready to listen to almost any other solution that sounded plausible. The Islamists filled the vacuum.

There had always been radical Muslim groups around who condemned the existing governments as insufficiently Islamic; it was a normal part of politics in Muslim countries. Their numbers grew and their critique sharpened as the secular Arab governments demonstrated their total inability to deal with the problems they confronted, and by the early 1970s they had achieved critical mass in a number of Arab countries: they became actual revolutionary movements. Their analysis of the problem was crude, but it had an undeniable appeal because of its very simplicity.

They began with a question. Why, after a thousand years of brilliant success in every field – political, military, scientific, commercial, and cultural – have Muslims been losing on every front for the past several hundred years? We Muslims presumably owed our successes to God's favour, for we are His people, so we must conclude that His favour has now been withdrawn. Therefore the key question is: What are we doing that has caused God to turn away from us?

As with all such rhetorical questions, the answer is only a split second away. It is that ever since we Muslims were first confronted with the challenge of the West a few hundred years ago, our dominant strategy for coping with the threat has been to *copy* the West. We have not only copied Western technology, but we have also adopted Western ideas, perspectives, institutions, and behaviours. In doing so, we have abandoned our own Islamic traditions and values – so God has ceased to help us.

It is a perfectly rational argument, if you accept the initial premise that all the successes or failures of Muslims in the world are directly dependent on God's favour (which is a premise that many Muslims are willing to accept). It is also a very attractive argument to people who are close to despair, because it says that the solution lies in your own hands. The problem is not that the Arab world is several generations behind the West in its technological skills, its industrial strength, its educational level, and its political and social ability to compete in a globalized world (which is a deeply depressing answer, since it means that it will take several generations to fix). Rather, the problem is simply that Muslims are living the wrong way – and that's easy to fix. All we have to do is start living the way God truly wants Muslims to live, and then He will be at our side again and we will start to win.

It is not a new argument. In fact, it has been deployed against many Muslim regimes for many centuries past. A Muslim ruler who crossed some powerful vested interest or had the bad luck to preside over a military or economic disaster could always count on some group of bearded fanatics with a political agenda proclaiming that he had strayed from the path of righteousness and no longer deserved to rule over good Muslims. It was the only morally correct solution to the problem of how to remove a Muslim ruler who theoretically governed with God's authority, the Islamic equivalent of the Chinese device of declaring that a divine emperor had "lost the Mandate of Heaven."

Of course, there was plainly something anachronistic about resurrecting this old argument and strategy in the latter half of the twentieth century, for use against secular, so-called socialist regimes that did not even bother to claim Islamic legitimacy for their rule. On the other hand, it could be a good way to mobilize people for yet one more try at breaking the stagnation and defeatism that paralyzed the Arab world, and what other arguments and strategies were left? As British diplomat James Craig reported back to the Foreign Office after a tour of several Arab countries in 1972, when Arab morale was at the very nadir: "One theory put to me was that, since Arab nationalism had manifestly failed, people are turning to the alternative of Islamic nationalism. I argued that this, too, had failed – indeed, it failed long ago. The reply was that the very length of time which had passed since this failure made it possible to consider giving it a second trial run."

You will have noticed how this discussion lurches back and forth between talking specifically about Arabs and more generally about Muslims. It does so because that is precisely what the arguments of both the Arab nationalists and the devout Islamists were doing in the late 1960s and early 1970s, as the old certainties of the secular modernizers lost credibility.

Theologically, the Islamist position is profoundly anti-nationalist. It comes out of the Salafist tradition, an intensely romantic vision in which the world's 1.3 billion Muslims, living in forty-odd countries spread across three continents, return to the ideals of the first generations of Muslims and live as one under Sharia law in a single, borderless community. Nation-states based on shared language and history are idolatry and blasphemy and only distract the attention of Muslims from the one community they really owe loyalty to: the *umma*, the worldwide community of all Muslim believers. As Osama bin Laden put it in a tape broadcast in February 2003, just before the U.S. invasion of Iraq: "The fighting should be in the name of God only, not in the name of national ideologies, nor to seek victory for the ignorant governments that rule all Arab states, including Iraq."

The paradox is that while Islamism is an anti-national doctrine, most of the Muslims who have been attracted to it are Arab nationalists – because Arabs are the only large Muslim group whose situation is so desperate that many of them have been tempted to turn to such a radical doctrine. Some people try to force Iran into the same category, but the "Islamic revolution" in Iran in 1978–79 was in no sense an Islamist phenomenon. It was another example of conservative Muslim revolt against a radical project for Westernization by a secular modernizer, Shah Reza Pahlavi, but it completely lacked the apocalyptic world-changing ambitions of the Islamists. As Shias, Iranians belong to a minority sect of Islam that is seen as verging on the heretical by Sunnis, who account for perhaps 90 per cent of Muslims worldwide. Shias could not rationally share the goal of a singe borderless Muslim world-state run by Sunni Islamist fanatics, whose first act would be to crush dissenters like themselves. The Iranian Revolution was just about Iran, and although the Iranian mullahs run a thoroughly oppressive theocracy, by no stretch of the imagination could they be called Islamists in the current measure of that word. Arabs are certainly not the only Muslim group that has been attracted to the radical doctrines of the Islamists. There is more support for Islamism among Pakistanis than in any other large non-Arab group because of the radicalizing effects of the long confrontation with India, and latterly there has been considerable radicalization among some small Muslim groups who have come under extreme pressure: Chechens and Bosnian Muslims, for example, although they used to be among the most secular Muslims on the planet. But it remains true that the great majority of the committed Islamists in the world are Arabs, although less than a quarter of the world's Muslims are Arabs. Support for Islamist ideals (if not always for Islamist tactics) probably ranges between 10 and 15 per cent of the population in most Arab countries, though there are no reliable opinion polls on this subject.

The grievances of Arab Islamists are overwhelmingly about the plight of the Arab world, though in recent years they have tactfully added the plight of Chechens, Moros in the southern

Philippines, and other small, beleaguered Muslim communities to their list. They reconcile their very Arab-centred priorities with their pan-Islamic ideology by arguing that there is a worldwide conspiracy of Christians and Jews to destroy Islam – the "Crusader-Zionist plot" – and that the plotters have chosen the Arab countries, the very heart of the Muslim world, as the primary target for their attacks. In defending Arab interests, they argue, they are effectively defending all of Islam, and one day their struggle will have the active support of all 1.3 billion Muslims. But you have to start from where you are, so in practice they began their active operations among the 300 million people of the Arab world.

Islamism is not just an ideology; it is a political program for changing the world so that Muslims are no longer victims. Having defined the phenomenon of continuous Muslim defeats during the past few centuries as a moral rather than a practical problem, the Islamists devised a two-stage project for turning history around. The first priority is to get God back on the side of the Muslims, which means forcing the masses to abandon their corrupt, half-Westernized ways and get back to the way of life that God really demands of good Muslims (in the extreme and rigid form that the Islamists view as God's will). This means in practice that the Islamists must seize control of the state and use its power to *force* Muslims back into the right ways. Islamists are of necessity revolutionaries, and the first stage of their project requires the overthrow of the existing government in every Muslim country and its replacement by (of course) themselves.

Having accomplished this not unambitious goal and reformed all the societies of the Muslim world to conform to God's true requirements, they would then move on to the second stage of the project: the unification of the entire Muslim population of the planet in a single transnational super-state. Then, with God on their side, the united Muslims of the world will take on the West's hated domination of the planet and destroy it.

The Islamists are a classic example of a group of people who are dangerous but not really serious. Their analysis is quite rational if you share their frame of reference (though the great majority of Muslims do not accept it). Bits of their program could work, like seizing power in one or more Arab countries, because there are a lot of very unhappy people in those countries, and Western overreaction to the Islamist terrorists is making them more unhappy. But taking power everywhere, uniting the whole Muslim world in a single super-state, and launching the final jihad against the infidels – that is dreaming in technicolour. If you doubt that, consider Afghanistan.

In 1996 a group of Islamists called the Taliban (literally, "students of religion") came to power in Afghanistan. Ten years of Soviet occupation and guerilla resistance, followed by seven years of civil war, had almost destroyed the country, and most Afghans were ready to accept any government that could stop the fighting. Even so, the Taliban would never have won without the strong support of Pakistan's Inter-Service Intelligence (ISI) agency, which saw them as a means of controlling a turbulent neighbour. But what happened once the

Taliban were actually in power is very instructive, for they did none of the things that normal governments do.

They paid virtually no attention to public health or education (apart from having girls expelled from school), or even to trade and commerce. Instead, they put most of their energy into obsessing about the smallest details of the public's dress and behaviour. Men were punished for not growing their beards (un-Islamic) or for secretly trimming them (also un-Islamic); women were whipped for appearing in public without the company of a male relative, or with a square inch of skin showing somewhere; music was banned, videotapes were ceremoniously hanged, every pettiness imaginable was indulged.

Arab Islamists are doubtless somewhat more sophisticated than their Afghan country cousins, but they do inhabit the same territory. Indeed, many of the younger Arab leaders of the Islamist movement were resident in Afghanistan throughout the Taliban period, and gave no sign that they disapproved of the Taliban's behaviour. What seem like mere distractions and diversions of effort to outsiders are actually the heart of the matter to Islamists: it is only by getting the details of dress and behaviour exactly right that Muslims will once more be living in a way that pleases God, and therefore once again enjoy his support. The trivial stuff *is* the important stuff: get that right and God will take care of the rest.

The fact that the Islamists really would behave like this if they ever got power elsewhere, which is now widely understood, imposes a ceiling of sorts on their potential support. That kind of society has strong appeal among the dispossessed and desperate because of its intense egalitarianism, and it appeals also to conservative men of any class who feel threatened by the social changes – especially changes in the status of women and the deference of the young for the old – that are underway in the Muslim world. (Christian fundamentalists, of course, are largely drawn from precisely the same groups.) These social groups would not normally comprise a majority in any Muslim society, however, and the images and stories coming out of Afghanistan under Taliban rule were profoundly distasteful and disturbing to most Muslims elsewhere. That doesn't mean that the Islamists can never win anywhere: one can imagine some cataclysmic revolution bringing hardline Islamists to power even in a relatively modern and sophisticated country like Algeria or Iraq. After all, something rather similar happened in Iran twenty-five years ago. But it isn't going to happen all over the place. Muslims aren't stupid, and the vast majority of them don't want to live like that. Moreover, the better-educated among them are well aware of how un-Islamic the Islamists are.

The Islamists have grafted the Western concept of the nation-state (founded in this case on shared religion, not common language or ethnicity) onto the traditional Islamic idea of the *umma*, which is a community of believers, not a state. Worse, they have borrowed the distinctively Western idea of transforming the world through terror – as practised by Jacobins, anarchists, Bolsheviks, and many lesser groups of fanatics down to Sendero Luminoso and the Baader-Meinhof Gang – in order to create a utopia. In the case of the Islamists, that utopia may have a rather medieval look to it, but they are thoroughly modern men with a huge Western component in their thinking. Osama bin Laden grew up in jeans, not robes.

"[Osama bin Laden's] utopian vision of the future – a harmonious world in which the traditional institutions of government are no longer necessary – is an echo of nineteenth-century European anarchism. Like the anarchists, bin Laden believes corrupt power structures can be destroyed by acts of spectacular violence. . . . When he calls on his followers to remake the world through terror, he speaks in a modern Western voice. . . . With its radical utopianism and boundless faith in the human will, al Qaeda belongs in our world, not the medieval past."

– John Grey, *Al Qaeda and What It Means To Be Modern* (2004)

All of the early Islamist attacks were in the Arab world, because that was where the Islamists themselves came from. Every existing Arab regime was their enemy, and they made no distinction between secular republics like Egypt and traditional monarchies like Saudi Arabia – nor, indeed, between pro-American regimes like both of the above and pro-Soviet ones like Syria. In the eyes of the Islamists all the existing regimes were equally corrupt. Their first attack was a commando-style assault on the Grand Mosque in Mecca itself, Islam's most sacred site, by several hundred armed men in 1979. They held it for more than two weeks before being overwhelmed in heavy fighting; the survivors were executed by the Saudi regime.

A common feature of all these early operations, like the assassination of Egyptian president Anwar Sadat in 1981 or the large-scale uprising by the Muslim Brotherhood in the Syrian city of Hama in 1982, was that the planners naively shared the old anarchists' faith in the transformative power of violence: they genuinely expected masses of people to flock to the Islamists' banner once they gave the signal with their attack. It didn't happen. There had been a drift back to the mosques in the Arab world in the last three decades of the twentieth century, in reaction to the perceived failure of the project for high-speed modernization on the Western model, but it didn't mean that large numbers of ordinary Arab men and women were willing to risk their lives to help bring the Islamists to power. And if they weren't willing to do that, then the Islamists could not win power.

If you are seeking to overthrow a government from below, there are only two ways that work. One is to find allies in the armed forces and have them do it for you through a military coup. This route was closed off to the Islamists from the start, because the officer corps of Arab armies were the stronghold of the secular modernizers – and ever since the military recognized the Islamist threat, they have been very careful to weed out young officers at the first sign of Islamist sympathies. The other way to overthrow a government is in the streets, either by violent revolution or even, in some recent cases, non-violently, but either of these tactics requires a very large number of people to get out in the streets and challenge the existing regime – and for the Arab Islamists, people were simply not willing to take that risk. Most Arabs do not love the governments they live under, but they do not love or trust the Islamists either. They stayed at home in droves when the Islamists raised the banner of revolt, and stage one of the Islamist project ran straight onto the rocks.

By the mid-1980s, stalemate had set in throughout the Arab world. The Islamist revolutionaries were still there in every major Arab country, carrying out occasional terrorist attacks, but they were making no noticeable headway politically. The general view was that they were a violent nuisance but essentially a spent force: when the Palestinian Islamist group Hamas was founded in 1987, the Israeli secret service at first encouraged and subsidized it as a useful counter-weight to Yasser Arafat's secular Palestine Liberation Organization, which was seen as a far more dangerous opponent. But there was one place where Islamists actually were making a difference: not an Arab country at all, but Afghanistan. And it was there that a new generation of Islamists learned to move beyond mere exemplary violence and discovered strategy.

The Soviet invasion of Afghanistan in 1979 was an apparent triumph of American foreign policy, which had been seeking for years to turn Afghanistan into "Russia's Vietnam." Under the Carter administration in the later 1970s, National Security Adviser Zbigniew Brzezinski authorized a secret flow of arms and money to the Afghan tribes to encourage them to rise in revolt against the modernizing, secular, and pro-Soviet regime in Kabul. It was a strategy that allied America not only with the most deeply conservative Muslim forces in Afghanistan but also with the most radical Islamists in the Arab world, and nobody in Washington minded. Like Anwar Sadat in Egypt in the 1970s, who initially courted the Islamists as a potential source of support and was eventually assassinated by them, or the Israelis in the late 1980s helping to set up Hamas in the occupied territories, the United States was confident that it could exploit and control the Islamists for its own purposes.

Washington's ultimate goal in backing the Afghan insurgents was to force Moscow to intervene militarily to save the Kabul regime. Then, once the Soviet Union had been lured into invading, the United States would ally itself with local and foreign Islamist forces to get a full-scale revolt going against the Soviet occupation. After all, as Brzezinski remarked long afterwards, in 1998: "What is most important in the history of the world? The Taliban or the collapse of the Soviet Empire? Some stirred-up Muslims or the liberation of Central Europe and the end of the Cold War?"

Brzezinski really believes that the ten-year Russian debacle in Afghanistan was the cause of the old Soviet Union's final collapse in 1991. The rest of us are free to doubt it, but the United States certainly did inflict a long ordeal on the Russians, who lost fifteen thousand soldiers killed before they finally withdrew from Afghanistan in 1989. The Afghan people paid a far higher price, including hundreds of thousands killed and millions made refugees. But Americans paid a price in the end too, because Afghanistan is where the new Islamist strategy that ultimately led to 9/11 gradually came into focus.

Young Islamists from all over the Arab world flocked to Afghanistan to fight against the infidel Russian invaders: it was simultaneously an opportunity to serve Islam and a way to escape from the demoralizing stalemate at home. (Many volunteers also came from Pakistan and a few from other Muslim countries, but most of the foreign Islamists in Afghanistan were Arabs.) Much of their money and most of their weapons came directly or indirectly from the Central Intelligence Agency, the Defense Intelligence Agency, and other covert organizations working for the U.S. government, which is why it is sometimes said that the United States "created" Osama bin Laden and al-Qaeda. It would be more accurate to say that it successfully used the Islamists to attain its goals – and inadvertently created a monster in the process.

It seems unlikely that the scattered Islamist movements of the various Muslim countries, each largely trapped behind its own frontiers, could ever have achieved even the limited degree of co-ordination they now have if thousands of their members had not spent years waging a jihad together in the crucible of Afghanistan. It is even less likely that they would have arrived at the new strategy of attacking the West directly without the experience of that war fought so far from home. In any case, it is clear that the first foundations of what we know as al-Qaeda (an abstract noun meaning "network" or "base") were laid in Afghanistan in 1989, in the triumphant aftermath of the Soviet withdrawal, by Osama bin Laden and other "Arab Afghan" veterans of the anti-Soviet jihad. Al-Qaeda was only one among many similar Islamist organizations, united in basic ideology and ultimate goals but divided by personalities and methods, that were springing up, merging, and dissolving amid the wreckage of post–Soviet Afghanistan, but bin Laden had charisma, money (he came from a very rich Saudi family), and real organizing ability, so his outfit grew fast.

From the beginning, one thing in particular distinguished al-Qaeda and its many rivals in Afghanistan from the existing Islamist movements in the various Arab countries. All of the latter aimed to overthrow the secular governments of the Muslim world, stage one in the Islamist project, by direct attacks against those governments. The Arab mujahedeen in Afghanistan believed that this approach simply wasn't working. Terrorist attacks inside the Muslim countries had propaganda value in getting the Islamists' program before the public, but they did not win enough support to get the Arab masses out in the streets in support of the Islamist cause, so the revolutions remained forever stalled. It was in Afghanistan that the "Arab Afghans" came up with the idea of attacking the West directly by terrorist means.

This idea may initially have been just an attractive option for men who had learned to think and act transnationally, and were ready to move on from attacking Russians to attacking Americans. Just a little further thought, however, would have revealed to them that such attacks could yield more than propaganda success. If their attacks could draw the Americans and other Westerners into striking back militarily against the Muslim world from which the terrorism was coming, then those counter-strikes might finally drive the masses into the arms of the Islamists, and they could at last get their long-stalled revolutions off the ground. It was a roundabout route to their goal, to be sure, but sometimes the longest way round is the shortest way home.

This was hardly an original insight. Almost all terrorism is a form of political jiu-jitsu in which the weaker side (the terrorists) tries to trick the stronger side (the government, the colonial power, etc.) into an overreaction that really serves the terrorists' goals. When military staff colleges teach the theory of guerilla war and terrorism to Western officers, the point they always stress is that the guerillas or terrorists are never trying to win a victory on the battlefield. They can't; they don't have enough force. Instead, they are using the very limited amount of force at their disposal in ways that will goad you, the army, into using your overwhelming force in ways that help their cause and hurt yours.

The struggle will be decided, in the end, not by who wins the battles but by which way the mass of the population jumps, into their camp or into yours – and it is all too easy to trick an army into using the huge amounts of power at its disposal in ways that will fatally alienate a population. The U.S. army won almost every battle in Vietnam but lost the war. The same was true of the British in Kenya, Cyprus, and Aden, of the French in Vietnam and Algeria, of the Portuguese in Angola and Mozambique, of the Russians in Afghanistan – the list goes on.

Some will object that those were guerilla wars, "people's wars," whereas pure terrorism conducted by small groups of ruthless ideologues has a much less impressive record: where are the Montoneros and the Red Brigades, the Weathermen and the Symbionese Liberation Army today? But big and successful guerilla armies like the Vietcong, the FLN in Algeria, and Frelimo in Mozambique all started out as small groups of ruthless ideologues employing purely terrorist means. They just managed to attract enough popular support to grow into larger organizations capable of full-scale military operations in the later stages of their liberation wars. The real distinction is not between terrorists (ideologues using force for evil ends) and guerillas (nationalists using force for more or less good ends). It is between revolutionaries who are using terror against their own people, and those who are using it against foreigners. The former almost never succeed; the latter usually do – so if you're stuck in the former group (as the Islamists of the Arab world still were in 1990), you would be wise to move yourself into the latter group.

Compare the Islamist revolutionaries who emerged in Algeria in the early 1990s with the original Algerian revolutionaries and freedom-fighters of the 1950s. They both had ideologies that were not shared by the majority of the population (Islamist in the latter case, Marxist in the former), and their goal in both cases was to turn the population against the existing government and take its place. The difference was that the FLN in Algeria in the 1950s had the French army and a million French settlers to attack. It used terrorism against collaborators among the Muslim population of Algeria too, but the reason for its eventual success was that its terrorist attacks against French civilians in Algeria and in France itself tricked the French army into savage repression and indiscriminate reprisals. The Muslim population was eventually driven into the FLN's arms, and although the French army was never defeated in the field it eventually gave up and went home, abandoning its local allies to their fate.

Contrast the fate of the Groupes Islamiques Armées (GIA) and the other Islamist fighting groups that proliferated in Algeria after the shadowy group of generals who rule the country cancelled the 1991 elections when it became clear that Islamic parties would win in the second round. The rebels began with a much broader base of support than the FLN did thirty-five years earlier – many Algerians had turned to conservative forms of Islam in reaction to decades of repression and growing poverty, though few were explicitly Islamist – and yet they are now virtually extinct. Their problem was that there were no targets available who weren't Algerian. The GIA began by trying to kill regime members, but since those targets were generally too well protected, they ended up mostly killing villagers who co-operated (often under duress) with the regime.

This was so counterproductive in terms of the struggle for public opinion that eventually the Algerian army started mimicking the terrorists' behaviour in order to reinforce the effect: it would send out soldiers disguised as terrorists to massacre yet more villagers who were co-operating with the government. In ten years, about a hundred and twenty thousand people were murdered, usually in ghastly ways, but you don't win people's hearts and minds by killing their relatives and friends: the Islamist terrorists in Algeria never built mass support and are now a spent force. How different it would have been if Algeria had still been occupied by foreign troops, and the GIA could have built its strategy, FLN-style, around getting those foreign troops to commit atrocities against ordinary Algerians.

The dilemma of the whole Islamist revolutionary movement in the Arab world in the 1990s was the GIA's dilemma writ large: their project was stalled at the first stage because their countries were formally independent, and there was nobody around to kill except Arabs. Assassinating leading figures in the local regimes was an unrewarding business, because governments are enormous bureaucracies that can easily fill the vacancies you create – and being local regimes, they were rarely stupid enough to commit indiscriminate massacres that would drive local people into the arms of the Islamists. Going the GIA route and directly trying to terrorize your own people into supporting you won't work either. What you need here is to get some foreigners involved.

The new Islamist strategy that emerged in the camps of the "Arab Afghans" at the end of the war in Afghanistan put the highest priority on attacks against Westerners, and above all Americans. Whenever possible, these attacks should be in Western countries. The aim was to lure Western governments into indiscriminate counter-attacks against Muslim countries, and ideally even invasions that put Western troops on the ground in the Muslim world. The ultimate purpose was to recreate the conditions of a classic liberation war, where every bullet the foreign troops fire creates another recruit to the cause, and ultimately the Islamists win and the Americans go home because the Islamists are local patriots and Americans are foreigners. Then, once the rebels are in power, they impose their Islamist ideology, force everybody into the right ways of believing and behaving, and move on to the second stage of the grand project for putting Muslims back on top.

The founders of al-Qaeda were sitting in Afghanistan at the end of a ten-year war in which the United States had lured the Soviet Union into invading a Muslim country; the Soviet army had been chewed to bits in the subsequent war; and the Afghan people had been so radicalized by the invasion that the local Islamists, the Taliban, would soon come to power there. What could be more obvious than to think about tricking the United States into blundering into the same trap? So they set about building an organization to do just that.

I meet some resistance from Western audiences every time I discuss this Islamist strategy in public, and there are three main objections. One: Terrorists are just evil, and we shouldn't concern ourselves with their motives and methods. Two: Islamists are ignorant fanatics with a medieval worldview, so they are incapable of such a sophisticated strategy. Three: There is nothing in their writings and statements that refers to this strategy.

So, then, one: Being wicked doesn't make people stupid, any more than being good makes them bright. If you don't understand the terrorists' motives and methods, they will run circles around you.

Two: Islamists are indeed fanatics, but they are thoroughly modern fanatics with laptops, well-used passports, and long lines of credit. The leading cadres are intelligent men who are fully familiar with modern theories and ideas: some of them will probably read this book, as they read everything that pertains to their trade and mission. They would be derelict in their duty if they did not understand the history and theory of their chosen technique, terrorism.

And three: They would be equally derelict if they ever discussed their strategy in public. They talk freely about their motives and their goals, but they obviously should never openly discuss a strategy that aims to recruit people to their cause by tricking powerful strangers into inflicting death and destruction on them.

The initial idea of a terrorist organization that specifically targeted the West was hatched in Afghanistan in 1989–90, but it took some time to build it because the recently liberated country soon tumbled into a destructive civil war between the ethnically divided local mujahedeen groups who had united only to fight the Russians. Osama bin Laden arrived home in Saudi Arabia in 1990, just in time to witness the panic in Riyadh when the Iraqi army invaded the neighbouring mini-state of Kuwait. (The Saudi media were not allowed to report the invasion for one hundred hours.) The story goes that he offered the services of his "Arab Afghans" to defend Saudi Arabia from Saddam Hussein's tanks, which may be true: he despised the cynical combination of religious conservatism and grotesque corruption that characterized the Saudi ruling family, but he loathed the outright secularism of Saddam

Hussein's regime even more. At any rate, the Saudi regime did not accept his services, opting instead to invite American troops into the kingdom – and at that point, bin Laden crossed the line and became an outlaw.

His open vilification of the Saudi regime for allowing infidel soldiers into the "land of the two holy cities" (Mecca and Medina) led to his expulsion from Arabia, and later to the cancellation of his citizenship. He took up residence in Sudan for some years, sustained by his own ample resources of cash and a growing flow of money from Islamists in Western countries. While he was in Sudan his network of contacts and collaborators grew rapidly, and his particular interest in Muslims living in the West became evident. In 1996, after the Taliban gained power in Kabul, he moved the operation back to Afghanistan and set up training camps in which the principles and techniques of terrorism were taught.

During the later 1990s, somewhere between 20,000 and 70,000 people from about fifty countries passed through al-Qaeda's training camps in Afghanistan – "a terrorist Disneyland where you could meet anyone from any Islamist group," in the words of Rohan Gunaratna of the Institute of Defence and Strategic Studies in Singapore – and through other camps that were open for shorter periods in Yemen and Sudan. Al-Qaeda members, almost all drawn from the old "Arab Afghans" who had fought the Soviets, taught them secure communications techniques, the use of explosives, all the usual terrorist lore, and then the graduates returned home – but most of them had no further direct contact with al-Qaeda. Having honed their ideology and their "craft," they were sent on their way to make up their own role in the struggle. Some would subsequently found their own Islamist organizations, or had already done so before arriving in Afghanistan; al-Qaeda's leaders didn't mind. It is wrong even to think of al-Qaeda as a franchise operation, though that is getting closer: one witness at the trial after the bombings of U.S. embassies in East Africa in 1998 referred to it as a "formula system" for terrorism, a formula that could be exported and adapted to any environment.

The truth is that al-Qaeda hardly even exists – at least, not in the sense that formal bureaucratic organizations like Shell Oil or the U.S. Marine Corps exist. Terrorist groups have always been highly decentralized and divided into a cellular structure to minimize the damage when security forces penetrate their organization, but al-Qaeda went further than that. Even at the time of its creation, it had no formal boundary that separated members from non-members. There was a geographically dispersed inner group of ideologues and planners, probably numbering only in the hundreds, who served as a resource centre and a clearing house for money, people, weapons, and ideas moving between the various Islamist groups within and beyond the Muslim countries. Beyond that, there were some tens of thousands of activists fully committed to the struggle, some hundreds of thousands of sympathizers who were trustworthy enough to be depended on for money, shelter, or other services – and tens of millions of Muslims who already shared some of the group's Islamist perspectives and might be moved to more active support by the right combination of pressures. The West's allotted role in al-Qaeda's grand strategy was to supply those pressures (unwittingly, of course) by overreacting to the Islamists' attacks. And they were in no particular hurry: As they put it themselves, "The Americans have all the watches, but we have the time."

The first large terrorist operations that were planned and co-ordinated by al-Qaeda cadres were the simultaneous truck-bomb attacks on U.S. embassies in Kenya and Tanzania in 1998, which killed twelve Americans and 289 African passers-by. Six months before the attacks, bin Laden had cleared his theological flank by issuing a fatwa (an Islamic religious edict) that stated: "The ruling to kill the Americans and their allies – civilians and military – is an individual duty for every Muslim who can do it in any country in which it is possible to do it, in order to liberate the al-Aqsa Mosque [in Jerusalem] and the holy mosque [in Mecca] from their grip, and in order for their armies to move out of all the lands of Islam, defeated and unable to threaten any Muslim." It was not theologically sound, for bin Laden is not a religious authority empowered under Islamic law to deliver a fatwa, but it made the point with the target audience and the words were followed by actions.

Planning and preparation for the 9/11 attacks on the United States began only six months after the East African bombings, and took two and a half years to complete. So focused was al-Qaeda on this single goal that in all that time it only carried out one other operation, a suicide motorboat attack on the destroyer USS *Cole* in Aden harbour in 2000 that killed seventeen American sailors. Taking the time to prepare thoroughly paid off: in the end, the attacks on the World Trade Center towers in New York and the Pentagon in Washington were successful probably even beyond al-Qaeda's expectations, killing almost three thousand Americans and others in a ghastly live-television spectacle that engraved the images of horror in every American's mind and guaranteed a massive American retaliation. Which was precisely what bin Laden wanted.

What did Osama bin Laden expect to gain from the 9/11 attacks? Clearly they would raise the profile of the Islamist cause in the Muslim world and produce some new recruits from amongst the devout and disgruntled young, but in terms of the limited numbers that his training camps could handle there was no shortage of recruits anyway. Just as clearly, it would not bring the United States whimpering to its knees, begging for mercy. Anybody who knew as much about the world as bin Laden would have been well aware that America would strike back massively. If he knew that would be the result, and he went ahead with the attacks anyway, then we must presume that he wanted that result.

What form did he think American retaliation would take? At the very least he would have expected it to match President Bill Clinton's response to the 1998 attacks on U.S. embassies in East Africa, which was to shower al-Qaeda's training camps in Afghanistan with dozens of cruise missiles. Given the far larger casualty toll of 9/11 and the fact that it happened on American soil, however, he would have been expecting and hoping for something more: an American invasion of Afghanistan. He was quite right to do so, as any American president – Al Gore just as much as George W. Bush – would have been under irresistible popular pressure at home to strike back decisively against the country that sheltered the terrorists who planned those attacks.

He also probably expected that the U.S. armed forces would have the same miserable experience in Afghanistan that the Russians had in the 1980s: an easy entry into the country (which had no defences to speak of), followed by a long and bitter guerilla war producing significant American casualties and a huge Afghan death toll. Muslims elsewhere, infuriated by this, might then turn to the Islamists and overthrow their pro-American regimes, at least in the Arab world. But it did not actually happen like that: the American conquest of Afghanistan cost relatively few lives, and so far no powerful Afghan resistance movement has emerged. The sole Islamist regime in the entire Muslim world was overthrown, and there has not been a single successful Islamist uprising elsewhere.

Moreover, the original al-Qaeda no longer exists in the form that it took between 1996 and 2001 in Afghanistan: its bases are smashed, its people are scattered, and they will never again regroup as a coherent organization. Capturing or killing Osama bin Laden at this point would make little practical difference to the Islamist movement's ability to strike against Western targets. As he said himself shortly after escaping from the American bombing of the Tora Bora caves in late 2001: "If Osama lives or dies does not matter. . . . The awakening has started." How much of an "awakening" ensues, however, is another question. The answer depends largely on how far the United States wades into the trap that he set. Unfortunately – and no doubt to bin Laden's great surprise and delight – President Bush, having dealt with Afghanistan, proceeded to invade Iraq as well.

"When it is over, if it is over, this war will have horrible consequences. Instead of having one [Osama] bin Laden, we will have a hundred."
– Egyptian president Hosni Mubarak, March 2003

The U.S. invasion of Iraq was an enormous stroke of luck for the Islamists, and there will undoubtedly be some hell to pay in the Middle East as a result, but it hasn't solved the basic dilemma of the Islamists. They still do not command the loyalty of enough people in any Arab country to pull off a successful revolution, and their project remains firmly stuck in the mud. Perhaps enough dead Iraqis (plus a healthy helping of dead Palestinians in the occupied territories) will finally drive the people of some Arab country to revolt against their pro-American rulers one of these days, but there are no signs yet of such a movement sweeping the Arab world as a whole, let alone the broader Muslim world.

The Islamists are marginal to Muslim society, and their closest approaches to seizing power by force in major Arab countries – in Egypt, in Syria, in Algeria – may already be behind them. The international terrorism they have gone in for in the past decade is more desperation than anything else, and their long, slow decline will probably continue unless there is a really dramatic boost in the inadvertent help they are getting from the West. Israeli nuclear weapons use on Arab cities, or an American military occupation of Arabia, might do the trick, but short of that the Islamists will probably never even accomplish stage one of their project.

The loosely linked array of Islamist successor groups still known collectively in the West as al-Qaeda has a high nuisance value. Their proven competence at low-tech terrorist attacks makes them a constant, high-profile threat throughout the West, but that just proves that publicity works. They do not threaten either world order or really large numbers of lives, and it is hard to see how they could do so unless they acquired not just one nuclear weapon but a whole arsenal of them. Their greatest international significance is not what they have done themselves or even what they might do, but rather the excuse they have furnished to another small group of determined people with a project to change the world.

CHAPTER III

THE NEO-CONSERVATIVE PROJECT

Oderint dum metuant. (Let them hate so long as they fear.)

– The unofficial motto of *Pax Romana*

Pax Romana, the Roman peace, was a quite viable project that delivered order over a large area at reasonable cost: Rome directly ruled more than half the population of the known world two thousand years ago, and could collect taxes and recruit soldiers from that very broad power base. Even so, *Pax Romana* really just created a zone of peace and safety within the vast reaches of the empire; Rome was frequently at war on its borders, and did not actually exercise much control beyond them. The Bush administration aimed higher than that.

Pax Britannica was closer to what the neo-conservatives had in mind, since it was an overseas imperial venture that was largely driven by commercial and financial considerations and was often content to settle for indirect rule. However, Britain also had a very broad power base. It ruled about a quarter of the human race at the height of the empire, say between 1857 and 1947, and for the early part of that period it also had between a third and a half of all the industrial capacity on the planet. Moreover, Britain's rulers had relatively modest goals for their empire: they were not ideological missionaries, and did not come around to the idea of implanting British parliamentary institutions in their non-white colonies until the empire was collapsing around their ears.

The original *Pax Americana* was much more benign, for it didn't formally involve an empire at all. It came into existence in the late 1940s, when a visionary generation of American statesmen and soldiers took upon themselves the responsibility of containing Soviet power *without* fighting the Third World War. They made many mistakes along the way, but they helped to rebuild the shattered states of Western Europe and Japan and fostered democracy in them, they created alliances that held the line without frightening the Russians or the Chinese into doing anything foolish – and they also backed the new international institutions that might one day replace the "balance of terror" as a way of running the world. Above all, they were patient, and after forty years their patience was spectacularly rewarded when their main adversary, the Soviet Union, set its own empire free and non-violently metamorphosized into a more or less democratic country. Terrible things were done by both sides in those forty years, but *Pax Americana* delivered the goods: there was no Third World War, and the totalitarians lost. By 1989 or 1990, in fact, the United States had effectively worked itself out of the job of being the "leader of the Free World," for the rival world was also becoming free.

The man who was president of the United States when this great change came, George H.W. Bush, welcomed it as a deliverance and began the process of reshaping American policy for a less confrontational era when the United Nations would finally come into its own and the great powers would co-operate in keeping the peace. There were vested interests in Washington (and in other capitals) that were going to be badly hurt by the end of the Cold War, but they did not seem powerful enough to stem a tide that was sweeping the world. *Pax Americana* was laid to rest, and through the early 1990s defence spending fell sharply in all the industrialized countries: you could practically hear the long sigh of relief as a generation that had lived their entire lives under the threat of a global nuclear war finally grasped that it had really been cancelled. Bad things happened to many innocent people in Rwanda, in former Yugoslavia, in the Caucasus and former Soviet Central Asia, in East Timor, and in a number of other places – in a world with almost two hundred countries, a few of them are almost bound to be in trouble at any given time – but for the great majority of humankind it was a time of peace and of hope.

It is still a time of peace, actually, in the sense that there are only three or four active wars of any size in the whole world – and it should still be a time of hope too, for nothing has drastically changed since the early 1990s except for a slight rise in the amount of terrorism. (Americans see it as a huge rise in the amount of terrorism, but that is due to one shocking event: in the three years that have passed since 9/11, more Americans have been killed by bolts of lightning than by terrorists.) But hope is not the dominant characteristic of the new century. Many Americans live in fear of a terrorist threat that has been deliberately and grotesquely exaggerated; most of the politically attentive people in the rest of the world live with the growing worry that something is going badly wrong. That something is American foreign policy: *Pax Americana* has been raised from its shallow grave, and it has turned nasty.

The new-model *Pax Americana* is much more ambitious than the original, which was limited to specific geographical areas and essentially defensive in nature. It aims at "full spectrum dominance" militarily, which requires not only the sort of strategic superiority embodied in nineteenth-century Britain's command of the sea, but overwhelming power everywhere on land as well. "The military must be ready to strike at a moment's notice in any dark corner of the world," President George W. Bush told West Point cadets in 2002. "America has, and intends to keep, military strengths beyond challenge." Moreover, this enormous military strength will be devoted not merely to maintaining order, but to the task of bringing about radical political transformations in a number of non-Western societies, by force if necessary – and since 9/11, the principal focus of that effort has been the Arab world. Tom Friedman, one of the head cheerleaders for the invasion of Iraq at the *New York Times*, wrote in October 2003 that "this is the most radical-liberal revolutionary war that the U.S. has ever launched – a war of choice to install some democracy in the heart of the Arab-Muslim world."

That is a rather tall order for the United States, a country eight thousand miles away where few people are Muslim and hardly anybody speaks Arabic – but then, the new *Pax Americana* project as a whole is a tall order for a country with as narrow a power base as America. The United States spends more on its armed forces than the next nine or ten countries combined, but it doesn't get a lot for its money in terms of usable military power. It has enough nuclear weapons to incinerate the planet several times over, and even without using the nukes it can bomb any country that doesn't have a modern air-defence system with impunity, but it hasn't enough ground troops to occupy a single country of 25 million people effectively, and it probably couldn't go on fighting anywhere once its casualties rose above ten thousand dead: public opinion at home would rebel.

The United States still has the biggest economy in the world, but its share of global gross domestic product (GDP) has declined from a peak of around 50 per cent in 1945 to about 20 per cent in 2004 and a further relative decline is sure to follow, as the biggest Asian economies are currently growing at more than twice the annual rate of the U.S. economy. It is also extremely vulnerable economically because of its huge trade and budget deficits. How did a country with such a fragile power base and so little to gain from establishing military hegemony over the globe – for it already enjoys most of the benefits that might come from having a global economic presence – ever let itself get lured into this foolish adventure?

"The battle for the mind of Ronald Reagan was like the trench warfare of World War I: Never have so many fought so hard for such barren terrain."

– Peggy Noonan, special assistant and
speech writer to Reagan, 1984–88

The founding myth of the neo-conservative project is the belief that Ronald Reagan destroyed the Soviet Union and won the Cold War. He did so, according to the legend, by a combination of huge defence budgets that the Soviet Union could not match and a single magical speech in which he called for the dissolution of the "evil empire" – by a combination, that is, of military and ideological power. The American trumpet sounded, and the walls came tumbling down.

This is a misrepresentation of Ronald Reagan, who was not really a crusader at all. The Star Wars project that allegedly forced the Soviet Union into bankruptcy was in Reagan's mind a genuine attempt to protect the United States from the consequences of a nuclear war – and to the despair of his advisers (who understood that it was really about seeking the ability to carry out a nuclear first strike against the Soviet Union without fear of retaliation), he wanted to share the technology with the Soviet Union. In 1986, at a summit meeting in Iceland, Reagan actually agreed with Soviet leader Mikhail Gorbachev on a plan for getting rid of all the offensive ballistic missiles on both sides, until his refusal to abandon Star Wars wrecked the deal. He did sleepwalk through his presidency, and most of those around him were devoted Cold Warriors, but on the danger of nuclear war, Ronald Reagan's heart was in the right place.

As for the notion that it was the Reagan administration's decisions that destroyed the Communist empire, that is a huge misunderstanding of what really happened. The Soviet command economy virtually stopped growing after the mid-1960s because of its own internal failings, but Soviet defence spending, always a bigger share of a much smaller economy, continued to track that of the United States, whose economy continued to grow. The Nixon and Carter defence budgets of the 1970s grew only slowly, but by 1980 the cumulative impact on Soviet military spending of trying to keep up was huge: defence spending was taking up to 30 to 35 per cent of the Soviet economy. Reagan increased the U.S. defence spending sharply beginning with his own first defence budget in 1982, but that came so late in the game that it was practically irrelevant: he was flogging a horse that was already dead.

The growing economic crisis in the Soviet system was masked throughout the 1970s by the very high price the country was getting for its oil exports, which brought in enough foreign exchange to sustain the reward system by which the regime bought the loyalty of the key 10 or 15 per cent of the population. When oil prices fell drastically in 1981–82, the foreign exchange dried up and an attempt at root-and-branch economic reforms became unavoidable – all this well before there had been time for Reagan's bigger defence budget to have any significant impact.

But the whole Soviet system was so rotten and overstretched that as soon as Gorbachev's economic reforms began to bite, it started coming apart at the seams. That drove Gorbachev to offer political reforms as well, in a last-ditch attempt to save Communism, but it was too little, too late, and the whole system collapsed non-violently between 1989 and 1991.

"The Soviet people want full-blooded and unconditional democracy."

– Mikhail Gorbachev, 1988

By the end of Reagan's second term in 1988, foreigners who spent a lot of time with the democratic opposition in Russia could see that Communist rule was really drawing to a close, though it still seemed an astonishing idea. However, there is no evidence that anyone in the Reagan administration actually saw it coming. In fact, they didn't notice that the Soviet Union was changing at all for a full year and a half after Gorbachev had come to power in 1985 – but then the Iran-Contra scandal broke at the end of 1986, implicating Reagan's close associates and advisers in a bizarre and highly illegal scheme to sell arms to Iran (despite the fact that his administration supported Saddam Hussein's attack on Iran at the same time), and to use the proceeds of these arms sales to fund guerrilla attacks on the Nicaraguan government.

Reagan escaped formal censure by insisting that he could not remember if anybody had ever mentioned it to him, but he was in desperate trouble politically, and one way of diverting attention from the unfolding scandal was to change tack on the "evil empire" and begin a high-profile courtship of Mikhail Gorbachev. The Soviet leader was more than ready to respond, and within a year the two men had become almost dependent on each other for their popularity with their respective domestic audiences: on his visit to Moscow in 1988, Reagan said that his talk of an evil empire was from "another time." But when Ronald Reagan left office at the end of that year, neither he nor any of his associates had the slightest inkling that the Soviet Union was just three years away from collapse. Communism fell of its own weight, and they just claimed credit for it after the fact.

Some of the more far-sighted members of the Reagan administration and the subsequent administration of George H.W. Bush did, however, grasp a new and unwelcome reality: when the Soviet Union finally died in 1991, so did the need for *Pax Americana*, at least as far as other countries were concerned. If the United States wanted to go on being the paramount power – if it even wanted to maintain its existing pattern of defence spending – it would have to find some new enemies.

"Institutions like to continue what they have been doing, always on a grander scale, if possible. When old enemies disappear, mellow or turn into allies, as frequently happens in international relations, new enemies must be found and new threats must be discovered. The failure to replenish the supply of enemies is the supreme threat facing any national security bureaucracy."

– Richard J. Barnet, *Roots of War* (1971)

By the start of the 1990s, it was already an unshakable part of American political mythology that Ronald Reagan had brought down the Soviet Union, and by extension that a combination of U.S. military power and the irresistible attraction of American political values could bring about huge transformations in other people's societies. It was not too long a journey from that belief to the conclusion that the United States could and should use these same assets to remake the whole world in its own image – a transformation that would, in the eyes of most Americans, simultaneously do everybody else a favour and make the world a safer place for Americans. This would require the renewal and refounding of *Pax Americana* on a much more unilateral basis, but there were lots of people in Washington who could live with that.

In official Washington in the early 1990s, there was a desperate scramble for a new rationale to sustain the patterns of military spending (including think-tank contracts) that had become normal during forty years of Cold War. Two whole generations of professional soldiers and civilian defence experts had devoted their careers to coping with the immense threat presented by the Soviet Union, and suddenly it wasn't there any more – but it was too late to change career, and families still had to be fed, so a frantic search began for some new threat or threats that could sustain the existing pattern of expenditure.

Terrorism certainly wasn't a big enough threat to justify defence budgets on a Cold War scale in the early 1990s (and it still isn't), so in the absence of plausible great-power enemies the default option was "rogue states." North Korea, Syria, Iraq, Iran, and Libya had all been under the same management for between ten and forty years at this point, and their regimes had all been much more hostile towards the United States in their early years than they were by the early 1990s, but suddenly, for want of anything better, they were promoted to the first rank of global threats. Of course, they couldn't really be inflated enough to fill the space vacated by the

Soviet Union unless they, too, were able to attack the United States with nuclear weapons, so suddenly that also became a concern.

"If we were truly realistic instead of idealistic, as we appear to be, we would not permit any foreign power with which we are not firmly allied, and in which we do not have absolute confidence, to make or possess nuclear weapons. If such a country started to make atomic weapons we would destroy its capacity to make them before it has progressed far enough to threaten us."

– General Leslie Groves, head of the Manhattan Project, October 1945

Leslie Groves was usually viewed as barking mad when he advocated attacking other countries that tried to obtain nuclear weapons, but almost half a century later, in a capital where a lot of good jobs were at risk, the people who gradually became known as the neo-conservatives got a much warmer reception. "Rogue states" with "weapons of mass destruction" became the new obsession – and what was so neat about them was that you weren't just confined to "defensive measures" like pouring money into the ever-popular Ballistic Missile Defense program. Because they were small and vulnerable countries, you could design forces (very expensive forces) for "going after them" and "taking them out." Pre-emptive war (to forestall an impending attack) and preventive war (to destroy a potential future threat) both became possible strategies in a way that they had never been against the Soviet Union – and on this foundation began to be built a project for the perpetuation of U.S. global domination based on the unilateral exercise of overwhelming American power. The first people to succumb to this fantasy were mostly men who had worked in the Reagan administration and were amazed by what they thought (in retrospect) that they had wrought. Men like Dick Cheney, Paul Wolfowitz, and Lewis "Scooter" Libby.

In the spring of 1992, when Cheney was secretary of defense in President George H.W. Bush's administration and Wolfowitz and Libby were relatively junior political appointees at the Pentagon, excerpts from a draft "Defense Planning Guidance" written by the latter two men was leaked to the *New York Times* and led a horrified Democratic senator, Joseph Biden, to denounce the document as a prescription "literally for a *Pax Americana*." Written in the aftermath of America's easy victory in the Gulf War of 1990–91, the document proposed a new strategy "to set the nation's direction for the next century" in which unchallengeable American military power would "establish and protect a new order" – but this was not the elder President Bush's idea of a New World Order built around great-power collaboration under the authority of the United Nations.

The Wolfowitz-Libby "Defense Planning Guidance" did not even mention the UN, and called for permanent American military pre-eminence over all of Europe and Asia, including the Middle East. The United States must be capable of "deterring potential competitors from even aspiring to a larger regional or global role," including current allies like Germany and Japan, and it must be willing to use pre-emptive force against states that it suspected of developing weapons of mass destruction. U.S. military intervention overseas would be a "constant feature" in the future, and it might well include the pre-emptive use of American nuclear, biological, and chemical weapons.

It was an ultra-radical, some would say half-crazed, manifesto for American world domination that had no place in an administration as conventional and conservative as that of George Bush Sr., and although it had presumably been written with Dick Cheney's encouragement, saner members of the administration, like Secretary of State James Baker and National Security Adviser Brent Scowcroft, successfully insisted that the document undergo radical surgery. Like George Bush Sr. himself, Baker and Scowcroft were old-guard Republicans with extensive international experience who believed that even American power was limited, and that the best way of maximizing U.S. influence in the world was usually to work through multilateral institutions within the framework of international law. But they all got dumped together when the Democrats returned to the White House under Bill Clinton at the end of 1992, and the proponents of a new and far more sweeping version of *Pax Americana* spent the next eight years gnashing their teeth in the outer darkness while the great opportunity, as they saw it, passed America by. No sooner had history opened the door to them than American voters closed it again.

But the temptation to go it alone was great and growing in a world where the sudden collapse of the Soviet Union meant that the United States, for the moment, was the one and only superpower, and Cheney, Wolfowitz, and Libby were not alone in their conviction that the United States should seize the "unipolar moment." In their long but comfortable exile from active politics in 1993–2000, they gathered allies, mostly former Reagan and Bush administration officials now working in the oil and defence industries or roosting in various hard-right think-tanks in Washington – and their enforced holiday from government gave them the time and the freedom for a well-coordinated ideological campaign that eventually led to a sharp radicalization in thinking on defence and foreign policy in the upper ranks of the Republican Party. Ironically, they were known as neo-conservatives.

The *neo* refers to the fact that many of the original neo-conservative inner circle began their careers as Democrats, although hardly mainstream members of the Democratic Party. Paul Wolfowitz, Deputy Defense Secretary in George W. Bush's administration; Richard Perle, who served as chair of the Defense Policy Board until allegations of conflict of interest forced him out in 2003; Douglas Feith, number three at the Pentagon; and Elliott Abrams, Bush's chief adviser on the Middle East, all served on the staff of Democratic Senator Henry "Scoop" Jackson in the 1970s, at a time when Jackson was the most hawkish Cold Warrior in the Senate. (His major legislative contribution in that period was the Jackson-Vanik Amendment, which required freedom of emigration in U.S. trading partners as a precondition of normal trade relations with the United States. Its main purpose and practical effect was to open the door to the mass emigration of Soviet Jews to Israel.) Wolfowitz, Perle, Feith, and Abrams all have long-standing links with the hard-line Likud bloc in Israel, and Perle and Feith collaborated in a 1996 study for incoming Likud prime minister Binyamin Netanyahu entitled *A Clean Break*, which prominently advocated the overthrow of Saddam Hussein in Iraq as an essential part of a new Israeli strategy that would break out of the constraints of the Oslo Accords.

A year later, on June 3, 1997, Wolfowitz and Abrams, together with William Kristol and Robert Kagan (co-founders of the neo-conservative house organ *The Weekly Standard*), Dick Cheney (later vice-president under George W. Bush), Scooter Libby (later Cheney's chief of staff), Donald Rumsfeld (defense secretary), Peter Rodman (assistant secretary of defense for international security affairs), Paula Dobriansky (undersecretary of state for global affairs), Zalmay Khalilzad (U.S. ambassador to Afghanistan), and Jeb Bush (governor of Florida, but perhaps more importantly George W. Bush's younger brother), signed the statement of principles of a new pressure group, the Project for a New American Century (PNAC). The PNAC's goal was "to shape a new century favourable to American principles and interests," and the way to do that was to return to what they held to be the policies of the Reagan years: "A Reaganite policy of military strength and moral clarity may not be fashionable today. But it is necessary if the U.S. is to build on the success of this past century and ensure our security and greatness in the next."

What did that actually mean? Part of the answer came in the open letter that the PNAC founders, plus new members Richard Perle and Richard Bolton (later undersecretary of state for arms control and international security in the Bush administration) and some other like-minded signatories including James Woolsey (former director of the Central Intelligence Agency and a member of the Defense Policy Board under Bush), wrote to President Bill Clinton on January 26, 1998. They urged him to adopt a new policy aimed at "the removal of Saddam Hussein's regime from power," because otherwise "the safety of American troops in the region, of our friends and allies like Israel and the moderate Arab states, and a significant portion of the world's supply of oil will all be put at hazard." The broader strategy behind the Iraq recommendation was first sketched out in an article, "Towards a Neo-Reaganite Foreign Policy," that Kristol and Kagan published in *Foreign Affairs* in 1996, in which they argued that the United States should seize the "unipolar moment" when it was the only superpower, and adopt policies that would extend its exalted status indefinitely. A resurrected *Pax Americana*, in other words.

The Project for a New American Century advocated preemptive military attacks on "rogue states" like North Korea, Iran, and Iraq, and reorientation of America's political and military strategy from the old enemy, Russia, to the emerging strategic rival, China. It could easily have been the late nineteenth century, when British pressure groups were urging a reorientation of the country's defence efforts from the old enemy, France, to the new challenger, Germany. Indeed, so far as the neo-conservatives were concerned, it *was* the late nineteenth century, with not a moment's thought given to multilateral and non-military ways of dealing with the problem of changing power relationships. As they put it in their open letter to President Clinton, "American policy cannot continue to be crippled by a misguided insistence on unanimity in the UN security council."

The last and most complete statement of the PNAC's vision for a unipolar, American-run world before the responsibilities of office forced its members to stop talking openly about their ultimate objectives was a document produced in September 2000 entitled *Rebuilding America's Defenses: Strategy, Forces and Resources for a New Century*. It began: "The United States is the world's only superpower, combining preeminent military power, global technological leadership, and the world's largest economy. . . . America's grand strategy should aim to preserve and extend this advantageous position as far into the future as possible. . . . Yet no moment in international politics can be frozen in time; even a global *Pax Americana* will not preserve itself."

So how could the United States extend this moment as far as possible into the future? The report advocated establishing an unchallengeable nuclear superiority based on "a new family" of more usable nuclear weapons, the restructuring of the air force "toward a global first-strike force," and the development and deployment of "global missile defenses to defend the American homeland . . . and to provide a secure basis for U.S. power projection around the world." The Anti-Ballistic

Missile Treaty must therefore be torn up, since the prerequisite for an American nuclear first-strike capability was the ability to prevent target nations from retaliating against the United States with nuclear weapons. The United States should also "control the new 'international commons' of space and 'cyberspace,' and pave the way for the creation of a new military service – US Space Forces – with the mission of space control."

On the ground, there must be enough American combat forces to fight and win multiple major wars at the same time. This would be made possible at an affordable cost by rapid exploitation of the "revolution in military affairs" (the move to high-tech, unmanned weaponry) "to insure the long-term superiority of U.S. conventional forces," and by the establishment of "a network of 'deployment bases' or 'forward operating bases' to increase the reach of current and proposed forces." Substantial U.S. forces would have to be based abroad to fulfill "multiple constabulary missions" around the world, and these forces should remain under American rather than UN command. "The presence of American forces in critical regions around the world is the visible expression of the extent of America's status as a superpower," the document argued, and the United States must not allow "North Korea, Iran, Iraq or similar states to undermine American leadership, intimidate American allies, or threaten the American homeland itself." In this way, it would be possible to "preserve *Pax Americana*" and a "unipolar 21st century."

On the specific question of the Gulf region, the PNAC document was remarkably frank about what an attack on Iraq should lead to: "While the unresolved conflict with Iraq provides the immediate justification, the need for a substantial American force presence in the Gulf transcends the issue of the regime of Saddam Hussein." The wider strategic aim was "maintaining global U.S. preeminence," which would be greatly enhanced by American control of the Persian Gulf oilfields, the main source of oil imports for the emerging Chinese industrial giant, since a principal purpose of the massive military buildup would be "to cope with the rise of China to great-power status." But although they were only months away from an election that could return a Republican president to the White House, the authors of *Rebuilding America's Defenses* were remarkably pessimistic about the likelihood that their project would be translated into policy any time soon, "absent some catastrophic and catalyzing event – like a new Pearl Harbor."

Such were the views of the neo-conservatives on the brink of taking power in the United States – and *none* of this discussion was taking place in the context of a "war on terror." It was a program for American global hegemony, and they were working hard to ensure that it could be done at a cost reasonable enough not to alienate American voters. It was not a conspiracy: the neo-conservatives, far from hiding their views and their ties, actively campaigned for their project. It did logically require the marginalization of the United Nations and it called for some wars that would probably be illegal within the existing structure of international law, but America's veto on the Security Council (like that of the other traditional great powers) existed precisely to exempt it from the UN's rules and from international law whenever it felt the need.

So it was an entirely viable project, at least in the short term, if the American public could be persuaded to back it. The only worry that might have clouded the day for historically conscious neo-conservatives was the fact that the kind of massive military reorganization they were proposing to underpin *Pax Americana* had only been undertaken in the case of its predecessors, *Pax Romana* and *Pax Britannica*, when the power of the empire in question was already slipping into irreversible decline.

"History is replete with examples of empires mounting impressive military campaigns on the cusp of their impending economic collapse."

– Eric Alterman, *Sound and Fury: The Washington Punditocracy and the Collapse of American Politics* (1992)

This is the point, just before Bush and the neo-conservatives take office at the beginning of 2001, where the answers to some key questions about the nature and purposes of the *Pax Americana* project become clear. First, the "big" conspiracy theory that Emmanuel Todd raised in his book, *Après l'empire*: Is the entire enterprise of reviving *Pax Americana*, this time on a truly global basis, really just a diversionary operation, intended to impress the world with America's strategic indispensability and military invincibility in order to distract attention from its extreme economic vulnerability? And is it, by the way, a bipartisan project? When you put it like that, it sounds pretty silly – and that suggests that it probably is.

There was certainly a shift in the American public mood towards impatience with international institutions and a growing obsession with America's military power as the 1990s neared their end. That mood was reflected in Clinton's last defence budgets, which started going back up after 1998, as well as in his inability to get such innocuous multilateral agreements as the land-mines treaty and the International Criminal Court accepted by the Congress and his own military. But the Democrats showed no interest in a resurrected *Pax Americana* while Clinton was in office.

The fact that a lot of them voted in 2002 for Bush's invasion of Iraq only proves that they were either gullible (and believed the cooked intelligence that they were served) or extremely cynical (and believed that they were giving Bush enough rope to hang himself). In the case of Senate Majority leader Tom Daschle and Senator John Kerry it was unquestionably the latter: they consistently and successfully argued that to attack Bush on the "war on terror," civil liberties, or the invasion of Iraq would be to walk into the trap set by Karl Rove, the president's political strategist. If Bush's war prospered, he would win the next election anyway; if it did not, at least the Republicans would not be able to blame the failure on the Democrats. There was no bipartisan conspiracy to recreate *Pax Americana*.

Very well, then, was there at least a Republican conspiracy that saw *Pax Americana* as a necessary strategy to deal with

America's economic weakness? Almost certainly not. The feet of clay beneath the U.S. economy today are the huge foreign trade deficit and the equally huge budget deficit, but only one of those feet had yet turned to clay in the late 1990s. The trade deficit began to soar in the last few years of the decade, but the Clinton administration had successfully wrestled the huge budget deficits inherited from the Reagan and the first Bush administrations to the ground. It is the *combination* of the two deficits that creates such an unstable and dangerous situation, and that only came into being after the younger Bush administration came into office.

None of the members of the Bush cabinet with the exception of Treasury Secretary Paul O'Neill (who was sacked for his temerity) ever said anything in public that suggested they were even dimly aware of the gravity of the problem. Indeed, it is unimaginable that they would have voluntarily created a massive budget deficit with their tax cuts if they had even understood the nature of the problem. What drove *Pax Americana* was hubris, not economics. And certainly not terrorism.

CHAPTER IV

TARGET IRAQ

"I expected to go back to a round of meetings [on September 12, 2001] examining what the next attacks could be, what our vulnerabilities were, what we could do about them in the short term. Instead, I walked into a series of discussions about Iraq. At first I was incredulous that we were talking about something other than getting al Qaeda. Then I realized with almost a sharp physical pain that Rumsfeld and Wolfowitz were going to try to take advantage of this national tragedy to promote their agenda about Iraq. Since the beginning of the administration, indeed well before, they had been pressing for a war with Iraq. My friends in the Pentagon had been telling me that the word was we would be invading Iraq sometime in 2002."

– Former White House counter-terrorism chief
Richard A. Clarke, *Against All Enemies* (2004)

If there were no "rogue states" in the world, and no "weapons of mass destruction" either, 9/11 would have happened in just the same way. Only one day after 9/11, the Central Intelligence Agency (CIA) was already certain that al-Qaeda had sponsored the attacks, but to counter-terrorism chief Richard A. Clarke's dismay Paul Wolfowitz, deputy to Defense Secretary Donald Rumsfeld, was insisting that such a sophisticated operation must have had a state sponsor. His candidate for the guilty party was, of course, Iraq. By the following day, Rumsfeld was talking about "getting" Iraq: "[He] complained that there were no decent targets for bombing in Afghanistan and that we should consider bombing Iraq, which, he said, had better targets. At first I thought Rumsfeld was joking. But he was serious and the President did not reject out of hand the idea of attacking Iraq. Instead he noted that what we needed to do with Iraq was to change the regime, not just hit it with more cruise missiles. . . ."

We now know that the Bush administration came into office already determined to invade Iraq: former treasury secretary Paul O'Neill has revealed that at the very first meeting of President Bush's National Security Committee (NSC) on

January 30, 2001, more than seven months before the terrorist attacks on 9/11, the invasion of Iraq was "Topic A." In an interview with CBS News in January 2004 that coincided with the publication of *The Price of Loyalty: George W. Bush, the White House, and the Education of Paul O'Neill*, a book by journalist Ron Suskind that chronicled the former treasury secretary's two years in the Bush cabinet, O'Neill said, "From the very first instance, it was about Iraq. It was all about finding a way to do it. That was the tone of it: the President saying, 'Go find me a way to do this.'" Within weeks O'Neill saw a secret dossier entitled "Plan for post-Saddam Iraq," and an attack on Iraq remained an abiding theme in subsequent NSC meetings. Indeed, reports O'Neill, nobody questioned the assumption that Iraq should be invaded, and even the calamity of 9/11 did not derail the neo-conservatives' fixation on Iraq. They simply appropriated the terrorist attack as a convenient vehicle for pursuing it.

But why were they so determined to invade Iraq? On the face of it, it made no sense, for Iraq wasn't threatening anybody. It had been under strict UN embargo since the end of the Gulf War in 1991, and Saddam Hussein was just barely managing to stay afloat. He wasn't even particularly hostile to the United States: Saddam came to be seen as a dangerous enemy by Washington after his monumental blunder in invading Kuwait in 1990, but he had been quite happy to be an informal ally of the United States during his war against Iran in the 1980s, and seems genuinely not to have understood that his invasion of Kuwait would irreparably damage that relationship.

(The record of his interview with U.S. ambassador April Glaspie just before the invasion strongly suggests that he was seeking a green light from Washington, and may have mistakenly concluded that he had got it.) Even after his defeat in the Gulf War of 1991, he had no motive to sponsor terrorist attacks against the United States, and every reason to avoid doing so in view of the likely retaliation. The White House's own counter-terrorism expert and the CIA would both have told Bush and his cabinet colleagues, if they had cared to inquire, that Iraq was not involved in supporting anti-U.S. terrorist activities. If they were concerned about terrorism, al-Qaeda was the one to worry about.

But they weren't concerned about terrorism. Richard A. Clarke recounts in his book *Against All Enemies* that it took him more than seven months from the time of his first request, until only a week before 9/11, to get an opportunity to address the Principals Committee (Vice-President Dick Cheney, Secretary of Defense Donald Rumsfeld, Secretary of State Colin Powell, National Security Adviser Condoleezza Rice, and the heads of the CIA and the FBI) on the threat from al-Qaeda. And the Bush administration wasn't really concerned about allegations of weapons of mass destruction in Iraq at this point either: the extent to which it finally ended up believing its own cooked intelligence about Iraq's mythical weapons of mass destruction is debatable, but the subject was not even on the table during the seven months before 9/11. The administration's foreign priorities at that time were focused on ideological issues – withdrawing from the Kyoto treaty on climate change, sabotaging the International Criminal Court, killing proposals for controlling the global trade in small arms and for strengthening the Biological Weapons Convention – and on global hegemony issues like getting the Ballistic Missile Defense program up and running (which required withdrawing from the Anti-Ballistic Missile Treaty) and invading Iraq. So again, why Iraq?

A number of geopolitical explanations have been offered for the choice of Iraq. Two of the minor oil-related explanations – that military control over Gulf oil supplies would be a strategic asset for the United States in a future confrontation with China, and that oil concessions in a conquered Iraq would allow the Bush administration to reward its major contributors in the U.S. oil industry – hold a certain amount of water, given the strategic obsessions of the neo-conservatives and the Bush administration's close, almost symbiotic relationship with the U.S. energy industry. But nobody would invade an entire country out of the blue for such remote or paltry reasons, and the seemingly bigger reasons – "security of oil supplies" or keeping the oil price down – simply do not make sense.

Popular wisdom may cynically believe that "it's all about oil," but it actually isn't. The notion of "strategic security of oil supply," if it ever had any validity, lost it at the end of the Cold War. Nobody is going to blockade or sink the tankers bringing oil to the consumers, and the producers themselves simply cannot afford to stop pumping the stuff and selling it to all comers: their people live off the proceeds. The Iranian regime may hate the Great Satan, but Iran has pumped oil right up to the limit imposed by the Organization of Petroleum Exporting Countries (OPEC) cartel every month since the Revolution in 1979 (and often beyond the limit), and willingly sold it to any Western country that wanted to buy it at the going market price. How else is it going to pay for the shiploads of frozen Australian lamb that sail up the Gulf most days to feed 70 million Iranians? You don't have to occupy oil-producing countries militarily at vast expense to get oil from them, you just write them a cheque: Saddam Hussein sold half of Iraq's oil exports to the United States (which was busy filling its strategic reserve in anticipation of the war) the month before the United States invaded Iraq. And as for keeping the oil price down: when did it become an interest of the U.S. oil industry, Bush's closest political ally, to keep the oil price down?

You can think of other reasons that might have been important in persuading this or that member of the administration to get on the "attack Iraq" bandwagon. The advantages to Israel of crushing that country's strongest remaining Arab opponent would have appealed to the members of the administration who had very close links to the ruling Likud Party in Israel. In a more tangled and arcane way, it would also have appealed to the radical Christian fundamentalists in the Republican core constituency who see the United States and Israel as players fulfilling the Biblical prophecies that herald the End Times. The desirability of acquiring an alternative military base in the Gulf that would allow U.S. troops to be withdrawn from Saudi Arabia, where they were a permanent irritant to Muslim sensibilities, has also been advanced as a motive for invading

Iraq (though it isn't clear why the United States couldn't just have moved the troops from Saudi Arabia to its existing bases in Qatar and Bahrain without the nuisance of a war). Then there are the supposed personal motives, like Bush's desire to take revenge for an alleged plot by Saddam to assassinate his father in 1993, or alternatively an almost Oedipal eagerness by George W. to demonstrate that he could do what his father couldn't – take Baghdad.

Assembling a coalition of people committed to a common goal, even within a group as ideologically focused as the Bush administration, always involves playing on the specific motives that most appeal to the various individuals who must agree. But none of these motives, singly or in combination, could have persuaded this large group of Washington insiders to back such a dramatic and politically risky initiative as an unprovoked invasion of a country in an explosive region halfway round the world. So what over-arching motive did unite them, or at least enough of them to get this project off the ground?

Given what we know about neo-conservative ideas, *Pax Americana* is the obvious candidate. With the exception of Secretary of State Colin Powell, virtually every senior political appointee dealing with defence and foreign policy in the Bush administration was associated with various neo-conservative studies and projects. And the main reason that this group had already been agitating publicly for an invasion of Iraq since at least 1996 was that they saw it as the ideal vehicle for relaunching *Pax Americana* on a new basis. They would never have put it that way in public – you can't tell the American public that you want their sons and daughters to die in a war overseas for something as abstract as global hegemony – but they were clever and experienced enough to understand that when you set out to change the global rules, you need to do something dramatic to get people's attention. The cheapest thing to do, in terms of the federal budget and of American lives, was Iraq.

Consider the problem. The old version of *Pax Americana* rarely resorted to naked compulsion. There were exceptions, but successive administrations generally preferred to work through alliances and multilateral organizations under the shelter of international law whenever possible. (It multiplies your leverage, and it annoys people less.) America's hegemony did not extend to the Communist-ruled third of the world, of course, nor did Washington bother to exercise it in those parts of the Third World that were not strategically or economically important to it, but the United States genuinely filled the role of paramount power in the industrialized West, still the world's economic heartland. Moreover, its power was generally accepted as a Good Thing (despite much grumbling), because most people in the West believed that there was a real clash of values in the Cold War and that America better represented their values. America's power was never greater or less questioned than when it faced the Soviet Union across a divided world.

Then came the collapse of the Soviet Union, and by purely military and economic measures America's relative power grew even greater. But at the same time American global power faced a crisis of legitimacy, because with the collapse of authoritarian regimes not only in Communist-ruled Europe but in major Asian countries and in apartheid South Africa between 1986 and 1994, the United States could no longer convincingly portray itself as the sole guardian of freedom. Democracy was winning all over the place, without American help for the most part, and there was no longer some great and universally feared enemy of freedom against whom Washington could rally the troops. So what would become of the international leadership role that had been such a long and pleasant part of the lives of those who govern in Washington?

The end of the Cold War destroyed the basis for the existing version of *Pax Americana*, but at the same time it seemed to enhance America's relative military power to the point where no other country in the world could defy it. (This was not really true, but most people in Washington believed it.) For those in Washington who want to "preserve and extend this advantageous position as far as possible into the future," the task was therefore to find a new rationale for America's immense military effort and its worldwide military presence. The "rogue states with WMD" story might work with the U.S. domestic audience, but it just wouldn't fly with other governments. In fact, there was *no* cover story that they would swallow: they would just have to be shown who was in charge. The old *Pax Americana* had been compatible with international law and a consultative relationship with America's major allies; the new version would be based much more frankly on naked American power. Perpetuating the "unipolar moment" meant bigger U.S. military budgets than during the Cold War, not smaller, and an effective end to the old consultative alliances like NATO (though the facade might be usefully preserved). More urgently, it required the removal of the restraints imposed by existing laws and treaties: the United States must be free to use its power unilaterally as it wished.

So how could the neo-conservatives let the world know in a dramatic but economical way that the rules have just changed and now the United States is in sole charge? One good way would be to pick some country that has repeatedly defied the United States in the past – but isn't actually attacking it right now, for we don't want this to look like mere retaliation – and to whack it very hard. Create a horrible example of what happens to those who get out of line, in other words.

But won't such an action look capricious? In fact, won't it actually be illegal under existing international law? Yes, of course, but that's fine; we *want* to let the world know that the rules have changed. We need to send a message to everybody that we are in charge now, and further defiance will not be tolerated.

The war mustn't be too difficult, however, because the American public is not up for a bloodbath. The United States, unlike the Roman Empire, is a democracy, and American voters are famous for disliking foreign wars that aren't about the country's survival but still send their kids home in body bags. (They don't like high taxes either, which also tend to be a consequence of foreign wars sooner or later.) So which of the countries that regularly defy the United States could fill the role of horrible example without being too hard to take down?

Several countries qualified as candidates for the treatment on the grounds that they were generally defiant but not currently aggressive. Knocking off North Korea, for example, would make a profound impression on all the other countries in the world, and since the Pyongyang regime was a well-established bogeyman in the U.S. media, invading it wouldn't be too hard a sale to make at home. The problem here was that the North Korean regime might have nuclear weapons. They couldn't reach the United States, of course, but unless American forces could get every one of them in a surprise first strike, Pyongyang's "revenge from the grave" (as the nuclear strategists put it) might destroy Seoul or even Tokyo. It would also be a very big war on the ground, and China's reaction to an American act of aggression on this scale right on its own borders was impossible to calculate. All things considered, North Korea was not the ideal candidate.

How about Iran, then? Iranians officially hated the "Great Satan" and Americans unofficially hated them, and Iran certainly qualified on the defiance scale. Tehran had done nothing particularly aggressive towards the United States in recent years, so it fitted the parameters in terms of non-provocation too. But there were two large drawbacks to attacking Iran. One was that it is full of mountains – sort of Afghanistan West, except richer, more urbanized, and much more sophisticated. The other was that it is full of Iranians, and there was absolutely no doubt that most of the 70 million Iranians would fight back if America invaded. Maybe Iran wasn't such a good idea either.

Well, then, how about Iraq? It's dead flat, for a start (apart from the northern Kurdish bit, which the United States already controlled). It's good tank country – and there's a lot of oil under that sand, which is a nice bonus. There are only 25 million Iraqis, and their ruler, Saddam Hussein, is a loathsome thug whom nobody loves, so they probably won't fight very hard to save him. Israel sees Iraq under Saddam Hussein as one of its most dangerous enemies, so attacking it will have a special appeal for the Likudniks among the neo-conservatives. And Iraq doesn't have nuclear weapons.

Iraq practically nominated itself. From the earliest moments when the neo-conservatives began to consider how to refound *Pax Americana* as a go-it-alone American project for the New Century, Iraq was at the top of their hit list – not because it was dangerous, but because it wasn't. Invading Iraq wasn't about terrorism, and it wasn't about WMD either; it was about sending the right message to the rest of the world without spending too much in American lives and money to get the message out. All the key foreign policy and defence players in the Bush administration (except Colin Powell) seem to have agreed on that from the first meeting of the National Security Committee in January 2001. The trick was to get the American public to go along with it, because nobody had so much as mentioned attacking Iraq in the election campaign recently past. Of course they hadn't. They would have lost the election.

The problem that faced the neo-conservatives after the election was that they had to send different messages to two different audiences. They had to come up with some argument that would persuade the American public that it was necessary to invade Iraq to protect the United States, while at the same time making it clear to other governments that Washington was unilaterally changing the rules by which the world worked. Other governments would get the message loud and clear if the United States invaded Iraq without any provocation, but that same lack of provocation would make it much harder to sell the war politically at home – especially if Saddam Hussein just sat there and didn't attack any foreign countries, which had been his pattern for the past ten years. The sheer intractability of this problem may explain why the question of attacking Iraq came up at most of the National Security Committee meetings between January and September 2001, and yet little was actually done about it beyond an updating of military plans. Time passed, treaties got torn up, and work on eliminating the budget surplus went ahead urgently, but the administration made little visible effort to prepare the American public for an invasion of Iraq.

Maybe it was just the press of other business: after eight years' exile from the White House, Republicans had a lot of friends to reward and enemies to punish, which took time. But there is also the possibility that even the devout neo-conservatives in the administration were daunted by the task of manufacturing a completely fake case for invading Iraq in the relatively calm and unthreatening atmosphere that prevailed in the months before 9/11. On the other hand, they sincerely believed that their project was for the long-term benefit of the

United States, so they kept the question of Iraq on the table while they tried to figure out a way to sell an invasion to the American people.

"The United States is the best and fairest and most decent nation on the face of the earth."

– George H.W. Bush, 1988

"We know how good we are."

– George W. Bush, 2002

"If we ever pass out as a great nation we ought to put on our tombstone 'America died from a delusion that she had moral leadership.'"

– Will Rogers, 1949

It is a peculiarity of American politics that foreign wars must be sold not in terms of strategic necessity but on moral grounds. This emphasis on moral principle is one of the most attractive aspects of American public life when it does not descend into mere sectarian dogmatism, but it does make it easier to sell wars to Americans.

Ivo H. Daalder and James M. Lindsay, in their book *America Unbound: The Bush Revolution in Foreign Policy*, make a careful distinction between ideologically oriented neo-conservatives and what they call "assertive nationalists," traditional hard-line conservatives who, in their view, include Bush, Cheney, and Rumsfeld. But it is a distinction without a difference, for nationalism, in its American version, is based on a value system that most Americans believe to be of universal relevance. They are right too, but it is very easy for Americans to confuse the nationalist and the universalist parts of it.

Most Americans do not even believe that they are nationalists; they see themselves instead as "patriots." In American eyes, nationalism is a narrow, backward-looking ethnic obsession, mired in old history and old grudges, that immigrants were expected to leave behind when they came to the United States. The American identity is founded not on common ethnicity but on shared democratic ideals. "There is no American race, but there is an American creed," as President Bush said in his Fourth of July speech in 2002. This ideological definition of American identity actually predates the beginning of mass immigration from non-British sources, going all the way back to the Revolutionary War, but it has subsequently been linked in American political rhetoric with the "melting pot" phenomenon of many ethnicities sharing the same society.

It is a very attractive ideology, and far less exclusively American these days than most Americans realize. The richer European countries, Canada, Australia, and New Zealand, thanks to decades of open immigration policies, now have populations whose ethnic variety approaches or even exceeds that of the United States, and their successes and failures in dealing with the resulting challenges are not very different from America's. But in Canada or France or Sweden, national identity in the early twenty-first century is an amalgam of local history and universal human values. Nobody thinks that they hold the copyright on those values, or that their particular mixture of universal values, local history, and local geography is a model for all humankind.

American national identity does aspire to universality, for understandable historical reasons: more than two centuries ago, the American colonies were the first society of more than one million people in human history to create a democratic and egalitarian society. But they didn't come up with the idea themselves: the revolutionary generation of the American "founding fathers," remarkable though they were, drew on a century of intellectual ferment in Europe, and a more radical and arguably more influential revolution broke out in Europe's most powerful country, France, only six years after the United States won its independence. But most Americans genuinely believe that their own revolution was the turning point of world history, and that the United States is, in former secretary of state Madeleine Albright's phrase, the "indispensable nation." This has led to certain unfortunate consequences.

The first is that it disguises the depth and intensity of American nationalism from Americans themselves, because they have been taught that nationalism is a retrograde ethnic phenomenon and that their shared ideals of "freedom" and "equal opportunity" somehow fulfill a different function. In fact, they serve exactly the same function of uniting huge numbers of disparate people in a single imaginary community, and many other countries use them in exactly the same way. American nationalism is unusually intense for a developed country, just as you would expect for a relatively conservative society that escaped serious damage in the nationalist wars of the past century, but it is different from French nationalism or Brazilian nationalism mostly in its intensity, not in its essential character.

When the World Values Survey asked the citizens of fourteen countries if they were "very proud" of their nationality in 1999–2000, no European countries except ultra-nationalist Ireland and Poland reached the 50 per cent mark. Americans ended up at 72 per cent, between the Indians and the Vietnamese. So much for the allegedly greater power of ethnic nationalism – and American nationalism has actually intensified recently. University of Chicago researchers reported that before 9/11, 90 per cent of the Americans surveyed agreed with the statement "I would rather be a citizen of America than of any other country in the world;" afterwards, 97 per cent agreed.

Yet most Americans honestly do not recognize that they are nationalists like everybody else, living in a country with a highly nationalistic foreign policy. When attacked, as they were on 9/11, they interpret it as an assault not on their foreign policy but on their ideals. "They hate our freedoms," says President Bush, as if Osama bin Laden gave a damn one way or the other about the political principles by which Americans run their own affairs. The particular character of American nationalism makes it easier for an administration to mislead people about "why they hate us."

It also makes it easier to lead Americans into crusades abroad on false pretenses, at least in the short run. In the United States, the explanation that a foreign adventure will bring the lucky recipient "American values" carries considerable weight, since most Americans believe that their values are superior to those of other peoples. Indeed, they generally believe that other peoples have little chance of achieving democracy without the example and perhaps even the direct help of the United States, which is therefore the chief moral actor in the current era of world history. This belief can occasionally be a constraint on the U.S. government's freedom of action, since it demands that every American use of force abroad have a moral justification, but speech writers usually bridge that gap without too much difficulty. On balance, it may even be easier for the U.S. government to use force, since there is a popular assumption that America *only* uses force for moral reasons.

"The U.S. cannot spread its liberalism without military power as well. . . . We're talking about the U.S. serving as an organizing principle for the gradual expansion of civil society around the world, and making moral statements simply is not enough to spur that expansion. You also need military power, and you have to periodically show that you are willing to use it."

– Robert D. Kaplan, *Atlantic Monthly*, June 2003

The United States was the first mass society ever to carry out a democratic revolution, which is an imperishable achievement: to a large extent, Americans invented the methods by which a society of equals can become self-governing. But that was more than two hundred years ago, and in the wider world the examples of the French Revolution (which raised issues of racial, class, and gender equality largely ignored by the American Revolution) and of the slowly evolving British model of parliamentary democracy have been just as influential in shaping the many dozens of democratic societies that exist today. In the past twenty years, non-Western societies of many different cultural backgrounds have demonstrated both their desire for democracy and their ability to seize it from corrupt and oppressive rulers by non-violent means, as have European countries living under totalitarian regimes. None of this is acknowledged in the largely self-referential American debate, however, and so it sounds perfectly plausible (within the United States) to argue that America must go to war "to make the world safe for democracy." It allowed President Woodrow Wilson to sell a plain, old-fashioned imperial war to Americans as a crusade for freedom in 1917, and it let President George W. Bush do exactly the same thing in 2003.

This brings us to the next question: Was George W. Bush himself a paid-up neo-conservative, or merely (in the old Leninist jargon) a "useful idiot"? The stock answer is that you have to be interested in ideas before you can be captured by an ideology, so he can't really be a neo-conservative ideologue himself, but that is obviously too simple. He does not seem to be a person who is intellectually engaged, but he is a sufficiently adroit politician to realize that if you do not have an explicit ideological framework yourself, you would be wise to surround yourself with people who do. Before he decided to run for the presidency in 1999, there is no evidence that Bush had any interest in or knowledge of foreign affairs beyond the disdain for alliances and international institutions and the preference for unilateralism that was ingrained in the old, mostly Southern-based Robert Taft wing of the Republican Party, but when he did he surrounded himself with a group of advisers, the so-called Vulcans, whose views were congenial to his own. "Nobody needs to tell me what to believe," as he put it, "but I *do* need somebody to tell me where Kosovo is."

The key members of the Vulcans were Condoleezza Rice and Paul Wolfowitz; others included Robert Blackwill (Rice's deputy responsible for Iraq, Iran, Afghanistan, Pakistan, and India), Richard Perle, and Richard Armitage (deputy secretary of state). It appears to have been Rice who shaped the distinctly neo-conservative flavour of this team of advisers – the name is taken from the statue of Vulcan, Roman god of fire, that overlooks her steel-making hometown of Birmingham, Alabama – and the Vulcans, in turn, steered Bush towards his surprise choice of Dick Cheney, neo-conservative *par excellence*, as his vice-presidential running mate. But this does not necessarily lead to a conclusion that he was the victim of an ideological kidnapping.

It is striking that none of the Vulcans had figured prominently among President George H.W. Bush's advisers. From the start, the younger Bush was determined to follow a different course, and while it is pointless to psychologize about how the relationship between the two men may have influenced this outcome, it seems clear that the older man, while maintaining a dignified silence, was not sympathetic to the worldview of the people who surrounded his son. George W. Bush may be a "gut player," as he said, rather than an intellectual neo-conservative, but he was definitely a fully committed member of the team.

Another question that is often raised is about the unusually high proportion of Zionists with close links to the Likud Party in Israel among the ranks of the neo-conservatives. Granted that there was a general consensus in the Bush administration on the desirability of resurrecting *Pax Americana*, how much was the obsessive focus on Iraq driven by the priorities of these Likudniks?

Just mentioning that a significant number of the leading neo-conservatives are Jewish Americans who have close connections with the Israeli government will bring accusations of anti-Semitism, but that is an inevitable cost of commenting on Israeli-American relations and must simply be borne. The Israeli tail succeeds in wagging the U.S. foreign-policy dog quite often – indeed, the last American president to defy Israel openly was George Bush Sr., who forced the Israeli government to attend the Madrid conference on a Middle Eastern peace in fulfillment of his promises to America's Arab allies in the 1990–91 Gulf War, and he is convinced that he paid a high electoral price for it – but that is a normal part of politics. Israel enjoys strong sentimental support among American voters, and all Israeli governments work hard to perpetuate the popular American belief that Israel is a vital U.S. strategic asset in the Middle East. The real question is whether this powerful Israeli influence has been shaping American foreign policy in ways that serve Israeli interests to the detriment of American interests.

The leading Jewish members of the neo-conservative group, like Wolfowitz, Perle, Feith, and Abrams, were not just Zionists, a nationalist movement that commands the loyalty of most but certainly not all Jews. They were Likudniks, closely tied to the ultra-nationalist right-wing party that first came to power in Israel under Menachem Begin in 1977 and regained power under Ariel Sharon in 2001, and it may be presumed that they largely shared Sharon's vision of an Israel permanently in possession of much of the occupied West Bank and permanently superior militarily (in alliance with the United States) to all of its Arab neighbours. Destroying the Baathist regime in Iraq was certainly part of that vision, but it seems to have had an equal appeal to the larger number of non-Jewish ultra-nationalists who make up the small core group of neo-conservatives. None of them saw any contradiction between the Likud's vision for Israel within the Middle East region and their own larger vision for America's strategic future.

Did George W. Bush's own evangelical faith shape his strategic vision, especially in the Middle East? He undoubtedly has a sense of divine mission. Stephen Mansfield recounts in his book *The Faith of George W. Bush* that the then-presidential hopeful told a Texas evangelist at the end of the 1990s: "I feel like God wants me to run for President. I can't explain it, but I sense my country is going to need me. Something is going to happen – I know it won't be easy on me or my family, but God wants me to do it." However, there is no evidence that the general atmosphere of religious fervour that characterized the Bush White House from the start directly translated into U.S. strategy in the Middle East. The fundamentalist Christian religious influence on U.S. foreign policy came much more from the Republican grassroots.

Although American voters are not generally swayed by foreign issues, the future of Israel and of the Middle East is of great interest to one large voting bloc: those among the born-again Christians who subscribe to the belief that we are living in the End Times, and who insist that the United States support the most extreme expansionists in Israel because they actively look forward to a great war in the Middle East. They hope not to have to experience that war themselves, since they expect to be swept up to heaven in the Rapture, but the forces of the anti-Christ – the leading suspects for this role are the United Nations, the Muslim world, the "axis of evil," or the European Union – will ravage the world during the seven years of the Tribulation until they are defeated in a great final battle with the forces of goodness in the valley of Armageddon, in northern Israel. At this point, just before the Messiah returns to walk the earth for a thousand years, all the world's Jews will either convert to Christianity or be destroyed, but at earlier points in the script the Israelis are needed to fulfill the prophecies: they must conquer the rest of the "Biblical lands" (most of the Middle East) and built the Third Temple on the site in Jerusalem now occupied by the al-Aqsa Mosque. And the United States must help them to accomplish these goals.

An estimated 15 to 18 per cent of American voters belong to churches or movements that follow these teachings, and since it would be virtually unthinkable for them to vote Democratic, they may make up as much as a third of the country's potential Republican voters. When President Bush had the temerity to ask Prime Minister Sharon to withdraw his tanks from the West Bank city of Jenin in 2002, he reportedly received a hundred thousand angry e-mails from Americans who believe these prophecies, and he never mentioned the matter again.

In the view of the End-Timers, it is their Christian duty to help realize the prophecies that will bring on the Rapture, the Tribulation, and the thousand-year reign of Christ on the earth by supporting the expansion of Israel and the expulsion of the Palestinians from the land God gave to the Jews – and they must not slow history down by working for peace. As televangelist Jim Robison said when delivering the opening prayer at a Republican National Convention: "There will be no peace until Jesus comes. Any preaching of peace prior to this return is heresy. It is against the word of God. It is anti-Christ." Moreover, the believers do specifically see the U.S. invasion of Iraq as part of the necessary preliminaries to the unleashing of the final war, since Revelations 9: 14–15 speaks of four angels "which are bound in the great river Euphrates" who will be set free "to slay the third part of men." Somewhere near Fallujah, no doubt.

The fervent desire of this key group of Republican voters for a greatly expanded Israel was not easy to reconcile with the Bush administration's formal position of support for a "two-state solution" in Israel/Palestine, but it was only verbal support and no more to be taken seriously than Ariel Sharon's lip service to the same ideal. The End-Timers had little to complain about in the actual actions of the Bush administration in the Middle East in 2001-04. Only one senior cabinet officer in the Bush administration, Attorney General John Ashcroft, was closely associated with the End-Timers; their influence on policy came more from their huge importance to the Republican Party at election time. But when you combine that outside influence with the less extreme but still devout fundamentalist Protestant majority and the Likudnik Zionist minority in the administration itself, the forces that drove the Bush administration's policies in the Middle East become more comprehensible. It was not so much a plot as a worldview determined almost entirely by religious and ideological beliefs and electoral calculations, with little reference even to American strategic interests. Did the Israel government exploit this situation? Of course it did, but how could it resist?

The attacks on the World Trade Center and the Pentagon on September 11, 2001, created a psychological atmosphere in which America was allegedly at war and the constitutional rules were unofficially suspended. The neo-conservatives' hesitancy about cooking the intelligence on Iraq vanished, and at the same time selling an attack on Iraq got a lot easier, for after 9/11 almost anything they wanted to do on their real agenda could be marketed as part of the "war on terror." The terrorist attacks were a godsend for the neo-conservatives – but first they had to deal with the awkward fact that the attacks had actually been planned in Afghanistan.

It grows clearer each month, as bits of evidence trickle out, that the invasion of Iraq moved from its previous position high on the neo-conservative wish list into the realm of seriously planned operations as soon as the 9/11 attacks made it a politically saleable proposition, and various preparations were set in motion. "We won't do Iraq now," Bush told Condoleezza Rice on September 16, 2001 (as reported in Bob Woodward's book *Bush at War*). "We're putting Iraq off. But eventually we'll have to return to that question." Former CIA director James Woolsey was sent off on a private mission to find any shred of intelligence linking Saddam Hussein to al-Qaeda (he came up blank), a steady drip-feed of administration leaks about Saddam's dangerous weapons of mass destruction began to flow to the media, and on November 21 Bush called in Donald Rumsfeld and told him, "Let's get started on this," ordering him to begin secretly updating the military's plans for an attack on Iraq. But politically it was an absolute priority to deal with Afghanistan first.

The U.S. invasion of Afghanistan was in no way related to the neo-conservative strategy, and could not be made to serve it. What the neo-conservatives wanted to do was to make a deliberate and unprovoked attack on an uncooperative regime and send a message to the world that the United States was now running things; invading Afghanistan would be simply a U.S. response to a flagrant aggression that sent no message other than "Don't attack the United States." But Afghanistan could not be ignored. It was where the al-Qaeda training camps were, where the 9/11 attacks had been planned, where Osama bin Laden himself was. American public opinion quite reasonably wanted that threat dealt with as soon as possible, and the Bush administration had to comply. If Al Gore had been president in Bush's place, *he* would have had to order the invasion of Afghanistan after 9/11.

One of the hallmarks of a good strategy is that it actually compels your opponent to do your will, and in that sense al-Qaeda's strategy for 9/11 was sound: the Bush administration was compelled to invade Afghanistan. The way that it went about it, however, confounded bin Laden's likely expectation, based on his experience of the long guerilla war against the Soviet army in Afghanistan in the 1980s, that he and his Taliban allies could entangle the invading American troops in another long and costly war. On the contrary, the planning and conduct of the U.S. invasion of Afghanistan was a model of how to do a difficult military operation with maximum speed and minimum casualties.

Getting into Afghanistan has never been that hard: a roll-call of invaders from Alexander the Great to nineteenth-century Britons and twentieth-century Soviets have managed it without too much trouble. The difficulty is in staying there: managing the fractious and xenophobic tribes, controlling the hills that overlook the roads, and dealing with the harsh climate, the scarcity of resources, and the sheer inaccessibility of most of the country. Foreseeing that the American strategists planning the invasion would try to enlist the support of the ethnic militias of northern Afghanistan, which had lost the 1991–96 civil war and now clung to some strips of territory up on the former Soviet border, Osama bin Laden arranged for the suicide-bombing assassination of the Northern Alliance's charismatic leader, Ahmed Shah Masood, in his Panjshir valley headquarters only two days before al-Qaeda's teams of suicide-hijackers hit New York and Washington.

The U.S. planners did aim for an alliance with the northern militias just as bin Laden foresaw, but their strategy was much bolder and less conventional than he expected. They decided to skip a ground invasion altogether. Instead, they combined the Northern Alliance's numerous but poorly trained troops, CIA and Special Forces teams on the ground, and the U.S. Air Force's precision-guided weapons and unmanned aerial reconnaissance vehicles in a strategy designed to break the Taliban's power quickly and without significant American casualties. It was just the sort of situation where Donald Rumsfeld's cherished "revolution in military affairs" doctrine could be deployed to maximum advantage, and he imposed it unhesitatingly on a doubtful army high command.

Sympathetic offers of military aid flooded in from America's friends and allies, including all the countries that would shun the illegal invasion of Iraq sixteen months later – Canada, France, Germany, Russia – although only a favoured few countries were invited to contribute forces to the combat phase of the operation. The Taliban rulers were formally asked by the U.S. State Department to hand over bin Laden and the other al-Qaeda leaders and to dismantle the terrorist training camps on Afghan soil, although it warned them that there would be no second chance if they became evasive and tried to haggle (as they predictably did). The UN Security Council did not explicitly authorize the invasion of Afghanistan, but its resolutions of September 12 and 28 implicitly gave permission for the U.S. attack, although the situation did not precisely fit the UN Charter rule that grants countries the right of self-defence, and so great was sympathy for the United States that no member of the Security Council sought to oppose the American invasion.

Pakistan and Russia were very helpful in providing supply bases and overflight rights, and in persuading the various Central Asian “Stans” north of Afghanistan to do the same. CIA teams with suitcases full of money and communications equipment made the deals with the various Tajik, Turkmen, Hazara, and Uzbek militias that held the northern fifth of Afghanistan and began to buy up various Taliban commanders. They were soon joined by Special Forces teams with target-designator equipment to guide American bombs very precisely onto the Taliban forces facing the Northern Alliance. By the time the first U.S. and British weapons fell on Afghanistan on October 7, legal and diplomatic niceties had been observed and the vast majority of the world’s nations had offered their support or at least their good wishes for the U.S. military operation.

A month later massive U.S. bombing cracked the Taliban lines open. When Kabul fell on November 13, there were still fewer than five hundred Americans on the ground in Afghanistan. With the capture of Mullah Omar's headquarters in the southwestern city of Kandahar on December 7, the war was effectively over: only two months from beginning to end. By then most of al-Qaeda's camps had already been bombed to rubble, most of the "Arab Afghan" fighters still in Afghanistan had been killed or captured, and bin Laden was on the run. Afghan civilian casualties had been lower than even the most optimistic estimates, because for the most part the bombing had not involved urban areas. It was a nearly flawless military operation.

What should have happened next was a flood of foreign soldiers and civilians pouring into Afghanistan, most of them under the UN flag, accompanied by ample supplies and money. Their jobs would have been to scour the countryside for fugitive Taliban and al-Qaeda leaders, bring the victorious northern warlords under control, build a democratic central government and a national army, feed and clothe the desperate rural population, bring the millions of refugees back, and rebuild the country's shattered infrastructure. In other words, eliminate al-Qaeda, de-Talibanize the country, and put it on the road to a more hopeful future. As for the U.S. military, any troops that were not needed in Afghanistan should have been sent home, because there were no more actual battles to fight in the "war on terror." Afghanistan was the only place where the Islamist terrorists had had real bases and the protection of a sovereign government. Elsewhere, they were just civilians living among other civilians, and an army was an entirely inappropriate instrument for chasing them down.

But none of this happened. Throughout 2002–03, almost all of the United Nations troops were confined to Kabul and its immediate neighbourhood, while the U.S. military retained control over the rest of the country in order to hunt the remnants of al-Qaeda and the Taliban down. Because the United States was reluctant to commit a large number of ground troops to Afghanistan, however, the physical control of rural areas was entrusted for the most part to the local warlords. The result was that, while a certain degree of security and normality was restored in the capital, the interim government under Mohammed Karzai that was installed under American auspices in December 2001 never succeeded in establishing its authority over the provinces, where the warlords and their militias retained control. Even Osama bin Laden's apparent escape during the battle of the Tora Bora mountains east of Jalalabad in late December 2001 was at least partly due to the fact that the U.S. command did not commit American troops to the fight, leaving it to Afghan militias and Pakistani border troops, some of whom were allegedly bribed to allow bin Laden to escape across the border.

It was only in late 2003 that the United States began to "encourage" (i.e., allow) the UN troops to move out into the provinces, but by then the window of opportunity had all but closed: the local militias were firmly in control in the plains and valleys, the Taliban were making a comeback in the hills, the opium industry (largely suppressed by the Taliban) was once again the world's biggest, providing much of the rural income, and the so-called national government was a despised shadow with little authority beyond Kabul city limits. Chronic insecurity had led to foreign and even local development agencies withdrawing from many rural areas (where girls were still largely excluded from schools), and the national elections originally scheduled for the summer of 2004 were postponed. How did it all go so wrong so fast?

Part of the reason was a U.S. reluctance to commit American troops to combat in Afghanistan. The U.S. army was well aware of the country's reputation as a place where military occupations always failed in the end, most recently in the case of the Soviet occupation, so senior army officers wanted to keep American troops out of combat: that way they wouldn't alienate the locals so much, and they'd keep their own casualties down. At the same time, however, they very much wanted to hunt down the remnants of the Taliban and al-Qaeda, and they didn't trust the troops of other countries, operating under the UN flag, to do that job properly. That left only the local militias – which meant that the warlords had to be left in charge of their local areas, which in turn meant no effective central government, no rural security, not much of anything to show for the American occupation. Add in the neo-conservative mantra about how the United States "doesn't do nation-building," and you have most of the answer. But there was one more thing: a lot of the American troops who might have gone to Afghanistan to help stabilize the place were being held back in readiness for the next war, and most of the political attention in Washington had already moved there.

"The mission begins in Baghdad, but it does not end there. We stand at the cusp of a new historical era. It is so clearly about more than Iraq. It is about more even than the future of the Middle East. It is about what sort of role the United States intends to play in the twenty-first century."

– William Kristol and Lawrence Kaplan, *War over Iraq: Saddam's Tyranny and America's Mission* (2003)

"We're going to be on the ground in Iraq, as soldiers and citizens, for years. We're going to be running a colony almost."

– Paul Bremer, to a business audience, early March 2004

Once Afghanistan was out of the way, the administration acted fast to move its real agenda into the public domain, carefully painted to resemble the "war on terror." In late December, chief White House speech writer Michael Gerson asked David Frum, a member of his team, to sum up in a sentence or two the best case for going after Iraq. It was a tough assignment, because there was no real link between Saddam Hussein and the Islamist terrorists who had attacked America and obviously he couldn't mention *Pax Americana*, but after working at the problem for a few days Frum came up with the phrase "axis of hatred." It was meant to evoke shadowy ties between all those people who allegedly hated America, and specifically between Iraq and al-Qaeda.

It was nonsense, of course. Even if Saddam Hussein did hate the United States, he could not possibly co-operate with Osama bin Laden. Saddam was a secular dictator, leader of the pan-Arab nationalist and socialist Baath Party, and an accomplished killer and torturer of Islamist radicals, whom he rightly saw as a threat to his regime. Bin Laden was an Islamist zealot who preached the overthrow of secular rulers, the suppression of Arab nationalism and other national identities among Muslims in favour of a single borderless Muslim loyalty, and quite specifically the destruction of the Baath Party and of Saddam Hussein. But not two Americans in a hundred understood enough about Arab and Muslim politics to realize that the two men could not conceivably work together, so Frum's phrase would sound good enough to sway the public. Gerson bought Frum's suggestion, pausing only to change it to "axis of evil" on the grounds that Americans prefer a more theological turn of phrase, and passed it up the line to the policymakers who were working on President Bush's State of the Union message. Condoleezza Rice added Iran and North Korea, and by the time the speech went out on January 29, 2002, the "axis of evil" included the entire front rank of the neo-conservative hit list.

They were packaged in a different way, however. Now it was the allegation that these three countries were working on or already possessed weapons of mass destruction that put them in the front rank – that, and the suggestion that they were ruled by madmen consumed by hatred of America who would readily give those weapons to terrorists to use against the United States. In the real world, none of these states had been involved with any terrorists targeting the United States for at least the previous ten years, and the idea that any of them would hand over their precious nuclear weapons (if they had any) to Osama bin Laden's Islamist fanatics was simply ridiculous. But this speech was directed at Bush's badly frightened domestic audience, still reeling from 9/11 and many subsequent terrorist scares, and it worked just fine with them.

Few of them, for example, would have realized how odd it was that, while North Korea claimed to have a few working nuclear weapons and Iran was accused of having a nuclear weapons program, it was Iraq, whose program had been comprehensively dismantled by UN arms inspectors after the 1990–91 Gulf War, that was Bush's main target. Iraq got five sentences in the speech, versus one each for Iran and North Korea. "States like these, and their terrorist allies, constitute an axis of evil arming to threaten the peace of the world," Bush told his 52 million viewers. "By seeking weapons of mass destruction, these regimes pose a grave and growing danger. They could provide these weapons to terrorists, giving them the means to match their hatred. . . . Time is not on our side. I will not wait on events, while dangers gather. I will not stand by, as peril draws closer and closer. The United States of America will not permit the world's most dangerous regimes to threaten us with the world's most dangerous weapons. . . . History has called America and our allies to action, and it is both our responsibility and our privilege to fight freedom's fight."

It was a paranoid masterpiece, with hardly a single verifiable fact in it, but what was new was the stark unilateralism and rejection of international law implicit in the promise that the United States would attack these countries as and when it chose. With this speech, the public focus of the Bush administration abruptly shifted from terrorists to recalcitrant countries that defied the United States, and the idea that the United States must act alone and above the law was suddenly presented as a necessary response to the "threat" from these states and their alleged terrorist friends. By the most amazing coincidence, the long-term U.S. response to 9/11, now that Afghanistan had been taken care of, turned out to require precisely the policies that the neo-conservatives had been advocating for years as the necessary preconditions for putting *Pax Americana* on a sustainable basis.

To put the question plainly: Did the neo-conservatives in the administration deliberately and consciously hijack the national panic over the 9/11 terrorist attacks in order to impose their own quite different agenda on U.S. foreign policy, starting with the invasion of Iraq? And while we're at it, we should also deal with the mother of all conspiracy theories, which holds that 9/11 was so useful to the neo-conservatives who dominated the Bush administration that they must have either (a) planned it or (b) deliberately ignored prior intelligence about it.

Version (a) is popular mainly among Arabs and other Muslims who want to deny any Arab or Muslim role in the events at all, and blame it instead on a conspiracy between the CIA and the Israelis. It is frequently buttressed by the outright lie, now treated by most people in the Arab world as established fact, that Jews working in the Twin Towers were warned not to go to work on the morning of September 11. (Jews were, of course, fully and proportionally represented among the victims of 9/11.) This conspiracy theory is unworthy of further consideration – but the other version has to be treated more seriously.

The idea that at least some people in the Bush administration had intelligence forewarning of the al-Qaeda attack, but chose not to act on it, is a myth that will eventually take its place alongside the conspiracy theories about the Kennedy assassination in the collective American subconscious. But conspiracies do happen from time to time, and they may even have happened in Washington from time to time, so what are the grounds for dismissing this conspiracy theory out of hand? After all, it is now generally accepted that at least some bits of information pointing to the 9/11 hijackers were floating around in the U.S. intelligence world. How come somebody didn't put them together and stop the attack?

This whole theory rests on a profound misunderstanding of the way intelligence gathering works. The conspiracy theorists imagine a single vital piece of intelligence that reveals the plot, rather than the reality of a stream of raw data flowing across analysts' desks, some of it reliable, some questionable, and some of it plausible but wrong, in which the analysts try to see patterns and connections that may reveal what is actually going on. Sometimes they spot genuine patterns and get it right, but they also get a lot of false positives, and they often miss patterns that really exist. It's like playing Connect the Dots with all but a few of the data points missing, and quite a few false ones scattered around for good measure. Stuff gets missed that a luckier guess might have discerned – and after the disaster happens, you can always go back into the old data stream, pick out the data points that should have been joined up, and hang the analysts for negligence. In other words, the fact that some relevant bits of good intelligence were floating around in the system did *not* mean that good analysts were bound to come to the right conclusion.

But let us suppose that some low-level analyst did realize what was coming and urgently passed the intelligence up the chain to the head of the CIA or the FBI. How many people would know by then that this vital information had been received? At least half a dozen, for the raw intelligence data passes through several levels before it reaches the director's desk. How could they all be silenced – and how many more people at the decision-making level would have to be brought into the picture before a decision could be made just to sit on the intelligence and do nothing? Half a dozen more, at the very least. What chance is there that a conspiracy involving so many people from many different backgrounds would remain secret for long? Approximately zero. What would be the penalty for deliberately ignoring such a warning in order to further a partisan agenda? The crimes involved are high treason and accessory to mass murder, and the penalty is death. What is the likelihood that any senior official, knowing all this, would propose a conspiracy to suppress the intelligence and just let 9/11 happen? Absolutely zero.

Once 9/11 actually happened, how many neo-conservatives high in the Bush administration deliberately used the panic as a way of advancing their own project? That is a quite different question, for an ability to seize upon passing events and use them to support your own agenda is a highly valued skill among Washington's bureaucratic warriors. The strategy of bait-and-switch is the same whether you're selling cars or political policies, and nobody in the neo-conservative circle would have seen it as illegitimate. The more sensitive souls among them probably preferred to avoid too close an examination of the way the sale was being made, but that's how politics works all around the world. If your motives are good and your policy is sound, in the view of most practitioners, then a little bit of legerdemain with the actual arguments is no crime.

The key thing about Bush's State of the Union speech, reiterated and amplified by public statements made by senior neo-conservative members of the administration over the following weeks and months, was the "new doctrine called pre-emption," as the president later referred to it. But it wasn't really about pre-emptive war, where a country facing an imminent and obvious intention to attack on the part of an enemy may, under strictly defined circumstances, act first to blunt that attack. Pre-emptive war is what Israel did to the Arab states in 1967, and it is sometimes legal under traditional international law.

"America will act against . . . emerging threats before they are fully formed," Bush wrote in the introduction to the annual *National Security Strategy* document. "We will not hesitate to act alone, if necessary. . . . The greater the threat, the greater is the risk of inaction – and the more compelling the case for taking anticipatory action to defend ourselves, even if uncertainty remains as to the time and place of the enemy's attack." That is not pre-emptive war; it is *preventive* war, where you attack a country because you think it might attack you or become more dangerous to you at some future time. It is never legal, but it is the doctrine that the neo-conservatives wanted and needed.

The administration's cheerleaders in the U.S. media were ecstatic about the State of the Union message. Charles Krauthammer of the *Washington Post* rhapsodized that "Iraq is what this speech was about. . . . The speech was just short of a declaration of war." America's friends and allies abroad understood that too, but were shocked and confused by the sudden swerve of U.S. policy away from the war on terrorism and towards an illegal and seemingly irrational war of aggression against Iraq. British foreign secretary Jack Straw tried to pass it off as a momentary aberration driven by domestic political considerations and "best understood by the fact that there are mid-term congressional elections coming up in November." Canada's foreign minister, Bill Graham, simply sounded puzzled: "Nobody is supporting Saddam Hussein, but everyone recognizes in international politics you have to have a process where, before you invade a sovereign state, there has to be a reason for it, or we are going to have international chaos." They doubtless knew who the neo-conservatives were, but they still hadn't grasped the fact that they ran the place.

They did run the place, and a few months after Bush's January speech Randy Beers, a former Foreign Service officer who had served in the White House in various intelligence, counter-terrorism, and foreign military policy roles under four presidents (three of them Republicans), stopped by Dick

Clarke's house in Washington for some advice. Beers had ended up in more or less the same National Security Council job that Clarke had left in frustration only a month after 9/11, co-ordinating counter-terrorism activities – but as Clarke tells it in *Against All Enemies*, Beers was now thinking of quitting too. Clarke opened some wine, and Beers spilled his guts.

"They still don't get it. Insteada goin' all out against al Qaeda and eliminating our vulnerabilities at home, they wanna fuckin' invade Iraq again," he told his old friend. The United States still hadn't caught bin Laden or Mullah Omar, the Taliban leader, and the Taliban were regrouping in the hills, but Washington was restricting its military commitment in Afghanistan to a token force and holding back the bulk of available U.S. forces for the invasion of Iraq. "Do you know how much it will strengthen al Qaeda and groups like that if we occupy Iraq?" Beers raged. "There's no threat to us now from Iraq, but 70 percent of the American people think Iraq attacked the Pentagon and the World Trade Center. You wanna know why? Because that's what the administration wants them to think! . . . I can't work for these people. I'm sorry I just can't." So Beers quit too. A year later he volunteered to serve as chief foreign policy adviser for John Kerry's campaign to unseat the Bush presidency.

"Frankly, [sanctions] have worked. [Saddam] has not developed any significant capability with respect to weapons of mass destruction. He is unable to project conventional power against his neighbours."

– U.S. secretary of state Colin Powell, Cairo, February 24, 2001

"When I left the Foreign Office in 2001, we all believed that the strategy of containment was working and was denying Saddam the ability to develop weapons of mass destruction. . . . The development that prompted the switch from containment to invasion was not any new intelligence on Iraq but regime change in Washington. . . . This was a war made in Washington by an administration that chose Iraq not because it really imagined Iraq was a threat, but because it knew the country was weak and could not resist. . . ."

– Robin Cook, former British foreign secretary
(resigned from British cabinet in 2003 over Iraq),
Independent on Sunday, July 18, 2004

The credible new intelligence data about alleged Iraqi WMD came into the hands of the U.S. and British intelligence services between 2001 and the invasion of Iraq in March 2003, so what happened? A huge amount of effort has gone into dissecting the way that intelligence data were misused in the year following Bush's 2002 State of the Union speech, both in the United States and in Britain, in order to produce a convincing case for attacking Iraq. Congressional and parliamentary committees and commissions have sifted the evidence, all agreeing that the flimsy scraps of "intelligence" that were produced to suggest that Saddam Hussein had weapons of mass destruction of some sort and represented a danger to the United States and Britain, and that he was in contact with al-Qaeda and in some way linked to the 9/11 attacks, were false. (Most came from deeply suspect Iraqi exile sources.) But these examinations either left the question of the political responsibility for these falsehoods unanswered until after the next election (in the case of the United States), or concluded that although huge mistakes had been made, no one was to blame (in the case of the United Kingdom). That was hardly surprising, since the inquiries were either appointed (very reluctantly) by the government in power, or dominated by members of that government's party in the legislature. They were useful in terms of keeping the question of the culpability of the two governments on the public agenda, but the details of these inquiries would fill another book – and in any case, they are not necessary to understand what happened.

In the United States, it was a straightforward selling job: come up with reasons that will persuade the American public that it's a good idea to attack Iraq. Given how traumatized most Americans were by the shock of 9/11, and how reluctant they were to question presidential leadership at a time of perceived crisis when patriotism was at fever pitch and solidarity was an obligation, it was not a very difficult task.

"For reasons that have a lot to do with the U.S. government bureaucracy, we settled on the one issue everyone could agree on, which was weapons of mass destruction. . . ."

– Paul Wolfowitz, *Vanity Fair*, June 2003

A certain amount of selective manipulation of intelligence was necessary in order to produce "evidence" for the Congress and for international diplomatic purposes (and a secret cell called the Office of Special Plans was set up within Rumsfeld's

Pentagon under the control of Doug Feith to mine the intelligence data for nuggets that had been rejected by the normal intelligence process as unreliable, but might help to "prove" the existence of Iraq's WMD and its contacts with al-Qaeda). The main sales job on the American public, however, was done with pure rhetoric. Over a period of a year, in almost every public speech made by President Bush, Vice-President Cheney, and other senior members of the administration, the words *Iraq* or *Saddam Hussein* were mentioned in the same breath as *weapons of mass destruction*, *al-Qaeda*, or *9/11* at least a couple of times. Bush and his colleagues, clearly acting on expert legal advice, were careful never to say explicitly that the Iraqi leader was responsible for 9/11, but their rhetorical campaign was so successful that by the time the invasion actually began in March, 2003, about 70 per cent of Americans believed that Saddam had sent the terrorists.

There was still a residual unease, however, about the fact that almost none of America's traditional allies saw things the same way: they had all volunteered for Afghanistan, but this time most of them weren't coming. The idea of *Pax Americana* was that the United States would make the decisions and other countries would obediently fall in behind, trusting American judgment or fearing American power, but they *were* expected to fall in. It was never the intention that the United States should do all the heavy lifting involved in running the world completely alone – and the American public, accustomed for half a century to seeing the same loyal allies alongside the United States in every crisis, was disoriented and even a bit dismayed by their attitude this time. Other governments could see what the neo-conervatives were up to (as they were intended to), and although diplomatic courtesy prevented them from saying that bluntly, some of them, like the Germans, the French, and the Canadians, were being quite vocal about why they thought an attack on Iraq would be illegal and unnecessary, or at least greatly premature. This caused further unease among Americans, so it became very important for Bush to have America's closest traditional ally, Britain, on board for the attack. That complicated matters considerably.

According to Sir Christopher Meyer, former British ambassador to Washington, President Bush first asked Prime Minister Tony Blair for Britain's support in attacking Iraq at a private dinner in Washington just nine days after the 9/11 attacks, and Blair "said nothing to demur," but his formal (though still secret) commitment to invade Iraq alongside the United States probably only came soon after Bush's key State of the Union speech, likely on Blair's visit to the Crawford ranch in early April 2002. As the time for the invasion approached, however, it became clear that Blair was going to have great difficulty in carrying British popular opinion, and perhaps even the House of Commons, with him. That was the principal reason that less emphasis came to be placed on "regime change" (which was all right with the American audience but was seen as an illegal act of aggression in Britain) and more on the imaginary dangers of Saddam's weapons of mass destruction. "Imaginary dangers," in the sense that even those intelligence services that had deluded themselves into believing that Saddam had WMD didn't think that he had anything except chemical weapons – and chemical weapons are not really weapons of mass destruction in any meaningful sense.

The reason that chemical, biological, and nuclear weapons all ended up in the same category of WMD is that they have all been the target of attempts to impose legal controls or bans on their possession or use – and quite rightly too. But they are not weapons of equal destructiveness. A really big nuclear weapon, exploded in the right place under the right conditions, could kill several million people, and even an average nuclear blast would kill a hundred thousand people or more if detonated in a densely populated area. A chemical warhead is a battlefield weapon, exceedingly nasty but limited in its effect: the worst poison gas attack of recent history, the Iraqi air attack on the town of Halabja in 1988, killed a maximum estimated figure of 6,800 people although it involved aircraft dropping a large number of nerve-gas bombs on the town. A more realistic example of the damage that chemical weapons would do in terrorist hands is provided by the one known case of such an attack, when the Aum Shinrikyo terrorist group released sarin (nerve) gas on a crowded Japanese subway train in 1995. Twelve people died, some dozens were seriously affected, and close to a thousand felt briefly ill. A big nail bomb would probably have killed more people (though it would not have had the same dramatic effect).

It is possible to imagine that the intelligence services of the United States and the United Kingdom believed that Saddam Hussein had secretly kept some chemical weapons despite the seven-year presence of the UN arms inspectors in Iraq in 1991–98. It is not easy to believe that they would have thought this an urgent danger and an adequate reason to invade Iraq. Almost *every* country in the Middle East has chemical weapons: Syria and Egypt certainly do (because Israel does); Iran certainly does (because Iraq used them against it in the 1980–88 war); and Pakistan almost certainly does, because of its confrontation with India. There are tens of thousands of tons of chemical weapons in the Russian Federation, some of them reputedly stored in unguarded depots secured with bicycle locks. Even the United States still had more than 15,000 tons of mustard gas and 13,000 tons of various kinds of nerve gas at the time of its last public accounting of them in 1997.

Even if Iraq also had had a few chemical weapons lying around somewhere, they would not have been a particular threat to anyone who didn't invade Iraq, and terrorists were no more likely to acquire chemical weapons from Iraq than anywhere else. The whole furore over WMD was just a pretext for an invasion that had other purposes and, at a level that will never show up in the reports of the various inquiries, virtually everybody involved in the process on both the intelligence and the governmental side knew it. As Greg Thielmann, then director of the Office of Strategic Proliferation and Military Affairs in the U.S. State Department's Bureau of Intelligence and Research, put it: "Everybody in the intelligence community knew that the White House couldn't care less about any information suggesting that there were no WMDs. . . ."

Still, it was a necessary fiction, and in an attempt to provide diplomatic and political cover for the British prime minister, Washington and London sought a UN Security Council resolution in November 2002 demanding that arms inspectors be admitted to Iraq to search for Saddam's alleged WMD. They probably assumed that he would refuse, but he did not (he knew he had nothing to hide, after all), which threatened to throw the Anglo-American timetable for an invasion seriously off schedule. The U.S. troop buildup in the region had already begun in the autumn of 2002, and Washington was anxious to get the war over before the extreme heat of summer arrived: the effective deadline to get it started was mid-March.

By February 2003, the major obstacle to an invasion was the UN arms inspectors in Iraq, who were getting unimpeded access to any sites they wanted, were following up every tip that Western intelligence services deigned to give them – and were finding nothing. This was perplexing to chief UN arms inspector Hans Blix, a hawkish figure who was convinced that Saddam Hussein *was* hiding WMD when he was called out of retirement to lead the Iraq mission. As all the leads confidently provided by U.S. and British intelligence ran into the sand, however, he began to talk privately about "faith-based intelligence gathering" and to suspect that the WMD did not actually exist. As he noted in his memoir, *Disarming Iraq: The Search for Weapons of Mass Destruction*, "It occurred to me [on March 7] that the Iraqis would be in greater difficulty if . . . there truly were no weapons of which they could 'yield possession.'"

Tony Blair had promised parliament that he would seek a second UN resolution specifically authorizing an invasion before he joined an attack on Iraq, but it was very unlikely that the majority of the Security Council members would pass such a resolution unless the inspectors reported that they were being hindered by the Iraqis in their work. Indeed, there was a growing danger that, given enough time, the inspectors would report that there were no forbidden weapons in Iraq, thus removing Blair's entire case for joining Bush's war. So he resorted to scare tactics.

"Fish mongers sell fish, war mongers sell war, and both may sincerely believe in their product. But I think the overselling came . . . in the spring [of 2003], when it looked as though the British people were not actually going to sign up to this project. . . . [T]he continual assessments of an imminent terrorist attack on London, advising housewives to lay in stocks of water and food, I mean all that stuff . . . tanks at Heathrow. I mean, I call that overselling."

– Sir Rodrick Braithwaite, former head of the [British] joint intelligence committee, *The Guardian*, July 14, 2003

". . . [T]he intention was to dramatize it, just as the vendors of some merchandise . . . exaggerate the importance of what they have. But from politicians, of our leaders, in the Western world, I think we expect a bit more than that – a bit more sincerity."

– Hans Blix, on BBC's *Breakfast with Frost*, February 8, 2004

Why did Tony Blair commit Britain to this adventure at America's side? The professionals in the Foreign Office would probably have advised him to support it, simply because they generally put preserving the "special relationship" with the United States above all other considerations, but he was under no obligation to accept their advice. There was certainly no appetite for it in Britain, and there could be no personal or party political advantage in it for him: his own Labour Party was acutely uncomfortable at his closeness to the most right-wing American president in living memory, and Labour supporters were even more opposed to the idea of a war with Iraq than other British voters. We are left with only personal explanations for his extraordinary choice.

One was undoubtedly his religious fervour: Tony Blair was probably the most enthusiastic Christian to become prime minister since William Ewart Gladstone left Number 10 for the last time in 1894. (Only 16 per cent of Britons say religion is very important in their lives, compared to 53 per cent of Americans.) One of the highlights of the 2003 television year in Britain was an interview of Blair conducted by Jeremy Paxman, the attack-dog of British TV interviewers, who asked the prime minister if, on his visits to the White House, he prayed with President Bush. Blair affected outrage at the question – a necessary response, given the allergic reaction of the British to displays of religiosity in public life – but he did not say no. While there was a doctrinal and stylistic gulf between the born-again fundamentalists who made up a large share of the White House's population and Blair's orthodox, mainstream Christianity, he shared with them a missionary enthusiasm and an unshakable confidence in the moral rightness of his actions.

As Gladstone had gone out into the streets of Victorian London, picked up fallen women, and brought them home to read the New Testament to them (whipping himself in private afterwards), Tony Blair had acquired the habit of going out into the world and rescuing fallen countries (though his views on self-flagellation are unknown). His principle experience of foreign affairs before Iraq had been three foreign military interventions – in Kosovo in 1999, in Sierra Leone in 2000, and in Afghanistan in 2001 – that had not cost many British lives, that were more or less legal, and that were arguably all on balance beneficial to the people of those countries. So it had been flowers, champagne, and a warm glow of moral righteousness three times for Tony, and he was not averse to more of the same. "I am truly committed to dealing with [Iraq], irrespective of the position of America," he told a *Guardian* interviewer on March 1, 2003. "If the Americans were not doing this, I would be pressuring for them to be doing so." And he told cabinet colleague Clare Short: "If it were down to me, I'd do [invade] Zimbabwe as well."

But how did Blair fail to notice that the Bush administration's motives for invading Iraq were utterly different from his own, and that this was a completely illegal enterprise? Sheer inexperience may be part of the answer: he had never held any government office before he became prime minister in 1997 (the Conservatives had been in power since 1979), but nevertheless often acts as his own foreign minister. It is questionable whether Blair spotted the critical distinction between the previous interventions and Iraq when George W. Bush first asked him to help in the invasion, probably at a time when there were no Foreign Office minders in attendance. At any rate, he said yes – and it is ten times harder to take back your given word than to say no in the first place. It's a poor reason to take a country to war, but when all Blair's other justifications crumbled, he was still able to take refuge in his conviction that overthrowing Saddam Hussein was a morally righteous act.

So it may have been, but it was not a legal act, nor necessarily a wise one, and by late February 2003 it was clear that only a small minority on the UN Security Council would vote in favour of withdrawing the inspectors from Iraq and authorizing an invasion. No banned weapons were being found in Iraq, there was no reason to rush into war, and President Bush's fulminations about Saddam Hussein's policy of "delay and deceit" were sounding increasingly hollow.

Indeed the United States was receiving increasingly desperate peace offers from Saddam Hussein's regime by multiple private routes, including approaches to Richard Perle and to Vincent Cannistraro, the CIA's former head of counter-terrorism, proposing to let several thousand U.S. troops and/or FBI agents into the country to search for the alleged WMD, to grant the United States rights over Iraqi oil, and even to hold internationally monitored elections within two years. But the CIA instructed Perle to reply, "Tell them we will see them in Baghdad," and Cannistraro got a similar response: "There were serious attempts to cut a deal, but they were all turned down by the president and vice-president." Nobody else on the Security Council was told about the approaches, but they were nevertheless deeply suspicious about the Anglo-American attempt to rush the UN into war without hearing the inspectors' report.

"We will not allow the passage of a planned resolution that would authorize the use of force. Russia and France, as permanent Security Council members, will fully assume all their responsibilities on this point. We are totally on the same line on this as the Russians."

– Dominique de Villepin, French foreign minister, March 5, 2003

It wasn't just France. De Villepin had met with his German and Russian colleagues in Paris – what Condoleezza Rice called the "non-nein-nyet" alliance – before issuing his statement. France was prepared to use its veto if necessary, but so was Russia: Alexander Konovalov, president of the Institute for Strategic Studies in Moscow, explained on March 5 that "this is a very strong signal to the United States not to put the second resolution up for a vote at all. After such strong statements, Russia [has to use] its veto if it does come to a vote." Russian foreign minister Igor Ivanov let it be known that China, which also had a veto, "shared the approach" of Paris and Moscow in opposing a premature resort to force. And Germany, which had a temporary seat on the Security Council but no veto, was equally adamant, Foreign Minister Joschka Fischer saying, "I don't see personally how we can stop the process of Resolution 1441 [which sent the weapons inspectors into Iraq] and resort to war." The results of the inspections, he observed, were "more and more encouraging."

In fact, opposition to war against Iraq was overwhelming on the Security Council. Despite an intense campaign of pressure by the United States and Britain, almost none of the non-permanent members had been persuaded that war was desirable, and the resolution was unlikely to get more than four votes out of fifteen (the United States, Britain, Spain, and perhaps one other). A veto would not be needed. A few weeks earlier, the Anglo-American allies had sworn publicly to force a Security Council vote on the issue, but faced with this united front they withdrew their resolution, falsely claiming that France would block any attempt to use force against Iraq. (France had actually said that it would veto any measure proposing to withdraw the arms inspectors and invade Iraq without completing the process and hearing their report.)

Having abandoned the UN, the United States and Britain declared that they would attack Iraq as soon as the UN inspectors were pulled out. They claimed that Saddam Hussein was obstructing the inspectors and was therefore in breach of Resolution 1441 (something that neither the inspectors nor the Security Council had said), that Iraq's alleged breach of 1441 automatically cancelled the cease-fire of 1991, and that they were therefore entitled to invade Iraq under the original UN Resolution 678 of 1990 that had authorized the use of force to liberate Kuwait (the same resolution that George H.W. Bush and British prime minister John Major had interpreted at the time as *not* authorizing them to invade Iraq and overthrow Saddam Hussein). Saddam let the inspectors leave unharmed, and the assault began on March 20, 2003.

It was like beating up a baby with a baseball bat. The Iraqi forces, which had received no new equipment since their catastrophic defeat in the first Gulf War twelve years before, were helpless under the shower of precision-guided munitions that destroyed them before they even saw their enemy. Some Baathists fought bravely, but most Iraqi soldiers showed little desire to die for Saddam Hussein. The kill ratio on the battlefield was close to a hundred Iraqis for every dead soldier of the "coalition forces." The allegedly elite Republican Guards divisions were stupidly committed to battle in the open south of Baghdad, where they were promptly annihilated by American air power. There was not even a last stand in Baghdad, the one place where the Iraqi forces could have slowed an American victory and inflicted serious U.S. casualties by forcing a battle in a large built-up area. Baghdad was left virtually undefended, and fell on April 9. It was a splendid success militarily – and a political disaster.

In the first Gulf War, the U.S. forces that liberated Kuwait were accompanied by contingents from almost every NATO country (including France, Germany, and Canada) and by a number of Arab armies. The entire war was waged under the authority of the United Nations, and most of the countries that did not have troops on the ground, like Russia, nevertheless offered their support in other ways. Even in Afghanistan in 2001, practically every country that mattered offered to help in the invasion, although relatively few of them were compatible enough with U.S. forces in equipment and operational procedures to be allocated an active role in the war by the Pentagon.

But in the invasion of Iraq in 2003, there were no Arab allies, and effectively no NATO allies except Britain – even the Turks had refused to let the United States use its bases in the country for the attack. In fact, the Americans and the British were all alone on the front line except for a couple of thousand Australians. (Australian defence policy consists primarily of sending Australian troops along to every American war, in the hope that if one day Australia needs to have the favour returned, Americans will feel grateful enough to come and help. If the United States invaded Mars, Australia would send a battalion along.) And of course, there was no UN authority to make it legal: it was just three English-speaking countries invading an Arabic-speaking country, ostensibly as a public service to the world.

This did not matter to the hard-core neo-conservatives, of course. Their whole purpose was to send a message to the world that the rules had changed, and Iraq would do that job just fine. They didn't mind a bit when the arguments about Iraqi WMD and links between Saddam and al-Qaeda on which they had based their public case for war fell apart, either, although it required some verbal gymnastics from President Bush and Prime Minister Blair.

"The Iraqi regime possesses and produces chemical and biological weapons. It is seeking nuclear weapons. ... Facing clear evidence of peril, we cannot wait for the final proof, the smoking gun that could come in the form of a mushroom cloud."

– George W. Bush, October 7 and 8, 2002

"We are asked to accept that, contrary to all intelligence, Saddam decided to destroy those weapons. I say such a claim is palpably absurd."

– Tony Blair, March 18, 2003

"He had the capacity to have a weapon, make a weapon. We thought he had weapons. He could have developed a nuclear weapon over time – I'm not saying tomorrow, but over time."

– George W. Bush, February 8, 2004

"I have to accept that we have not found them and we may not find them. He [Saddam] may have removed or hidden or even destroyed those weapons."

– Tony Blair, July 6, 2004

The Iraqis almost certainly destroyed all their banned weapons in the summer of 1991, just as they always said they had, although they continued to hide some production and research facilities until the UN arms inspectors tracked them down in the mid-1990s. "I don't think they existed," said David Kay, head of the post-war Iraq survey group tasked with finding the WMD, when he resigned from the position after nine fruitless months of hunting for them in January 2004.

The collapse of the "intelligence" on which they had made their case for war severely damaged public trust in Tony Blair in Britain and in Prime Minister John Howard's government in Australia, the only other country to have joined the United States' invasion of Iraq, but it had significantly less impact in the United States. A survey by the University of Maryland found that as late as April 2004, 57 per cent of those interviewed "believe that before the war Iraq was providing substantial support to al-Qaeda," and 65 per cent believed that "experts" had confirmed that Iraq had WMD. The decline in American popular support for the war in Iraq is more likely to be due to mounting U.S. casualties there.

And meanwhile, the other great powers continue to ponder the message that the United States sent them by invading Iraq. They received the message loud and clear, but apart from Britain they have not come to heel. France, Germany, Russia, and China offered only verbal criticism of the invasion of Iraq, but it is clear that they are reconsidering their options in a fundamental way.

CHAPTER V

THE SYSTEM (SUCH AS IT IS)

The voice from the telescreen paused. A trumpet call, clear and beautiful, floated into the stagnant air. The voice continued raspingly:

"Attention! Your attention, please! A newsflash has arrived this moment from the Malabar front. Our forces in South India have won a glorious victory. I am authorised to say that the action we are now reporting may well bring the war within measurable distance of its end. Here is the newsflash –"

Bad news coming, thought Winston. And sure enough, following a gory description of the annihilation of a Eurasian army, with stupendous figures of killed and prisoners, came the announcement that, as of next week, the chocolate ration would be reduced from thirty grammes to twenty. . . .

"Oceania, 'tis for thee" gave way to lighter music. Winston walked over to the window, keeping his back to the telescreen. The day was still cold and clear. Somewhere far away a rocket bomb exploded with a dull, reverberating roar. About twenty or thirty of them a week were falling on London at present.

– George Orwell, *Nineteen Eighty-Four*

If we could have a safer, fairer global order through the unilateral exercise of American power, many people in the West (though not elsewhere) would reluctantly accept that solution. After all, the United Nations has not exactly been an unqualified success. But most people suspect that *Pax Americana* won't work, because Americans will not be willing to bear for long the burden of high casualties and high taxes that such a policy involves.

What we risk ending up with instead is a world in which all the old institutions of international governance have been destroyed or gravely undermined by the actions of the neo-conservatives, but the rival American bid to provide world order has crashed and burned. We may end up with nothing, in other words. No working multilateral institutions, little by way of international co-operation, and a world whose geopolitics is loosely modelled on George Orwell's *Nineteen Eighty-Four*.

The world of *Nineteen Eighty-Four* as Orwell depicted it never came to pass, though it seemed plausible enough when he wrote the novel in 1948. The post–Second World War world did begin to divide up into the three perpetually warring blocs he imagined, Eurasia, Eastasia, and Oceania (the Americas plus Britain), but the division remained incomplete. China never became the core of a united Eastasian bloc, and the line between Russian-dominated Eurasia and Oceania ran down the middle of Europe along the NATO–Warsaw Pact frontier, not down the English Channel. More importantly, these blocs did not end up perpetually at war with one another, although there were numerous clashes between Oceania and Eastasia (most significantly in Korea and Vietnam) and a terrifying forty-year nuclear confrontation between Oceania and Eurasia.

Most important of all, Oceania – the West – did not succumb to the totalitarian template that defines all three blocs in Orwell's novel. Stalin's Europe and Mao's China came pretty close to the Orwellian nightmare during the 1950s, but the brief interlude of the McCarthy witch hunt in the United States was the closest approach in the West, and it was not close at all. By the 1970s both the Soviet and the Chinese regimes were retreating from the full totalitarian model, perhaps because such regimented viciousness is hard to sustain over long periods of time. Then came the non-violent revolutions of 1989–91, bringing some kind of democracy to most of the countries of Eurasia and ending the Cold War, the main military confrontation in the world. At the same time, China (Eastasia) relaxed politically and integrated into the emerging global economy without a revolution. Orwell's book became a frightful vision of a future that might have been, but never was.

Why didn't it come to pass? One reason was certainly the existence of nuclear weapons, which made any direct military clash between the blocs insanely dangerous. Orwell just ignored their existence. In *Nineteen Eighty-Four* the three blocs fight endless, ritualistic, deliberately indecisive wars whose purpose is to justify domestic repression everywhere, and only conventional weapons are used: the "rocket bombs" he writes of are not nuclear-tipped ICBMs, but near descendants of the Nazi V-2s that did fall on London in 1944. In the real post-1945 world of widespread nuclear weapons, however, you could not have had twenty to thirty Eurasian (i.e., Russian) "rocket bombs" per week falling on London for very long without escalation to all-out nuclear war.

But the more profound reason that *Nineteen Eighty-Four* remained a fiction was that the most powerful of the three proto-blocs, the West, would not abandon its clumsy, seemingly inefficient democratic system despite the temptation to mobilize for total war, and flatly refused to embark on any kind of ideological crusade. This was largely due to the wisdom of a generation of American leaders in the early postwar years who coped with the Soviet threat, to the extent that it actually existed, by relying on nuclear deterrence to contain the Soviet Union militarily while subsidizing the reconstruction of democracies in western Europe and Japan. Relations between Oceania and Eastasia superficially seemed closer to the Orwellian model for a while, with Western armies fighting limited (non-nuclear) wars around the borders of China almost continuously from 1950 to 1973, but then the West finally figured out that most of these conflicts were really about national liberation from imperial rule and who gets to rule locally afterwards, and direct involvement by Western armies ceased.

There was also a third reason why Orwell's future did not happen, though it rarely gets the credit it deserves. The structure of international laws and rules that came into being with the creation of the United Nations in 1945, and the powerful idea of a global community that it embodied, helped to stave off a descent into a world of universal violence and repression. Even in the darkest days of the Cold War, the superpowers were able to back away from potentially lethal confrontations without loss of face by deferring to the legal authority of the UN Security Council in matters of war and peace. And even in the deepest pits of repression, democrats like the Czech dissidents of Charter 77 and Daw Aung Sang Suu Kyi in Burma could gain some protection by appealing to the world of law imagined by the UN Charter and the International Convention on Human Rights. The law was broken daily, even hourly, but it made a difference that the oppressors generally felt obliged to deny their misdeeds or cloak them in fake legality rather than simply doing them boldly and openly. Nowhere, not even China in the days of the Cultural Revolution, was as bad as Orwell's world.

Nobody wanted *Nineteen Eighty-Four* to come true, least of all Orwell, and he would have been delighted had he lived long enough to learn that his model of the future had been aborted. But history is full of potential turning points, some of which get taken and some of which do not: the real world turned out so much better than Orwell's terrible vision (if still well short of perfect) because individuals and countries made particular decisions and adopted specific policies at certain times.

It is hard to imagine any realistic outcome that would have matched the awfulness of *Nineteen Eighty-Four*, which is after all a novel, but other decisions and policies would have led to other outcomes in the real world, and some of them would have been extremely grim. Which brings us to the present, for the game is never over. There are decisions being made and policies being adopted right now that, if they stand, will deliver us into a world that is much worse than the present, and a good deal closer to Orwell's fantasy.

"This organization is created to keep you from going to hell. It isn't created to take you to heaven."

– Henry Cabot Lodge Jr., Republican senator and U.S. delegate to the UN, 1955

"I believe that I made the right decision, but I accept it is a big responsibility," said British prime minister Tony Blair in October 2003, six months after the invasion of Iraq. "You are, and should be held to account for such decisions. . . . Those who started the war must finish it. The judgement will be made by whether we make life better [in Iraq] or not." That was about all that Blair had left to say at that point, given the total absence of the alleged weapons of mass destruction that were his original pretext for attacking Iraq, and a comparable shift of emphasis in justifications for the war occurred in the United States for the same reason.

But even if the American and British governments genuinely felt the pain of oppressed Iraqis (while remaining strangely numb to the pain of oppressed Burmese, Belarussians, and Burundians), the welfare of the Iraqi people was not an adequate legal justification for the unprovoked invasion of a sovereign country. Even if Iraq were to become a bastion of peace, prosperity, and democracy in the Middle East as a result of the Anglo-American invasion – a highly improbable outcome, on present evidence – the attack would remain an act of aggression contrary to international law.

At this point in the argument, a chorus of "so what?" arises from all those who see their short-term purposes served by the elimination of Saddam Hussein's regime, and they are quite numerous. Americans and some others who obsessed about terrorism and believed the myths about Iraqi WMD and Saddam's alleged links with al-Qaeda; U.S. neo-conservatives who saw the Iraq War as the opening shot of their campaign to impose *Pax Americana* on the world; Israelis who regarded Iraq as the largest remaining threat to their military hegemony in the region – they all feel that the benefits of an armed invasion of Iraq outweighed the damage to the international rule of law, which is longer-term and less easily comprehended. The humanitarian argument that Iraqis are better off without Saddam Hussein, the fallback justification for the invasion after the alleged WMD evaporated, may well be true – we'll know in a year or two – but even if that really had been their motive, it wouldn't be enough. The implications of the illegal invasion of Iraq for the international system are huge and entirely negative, and the fallout from that deed may blight our world for many years.

We are not dealing here with the obvious first-order consequences of the invasion, like the guerilla war in Iraq against the occupation forces, the further alienation of Arab and Muslim countries, and the likely boost that this will give to the phenomenon of international Islamist terrorism. It is the international system itself that is at risk, for when the United States and Great Britain, both permanent members of the UN Security Council, invaded Iraq in the teeth of opposition from almost everybody else, they attacked the foundations of the entire post–Second World War international order. Such an action can have far-reaching consequences.

On March 15, 2003, on the eve of the U.S. attack on Iraq, Professor Gwyn Prins of the London School of Economics wrote in *The Guardian*: "We are at the passing of the age of Middle Earth. All the agents and the institutions of that age will be profoundly affected. The previous breakpoint of equivalent importance was in the late 1940s. Emerging from the ashes of the destruction of the Third Reich, and led by the U.S., the victors found collective will to act, and in that time, they engendered the universal declaration of human rights and initiated the three main multilateral adventures of the next half-century: the U.N., NATO, and the EU. Today, simultaneously, we are seeing the draining of power from all three, and transformation of the residuum. The catalyst to this profound and rapid change has been Iraq." He may well be right – and in that case, we are all in trouble.

The great achievement of the twentieth century was to make aggressive war illegal. People tend to sneer when they hear that assertion, since the twentieth century was obviously full of wars, but that's because they don't understand how very much worse the world was before we changed the rules. Few people realize that until the mid-twentieth century, it was perfectly legal for one country to attack, carve up, or even swallow another. Indeed, it was done all the time: at least 90 per cent of all the states that ever existed have been destroyed by war.

There have been interludes in various parts of the world where the impact of war was limited by common agreement. During the seventeenth and eighteenth centuries, for example, Europe fought its wars by a set of unwritten rules that prevented any of the great powers from going under (though countries as large as Poland could simply disappear, at least for a time). However, those rules broke down during the French Revolutionary and Napoleonic Wars of 1793–1815, when many smaller countries were simply swept away and even the biggest ones faced military occupation and regime change. Within the space of two years in 1812–14, there were French troops in Moscow and Russian troops in Paris. The badly shaken survivors of the Napoleonic Wars did manage to revive the old rules for the remainder of the nineteenth century – only to see them collapse entirely in the course of the First World War.

The 1914–18 war was not very different from the War of the Spanish Succession two hundred years earlier (1702–14) in its motives, its list of participants, or the stakes that the participants thought they were playing for when they entered the war: a colony here, a border province there, and of course prestige. But the mass death inflicted on conscript armies of ordinary citizens by the new weapons of industrialized slaughter during the Great War, as they called it at the time, was so great that the war had to be redefined as a cosmic struggle between good and evil. It gradually came to be seen that way in the minds of the warring populations and even of their leaders, not because the political stakes were unusually high or some great moral issue was involved, but because it was consuming hundreds of thousands of lives a month.

You can only justify the sacrifice of so many people by elevating your mundane war aims to an altogether higher level and transforming the struggle into a crusade against evil – but since it is impossible to compromise with evil, any possibility of a negotiated peace on the old pattern becomes impossible and diplomacy fails by definition. In the end, every regime on the losing side was destroyed, and two great empires of half a millennium's standing, Austria-Hungary and the Ottoman Empire, were chopped up into a dozen successor states.

"A general association of nations must be formed under specific convenants for the purpose of affording mutual guarantees of political independence and territorial integrity to great and small states alike."

– Woodrow Wilson "Fourteen Points"
Speech to Congress, January 8, 1918

Whole populations were in shock by 1918. Matters had got so far out of hand that there was wide support for U.S. president Woodrow Wilson's radical proposal that there should be new rules for international conduct and a new institution to enforce them: the League of Nations. It was duly created (though the U.S. Congress refused to let the United States join) with the task of preventing further wars, especially among the great powers.

The League of Nations incorporated revolutionary ideas like the right of peoples to self-determination, and from the start it aroused a great deal of sullen resentment among the foreign policy professionals, who felt (as do today's American neo-conservatives) that the new institution in Geneva imposed unnecessary constraints on their freedom of action. Lord Robert Cecil, a strong supporter of the League, observed that the British government regarded it as "a kind of excrescence which must be carefully prevented from having too much influence on our foreign policy. Geneva, to them, was a strange place in which a newfangled machine existed to enable foreigners to influence or even to control our international action."

The League of Nations failed, of course, and not only because of the resistance of those who were still enmeshed in the old notions of absolute national sovereignty. It was born into a world where Communist and fascist totalitarians vied for power in Europe, two-thirds of the planet's people lived in somebody else's empire, and the United States had retreated into isolationism. The idea of a forum where all the world's governments would be present all the time to deal with the world's problems collectively was a great leap forward, and preventing the outbreak of another war like the last was hugely important, but the League was doomed to fail.

The Italian invasion of Abyssinia (Ethiopia) in 1935, in defiance of the new international rules, showed that the great powers, despite their commitments, were in practice not ready to unite to prevent aggression. Multilateralism was a new and uncomfortable idea, and every country began to seek safety instead in private deals and alliances that quite closely mirrored those of the time before the First World War. Abandoning hope of multilateral action, Britain and France gave bilateral guarantees to Poland after Hitler seized the Czech lands in 1938; when he ignored those guarantees and invaded Poland in September 1939, it triggered the Second World War.

It is worth pausing at this point to consider what the League of Nations could have done about Hitler even if the United States had been a member and all the democracies had been willing to stand by its principles, for there is a great deal of naivete about the nature of both the League and its successor, the United Nations. If Adolf Hitler had confined himself to murdering Jews, gypsies, homosexuals, and domestic political opponents, and never invaded Poland or his other neighbours, he would have died in bed sometime in the 1960s, and the Third Reich would have lasted until such time as the Germans themselves got sick of it.

The League's job was to prevent international aggression, not to police the behaviour of governments within their own borders, and it would have been against international law for the League to sponsor a military intervention to close down Dachau – not that it would have found any volunteers for the job. The democratic governments of Britain, France, and the United States would have wrung their hands and begged the Nazis to be nicer, but they would not have gone to war with

Hitler over the concentration camps. They would probably even have gone on trading with Germany, so long as its leaders were reasonably discreet about the details of their extermination program. Hitler's mistake was to attack and annex his neighbours and challenge the international balance of power.

If you doubt this, consider the fate of Stalin, who killed many millions more than Hitler but knew the international rules and was punctilious about observing them. Soviet troops occupied most of Eastern Europe at the end of the Second World War, but only with the consent of Moscow's allies, the other victorious great powers. The Soviet army forgot to go home again after that, but it never tried to move any farther west, so Stalin died a natural death, and his regime survived him by more than thirty years. It did so because the Soviet Union's rulers understood the basic rule of international law in an era of absolute sovereignty. You can do what you like to your own subjects, so long as you don't attack the neighbours. *Cuius regio, eius religio* (If he's your king, then that's your religion), as the Religious Peace of Augsburg put it in 1555, at the start of Europe's long domination over the world, and that is the way it has worked ever since.

So it would be a mistake to expect international law to protect you from your own government: the great twentieth-century experiment has been to see if it might at least be expanded to the point where it protects people from being killed by foreign governments. At the end of the Second World War, with some forty-five million dead and half the cities of the developed world bombed flat, rebuilding an international organization that would be capable of taking on that job was the highest priority, and it was once again Americans who took the lead. The League was dead beyond hope of resurrection, but the surviving governments in 1945 went right out and cloned it (with some major improvements) as the United Nations Organization. They did it because they felt that they had to. One more great-power war like the one just past, but this time with every great power in possession of nuclear weapons from the start, and there would be nothing left. Changing the traditional way that the international system worked would be hard; not changing it would be fatal.

"More than an end to war, we want an end to the beginning of all wars – yes, an end to this brutal, inhuman and thoroughly impractical method of settling the differences between governments."

– President Franklin D. Roosevelt, April 1945

The United Nations as constituted in 1945 was a profoundly cynical organization, more explicitly so even than the League of Nations. It accepted without demur that its member states enjoyed absolute sovereignty and would never be forced to submit to intervention in their internal affairs (with the sole and uncertain exception that acts of genocide might trigger international intervention). The UN Charter made absolutely no moral or practical distinction between the most law-abiding democracies and the most repressive dictatorships among its membership. How could it, when more than half its members were themselves dictatorships? The UN was not about love, or justice, or freedom, although words of that sort are sprinkled freely through the preamble to the UN Charter; it was about avoiding another world war.

The problem that the surviving governments faced in 1945, in an even starker version than their predecessors in 1918, was this: the existing international system, which gives each sovereign state the right to use war as an instrument of policy, is bankrupt in an era of weapons of mass destruction. The world cannot afford to allow countries armed with nuclear weapons to go to war with each other. It can certainly never again go through one of those generalized great-power mêlées (latterly called "world wars") that in the past were the main way of adjusting the international system to accommodate the changing balance between the great powers. If we fight that kind of war just once more, with thousands of nuclear weapons available to the major powers, the whole northern hemisphere will fry, so we have to stop doing it. We have to change the system. In fact, we have to outlaw war.

Because "outlaw war" sounds like a naive slogan on a protester's banner, people fail to grasp how radical a change it was for the great powers of the world to sign up to such a rule in 1945. Ever since the first city-states of Mesopotamia five thousand years ago, war had been a legitimate tool of statecraft, with no lasting opprobrium attached even to waging "aggressive war" so long as you were successful. Empires rose and fell, the militarily competent prospered, and the losers didn't get to write the history. Now, all of a sudden, it's over.

Since 1945, according to the UN Charter, it has been illegal to wage war against another country except in two tightly defined circumstances. One is that you have just been attacked, and are fighting back in immediate self-defence pending the arrival of international help. (There is no possible reading of this rule, Article 51 of the UN Charter, that would extend it to cover preventive war, where one country attacks another because of something it fears the other might do in future.) The other exception arises when the UN Security Council authorizes various member states to use military force on its behalf to roll back an aggression, or to enforce its decisions on a tightly limited number of other questions.

And that's it. Apart from these exceptions, international war – that is, war waged by a sovereign government across an international border – has been illegal since 1945. It is illegal to attack a country because it is sitting on territory that belonged to your country in your grandparents' time. It is even illegal to attack a country because it is ruled by a wicked dictator who oppresses his own people. The rules had to be written like that because to allow exceptions on these counts would have left loopholes big enough to drive a tank through – and because many of the countries that had to be persuaded to sign up in order for the new United Nations to become a truly universal organization were themselves ruled by wicked dictators who oppressed their own people. The founders of the UN in 1945 were not trying to create an organization that would impose democracy, justice, and brotherly love on the world. They were just trying to build an institution that would prevent a Third World War, and as many other wars as possible.

Making war illegal does not mean that all wars have stopped, any more than making murder illegal has stopped all killings, but it has transformed the context in which wars take place. The United Nations does not always act to roll back a successful aggression, because that requires getting past the vetoes wielded by all five permanent members of the Security Council and then finding member states willing to put their troops at risk on the ground, but it almost never recognizes border changes that are accomplished by war.

For twenty-six years, it refused to recognize the annexation of East Timor by Indonesia as legal – and in the end, East Timor got its independence back. For twenty-four years, it refused to accept the occupation of South West Africa (now Namibia) by the apartheid regime in South Africa as legitimate, and in the end, Namibia got its independence too. For thirty-seven years it has refused to recognize the Israeli annexation of East Jerusalem after the 1967 war, even though nobody can currently imagine how that could ever be reversed. The point of the rule, quite explicitly, is that no country must ever profit territorially by its military success, for that would encourage further military adventures. And occasionally, as in Korea in 1950 or in Kuwait in 1990, the UN does manage to authorize an international military force to repel an aggression.

There is also, however, much that the UN cannot do. First and foremost, it cannot act against a perceived interest of any of the great powers, for in order to get them all to sign up it had to offer them a special deal: vetoes that allow the United

States, Russia, Britain, France, and China to block any UN action they don't like. It's neither fair nor pretty, but how else were the founders of the UN going to get the great powers to sign up – and what use would the organization be if some of them were outside it?

In practice, the interlocking vetoes of the great powers on the Security Council meant that during the long years of the Cold War, when most world issues had been absorbed into the general confrontation between NATO and the Warsaw Pact, the UN was paralyzed in large parts of the world. It could only step in if both sides decided that getting the UN involved would enable them to back away safely from some dangerous confrontation (like the Cuban missile crisis) without loss of face.

The United Nations cannot intervene in a sovereign state – or at least it could not until recently – even to stop the most horrendous violations of human rights. The UN not only failed to intervene to stop the genocide in Cambodia in the late 1970s (for the Khmer Rouge, the perpetrators of that atrocity, were also the recognized sovereign government). It even continued to recognize the Khmer Rouge government-in-exile through most of the 1980s because it had been illegally displaced by a Vietnamese invasion. Matters might have been different if the United States, still bitter over its defeat by Vietnam, had not backed this policy so firmly, but in strict law the fact that the Vietnamese invasion had been intended in large part to stop the killing (particularly of the Vietnamese minority in Cambodia) simply did not count against the fact that Vietnam had violated the sovereignty of a neighbouring state.

And yet the UN is a central and indispensable part of the modern world. It is the institution through which a politically conscious global society first came into existence, and its specialized organs are still the arena in which most of the world's large-scale deals are made on matters ranging from telecommunications frequencies and trade to public health and the environment. It is the organizer and command centre for many of the peacekeeping missions that hold old enemies apart and try to minimize the level of violence in failed states, and the source of legal authority for most of those peacekeeping missions that it does not directly control. Since the end of the Cold War, it has become considerably more active in this field, in some cases even bending its own rules to ratify intervention in (smallish) sovereign states against the local government's will to end genocides and similar massive abuses of human rights. And most important by far, it is the repository of the new international law that bans the use of aggressive military force, even by the great powers.

It is not generally realized how important this law is because it is so often broken, especially by the really big powers. Repeatedly during the Cold War the superpowers of the time sponsored coups against the governments of recalcitrant countries within their own spheres of influence or even invaded them – the Soviet Union in Hungary, Czechoslovakia, and Afghanistan, the United States in Chile, Grenada, and Panama

– and the lesser powers were not far behind. The British, French, and Israelis plotted to attack Egypt in the Suez War of 1956, Egypt and Syria launched a surprise attack on Israel in 1973, China fought border wars with both India and the Soviet Union, and India and Pakistan fought three wars of their own. Yet the fact that we now lived in a world where most of these actions were illegal did impose limitations on the traditional behaviour of states.

The superpowers disciplined their satellites without hindrance, but even they were careful to give lip service to international law in most cases: the Russians always found some local Communist who could claim to be in power to invite them in when they invaded their satellites, and the United States went to the trouble of manufacturing a fake North Vietnamese naval attack on U.S. ships in the Gulf of Tonkin before starting the bombing of North Vietnam. And most of the wars not backed by the veto-wielding superpowers lasted only a short time before international diplomatic intervention stopped them.

The Security Council would busy itself with appeals for a cease-fire and offers of peacekeeping troops, and at least one side (generally the one that was losing) would be eager to comply, which made it hard for the other side to go on fighting. So wars rarely ended in decisive victories any more, and territory almost never changed hands in a legal and permanent way no matter who won or who lost. These very significant constraints may also explain why nuclear weapons, which were used in the Second World War just as soon as they were invented, have not been used in war again for the past fifty-nine years.

Of course, these same constraints can feel very burdensome if you happen to be the greatest power in the world, with overwhelming superiority in both nuclear and conventional weapons. You might even wind up filled with frustration and fury because all these Lilliput nations are trying to use the rules of the United Nations to tie you down like Gulliver.

The best measure of any institution's real importance is how much its enemies hate it. Richard Perle, a.k.a. the Prince of Darkness, house intellectual of the neo-conservative group since the mid-1980s and chairman of the Defense Policy Board at the Pentagon until allegations of conflict of interest compelled his resignation in early 2003, hates the UN a lot. In late March 2003, just as the U.S. invasion of Iraq got underway – an invasion Perle and his fellow neo-conservatives hoped would destroy the Security Council's moral authority and its ability to put a brake on American power for good – he wrote an article for *The Spectator* in which he did a little jig of joy on the UN's presumptive grave. It is worth quoting at some length, because it gives a sense of the rage that the UN inspires in these circles.

> *Saddam Hussein . . . will go quickly, but not alone: in a parting irony, he will take the UN down with him. Well, not the whole UN. The "good works" part will survive, the*

low-risk peacekeeping bureaucracies will remain, the chatterbox on the Hudson will continue to bleat. What will die is the fantasy of the UN *as the foundation of a new world order. As we sift the debris, it will be important to preserve, the better to understand, the intellectual wreckage of the liberal conceit of safety through international law administered by international institutions. . . .*

[For many liberals], the thumb on the scale of judgment about this war is the idea that only the UN *security council can legitimize the use of force. . . . This is a dangerously wrong idea that leads inexorably to handing great moral and even existential politico-military decisions to the likes of Syria, Cameroon, Angola, Russia, China and France. . . .*

Facing Milosevic's multiple aggressions, the UN *could not stop the Balkan wars or even protect its [sic] victims. . . . We will not defeat or even contain fanatical terror unless we can carry the war to the territories from which it is launched. This will sometimes require that we use force against states that harbour terrorists, as we did in destroying the Taliban regime in Afghanistan. The most dangerous of these states are those that also possess weapons of mass destruction. Iraq is one, but there are others. . . . The chronic failure of the security council to enforce its own resolutions is unmistakable: it is simply not up to the task so we are left with coalitions of the willing. Far from disparaging them as a threat to a new world order, we should recognise them that they are, by default, the best hope for that order, and the true alternative to the anarchy of the abject failure of the* UN.

An invigorating rant by a master of sophistry, wonderfully compendious in its conflation of every half-truth, elision, and blatant lie that is deployed from time to time in arguments of this nature. There is the parochial sneer at the ridiculous idea of Americans having to share decisions on the fate of the world with countries "the likes of Syria, Cameroon, Angola, Russia, China and France." (But hang on a minute. If the United States is not willing to share those decisions with other great powers like Russia, China, and France, then it will have to compel their obedience by overwhelming military and financial power for the rest of eternity, and maybe have to fight them anyway in the end.)

There is the assertion that fighting fanatical terror "will sometimes require that we use force against states that harbour terrorists, as we did in destroying the Taliban regime in Afghanistan," as though this explains why the UN has become an obstacle to sane policy. Perle is counting on his readers to forget that the Security Council did effectively support military action against Afghanistan, agreeing that the United States had a legitimate case – and that since the war was not illegal, almost all the allies and friends of America who later baulked at joining the invasion of Iraq offered troops for the Afghan operation. There is the usual attempt to force Iraq into the same frame of reference by completely unsubstantiated and false assertions that it harboured terrorists and had weapons of mass destruction.

And so it goes on, with the UN portrayed one moment as an irrelevant excrescence and the next moment as an arrogant and uncaring organization of great power. Perle shamelessly serves up the familiar half-truth that "the UN could not stop the Balkan wars," as though it were an entity capable of acting independently of its most powerful member states. If it really were, then he would be the first to lead a revolt against it, but at this point in his argument it is a useful rhetorical device to mask the fact that it was the veto-wielding great powers on the Security Council – just as much the United States and Britain as Russia and China – that blocked the decisive use of UN-backed force to halt the fighting in the Balkans in 1992–95.

The failings of the UN in the Balkan Wars of the 1990s were the failings of the countries that made it up, and above all of the great powers with permanent seats on the Security Council. Since the Security Council is a veto-driven body, it can only be as determined to act as its most weak-kneed permanent member, which is a large problem if you have ambitions to see the UN become the full-time policeman of a new world order, fighting evil wherever it appears.

The problem is exactly the same, however, if you propose to fight evil instead with Richard Perle's "coalitions of the willing" – in the case of Iraq, the United States, Britain, and whichever countries they could beg, bully, or bribe into coming along. Just as there are some jobs that the Security Council will take on and others that it cannot agree upon, so there are some evils that Washington wants to fight, and others that it either doesn't care enough about – the Burmese dictatorship, for example – or does not dare take on, like North Korea or Iran.

In any case, the United Nations was not created to fight evil wherever it appears. It was designed primarily to stop the kind of straightforward cross-border aggression that had triggered both the First and the Second World Wars, but must not be allowed to cause a Third – and indeed, unprovoked invasions of the classic kind have been remarkably rare since 1945, presumably because the new international rules embodied in the UN Charter really do have some deterrent value. Since the veto-wielding permanent members of the Security Council stand to lose everything themselves in another world war, they have often been able to act in a surprisingly co-ordinated and decisive manner at the UN when events elsewhere threatened to drag them into such a conflict.

The first real test of the new rules came in June 1950, when North Korea invaded South Korea. The Security Council passed the test with flying colours, promptly authorizing the dispatch of a UN military force under American command that fought a three-year war to repel the aggression. True, that resolution probably only passed because the Soviet Union, North Korea's ally, was boycotting the Security Council at the time over the issue of who represented China membership and therefore was not present to cast its veto.

Stalin in his final years was not wholly sane, and post-Soviet research in Russia suggests that he encouraged North Korea to invade the South. But Stalin's successors in the Soviet Union were generally as aware of their duty to avoid another world war as their Western counterparts, and when real crises came along the Security Council functioned fairly well. It managed to obtain rapid cease-fires in the various Arab-Israeli and Indo-Pakistani wars that dotted the last half of the twentieth century.

On the other hand, the veto meant that it could take no collective stand on aggressions that occurred entirely within the sphere of influence of one of the superpowers themselves, like the Soviet invasion of Czechoslovakia in 1968 and the U.S. invasion of Grenada in 1983. And the Security Council completely dodged the Iraqi invasion of Iran in 1980, mainly because both Washington and Moscow solidly supported Saddam Hussein's attack on his neighbour.

Saddam's subsequent invasion of Kuwait in 1990 was different, and not only because it threatened American interests in the Gulf. Although all Iraqi governments since independence had maintained a territorial claim to Kuwait, there was no recent history of tit-for-tat interventions and provocations as there had been between Iraq and Iran: the invasion of Kuwait came utterly out of the blue. It was one of the most blatant cases of unprovoked international aggression since Korea in 1950, and Saddam's declaration that he was annexing Kuwait compounded the offence: for the first time ever, a member of the UN was being conquered and absorbed by another member.

The situation was almost identical to the Italian invasion of Abyssinia in 1935 that had demonstrated the inability of the League of Nations to respond to aggression and so initiated the slide into the Second World War, and leaders who understood that history were determined that the United Nations should not go the same way as its predecessor. As it happened, the historically minded people in power at the time included Soviet president Mikhail Gorbachev and U.S. president George

H.W. Bush, both of whom were strongly committed to using the Security Council more vigorously to ensure global order in a post–Cold War world. So there was virtually no hesitation: the Security Council voted full legal authority for an American-led army to drive Saddam out of his conquest, and Bush did everything possible to ensure that the Gulf War of 1991 would be a useful precedent for future UN military operations to contain aggression and enforce international law. The elder Bush was a man of immense international experience – former U.S. ambassador to China, former head of the Central Intelligence Agency, global business connections – and he actually understood the way the world works. In particular, he was conscious of the limitations of U.S. power, the importance of restraint in military operations, and the absolute primacy of international law.

"We have before us the opportunity to forge for ourselves and for future generations a new world order – a world where the rule of law, not the law of the jungle, governs the conduct of nations. When we are successful – and we will be – we have a chance at this new world order, an order in which a credible United Nations can use its peacekeeping role to fulfill the promise and vision of the UN's founders."

– President George H.W. Bush, announcing the start of hostilities in the first Gulf War, January 16, 1991

Bush Sr. actually meant it too: what he was going to do in Iraq was precisely what the UN Security Council had authorized him to do, and not a bit more. "Trying to eliminate Saddam, extending the ground war into an occupation of Iraq . . . would have incurred incalculable human and political costs," George Bush Sr. wrote in his 1998 book, *A World Transformed* (co-authored with his former national security adviser Brent Scowcroft). ". . . We would have been forced to occupy Baghdad and, in effect, rule Iraq. The coalition would instantly have collapsed, the Arabs deserting it in anger and other allies pulling out as well. There was no viable 'exit strategy' we could see, violating another of our principles. Furthermore, we had been self-consciously trying to set a pattern for handling aggression in the post-Cold War world. Going in and occupying Iraq, thus unilaterally exceeding the United Nations mandate, would have destroyed the precedent of international response to aggression that we hoped to establish."

George Bush Sr. did not want Saddam Hussein to go on ruling in Iraq. He even encouraged rebellions against Saddam in the Shia south and Kurdish north of Iraq, although he probably regretted that in the end because without direct American support the revolts simply got a lot of people killed for nothing. (Most of the bodies found in the mass graves in Iraq after the 2003 invasion were people killed in the unsuccessful revolt against Saddam in 1991.) But he was unwilling to order U.S. forces to invade Iraq and overthrow Saddam Hussein even though the road to Baghdad was open, because that would be going beyond the law.

The elder Bush also had grave reservations on a purely military level about going to Baghdad – "Had we gone the invasion route," he wrote in 1998, "the United States could conceivably still be an occupying power in a bitterly hostile land" – but his first concerns were the United Nations and international law. He believed that the end of the Cold War had created an opportunity for the UN Security Council to begin functioning as a real enforcer of international peace and order, and he was not going to throw that away by exceeding his legal mandate from the Security Council. When he spoke of a "New World Order," he really meant it. He had lived his whole adult life under the threat of a major nuclear war, and for him the strengthening of international law was an absolute priority. There was much more at stake than the fate of one tinpot dictator or even the fate of the Shia rebels, so once he reached the limit of his UN mandate to liberate Kuwait, he stopped.

Twelve years after George H.W. Bush fought a war to defend the sovereignty of Kuwait, his son George W. violated the sovereignty of Iraq and invaded and occupied the whole country without plausible provocation, legal justification, or Security Council approval. His administration had formally adopted a U.S. national strategy of maintaining absolute military superiority over any rival power or combination of powers on the planet in perpetuity – an absurd ambition, but no less serious for all that. His challenge to the United Nations on the eve of his invasion of Iraq contained a scarcely hidden threat that the organization would henceforward be ignored by its most powerful member if it didn't follow Washington's lead: "All the world faces a test and the UN a difficult and defining moment. Will it serve the purpose of its founding [by giving Washington permission to attack Iraq], or will it be irrelevant?" And there was no coherent criticism of this blatant rejection of international law by the Democratic presidential candidate during the 2004 campaign either; just promises to pursue the same course more efficiently and with more attention to bringing important allies along. How did we get from the elder George Bush's "New World Order" to this desperate situation so fast?

It was not a straight downward path. In the afterglow of the successful Gulf War in 1991 and with better co-operation among the veto-wielding permanent members of the Security Council, there were several attempts to expand the UN's ability to intervene in armed conflicts beyond the limits laid down by the Charter. The various UN peacekeeping forces that had been sent to troubled corners of the world during the long decades of the Cold War had always gone at the request or at least with the consent of the "host" governments, since the UN's own rules forbade it to intervene in the affairs of sovereign member states without permission, but in the 1990s some peacekeeping missions and more robust "peace-enforcement" operations began to edge beyond the traditional boundaries.

The first of these, the ill-starred Somali intervention in 1992, was undertaken without any invitation or request for help from the host government because there simply wasn't any central government any more: Somalia had become a mere battlefield where rival militias fought amid a starving populace. In the minds of some of the authors of the action, in particular that of President George H.W. Bush, part of the attraction of "doing" Somalia may have been precisely that it gave the UN an opportunity to redefine and expand the nature of peace-keeping operations in a case that was not strictly illegal under the Charter. Nevertheless, it was an operation quite startling in its altruism, for none of the intervening powers had anything to gain from the intervention, nor did the chaos and misery of Somalia threaten any of their vital interests.

Unfortunately, it was also a very difficult operation in an intensely hostile environment. For the United States, which lost eighteen soldiers killed in a single day in Mogadishu in an ill-advised and badly managed raid (the "Black Hawk down" episode) that also killed up to a thousand Somalis, it ended up being perceived as an abject failure. One of President Bill Clinton's first acts in office in 1993 was to pull the whole U.S. force out of Mogadishu, and the experience left such deep scars on the new administration that Clinton flatly refused to allow the UN to mount a major military operation in Rwanda in 1994 to stop the genocide there. It was not so easy to ignore the savage wars that began to wreck the countries of former Yugoslavia in the early 1990s, however, and gradually and reluctantly Clinton's administration was drawn back into the business of military intervention.

The Balkan military interventions of the 1990s – Bosnia in 1995 and Kosovo in 1999 – were undertaken in a quite different political atmosphere from Somalia. They were in a part of the world where the great powers had major political and security interests (and even, in the case of the Russians, strong emotional ties). They ran straight up against the ban on UN intervention in the internal affairs of sovereign states: Serbian dictator Slobodan Milosevic was a vicious sponsor of ethnic cleansing and mass murder, but he was definitely the legitimate ruler of a sovereign state, and bombing Serbia to make him stop what he was doing definitely constituted intervention in its internal affairs. Russia, where public opinion is instinctively pro-Serb and anti-Muslim for historical reasons, and China, which is perennially nervous about any change in the rules about sovereignty that might expose it to future intervention, were both reluctant to authorize offensive military operations in the Balkans under UN auspices, and at first the United States and Britain were equally opposed.

Nothing could legally be done to stop the slaughter of Muslims by forces operating with Milosevic's tacit approval in Bosnia and later in Kosovo – yet something had to be done. The solution, once the Clinton administration got over Somalia and worked its nerve up for another intervention, was to wage limited air-only wars against Serbia using "coalitions of the willing" (in practice, the forces of the NATO alliance) that operated on a nod-and-a-wink basis, with the unspoken understanding that these operations would receive UN approval after the fact. The Kosovo War in 1999 was a particularly dodgy business from the legal point of view because Kosovo, unlike Bosnia, was still part of Serbia and so the horrors there were, strictly speaking, a Serbian domestic affair.

NATO undertook the Kosovo operation only because all the major powers understood that the Russian government, while obliged by public opinion at home to veto any proposal for military action against Serbia that came before the Security Council, wasn't really planning to die in a ditch to stop it from happening. It was virtually certain that the Russian government, which was run by quite sensible people, would allow the UN to take ownership of the occupation and retrospectively legitimize the war once the shooting stopped – and so would the Chinese government, which had no wish to isolate itself further in a world where every other major power is at least formally democratic.

If it was acceptable for NATO to attack Serbia over Kosovo in 1999 without Security Council authority, on the assumption that the legal details could be tidied up later, then why was it wrong for the United States to invade Iraq without UN authority in 2003? The answer is that in 2003 there was not even tacit support for the U.S. action among a majority of the members of the Security Council.

When the UN's members, driven mainly by humanitarian considerations, began to stretch the rules against outside intervention in the internal affairs of sovereign states after the end of the Cold War, they did so on the understanding that it would always be done on the basis of a broad consensus, and there was no such consensus on Iraq. On the contrary, few governments believed the Bush administration's allegation that Iraq represented a threat to world peace urgent enough to justify the unprovoked invasion of an independent country, nor was the humanitarian situation there any worse than it had been for the previous ten or twenty years. Other countries simply did not believe Washington's "evidence" or trust its motives, so the Bush administration went to war virtually alone.

In attacking Iraq in March 2003, Washington not only violated international law, but it also abandoned the multilateral consensus that had more or less legitimized the various attempts to move beyond the strict UN rules in the name of humanitarian intervention during the 1990s. There are those who would argue, with the wisdom of hindsight, that those attempts to move beyond the old ban on invading a sovereign state even for humanitarian reasons were therefore a mistake, since they gave Washington a precedent of sorts to work with. However, this argument implicitly assumes that the Bush administration actually cared about the UN rules and merely wanted to expand the scope for legal intervention further to embrace cases like Iraq. This was not the case.

"I think in this case international law stood in the way of doing the right thing. . . . [There was] no practical mechanism consistent with the rules of the UN for dealing with Saddam Hussein. . . . International law . . . would have required us to leave Saddam Hussein alone."

– Richard Perle, November 20, 2003

The real ambition of the neo-conservatives who came to power with George W. Bush, frankly expressed in their speeches and writings, was to sweep aside all impediments to the unilateral exercise of American power, starting with the legal authority of the Security Council. Many of them were therefore quietly pleased when the United States ended up invading Iraq illegally and virtually alone apart from Britain: that helped to drive home to everybody the fact that America's actions were showing the United Nations to be, in Bush's favourite word, "irrelevant." In a nod to the old rules, the U.S. government's international lawyers did throw up a legal smokescreen of claims that the United States was free to attack Iraq without explicit UN authorization on the basis of old Security Council resolutions dating back to before the first Gulf War in 1991, but there was scarcely an independent expert on international law in the world who accepted those claims – and the neo-conservatives couldn't have cared less.

So they got their war, and of course they won it easily (annual U.S. military spending was about 140 times greater than Iraq's). To a considerable extent, they also succeeded in sidelining the United Nations, which lacked the ability to stop the American action and realized that it would be counter-productive to condemn it openly. But if the UN sinks into irrelevance, what replaces it? Will the other countries of the world – the other 96 per cent of the human race – accept the unilateral exercise of U.S. power as an adequate substitute for the rule of law in international affairs? Certainly not.

The entire international community is now in a state of suspended animation. Most other governments deplore what the Bush administration did, but they are so appalled by the choices they would have to make if this turns out to be a permanent new reality that they have put everything on hold until at least early 2005. They continue to believe that the United

Nations is our only real bulwark against a return to the lethal old world of international anarchy, and they do not want to abandon the work of sixty years in response to the actions of a unilateralist U.S. policy that might prove to be only a passing phase in America's adjustment to the changing global balance of power. They even devised a strategy of sorts for trying to shepherd the United States back inside the system without a confrontation.

In October 2003, the Security Council passed a unanimous resolution that recognized U.S. responsibility to hand over control to a new Iraqi government as soon as possible, and in June 2004 it passed a further resolution recognizing the "sovereign government" that the United States had selected to replace direct U.S. rule. On the surface, it looked as if the invasion of Iraq had been just another Kosovo-style exercise where a "coalition of the willing" was given a nod and a wink from the UN to do the job, with legitimation after the fact by the Security Council a foregone conclusion. But it was nothing of the sort.

The United States was given the quasi-legitimation of the two post-war Security Council resolutions on Iraq because the only real alternative would have been to condemn the organization's most powerful member as an international outlaw. Such an action would have elicited only defiance and abuse from the Bush administration, and would have alienated precisely the American voters on whom everybody else was counting on to remove the Bush administration in November. Better to paper over cracks for the moment and pretend that the United States was still committed to the United Nations –

though it will be noted that the two resolutions shook loose very little new money and virtually no extra non-American troops for the U.S. occupation forces in Iraq.

But time is running out on these stalling tactics. If the outcome of the November 2004 election in the United States is a second Bush administration that dumps the leading neo-conservatives and abandons its unilateralist adventure, or a Kerry administration that clearly accepts the primacy of international law, then the panic will be over and the relatively benign international climate of the 1990s will return (although there will be a lot of repair work to do at the UN). But if the Bush administration embarks on another four-year term with the same crew in charge, or if a Kerry administration shows itself to be infected with the same unilateralist virus, then other major countries will start moving to protect their own interests by creating countervailing centres of power. They will not be called alliances at first, but that is what they may become.

"A war which lacks legitimacy does not acquire legitimacy if it is won. . . . We have a vision of the world based on the view that war should not be used to settle a crisis which can be resolved by other means. War must be the ultimate resort. The world today obliges us to seek a consensus when we act, and not to act alone.

"The U.S. has a vision of the world which is very unilateralist. I hold a vision of a multilateral world which apparently – and I say apparently – is opposed to this. Europe is, and certainly will be in the future, here to stay as a major world power. Then we have to take account of

the emergence of China on the world stage, and India too. . . . Whether you like it or not, whether you want it or not . . . we are moving towards a multipolar world."

– French president Jacques Chirac, at the G8 Summit, Evian, France, May 25, 2003

You can live safely in a multipolar world that has multilateral reflexes and a respect for international law, but great-power politics is lethally dangerous in a multipolar world with no effective international institutions. The Cold War was a bipolar world with a partially effective UN as a buffer between the two blocs, and the 1990s was a time of unprecedented international amity when it could truly be said that no great power had good reason to fear the intentions of any other. The best recent historical parallel for the process we may soon embark upon is the early twentieth century, when the alliances that later fought the First World War initially took shape.

There was a paramount power, Britain, that had allowed itself to become isolated. There were anxious established powers that had already been in relative decline for some time: France, Austria-Hungary, and Turkey. There were ambitious rising powers: Germany and Japan. There was absolutely no system of collective security – countries were free to attack one another, seize colonies, and even annex parts of each other's homelands – so the only way to protect yourself was to band together with other countries in alliances. And there was a very gradual, often secretive process in which the major powers did move into alliances over a period of years. Any resemblance between this history and the process that we may embark upon in the next ten years is all too plausible.

History does not repeat itself, but patterns of international behaviour do. In a world where the UN has been gutted and the law of the jungle has returned, you would expect nations to respond by increasing armaments and forming something like the alliances that emerged in the years before 1914. That does not mean that the public will read about it when it happens, or that these new arrangements will be formal alliances like NATO and the old Warsaw Pact, with joint military command centres and the like. Indeed, the husk of NATO may survive, like the Holy Roman Empire of former times, even as its members informally align themselves with new partners – and *informal* is probably the key word if we go through this pattern again, for formal military alliances with no ideological cement have been unfashionable for a long time. Even a hundred years ago, the arrangement between Russia, France, and Britain, though in reality an alliance was known simply as the "Friendly Understanding" (Entente Cordiale).

It's not all that hard to guess what the global lineup would be *circa* 2015 if Washington continues to pursue its unilateral fantasy of absolute power and there is a global retreat from multilateralism. The choice of potential alliance partners is never that wide for any country, as it is driven by geography, shared concerns about the behaviour of certain other countries, and the question of whether a given relationship is a good military and political fit.

Every single alliance relationship that is sketched out below has been a reality at some point in the past 150 years, with the sole exception of the United States and India.

NATO would certainly be the first victim of a realignment of the great powers, though it is not true that "the Atlantic is getting wider," as some claim: the body of water that is rapidly expanding is the English Channel. Of NATO's three militarily significant European members, France and Germany have taken the lead in opposing the trend of American policy since 2001, while Britain remains indissolubly wedded to the United States not only by the Blair government's choice but more profoundly through its dependence on the United States for key elements in its "independent" nuclear deterrent force. Although many people in Britain feel very uncomfortable about it, the Anglo-American alliance, now almost a century old, will probably remain as firm in any plausible future that starts from here as it was in Orwell's *Nineteen Eighty-Four* (where Britain was Oceania's "Airstrip One" off the coast of Eurasia).

America's other allies in this changed world would include Canada (whether it likes it or not), Australia, Israel (by far the greatest military power in its own region despite its small population) – and probably India. This is a world in which the American military presence in the Muslim Middle East would persist and might even expand, with possible invasions of Syria and Iran following those of Afghanistan and Iraq to create a solid block of U.S.–controlled territory from the eastern border of Israel to the western border of Pakistan. Since India's immediate security concerns focus mainly on Pakistan and to a lesser extent on other Muslim countries that back Pakistan in the Kashmir dispute, it would be hard for any Indian government to resist the temptation to throw its lot in with an America that had effectively subjugated its Muslim near-neighbours. It would be equally hard for the United States to resist the attraction of Indian military manpower if it were bogged down in a series of occupations of Middle Eastern countries (though this raises the question of what would become of America's current alliance with nuclear-armed Pakistan). An Indo-American alliance is a particularly good fit because strategists of a traditional bent in both countries see China as their emerging strategic rival, in India's case for dominance in Asia and in the U.S. case for global domination.

China, as usual, would be global odd man out: none of its larger neighbours trusts its current government enough to contemplate a close security relationship with it, although as the international outlook darkens, the Europeans are working to ensure that it does not feel cornered by a uniformly hostile West. President Bush's National Security Strategy statement of 2002, seeking to provide a rationale for fearing China, stated: "In pursuing advanced military capabilities that can threaten its neighbours in the Asia-Pacific region, China is following an outdated path." (As if the United States had ceased to pursue advanced military capabilities.) But in early 2004 France became the first European country to conduct joint naval exercises with China, and European Union chief Romano Prodi has made sure that China has access to key technologies such as Europe's satellite geo-positioning system so that Beijing can target its missiles more accurately.

Just straws in the wind, at this point, and they are not the precursor to some European-Chinese strategic alliance. Quite apart from the political gulf between democratic Europe and autocratic China, the sheer scale of China makes the whole business of building an alliance less urgent in Beijing's eyes, and its rapid growth towards full industrialized country status reinforces its go-it-alone distaste for alliance games.

Beijing has been playing a very long game since the death of Deng Xiao-ping, seeking to avoid any confrontation with the established great powers and especially with the United States while it grows back into great-power status itself. But at a certain point the aggressive promotion of *Pax Americana* would invalidate this strategic policy: China would definitely act to constrain the unilateral exercise of American power in its part of the world, where unresolved questions about the future of Taiwan and North Korea offer plenty of potential for confrontation. If there's a return to the old world with the old rules, then China would urgently build up its own military power, including most especially its nuclear deterrent power. It was genuine restraint, not lack of resources, that held China to fewer than two hundred long-range nuclear-tipped ballistic missiles all these years. It is already moving past that self-imposed limit with the Type 94 ballistic missile submarines that carry sixteen missiles each, and there is no treaty that would prevent it from going up to thousands of warheads.

This would leave us with not a two- but a three-bloc world, however, for it is hard to imagine that either the Western Europeans or the Russians would find an alliance with China attractive or even comfortable. However, they might well make an alliance with each other. Within the European Union, France and Germany were already moving towards closer military and political co-ordination outside the NATO framework, but even with the addition of most of the smaller members of the European Union, a Franco-German alliance would not counter-balance the military and economic power of the United States. Paris and Berlin would have to find a great-power partner with a big resource base and a serious nuclear weapons capability, and the obvious candidate is Russia.

Would Russia be attracted by such an alliance? Moscow greatly prefers the current world where it is not forced to choose between the United States and Europe, but in the end the Russian leadership knows that it is European. Its great ambition is to join the European Union, and the reward that the Western European great powers could offer in exchange for EU access to Russia's huge natural resources and nuclear weapons capabilities is accelerated EU membership (though it might by then be membership in a European Union that has lost the United Kingdom). If Russia concludes that its dream of a real partnership with Washington, even a junior partnership, is just a fantasy – and it is already pretty close to that conclusion – then a Paris-Berlin-Moscow deal is not a far-fetched alternative.

There have already been cautious diplomatic explorations

of this strategic option. In the months after the invasion of Iraq, Paris and Berlin began for the first time to talk seriously of a "union of France and Germany" that would merge their foreign and defence policies. (French foreign minster Dominique de Villepin called it "the only historic gamble that we cannot possible lose.") If it came into existence, such an entity, with about 140 million people, would be able to approach Russia (population 145 million) as an equal in any discussions about a possible alliance – and such discussions, in the most tentative and informal way, may already have taken place. In July 2003, Alain Juppé, a former French prime minister and foreign minister who was then the leader of President Chirac's reformed Gallist party, visited Moscow. What was said in private is not know, but Juppé afterwards commented that "the idea of a strategic partnership between the European pole and the Russian pole" did not exclude "dialogue with the other poles, the American pole, of course, and China." And he added: "The world of the coming decades will function this way."

This would give pleasure to some in France, where it is commonplace to discuss NATO as "a tool to prevent Europe from having a common defence," but it would not please most Germans or Russians, and the notion has now been placed on a back burner while the prospective strategic partners wait to see which way the United States jumps. But they could make such an alliance work if they felt they had to, and it could grow into a serious strategic competitor to the United States in less than a decade.

As for the "New Europe" (as Donald Rumsfeld called it) of former Soviet-bloc countries in Eastern Europe whose governments have aligned themselves with the United States over Iraq, they would have little choice but to go along with this sort of continental European alliance in the end. They want to be in the EU even more than they mistrust the Russians, and a large majority of their own citizens already strongly opposes the commitments their governments have made to support American policy in the Middle East.

Among the major players there remains only Japan, whose relatively isolated and invulnerable position suggests that its future may be that of a giant Asian Switzerland, heavily armed but increasingly neutral. Other middle powers like Italy, Spain, Turkey, and South Korea, currently in U.S.–led alliances, would have a difficult time deciding where their future lies, though the first three would probably end by opting for Eurasia. This would be an inherently unstable situation, since it would mean that much or most of the Middle East was effectively U.S.–occupied territory, but for quite a long while, nothing terrible might happen.

In sketching out this possible world of ten years hence, I am drawing a not-quite-worst-case scenario that may never come to pass. It is possible that a change of course or of administration in Washington will quickly return us to the relatively safe and orderly world of the later 1990s, with little to remind us of this interlude except the mess in Iraq and a heightened consciousness about the risk of terrorist attacks. But if these informal alliances do begin to take shape, then the level of trust in the world will go down dramatically – think how short a time it took during the runup to the invasion of Iraq for many Americans to become persuaded that France, of all places, was their enemy – and vicious circles of entirely familiar historical types will start to rotate. At that point we would be in a situation that is probably more dangerous, though less overtly hostile, than the Cold War.

It would be less overtly hostile, because the immense movements of people, goods, and money around the world that are the hallmark of this globalized era would not cease, though they might diminish, and because international information flows would continue to be relatively free, if only for economic reasons. It would be a situation reminiscent of the early twentieth century, another globalized, free-trading era when most ordinary people did not even need passports to move between countries – but the level of international mistrust was very high, and the lethal military calculations of the alliances lurked behind the peaceful facade of everyday life. The danger is not that some madman might launch a deliberate war of conquest; it is that various governments would begin to worry once again that local clashes between the alliances or their proxies might escalate, and that threats might be made which must be deterred to preserve their credibility, and that they therefore have to think about what they would do in the awful contingency that deterrence doesn't work or that somebody misunderstands. . . .

Neither of the great alliances of the Cold War ever seriously considered launching an all-out nuclear attack against the other except as "pre-emption" of an anticipated surprise attack, usually in the midst of some escalating local crisis, but they still came quite close to war a number of times. If only evil dictators bent on world conquest began wars, we would be fairly safe, but a belief that pre-emption ("first strike," as they called it back then) might mean survival for the people on our side can persuade even normally sane and moral people that destroying millions of foreigners' lives with nuclear weapons is a rational option. The psychologists who regularly tested the crews in the missile silos for reliability during the Cold War looked for exactly that sort of rationalization in their clients, and they had no trouble finding it. They probably still don't.

For more than half a century, far-sighted people in many countries have been working on a project for international law and order that is our best and perhaps our only chance of avoiding global disaster on an unprecedented scale. It is obviously a hundred-year project at the very least, for it flies in the face of history and of traditional ideas about human nature, as most of its supporters were well aware from the start. They had to try anyway, because all the alternative outcomes were so much worse in a world of nuclear weapons, and they have made encouraging progress towards their goal. By the late 1990s it was becoming possible to believe that the project might actually succeed, and that the worst of the horrors that infested our future might never come to pass. Now all that is at risk.

CHAPTER VI

SURVIVING THE TWENTY-FIRST CENTURY

"This is a century which is going to see China emerge as the largest economy, and usually with economic power comes military clout. In the world we are constructing, we want to know [that the system] will work whoever is the biggest and the most powerful. It would be very easy for a country like New Zealand to make excuses and think of justifications for what its friends were doing, but we would have to be mindful that we were creating precedents for others also to exit from multilateral decision making. I don't want [those] precedents set, regardless of who is seen as the biggest kid on the block.

We saw the UN as a fresh start for a world trying to work out its problems together rather than a return to a nineteenth-century world where the great powers carved it up. . . . Who wants to go back to the jungle?"

– Helen Clark, prime minister of New Zealand, May 2003

New Zealand refused to send its troops to join the United States, Britain, and Australia in invading Iraq because Helen Clark's government understood that what we do now affects the future. The day will come when the United States is no longer the superpower bestriding the world, but New Zealand's geography will always be the same as it is now, so it needs a global system that will protect it from harm even when China is the greatest power: a system based on law and multilateral consensus. So does everybody else.

It's not hard to run the world when things are as easy as they are now. There is an established set of great powers, their relative rankings virtually unchanged for the past fifty years except for the Russians, who have accepted their fall from superpower status with remarkable grace. There are no rival alliance systems, and no great power has a major grievance against any other. The global economic climate is benign, the physical climate is not yet changing radically, and painful decisions that require serious sacrifices can still be postponed. A world where terrorism is seen as the biggest problem is a world without big problems. But this happy scene is going to change.

Global warming and other environmental problems are going to hit us very hard over the next fifty years. How fast they will hit, and how great the resulting upheavals will be, cannot be known in advance, but very few people apart from the usual suspects in the United States any longer doubt that climate change is a reality, and that it will hurt some countries a lot more than others. There will probably be major disruptions in food supply and mass movements of population in some parts of the world – including some technologically competent parts of the world that have access to the full range of modern weapons. It will not be possible to ignore their suffering, as they will possess the means of drawing it forcefully to everybody else's attention, so there had better be a system in place that enables us to spread the burden of coping with these changes.

At the same time, the pecking order of the great powers is starting to change again. In a globalized world where regional differences in the level of education, technological ability, and commercial competitiveness are gradually being erased, small countries with a big lead like Portugal in the sixteenth century or Britain in the nineteenth century can no longer be in the first rank of the great powers; only countries of a semi-continental scale can be contenders. The five biggest powers of 2040 will be China, the United States, India, Russia, and Brazil – probably in that order. This ranking is implicit in the current long-term growth rates of these economies, projected one generation out, and while some specific country might surprise us by growing faster or slower than the projections suggest, the overall pattern is practically carved in stone.

The last time the world went through a change of this order, it ended up in the First World War. Long before we get to 2040 – within the next ten years, in all likelihood – the strains and stresses that these gradual shifts in relative power are putting on the existing great-power system will begin to show through. If we have a working multilateral system in place, these stresses and strains can probably be contained and channelled, and everybody will have time to accommodate themselves to the emerging realities gradually and peacefully. If not, then we may look forward to a process quite similar to that before the First World War, with everybody seeking shelter in alliances of one sort or another.

It would be a less stable situation than the Cold War, for that was a relatively simple time where there were only two blocs, when the threat of nuclear weapons proliferation beyond the five declared nuclear powers had been largely contained, and when terrorists were a good deal less imaginative than they are now. Getting through the next half-century was going to be tricky enough even if the great powers went on trusting one another and the United Nations worked well. It will be hopeless if we end up in alliances and arms races again, but the current U.S. bid to impose a new and unwelcome *Pax Americana* on the world could set off a slide back into that old pattern and foreclose on our future.

The risk is compounded by the very fragile state of the U.S. economy. The U.S. dollar's prolonged act of levitation must end one way or another, and the possibility that it will end in a sudden crash cannot be excluded. Just as it is in everybody else's interest to offer the United States a non-humiliating path of retreat out of Iraq (hence the unanimous UN resolutions of October 2003 and June 2004), so it is in the interest of investors and central banks everywhere that the dollar does not suddenly collapse, and they will do what they can to avoid it. But if it happens anyway, there could be an extreme political reaction in the United States. It cannot be presumed that blame would automatically be cast on the right culprits. Indeed, it can safely be assumed that there would be an enormous political effort in the United States to shift the blame onto foreigners, accompanied by a steep increase in American popular hostility towards those countries that are seen as having opposed U.S. policy internationally.

It could get quite ugly, in other words, and we could end up with a world we do not like a bit. The objective is to get through what promises to be a very difficult half-century without a world war, and what happens in the next couple of years may be decisive. Either we get back to building the international institutions we started working on sixty years ago, or we get used to the idea that we are working our way up to the Third World War. So it is important that the United States does not succeed in turning Iraq into a Middle Eastern base for *Pax Americana*, and that Americans come to see the whole project for global hegemony as an expensive mistake. But it is also important that other countries give the United States the softest possible landing. Not only does the world not need an angry and resentful America, it needs a United States that is actively committed to the project for building a law-based international society.

"There were times when it appeared that American power was seen to be more dangerous than Saddam Hussein. I'll just put it very bluntly. We just didn't understand it. "

– Condoleezza Rice, May 30, 2003

At the G8 Summit after the invasion of Iraq, U.S. national security adviser Condoleezza Rice was like a schoolteacher reading out the end-of-term reports for a group of children who had failed to live up to their potential. "There was disappointment that a friend like Canada was not able to support the U.S. on what we considered a very important issue," she said. "There was disappointment in the response of the German government, too." And the behaviour of France was "particularly disappointing." It was ridiculous, but it was also very revealing. The United States had just carried out an entirely unprovoked and illegal act of aggression, everybody else knew that it was bound to end in tears – and yet Rice felt fully justified in rebuking them for failing to go along with it. It suggested an almost total inability to see the administration she served and its policies as others saw them.

It was not an isolated incident. The neo-conservatives never intended the United States to become as isolated as it has. They imagined that when they displayed American "resolve" and demonstrated that they were now in sole charge of the planet through an exemplary war or two against universally unpopular regimes, all their old friends and allies would fall into line under *Pax Americana* more or less willingly. They were not supposed to respond as they have. Nobody in Washington in 2001 could have imagined that only two years later half of the European Union's citizens (according to an 18,000-person, 15-country survey conducted six months after the invasion of Iraq) would see the United States as a danger to world peace rather than a force for good.

This peculiar inability to predict the responses of others is largely due to the very enclosed world in which American debate on these issues has taken place in recent years. From Samuel Huntington's *The Coming Clash of Civilizations* in the mid-1990s – immensely influential in the Washington bureaucracy and various think-tanks that were desperately seeking a new enemy, but mostly seen as highbrow propaganda outside the United States – to Robert Kagan's 2003 book, *Paradise and Power*, which explains that the United States must take over the world but the Europeans won't understand why because "Americans are from Mars, Europeans are from Venus," the key books and articles that have set the intellectual tone inside the Beltway in Washington have addressed a world that bears little resemblance to reality as experienced by most non-Americans.

The fact is that neither Europeans nor Asians nor (above all) Middle Easterners agree with mainstream American political opinion any more. They don't think al-Qaeda is a global menace. They don't live in fear of rogue states. They don't think we are living in the opening stages of a "clash of civilizations" (though they worry that Washington's efforts might yet make it happen). They don't agree with pre-emptive and preventive wars, and they don't believe that 9/11 "changed everything." And no amount of lecturing by American officials and academics who tell them to "grow up" is going to change that. It is a genuine difference of perspective, not anti-Americanism – but pushing *Pax Americana* much further could turn it into that.

Meanwhile, what about the poor Iraqis?

"I tell you, it is never boring in Baghdad these days. . . . You go out of your house in the morning never knowing if you will get to work at all. Some days it is bad: huge checkpoints with tanks, where everybody has to get out of their cars. What is amazing is that the Americans have still not learned their lesson and always bring just one translator – actually, strike that: the translators have stopped going to work, so we are lucky if there is one at all. . . .

"The weather is fine, and when the sun sets we sit in an outdoor tea-house listening to pro-Fallujah songs blasting from a car stereo while teenagers stand beside the car trying to look tough. If we get sick of that we go to a friend's newly opened mobile-phone accessory shop in Adhamiya, where he has to dodge demands for phone covers with pictures of Saddam on them. Even more surreally, a kid came in asking if he had any of the old 'Saddam, we love you' songs that he could use as a ring tone.

"Did I tell you that I don't understand my country any more?"

– "Salam Pax," *The Guardian*, May 5, 2004

Iraqis are not the passive, helpless people whose allotted role in the neo-conservative fantasy was first to stand cheering by the side of the road while the U.S. army liberated them and then to receive "freedom" and democracy gratefully from American hands. (And, of course, to make fourteen permanent military bases in their country available to the U.S. armed forces in partial recompense for this American generosity.) Iraq used to be the most literate of all the big Arab countries, and in the 1970s, before Saddam's wars impoverished the country, it was also the most developed and prosperous of the large Arab states, with a big middle class, a diversified economy, and social services of a near-European standard. It could be all of those things again, and democratic to boot – and it does not need American tutelage to get there.

Nobody needs American tutelage to get there. Democracy is not a copyrighted American process that can be implanted elsewhere by force. It is a way of running the affairs of large societies that is available to anybody who wants it, regardless of their particular culture, and the history of the past twenty years demonstrates that people of every culture want it and know how to get it: Filipinos, Bangladeshis, South Koreans, Russians, South Africans, Indonesians – and, one of these days, Arabs too. It could easily take root in Iraq, but it has to be left to the Iraqis. It cannot come as part of a package that also involves making Iraq an American client state, because that makes those who are in power collaborators and discredits any project with which they are associated.

The wave of violence that has swept over Iraq since the American occupation does include a number of attacks by Islamist terrorists who have been attracted to the country by the presence of American forces, but it is primarily a homegrown resistance movement driven by anger at the American presence. A more competent occupation regime than the chaotic Coalition Provisional Authority might have postponed the growth of a resistance movement – disbanding the Iraqi army and turning several hundred thousand military men out on the streets *with their weapons* has to rank among the ten stupidest decisions of the past century – but if it had not emerged now, then the United States would have pressed ahead even more determinedly with its plan to turn Iraq into its main Middle Eastern base, and the resistance would just have emerged a bit later, as America's plans for Iraq became clearer. One way or another, the American military presence was going to elicit an Iraqi resistance movement.

What would happen if the United States just pulled its troops out? Not necessarily the civil war that U.S. propaganda insists is the only alternative to a continuing American military presence in Iraq. There have been bitter clashes between predominantly Arab governments in Baghdad and separatist-minded Kurds on a number of occasions in the past (and that could happen again whether the United States stays or goes), but Arab Iraq has never had a civil war. Politics was an extremely rough game in Iraq during the forty-five years between the overthrow of the British-imposed king in 1958 and the destruction of the Baathist regime by U.S. military power in 2003, but Iraqis always understood that they were all in the same boat and that it made no sense to sink it. There was no civil war then, and it's not clear why there would be one now.

It would be helpful if UN troops, preferably mostly from Muslim countries, were to arrive in Iraq as American troops were leaving, because there is a genuine problem of public security in Iraq. But even if other countries refuse to send their soldiers into Iraq now that things have got so far out of hand, the American troops should still go – and go very fast. The Iraqis may not succeed in composing their differences peacefully and refounding their country as a democratic state, but their chances of doing so are far greater if they do not have to contend with the American occupation and the violent resistance to it. As for the "war on terror," Iraq was the wrong place to fight it anyway, but more generally it must be taken away from the armed forces and given back to the people who really should be waging it, the intelligence services and police forces of the world.

And if all this happens, what becomes of America's position in the world? No more dreams of global hegemony, obviously, but the United States remains the first among equals for at least another generation. None of the other great powers wants to take that role away from it; they just want it to play by the rules, and carry its share of the load in building an international system that is capable of withstanding the storms that are coming.

"It is . . . a trait no other nation seems to possess in quite the same degree that we do – namely, a feeling of almost childish injury and resentment unless the world as a whole recognizes how innocent we are of anything but the most harmless and generous intentions."

– Eleanor Roosevelt (wife of FDR), 1946

The hardest thing Americans are going to have to do in this generation is to get used to the idea that the United States is just another country. Still a very big and powerful country, to be sure, but not the "indispensable nation," not a beacon of liberty shining into the darkness, and not the only great power that really matters. Most other countries are now democratic too, and they do not look to the United States for example. No other country yet rivals the United States in military power, but that is not as important as Americans think because their enormous military machine can only be used, in practice, against very weak countries: war with a serious opponent would lead to a level of American casualties that the U.S. public would not tolerate for long. And the world does not *need* America in the same sense that it did when totalitarian Communist powers controlled the heart of Eurasia. But neither does it need America to go into a gigantic sulk about its lost status.

It is hard for any country to come to terms with a loss of power. Spain, the superpower of the sixteenth and early seventeenth centuries, took more than three centuries to get over the shock of losing its leading place in Europe. France, the dominant European power for the latter half of the seventeenth century and all of the eighteenth, had pretty much overcome its bitterness by the latter part of the twentieth century – say, a century and a half to recover. Britain, the superpower of the nineteenth century, has made a quicker recovery, but its consistent attempts to "punch above its weight" in international affairs by hitching a ride on America's coattails suggest that it has not fully come to terms with its real status yet. How long will America take? Nobody knows, but the course of the next fifty years will be determined in large part by how well or how badly Americans cope with the change.

The particular problem for Americans who have to make this adjustment is that they are quite unaccustomed to thinking of the United States as simply a large, English-speaking democracy with considerable ethnic diversity that occupies the middle band of the North American continent. American nationality has always been defined in ideological terms, and pretty sweeping ones at that: the cradle of democracy, to begin with, but latterly also the head office of the perfect economic system: free-market capitalism. Letting go of these illusions is bound to be painful, and there are powerful interests in Washington and elsewhere that will fight hard to keep them alive. They may not win, but if they do, Iraq will just be the first stage of a very rough ride.